The

KING

of

NOTHING

MUCH

JESSE EDWARD JOHNSON

PAUL DRY BOOKS
Philadelphia 2020

First Paul Dry Books Edition, 2020

PAUL DRY BOOKS, Inc.
Philadelphia, Pennsylvania
www.pauldrybooks.com

Printed in the United States of America

Library of Congress Control Number: 2020931611

ISBN-13: 978-1-58988-144-0

for Ruby and Quinn

Who is it that can tell me who I am?
—KING LEAR

I've got static in my head
The reflected sound of everything
—ELLIOTT SMITH

The

KING

of

NOTHING

MUCH

Weldon stood at the end of a line of silent men, waiting for someone to mention the weather. Fathers at a
child's birthday party, stooping over little paper plates
with cake on them, or the shrapnel of cake, crumbs and
smears of frosting slowly crusting over.

This was a formation he knew all too well: dads at
the side of a room, trying to find something to say. If
there was a game to talk about—one just played by a lo
cal team, or one that was about to be played—you could
talk about that. If there was news about a celebrity that
men were permitted to discuss in public, you could talk
about that. You could talk about the cake.

On the other side of the glass, a horde of young kids

ran amok in the Fun Zone, herded by teens in canary yellow T-shirts with the JumpFest logo printed in red across the front. The glass was not enough to block the noise. And the music: the music was kid music, of the very worst variety. Weldon's wife Deb—God bless her—was in there too, shoes off, socks on, shepherding the twins through the tunnels and into the bounce-house and up and down the long tall slide. This was their deal: they were hers to handle at parties; they were his to handle for most of the rest of the week. Weldon had had the option to stay home with Presley, their older daughter, doing nothing whatsoever, but, for reasons he couldn't quite fathom, he hadn't.

Someone mentioned Spotify. Playlists. User interfaces. Amazon music, someone said. Still they held the weather in reserve.

All men are alpha males. Weldon had read that somewhere. Was it true?

One dad said something about his vegetable garden. That thread didn't extend very far. Another said something about a new bagel shop. Weldon raised his eyebrows, pursed his lips. That could be good. There weren't—that dad pointed out—very many bagel shops in the Seattle area. And then he launched, abysmally, into a multiple-sentence disquisition on the years he'd lived in New York.

Weldon decoupled himself from the fathers and wafted over toward the cake table. Wrong move. For standing guard beside the cake was Maureen Glazier, mother of the birthday boy, a worthy Scylla to the Charybdis that was the line of fathers and their talk of bagel shops.

Weldon had no memory of having seen Maureen—either of the Glazier parents, for that matter—at any Dixon School events. There was a deer-like meekness about her. And she was intimidatingly tiny. She was clad in a certain kind of Eastside uniform: running pants and running shoes, a lilac-colored top. Hair pulled back into a pony tail. A harried expression. Really, really worried: that's how she looked. (*Be afraid*, Weldon often said to the twins, in the voice of the Bedtime Monster. *Be very afraid*.) He felt kind of bad for her, feeling so keenly, as it seemed she did, the need to be on top of the situation, to keep track of every little thing that happened. He decided—what the hell—to introduce himself.

"Hi," he said, extending his hand. "I'm Weldon. Weldon Tines. I'm Reese and Danny's dad."

Maureen appeared surprised to have been approached in such a direct, disarming way, but forced a smile and shook his hand. Hers was a cold and bony hand. Teeny tiny. "I'm Maureen. I'm Perry's mom."

Now it fell to Weldon to say something. But what?

"Good turnout," he said.

She shook her head, worriedly, "I hope we have enough cake."

Weldon, eyeing the cake, whose bottom layer hadn't yet begun to be explored, wasn't worried.

"Is your husband—" he started the question before he knew how to finish it, and without appropriate regard for the assumptions with which it was laden.

"He has to work. Big client in town."

"I see."

Weldon found himself longing for the predictable discomfort of the fathers. Fertilizer. Fairways. Fenway Park.

On the opposite side of the glass, Perry, the birthday boy, a scrawny blond kid with a ludicrous hipster haircut, was leading a train of kids up-castle. He was a classmate of the twins at Dixon School, a private elementary school in Redmond. Yes: private school. For kindergarteners. It was just one of those undiscussable things between Weldon and Deb: the kids were going to go to private schools. Presley had graduated from Dixon—and had since moved on to the middle school it fed—and now the twins were following suit. Twenty-four grand a year. Twenty-one for a sibling. Forty-five grand a year. Weldon thought, sometimes, about the things they could have done with that money and the kids in public schools. A bigger house. Hawaii. But he knew it wasn't up to him. He wasn't the one making the money. And, more importantly, Private School had been ingrained in Deb's psyche since before she had any idea that a man named Weldon Tines existed. She'd been raised in the glossy private schools of greater Orange County, had gone to a private university (Duke) for her B.A., and then another (Yale) for her law degree. And the whole *raison*, it seemed, for having done so was to be able to send *her* kids to private school. The kids had been going to go to private school since before they were born, and now they were. Which meant that all the school events they went to were infested with Mercedes and Audis and Maseratis. Weldon had gotten so used to feeling vaguely inferior at these events that he'd come to inhabit that feeling with a sense of pride and defiance. He'd wear sweatpants to school on a regular basis. A soiled baseball cap. He'd bring cheap doughnuts to a parent event. It was petty, he knew, but he couldn't help himself. One time he stole a bowl.

On the opposite side of the glass, the Tines twins—Danny and Reese, all of five years old—were rolling around on the floor in perfect glee. Weldon smiled, arms crossed, clamping his fork to his plate with his thumb.

It wasn't that they couldn't afford private school; it was that they could *barely* afford private school. Everything else about their lives was solidly, straightforwardly middle class. Their house, their car, their clothes. But there was this giant tumescent bulge in the family budget which represented the Dixon tuition. To Weldon it still looked like a typo. But it seemed like the Dixon tuition was, for all the other Dixon parents, another right-sized item in the family budget. Like a grocery bill, or a trip to the barber. It fit right in. No bulge.

"Daddy"—Reese, bursting through the door to the Party Room, pigtails bouncing—"come in the tunnel house with us!"

"Nope," said Weldon. Not a chance. "Today's my day off." He gestured toward his sweatpants—Seahawks, white—to demonstrate the point.

"Come on, Wel," said Deb, who had followed their daughter into the room. She gave him a wink. "Go in the tunnel."

Et tu, Deb?

"Please Daddy, please Daddy, pleeeeease?" Now Danny was in on it too.

Reese ran up and, taking Weldon's plate-hand by the wrist, began to pull. Danny came for the other, and the two of them leaned forward toward the door to the Fun Zone, dragging Weldon forward like a stubborn ox.

Weldon sighed and glared at Deb—who was smiling in great amusement—and went. Out of the frying pan and into the bouncy-house.

It didn't take long for Weldon to warm up to his surroundings. He was the twins' prisoner—a part he played frequently and knew how to embellish. They led him wherever they wanted, one twin per wrist. First to the ball pit, where he bellyflopped solemnly to his death. Then to the tunnel, where the twins—joined now by a gaggle of other kids—kicked and prodded him until he was in and then (mercifully) out the other end. He perished theatrically several more times at the hands of his captors. The teens in yellow shirts let them be. The other parents in the room, all mothers, cast wary glances at Weldon—nothing he didn't know how to ignore.

"Slide time!" Danny, Captain of the Guard, exclaimed.

Oh shit. "No," said Weldon.

"Forward, prisoner!" shouted Perry, with genuine malice. Then, with his hair falling ludicrously into his eyes, he began to prod Weldon in the hindquarters with a large foam sword. The other kids followed suit, and their prisoner was compelled to climb the quaking metal stairs.

The view from the top was impressive. Through the glass that gave onto the Party Room, Weldon could see the Wall of Fathers watching him, smug in the knowledge that they would never come to such a fate.

"Now everyone go down," said Danny. "Except me. I'm the Captain of the Guard."

One by one the other kids whistled past Weldon and down the slide and into the pit of balls below. And then, at Perry's urging, they formed a gauntlet at the bottom of the slide. A nice touch.

"Blindfold him!" shouted Reese.

The gauntlet agreed, and began to chant: "blind-FOLD, blind-FOLD, blind-FOLD."

"Give me your sweatshirt," Danny commanded.

Weldon removed his sweatshirt and tied the arms around his head. Shrouded now in darkness, he began to feel genuine fear. But there was no time to deliberate, for the Captain of the Guard was prodding him, and shouting a command: "Forward, prisoner!"

Weldon launched his paunchy body down the slide. His sphincter leapt into his stomach, and he heard himself squeal in true exhilaration as he came careening into the balls.

And then there was wailing. Weldon, rising, stupefied, ripped the sweatshirt from his eyes. And there, bent before him, was Perry Glazier, birthday boy, wailing, the index finger of one hand clasped in the other. His ears bright red, his sculpted locks draped in a thick blond wedge.

Instantaneously, as if ex nihilo, Maureen too was there, rocking the wailing Perry back and forth, and glaring up at Weldon. Someone cut the music.

"Come on, Perry," said Maureen. "Let's go find some ice."

The kid was crying even louder now. "I don't want to!" He wrenched himself from his mother's slender arms but was caught again by the elbow and dragged forward toward the Party Room.

Weldon jogged behind and caught them at the door. "Hey, I'm—"

"Can someone get some ice?" Maureen looked around frantically as she said this. One of the fathers moved in the direction of plausible ice.

Reese and Danny joined Weldon at the threshold of the Party Room.

"Do we have to go home now?" said Danny.

"I don't know."

Weldon found Deb across the room and shrugged. Her eyes bored into him, and the little dimples that appeared above the bridge of her nose when she got mad, which wasn't all that often, had made a timely appearance. They were like little parentheses enclosing her ire. Weldon couldn't help but think how hot she looked with those furious forehead dimples and those darkly scorching eyes.

With her searing eyes and hot dimples, Deb directed Weldon toward Maureen, who was sitting on a chair by the cake, with little whimpering Perry on her lap. This gesture meant that Weldon was supposed to Do Something.

Weldon went over to Maureen. "I'm so sorry," he said. She didn't look at him.

The ice pack was comically massive, far too big

for Perry's tiny finger. More than hurt or sad or mad he looked worried. Really, really worried. Eyes wide, hair dripping into his eyes.

One of the other fathers—possibly the one who had manfully secured the outsize ice pack—came to Weldon's side. Looking down at the injured child as if he were inspecting a busted water pipe or buckled floor, he placed a hand on Weldon's shoulder and, with a maddening smirk, pronounced his sentence: "Looks like you'll be hearing from Pike."

Looks like you'll be hearing from Pike.

Weldon had been summoned—there was no other way of putting it. He had come because, from wife to wife, Maureen to Deb, the Duke of Glazier had subpoenaed him.

The trip to the Glazier household filled Weldon with dread, and yet it carried with it a certain relief. It was good—almost—to have something new and strange and a little bit frightening to do. A different road to drive on. A break from the routine. The roiling of the week: kids to school; meals made; kitchen cleaned. Shits taken. Magazines flipped through. Leaves not raked. The roiling, roiling of the week. The arrival of the bus in the afternoon. Kids running down the driveway. Opening and closing the mailbox. Sifting through the mail on the amble down the driveway. Wet grass; yet more leaves—always more damn leaves. The dismantling of backpacks and lunchboxes. Shoes and boots on the shoe-boot shelf. Hands washed. Snacks made, eaten. Toys brought out, then put back or not put back. Dishes washed again. Pills taken. Beds made and flung back open. Netflix. Presley at a friend's. Presley always now, it seemed, elsewhere. The endless roiling of the endless weeks.

The Glazier house loomed up over the eastern shores of Lake Sammamish among an enclave of large homes on large lots. It was big and dark, with various rooflines at various levels sloping down in different sorts of ways. A fifty-year roof, if Weldon wasn't mistaken. Impressive. The paint looked great. The trees were nice, and nicely mulched. And the mulch didn't stink, like the mulch that Weldon's friend Dell had brought to Weldon's house in the spring. That mulch, the Dell mulch, had smelled like diarrhea. But the Glazier mulch was dark and rich and perfectly laid about the feet of the perfect trees and shrubs. Weldon didn't get down on his knees to smell it, but he felt that if he had, he'd find that it smelled marvelous, like dark mushrooms or the spirit of the age.

There were five garage doors, enclosing what, Weldon thought to himself, we dare not seek to know. It was a line from a movie, or a book, or nowhere. He hiked up his jeans and strode doorward with dread.

Weldon rarely wore jeans anymore. He mostly wore what he liked to call, with a raise of the eyebrow—and, when he said it to Deb, a horseshit British accent—*athletic trousers*. Adidas, for example, stretchy and striped along the outside of the legs. Puma, too. Or Nike. The kind that you could find splayed out disastrously, like so many corpses, in those massive bins at Costco. $16.99. Too little too late. He'd reached a point in his life where many of his shirts had begun to harbor creative differences with his torso. Different views of the future. The shirt he had chosen for this occasion, this hearing-from, was the shirt he felt still fit him best, a checked affair in blue and white. Good jeans. Reliable leather shoes.

There was a nice wooden trellis with a pretty vine on it next to the front door. At the base of the vine sat a little granite basin with water streaming down the sides. There was a grill out back, Weldon felt he knew, that cost thousands of dollars and never got used.

The knocker was big and brass and heavy. With a chuff of an exhale, Weldon lifted it and let it thud down clangingly into the door. That felt kind of good, he had to admit. He knocked with it again, then rang the doorbell.

The person who answered the door was not Pike Glazier—Pike from whom Weldon would be hearing, Pike from whom Weldon had heard. No, it was a pert young woman with shoulder-length brown hair and a clipboard pressed against her chest.

"You must be Weldon," she said, extending her hand, "I'm Sherry. I'm Mr. Glazier's personal assistant." Fuck: a Personal Assistant? "Come on in."

Weldon crossed the threshold. The entryway had a very high ceiling, dominated by a massive chandelier, a nebula of shards and squares and crystal spearheads. Directly before them was a spacious sunken living room, with high glass windows giving onto the lake. At one end was a large stone fireplace, in which a low gas fire glowed in just the way it should. On the opposite wall, across the sky-wide living room, was the largest screen that Weldon had ever seen.

"Mr. Glazier will be right down," said Sherry. "Can I offer you some water?"

"No thanks," said Weldon, even though his mouth felt full of desert sand. "Can I use your restroom?"

"Of course. Right this way."

She led him down a hallway to the left.

"The powder room's right there," she said, with a practiced gesture, the kind of gesture you'd use to show a dignitary his seat at the table.

It was only the guest bathroom—the *powder room*—but this was a premium shitter, with two sinks and a complicated Japanese toilet. Weldon dropped his jeans and sat.

He had established the practice of sitting while he peed when the twins were toddlers, and he had to carry them up to his bed in the dead of the night. If, after dropping them off in the warmth of the covers, he peed sitting down, with his eyes closed, he could persist in dream, and not have any trouble getting back to sleep. But if he turned on the light in the bathroom and stood to pee, it woke him up. These were the tricks of the trade. But over time the practice of peeing while seated had evolved as a way to allow for a quick check of his phone while he was sitting there—and a game or two of solitaire. It had become a kind of minor addiction. Better than smoking, but still.

He got out his phone and started a game and played it, then went about checking his balls. After Weldon got his vasectomy, a node of something formed on the eastern border of his scrotum. It was still there. It didn't hurt. It was just a node. A bolus. At first it freaked him out. But the doctor said it was probably just a *spermatocele*. And had said this as if everyone alive knew the meaning of the word *spermatocele*. As if everyone tossed that word around like all the fucking time. Weldon had googled it: *a painless, fluid-filled cyst in the long, tightly coiled tube that lies above and behind each testicle (epididymis). The fluid in the cyst may contain sperm that are no longer alive.* Weldon wasn't sure how he felt about the idea of sperm that were no longer alive. Dead sperm that couldn't really die, that were mummified and entombed. His balls' version of the Valley of Kings, those little sperms his Tut and family. He would grab hold of this spermatocele, between thumb and index finger, from time to time, to make sure that it hadn't gotten bigger. He pinched it. It hadn't.

Weldon started another game of solitaire but then, thinking better of it, rose and hiked his jeans and, after finally figuring out which button meant flush, he went to the sink. An array of products stood at the ready: cotton balls, lip balm, lotion, cologne. You never knew what you might need. Weldon washed his hands, then doused them in cologne and slapped it on his jowls. Then he leaned in to examine the specimen of man before him.

When you hit thirty-five, a pilot's voice may as well have come over the airways in your heart and mind and said, *We are now beginning our initial descent into shittiness. Please make sure your backs are slouched and chins and bellies are in a fully down-sagging position.* Weldon's hair—which he kept cut short—was brownish, and graying in places, and curly in a way he didn't like. If his hair was the ocean, and his forehead was the beach, the tide was most definitely on its way *out.* And he was pretty sure that he could detect the very beginnings of a vortex of baldness at the top of his head. A little swirl of thinning. (Thinning: there was something to that word.) His eyebrows, by contrast, were accumulating material. It was as if all the hair that was fleeing the top of his head was migrating to his eyebrows and setting up a refugee camp above his eyes. And *protruding*: yes, protruding was the word, shooting out at every conceivable angle. Extending out into the Z axis. His eyes were grayish green and, he felt, an attribute. But his nose: his nose was too small for his face, somehow. Kind of round at the tip and receding from the viewer, smashing back in on itself. A rounded chalk-nub of a nose. But worst of all: his chin. There were at least two problems with his chin. First, it was kind of chiseled out, like this little round nub that had a shape, like the chin of a mall Santa. A little button-type protrusion. Its own little island of flesh. A cartoon chin. But then add to that the pouchiness, and you had real problems. Because the chin was both really well-defined—too well-defined, too shaped—and also giving birth to this pouch of flesh below, a horrible mock-pedestal for displaying the little round protrusion at the bottom of his face. A pedestal in the shape of a sagging balloon. It was hard to accept.

Weldon looked, he felt, a little like the newspaper editor on *The Wire*, the guy who also played the merry chemist on *Breaking Bad*. But his face was wider than that actor's face. Pouchy, flabby, way too thick of cheek. Danny liked to grab great handfuls of his cheeks and squish them and squish them, obliteratively. Weldon didn't mind. But he did wish there wasn't quite so much to squish.

There was a knock on the door. Three quick raps. Decisive, efficient. Weldon opened the door to find a brimming, beautiful face, a male face, well made, well kept up. A white man with good hair and bright eyes. Rob Lowe-esque. A man in his early fifties, maybe—maybe just his forties. Weldon wanted to think that he was in his fifties but still looked like he was in his thirties. But maybe he was in his late forties and looked like he was in his early forties. Whatever the case, he looked a lot better than Weldon. He was trim and fit. A man who dealt in *reps* and *sets*. His clothes—a sheeny blue button-up shirt, rolled up to the elbows, black slacks, and shiny black shoes—looked expensive.

"Pike Glazier."

"Weldon," Weldon said.

Pike's handshake was firm and good and dry. He didn't look like Tim Tebow, but if he'd told Weldon that he knew Tim Tebow, Weldon would not have been surprised.

Rushing yards. Yards per attempt. Yards after contact.

As Pike led Weldon into the living room, Weldon glanced outside. There it was, out on the expansive deck: the grill, big, tucked under a blemishless cover.

"Please," Pike said. "Make yourself at home. Mi casa es tu casa."

Nope. Pike's casa most definitely was *not* Weldon's casa. There were no forsaken children's socks strewn about the room. And he doubted he'd find any rock-hard pizza crust in any of the couches. And he was pretty sure that all of the battery covers on all of Pike's remotes were still attached.

They sat on leather sofas at the fireplace end of the living room, facing each other over a sleek low hardwood table, on top of which sat a dark brown leather portfolio. The edges of the portfolio lined up perfectly with the edges of the table.

"So what line of work are you in?"

Weldon immediately regretted having asked this question. For whenever you asked this question, it would then be asked of you.

"Consulting. You?"

Consulting: what a loaded word! There were so many questions Weldon wanted to ask. Consulting whom, about what? And to what purpose? And how could you consult enough to afford that kind of house? And why wasn't he at work right now? Or did he just work whenever he wanted to? Was he about to hop in a jet? So many questions. Such expensive-looking shoes.

"Well," said Weldon, feeling The Dampness begin to coat his body. "I'm basically a stay-at-home dad. Well, I *was.*"

One of Weldon's problems, he felt—though it hadn't always felt like a problem—was that he didn't have much of a desire to make money. He didn't *love* money. It didn't really make sense to him as a way to organize your life. It wasn't that he was anti-capitalist or anything like that—you could make money if you wanted to. But

Weldon hadn't ever wanted to. You needed some money to be comfortable and comfort was good but beyond basic comfort it seemed kind of pointless and stupid. But what else did the Pike Glaziers of the world have? What other sword to shove into the stone?

"Did you get fired?"

"What—"

"I'm kidding!" said Pike. He leaned over the table to deliver a soft rap on Weldon's knee.

"Yeah," said Weldon, forcing a smile. "Right. Well. Is that your boat?" he said, pointing at a picture of a boat on a nearby wall.

"Work hard, play hard," said Pike, with a glazed Glazier smile.

"Is it a yacht?"

"Not quite," said Pike. "I guess I can't retire yet!"

Weldon nodded, raised his eyebrows. "How's Perry?"

Pike waved a hand dismissively. "He'll be fine. I'm going to get him a puppy."

Inexplicably, Weldon started to talk about his childhood dog, a golden retriever named Rouser. Pike listened intently—or almost intently. He had this air about him, Weldon noticed, of being totally intent on you while always also thinking about something else. As if you were incredibly important to him, but not as important, say, as this other thing he had to do. More than once he glanced at his phone. His phone had no protective case or cover. Imagine that. That was, to Weldon, a state of elevated existence. An existence in which you didn't worry about dropping your phone.

"Let's get down to brass tacks, shall we?"

Brass tacks: there was a phrase for a man like Pike to use. Weldon pictured a big mahogany closet in the basement of that mansion with a big tin basin full of tacks made out of brass. He laughed. "Yeah, sorry. I don't mean to waste your time."

Pike laughed a sudsy laugh, then undid the metal clasp on the portfolio, without opening the cover.

"I don't want you to feel threatened, okay?" he said, pressing the tips of all ten fingers into the smooth brown leather. "I'm not trying to threaten you here."

Weldon raised an eyebrow. His mouth felt dry. He felt threatened.

"Listen," said Pike. "This thing with Perry—there's a simple way to resolve it."

Weldon raised his eyebrows. How much would he have to pay?

"Let's face it," said Pike, "most people would go to a lawyer. But I'm not most people. That's not my style."

Then why the summons? Why the portfolio? Why not just let it go?

"I appreciate that," said Weldon. With his right hand he was rubbing his left arm. The planks of the floor were dark and clean and smooth.

"We all make mistakes, right?" said Pike, with a laugh which Weldon did his best to match. "But," said Pike, punctuating himself with an index finger pointed in the air, "there *is* something you can do for me."

Weldon felt as if he'd just walked into a movie. As if he was about to be asked to kill someone, or deliver a briefcase full of something bad.

"Listen, Perry's real beat up about this."

"Really, Mr. Glazier, I am *so* sorry. I have no idea what I was thinking."

"He was going to go out for the football team."

He was? Weldon tried to picture Perry—worried Perry, dripping-haircut Perry—playing football. It was not a pretty picture. He had to work to suppress a guffaw.

"They have football at their age?"

"Yeah. Pee-wee bullshit. No hitting. But it's a start."

What was the finish? Perry on a stretcher? Perry placekicking terribly? Perry bringing water to a giant of the forest?

"What do you want me to do?"

"Perry mentioned," said Pike, glancing down at his fingernails, "that you have this family trip you're planning. For the weekend? Some lake in the mountains?"

Oh shit. Seriously? Weldon feigned confusion, but he knew exactly what came next.

"He doesn't get out much, you know? Not nearly enough. A trip to that lake– that would mean the world to him."

To him, or to you?

"Can—" stammered Weldon. "I should talk it over with my wife."

"Of course," said Pike, with another quillion-dollar smile. "You can text me later on today. Fifty-two-GLAZE."

"What?" said Weldon.

"That's my number. Fifty-two-GLAZE."

"Okay. Right."

"Text me."

"Okay, sure," said Weldon. "Text is fine."

"I mean right now. Then I'll have your number. Fifty-two-GLAZE."

Weldon got out his phone and entered the numbers—the fucking letters—and hit send and Pike's phone dinged.

"Perfect," said Pike, rising, and extending his warm dry hand.

Deb sat on the floor of the living room, head bowed. Weldon was on the couch behind her, driving his elbows into her shoulders. This was how he earned the right to watch *Monday Night Football.*

"I went over to Pike Glazier's house today."

This was the time of day—no kids, no noise—for Weldon and Deb to Talk Things Over.

"That's right. How'd it go?"

Weldon muted the game and told her about the encounter—the house, the Personal Assistant, the premium shitter, his conversation with Pike on those black leather couches—sprinkling in plenty of color commentary along the way. He saved the upshot for the end, knowing that Deb would not be pleased. And pleased she wasn't.

"Are you serious?" she said, turning to grill him with her dark, almond eyes. There they were: those hot downslashing dimples, the ones that formed above the bridge of her nose when she got mad.

"That's what he said."

"Weldon, you have to tell him no."

Even under optimal conditions, Deb wasn't crazy about going to the cabin. Adding this extra variable, in the form of an extra five-year-old, might well be enough to topple their teetering detente.

"You have to call him tomorrow," she said, rising slowly from the floor.

Which reminded Weldon that he'd said he'd text tonight. *Fifty-two* GLAZE.

"I know," he said, softly, picking a fragment of popcorn from the fabric of the couch. "But what about that portfolio?"

"What about it?" she said, smoothing her long dark hair into a ponytail.

"There were documents in there."

"And?"

Deb, who worked as in-house counsel for a high-end sportswear company, knew her documents. The company made really cool things—jackets and pants and sweaters and hats and sunglasses; the kinds of things that people like Pike Glazier bought and wore and talked about—and was doing very well. Deb's salary kept getting better, and her workload was mostly comfortable and fine. And they got lots of deeply discounted off-season sportswear—jackets and mittens and vests and such. Whenever Weldon was wearing one of those jackets, he felt like it didn't quite belong on him. He felt that someone Glazier-esque

would try to strike up a conversation with him about ski-
ing or cycling or backpacking or kayaking. And sometimes they did. And Weldon would smile and nod.

"Can he sue us?" said Weldon, following Deb into
their bedroom, then through the bedroom into the master bath. One sink. Zero fancy toilets.

"Anyone can sue anyone."

And that was the point, wasn't it? Pike knew he
didn't have to win to win. He only had to throw his
weight around.

"He's just posturing," said Deb, applying toothpaste
to her brush. "You have to tell him no. This is our family
vacation, Wel."

Weldon nodded absently. It could wait until the
morning. He joined Deb at the sink and made a stupid
mirror-face. Deb smiled with the edges of her eyes.

Weldon cherished these moments with Deb, their quiet evening rituals. Brushing their teeth. Applying cream.
Utilizing Q-tips. The way she lay on her side of the bed
reading, most nights, with her hair spread wide across the
pillow, like the rays of the sun in an old religious painting.

They had met at the wedding of a mutual friend. He'd
made her laugh. He could still do that. Sometimes he felt
that that was the only thing he had to offer. And sometimes he felt that that was all that he *needed* to offer.

She was a true diamond in a rough. Goddamn. Funni-
er than met the eye. Smarter. Wiser. Better in all regards.
She aged so well that it just didn't seem fair. In every respect. Soon after they'd started dating, Weldon began to
fear that he'd lose her. That he'd fuck it up. That he had

to take some action, some action he couldn't possibly perform in time, to make sure that she stayed with him. But when she was with him, she put him so at ease that he forgot all about that and dwelt in her presence and, as a result, did exactly what he had to do to keep her by his side.

He liked to lie there at night with the sheets pulled tight to his chin and his hands on his chest. Perfectly still. Deb would fall asleep, perhaps, with her hand on his chest and her head on his shoulder. And Weldon would lie there, eyes open, still as a loaf of bread, listening to the rising and the falling of her breath.

"Do you think I could run my own business?" He was speaking to the ceiling as he said this.

Deb, mid-dream, humphed a muffled, half-asleep response, a hum of dull warm sound.

I could, Weldon would think, from time to time. But there wasn't ever a satisfactory end to the sentence. It was a refrain without a moral, a joke without a punchline. *I could* – He'd taken to wafting these words through his mind—even speaking them out loud, at times—but there was never a good-feeling end to the sentence. It was as if, having given himself over to full-time fatherhood for so many years, he had completely forgotten how to be a person in the world. Now that the twins were in school all day, five days a week, he had no idea how to fill the newly vacant hours, hours that daily yawned before him like a cavernous maw.

But today would be different. Today Weldon was ready to burst into action, in the form of a full-frontal assault on the blackberries behind the garage. Their silent incursion on his family's territory had gone on far too long. No more excuses. He had some coffee and breakfast and played three games of solitaire, then went outside. *You're all mine, bitches*, he said to himself, assessing the enemy position, then went into the shed for gloves and a pair of rather rusty loppers. He held them up, opening and closing them with great satisfaction, then circled the garage and got to work.

The work—*goddamn*—was great, was just what he needed. This might even be considered a perk, he was seeing now, of his newly child-free days. You could stake out an entire weekday morning just for blackberry removal, and no one would ask you to do something else. He cut long, fibrous, corded, thorny stalks and yanked them from the mess of brambles and folded them up and tossed them onto a pile at the side of the shed. (What was he going to do with that pile, once it had been piled? TBD.) His phone vibrated twice in his pocket—Pike Glazier. *Fifty-two*-GLAZE. Weldon ignored it both times. *Sorry, Pikester, I got shit to do.*

There was something fantastically empowering about battling those baleful blackberries. He was clearing new land, expanding his holdings. Protecting his property. Restoring what was rightfully his. Defending his family from nefarious forces. Anything seemed possible. *I could start a business. I could write a novel. I could join a gym.*

Mere minutes into his foray against the blackberries, Weldon was dripping with sweat. He set the loppers down against the back wall of the garage—which needed to be repainted, didn't it?—and wiped his brow and went inside to get some water and—why not?—his portable radio. He tuned the radio to AM sports talk. Sports talk: so comforting, in a way. They always said exactly what you knew they were going to say. There was a script; they stuck to it.

I could start jogging. I could start whittling. I could eat less dairy.

His phone rang, yet again. *Fifty-two-SHITHEEL.* Pike had this way of talking, it now occurred to Weldon, as if he was making a PowerPoint presentation at all times. *Fifty-two-ASSHAT.* He grabbed the end of a thick blackberry stalk and pulled and lost his grip and fell backward and hit the back of his head on the wall of the garage. *Fuck.* His glove had come off, held hostage by those malevolent thorns, and as he reached back to get it he slashed the back of his hand on a neighboring stalk, opening a long cut on the back of his still gloveless hand. *"Goddamn it."*

He stood there, watching the blood fill the little fissures in his skin, for several heaving breaths, then cast his gaze across that sea of blackberries. What was he doing? What was the fucking point of cutting them down? They'd only grow back. And then he'd have to cut the new ones down. And on and on.

He lopped another stalk and folded it over onto itself and tossed it onto his puny pile—*what the hell am I going to do with that pile?*—and then returned to the little wedge of space he'd cleared, which was smaller than seemed just. There was still an awful, awful lot to do. His shirt was soaked.

"I should be getting the roots," said Weldon, looking down at the clustered nubs of blackberry stalks sticking out of the dirt. If you didn't get the roots, they just grew back. The thought of this made Weldon very tired.

He could take a fifteen-minute break. He could have a power snack. He could hire someone with bigger equipment.

His phone rang. He answered it.

"Hello?"

"Yeah, Weldon. Pike. Pike Glazier. I've been trying to reach you all day."

It was 9:48 A.M. How long was Pike's day?

"Yeah, sorry," said Weldon. "I—"

"Have you considered my proposal?"

My proposal. This man was full of proposals. He was a walking, talking *proposal.*

Weldon looked down at his hand. His bitten nails. The cuticles in disarray. That bright red scratch underscoring his knuckles.

"Yeah," he said, softly. "I'll do it." He could feel his jaw harden as he said this, his lower molars locking into his upper molars. "I'll do it."

Silence: this was Weldon's punishment. Not beratement; not indictment. Silence. Deb was not amused. He had his work cut out for him. At least she'd gotten in the car.

Deb was game for most things. She was a dream of gameness, really. Upbeat, energetic. But not, for whatever reason, when it came to going to the lake. Weldon loved the lake. The kids—even Presley, maybe, still—loved the lake. But Deb was a hard sell. She was always coming up with reasons not to go. (And when Weldon had floated it as a potential honeymoon desti-nation, all those honey-dripping moons ago, she had re-jected the idea with unusual vehemence.) But this time

Weldon had put his size 11 foot down, and told Deb, in nonthreateningly direct terms, that she was coming too. Because the twins just started kindergarten, and were starting to stream away from them, just as Presley had.

Their life together as a family was a river, he had tried to suggest. In early life, the kids were with you in a big yellow inflatable boat. The rapids were considerable, but the boat was big enough to handle it, with Deb and Weldon paddling around the rocks. But the older they got, the less stable the boat became. And then Weldon and Deb found themselves outside the boat, swimming alongside, checking, only, in ever more cursory ways, to make sure that the boat—ever lither, ever sportier—could handle the obstacles on its own. And before you knew it, there'd be no boat at all. The kids would be fully immersed in the river, in body and in soul, and swimming before you, and then downstream from you, where you could barely see them, and certainly couldn't catch up to them, and you'd be fearing—fearing constantly, perhaps—that you'd lose sight of them for good.

But when they were at the lake—when, even better, they were in the car on the way to the lake—you could feel for a moment that your kids were still moored to you, if only temporarily. For that brief stretch of time, it could seem they weren't streaming away.

Weldon eased their family car, a Honda Odyssey which he had dubbed the *Landshark*, through the gates of the Glazier Compound and up the paved driveway.

"Wow," said Deb, her silence broken by the spectacle of the house. "Do you think they have enough garages?"

Frail young Perry was waiting by the front door with his mother, alongside two suitcases that were just about as tall as he was. He looked like a young Macaulay Culkin, but somehow even paler and bluer.

"My god," said Deb. "Is he bringing all of that?"

Weldon got out and said hi to Maureen—no sign of Pike—and regarded Perry's outsize baggage, holding back his jokes, then sized up the boy himself. His hair was freshly shorn. He looked forlorn. There was a U-shaped metal brace on the finger that had met with Weldon's hurtling foot at JumpFest.

"How's that bum digit?"

"I can't do iPad with my brace."

Weldon bit his tongue.

The side door of the Landshark slid open, and out popped the heads of Reese and Danny. "Perry, come on! We're making a game." Perry slithered around Weldon and into the van.

Weldon turned to Maureen, then back to the bags. There were so many questions he wanted to ask her, all of them sarcastic. He said nothing.

"One of them is bedding—Perry is very particular about his bedding."

Weldon nodded. There was no use pushing back. But getting those things into the Landshark would be another matter.

"Does this cabin have a phone? Is there cell service out there?"

Weldon gave Maureen the number, and assured her that there was. Then he wheeled the massive bags—

trunks felt like the right word, as if this were a nineteenth-century journey by rail—toward the open back hatch door and sighed. This was going to be a chore.

"Step aside," said Deb, arriving on the scene. "The Master is here."

Deb was the undisputed champion of packing the Landshark. She could fit four rhinos in the back, with room still for a baby elephant. Happily leaving her to Tetris the suitcases into place, Weldon returned to the driver's seat.

I could be a chauffeur. I could start a high-end transport company. I could work for the federal government.

Weldon almost always drove almost every mile of almost every trip. He liked driving. It was like a moving oasis in time. Everyone was together and doing just fine, the world was moving past you at a perceptible rate, and very little was expected of you. Almost nothing at all. Hands at the wheel, mirrors in place. Heated leather seats, full entertainment package. GPS display. And there, in that car, from your position behind the wheel of the majestic Landshark, you could, by way of your rearview mirror, Assess the Cargo.

In the very back, in a spot where Weldon had to really crane his neck to address her, was Presley. Twelve now. Holy shit. Seventh grade. Looking more and more like Deb with every passing day. Dark eyes, straight brown hair with arched bangs. Braces that you almost never saw. Wicked smart, but quiet of late. She was great with the twins—all-world, really, in the big sister department—but skeptical of most things Weldon. Weldon had been a little nervous about naming her "Presley." So many kids' names these days were such show-pieces, it seemed, like brand names you could plaster on your Christmas cards. But as soon as he mentioned it as a possibility—it had been his maternal grandmother's maiden name—Deb fell in love with it. So that was that. He was glad now that she had that name. It was aging well.

Moving to the middle row: the twins. Danny. Daniel: Daniel was a check, felt Weldon, against the frivolity of modern child-naming. Daniel was solid, timeworn, built into the bedrock of American naming. Reese was a little more questionable, but fit. She was by far the more spirited of the twins, full of energy, and often doing things that were at once completely charming and a complete and total pain in the ass (like the gorgeous watercolor painting she did on the wall of the master fucking bedroom, or the mud sculpture—a girl-knight on a boy-horse—installed under the dining room table). Just now, she was singing silently to herself, and rocking her head from side to side.

My purpose on this earth, Weldon said to himself, to her, for the four-hundred-seventy-seventh-time, *is to protect you.*

Danny was the one who understood what it took to get safely across a road. Reese was mostly in the clouds—and if clouds had clouds, she would be in those. When they played tee-ball for the first time in the spring—with Weldon serving as assistant coach, which basically meant that he was in charge of the herding of kids and the herding of balls and the herding of kids herding balls—Reese was the kid wandering the outfield looking for flowers, hat long gone. Danny assumed, in contrast, the ready position, no matter where he was. Hat pulled down tight over his forehead. Glove glued to the ground, even way the hell out in center field, where zero kids would ever hit the ball. But if they did (they wouldn't), Danny would be ready.

When Weldon and Deb found out they were having twins, they freaked out. And then the twins came, and they freaked out again. It was hard. It was impossible. It was a blur. A daze. The fog of war. A fog which still lay thick on them, in places. But the sun had begun to burn it off—the sun, in this case, being the sheer wonder of who they were and who they were becoming. Danny and Reese Tines. They were also the sun in the sense that they'd become the center of the Tines Family Solar System, the binary system around which everything revolved. What did The Twins think? What did The Twins want to do? What was best for The Twins? Weldon had sunk himself into them, had dissolved into their overwhelming needs. And now that they didn't need him as much as they'd needed him before, a part of him had vanished down a hole, maybe never to return. Weldon was partially Weldon-less now. Twinned into oblivion. But he loved them. He loved nothing more than them.

Weldon, cruising down a big broad straightaway, craned his neck to get a glimpse of Presley. Her eyes were glued to the screen of her new phone. This was a new reality: Presley plus phone. Weldon had opposed her getting a phone, but Deb had vetoed his veto; and he couldn't really deny that it was unfair to deny Presley a phone when he was on *his* phone all the fucking time—usually playing solitaire—so they'd gotten her the newest iPhone. Weldon had argued for an earlier model, to no avail. It was, they said, a way for them to reach her. And it was. It was. But it was also a way for her to stream ever farther away. She played on the volleyball team, but didn't want Weldon to have anything to do with it. She permitted him to attend her matches—home matches only—but he was not allowed to make any audible sound. There was such beauty in that volleyball. The empty gym. The uniforms. The dust in the air. The feeling of a space being *used*. And the chance to be in the same room with his daughter for an extended period of time. To know where she was and where she was going to be. He would stand at the end of the bleachers, arms folded. And if the twins were there—they often came along—they'd be playing on the bleachers. They were in the room too. They were all of them in that big wide empty dusty room together. Weldon Tines and Presley Tines and Reese and Daniel Tines.

The car produced the same effect. Weldon had always loved road trips, but his reasons for loving them had changed over time. Now he loved them, he felt, because his wife and his kids and he himself were all in the same small space together, going somewhere.

But now this little bleating Perry Glazier had thrown off that perfect balance. At the twins' insistence, and with no small quantity of cursing, Weldon had installed the middle seat of the second row of the Landshark so that Perry could sit between them. And there he sat, at the center of the action, an inevitable fact of Weldon's rearview vision. And, it quickly became clear, a shrilly *audible* presence. *You're going over the speed limit. Your blinker's still on. How come we can't do our own A/C?*

At last Weldon got him to agree to a movie, and he and Deb were granted a spell of cherished silence. This was another beautiful thing about being on the road: a solid stretch of time with Deb, with minimal distractions. The way she sat there, in the passenger seat of the Landshark. Squinting through the windshield. On most days she parted her hair neatly on the side, but on road trips she put it up in a bun. Her legs crossed on the seat, big toes pointing forward. How did she do that? She was small, that's how, a little feisty bundle of wonder. She liked to wear a whole bunch of bracelets, all at once. On Fridays she worked from home, and it was understood—especially now, praise be to whomever, that the twins were in all-day kindergarten—that Friday afternoons presented a window of opportunity, as far as marital interactions were concerned. But Weldon wasn't holding his breath about tonight. Part of the price you had to pay to take a trip.

In that respect—in the marital-interaction department—Weldon was very good at what he did.

A reddish sedan passed them on the left, with the words *Just Married* scrawled over the back windshield. Someone Weldon once knew said that there was no such thing as a happy marriage, and no such thing as an unhappy marriage. You weren't happily married or unhappily married, the guy had said. You were *just married.*

The poor bastards in that car didn't realize how much truth was frothed into that shaving cream. One sense of *just* would soon give way to another, all too quickly. But still.

They were making good time—they'd be at Smokey's Smoke Hut very soon. A stop at Smokey's was one of a handful of essential traditions of the Tines Family Journey out to the cabin. Weldon and his family had been going there—where *there* was a roadside burger-shack in the foothills of the Cascades—for as long as he could remember. He loved the burgers, the thick shakes, the impossibly greasy fries. The little paper cups for ketchup. The waxy soda cups. And he loved the repetition in the name of the place, the echo of *Smokey* and *smoke*. The Moonlight Burger had everything that a reasonable person might ever expect to have, wedged between two lovely moons of bun: two patties, bacon, cheddar, shredded lettuce, tomato, diced onions, thousand Island, ketchup, mustard, mayo. Damn. The kids loved it too. And Deb: Deb ate very healthfully in general, but she did love a good burger, and Smokey's had the best there was. A million-way tie for the best burger ever.

So as Weldon swung the Landshark onto the damp bald asphalt of the parking lot at Smokey's—another layer of pavement had long been needed there but hadn't ever been laid—he was excited and ready, but a hint of dread was also clouding over him. The Glazier kid: the Glazier kid would find a way to fuck it up.

"What is this place?" said Perry, awakened to the world outside the movie.

"This," said Weldon, "is paradise on earth."

"It looks gross. Can we go to McDonald's?"

This kid.

"Yeah," said Danny. "McDonald's!"

Deb looked amused. She liked watching Weldon squirm.

"No," he said, "we're not going to McDonald's. This is where we always stop. And we only make one stop."

"But I don't like hamburgers," said Perry.

"Get a chicken sandwich."

"I don't like chicken sandwiches."

"Get some fries."

"French fries make my tummy hurt."

Weldon got out of the car. Was joined by no one else. No matter. Zipping up his plaid fleece jacket, he headed for the counter. There was no seating at Smokey's. Only a counter. You ordered your food, they gave it to you, and then you were on your own. Magnificent.

Weldon ordered.

"I have to go to the bathroom."

Now the Glazier kid was on the loose, and coming straight for Weldon, his metal finger-brace between his legs.

The bathroom at Smokey's was off in an outbuilding. Weldon got the key. "Come on."

"I don't want to use that one."

This fucking kid. "Can you hold it?"

"Not really."

"Come on," said Weldon. "Let's go over to the bushes."

"No way!"

Fuck.

"Can't we just go to McDonald's?"

There was something far too on-the-nose, far too symbolic, of something, Weldon thought, as he swung the Landshark into the McDonald's parking lot, about that bag of cooling burgers on the console.

He didn't get out. He stayed in the car and ate in peace.

I could start playing guitar again. I could learn to play the drums. I could give up solitaire for good.

Deb came back with an extra large McDonald's plastic cup—iced tea, larger than anyone needed. Her road trip staple.

"Traitor," Weldon said.

Deb took a long sip in defiant response.

"Where are the kids?"

"I sold them," she said.

Then he asked a question whose answer he knew before he'd finished asking it, and the answer was yes, Presley *was*—goddamn—old enough to handle all the kids inside McDonald's by herself.

"How are you doing?" asked Deb.

The simplest of questions; the hardest to answer.

Weldon held up the grease-blotched paper bag of uneaten Smokey's burgers in response. His counter to her tea. "I think," he said, "that I'm about like this."

She cracked a smile and patted him on the shoulder, then dug in with her fingers. Goddamn.

"Let me get a sip of that," he said.

"Hell no."

In college the point had been to be as blasé as possible about everything. You spent New Year's on Thom Yorke's yacht? No big deal. You got into Geoffrey Chaucer's graduate poetry workshop? Not that big a deal. You had sex with Hester Prynne? It was OK. That attitude had carried Weldon forward into his years as a record store employee and goer-to of shows in Hollywood and greater Los Angeles. Everything was fine. OK. No big deal. Then came Deb. Deb was a big deal. Deb was a big fucking deal. She was the flood of warm everything that had swept him out of his abiding emotional reticence. Weldon fell instantly in love with Deb. He knew right away. He never wavered. And he'd had to be persistent. He'd had to keep emailing her, and calling her, and fabricating little bouquets from the decorative grasses that grew outside his apartment building. It was a full-on assault, but an assault which he did his best to make as low-key—or *low-presh*, as he described it to himself—as possible. A low-presh onslaught, which took the form of cards and grass-bouquets and emails and phone calls. He tried to keep his voicemails funny and light-hearted. She finally consented to a date. And that was that. He wasn't about to let her go. After their third date, as he stood with her at the base of her apartment building on a side street in West Hollywood, he pulled from his pocket a folded-up piece of paper and unfolded it and handed it to her. At the top of the sheet—which was handwritten; he'd taken his time to make his writing look less shitty than it usually did—he'd written, *How's my driving?* Below that, he'd written out eleven questions, and next to each question—i.e., on the right side of the page—there was a scale from 1 to 5. A 1 meant *not at all —like, not at all!*; a 2 meant *not really (or like, barely)*; a 3 meant *sort of (like, a little)*; a 4 meant *quite a damn bit*; and a 5 meant *Hell yes!* He watched her as she read the sheet, laughing in her kind of muffled way, hand to her mouth—like she both did and didn't want you to know she was laughing. He was hoping she would fill it out right then and there, but she didn't. She gave him a look—what did it say, that look?!—folded the paper twice, and slid it into her purse. Then she kissed him on the cheek and went upstairs. The next morning, the completed worksheet lay at the doorstep of his studio apartment in Echo Park. He read it right away. He got six 5s—for *Am I friendly?*; *Am I funny?*; *Do you think about me when I'm not in the room?*; *Is my breath OK?*; *Do you like my taste in music?* and *Do you think I'm hot?*; two 4s—for *Does my car smell OK?* and *Am I performing my gentlemanly duties in a satisfactory manner?*; one 3—for *Is my haircut up to snuff?*—one 2—for *Do you like the way I dress?*—and one lone 1, for *Is my footwear acceptable?* Even as he'd written that question he knew it was a problem. The way he'd written it. Because, before meeting Deb, Weldon had found what he felt was a reliable solution to the problem of what shoes to wear, at all times, and for all occasions. To Weldon, when he was in his 20s, it was a really funny joke to wear Doc Martens well after they'd plunged out of vogue—but not so late as to be retro. It was a play on the idea of retro-ness. Retro before the fact. He'd wear those Docs and jeans and a white button-up shirt and a black blazer with a cigarette hole in the right sleeve which he had purchased at a Goodwill in the Valley. (He still had that jacket, and had worn it to the Dixon School Auction & Gala the year before, and wondered why he hadn't thought of doing so earlier.) He liked that jacket because, even though it was basically a piece of shit, it made you look dressed up. Which called various things into question. Which was, Weldon felt, worthwhile.

As Weldon of Now, piloting the Landshark toward the foothills of the mountains, thought back to Weldon of Then, he marveled at his ballsiness, his *confidence*—which seemed totally unfounded, totally made up. But wasn't that the nature of confidence? It was like the price of a stock, just this arbitrary, made-up thing, which fluctuated according to principles which may or may not have anything to do with tangible reality. But he was young and in good shape and involved in the culture. He knew what was going on, more or less (despite his refusal to buy nice shoes). He was good-looking and funny and read the *LA Weekly* every week. He worked a couple shifts at Amoeba in Hollywood, on top of his gig as a process server. He kept track of the opening of new restaurants—especially the ones he could afford. Even the ones he couldn't. Pop-ups downtown. And art shows in cold and dangerous buildings. And the Bradbury Building, its atrium: he'd taken Deb there once. She hadn't been before.

In that time and place, that Los Angeles of a decade and a half ago, there had been a sense in the air of all that you could do. The warm spring nights with Deb at his side. They'd walk for hours and hours and hours, sometimes in circles. They'd sit on the verandah outside Weldon's apartment, eating fruit and drinking cold white wine. The dusk. The smell of jasmine on the air.

Now they lived in the suburbs, and had kids, and Deb worked a good job, and Weldon didn't know what the hell to do.

I could learn another language. I could get an app for that. I could get a weight-loss app.

"This movie is boring." Perry—implacable, unrelenting, unsilenceable Perry. "Can I play with my iPad now?"

Weldon wanted to scream. This fucking kid. Deb put a hand on his arm. They shared a look.

"Sorry, Perry," Deb said, with otherworldly calm. "But it just wouldn't be fair."

"Danny can watch me play my game. And Reese can have my iPod."

An iPad *and* an iPod? Fucking hell.

"Yeah dad!" said Danny. "Pleeeeeease," he added, joined by Reese. Big old gap in the front of her mouth where her teeth no longer were. Weldon was vanquished. On he drove.

For one of their earliest dates, Weldon had taken Deb to the Echo on Sunset, preceded by sushi at a hole in the wall nearby. And as she sat there on a mat on the floor, legs crossed, rubbing her chopsticks together with such elemental vigor, he knew he wanted to marry her. He knew then, at that moment, as her chopsticks scraped against one another, that he couldn't let her go. That he had to do whatever he could to hold onto her, and marry her. Sell his Les Paul. Sell his Astro van. Hell, sell all his records. Max out his credit cards. Whatever it took. It didn't matter. He couldn't let her go. Such fire in her eyes, in everything about her.

The road bent upward into the mountains along a river. On the Nav screen, Weldon could see that there were a lot of sharp turns ahead. The pass was getting closer. Deb looked drowsy. Everyone was silent.

I'm over halfway done, Weldon would think to himself, from time to time. *My life is over halfway over.*

By the time they reached the pass, Deb was asleep. She'd had a hard week. The rest was well-deserved. The problem, however, was that that left only Weldon to bear the brunt of Perry's ceaseless questions and comments. *How much longer? You have ketchup on your lip. Pike's car has heated seats in back.*

What were iPads for, if not to stopper the mouths of plaintive kids?

Weldon didn't let the Glazier kid's interrogations keep him from enjoying the passage from west of the mountains to east of the mountains. West of the mountains, everything was wet and green and gray and kind of crappy. Strip-malls in cloud-cover, was the feel of it, often. By contrast, east of the mountains the sun shone pretty much constantly, and there were pines in place of firs, and grasslands, and scrublands. It was arid. It dried you out, somehow, to go there. He liked that. And he liked that you didn't even really notice the sudden change of it, unless you were paying attention, which usually you weren't. Especially if Perry fucking Glazier was in the van, which he was, and piping up, just as they were coming into Weldon's favorite part of the drive, where the big steep catastrophic mountains rose up directly from the road, glowing with the tones of early fall.

As they crested the pass and began their eastward descent, Weldon beheld Perry in the rearview mirror, with his new foam toy in one hand, his iPad in the other. His McDonald's soda cup clamped between his knees, and a wad of cold McNuggets in his cheek. His pain and suffering did not appear to be considerable.

And there was Reese, gazing again out the window. Reese who still couldn't hack a whole night in her own bed. She came up at all odd hours of the night, and Weldon would either patiently, quietly, tiredly escort her back to her room or just let her take his spot alongside Deb and go to her bed. He probably slept as many hours in Reese's bed as he did in his own. Once in a while—once in a great damn while—she made it through the night, and when she did, she was very, very proud. She'd get there. Wait.

"What are you doing, Reese?"

"I'm imagining what stars would be in daytime."

And Danny, gazing intently at the screen of Perry's iPad. On a cold recent morning at the bus stop—the only genuine hint of fall they'd yet experienced—Danny put his hands in Weldon's pockets and Weldon put his hands over Danny's hands and sort of curled them over them to keep them warm.

Streaming away from you. Streaming away.

"When we get to the cabin," Perry said, without looking up from the screen of his device, "I should have first choice of beds, since I'm the guest."

When they got to the cabin, it was already late afternoon. Weldon opened the door and inhaled deeply. Yes.

There was always a smell about the place. It was the smell of camping, maybe. Smoke and wood and trees and stale bread. Weldon loved that smell, that mix of smells. It reminded him of something.

There was nothing thoroughly amazing about the cabin. It had two bedrooms—one for Weldon and Deb, one for Presley—and a sleeping loft for the twins (and shrill young guests with minor finger woes). It was—not unlike himself, Weldon felt—simple and solid. Doing its job. Not trying to do too much. Decent, grounded. On the fucking lake—what more important job could it have than being on the lake?

And the lake itself: the lake itself was beautiful, as beautiful, really, as anything could be. Long and narrow. A bright deep blue. On the far shore the mountains rose abruptly, in places, beige in their baldness and flecked with trees and rocky ridges. Beautiful.

"Hey," said Weldon, "today's the solstice."

"What's the solstice?" Perry said.

"The official change of seasons."

"It's not the solstice, dad," said Presley, passing him on the way to her room. "It's the equinox."

"Same diff," said Weldon.

I am over halfway done.

This wasn't the first time that Presley had corrected him, and it wouldn't be the last. In fact, it seemed that it was just beginning, this cascade of corrections. The older she got, the more she would correct him. He'd get wronger as he got older, and she'd continue to get brighter and more right. And he had this vision, this winding, spiral-type vision of a future in which all of their conversations would hinge on her correcting him. That he might someday just start saying things blatantly wrong on purpose so that he could hold on to that little shred of fabric that remained between them, which was this propensity for him to be wrong and for her to be right and for her to show him how he was wrong. He might hold onto that.

Weldon lugged in all the bags and Deb began to put the clothes in drawers. This was something she always did, no matter where they were, no matter how short their stay. The clothing always went in drawers. Weldon knew she would have much preferred to stay at one of the resorts that lined the far end of the lake, and he was glad not to have that wish spoken out loud for the thirty-ninth time.

As Deb unpacked, Weldon drifted into the living room. Yes: this was home. All the raw wood surfaces. The hard industrial carpet. The cassette player. His father's collection of sappy jazz. There were old wool blankets in the closet, and pillows that were lumpy and scratchy. And a cupboard full of old games: Monopoly, Parcheesi, Stratego. The floor in the dining area was wood and scuffed and old, with a ratty, ropy oval rug under the table. There was a picture of his mother on the wall. And a photo of his father waterskiing many years ago—in the early '70s, say, one of Weldon's favorite photos of all time. In the photo, his father, young and with a head still full of hair, was gliding across the water toward the camera on his skis with his hands raised in the air and a wide smile on his face—without any sign of a boat or rope. He just stood there on the water, gliding, frozen in time.

Weldon stopped coming to the cabin for a couple of years after his dad died. Then his brother Ben convinced him to go back, and he was glad he had. It wasn't bad or sad at all. It was the same great place to be. But now Ben wanted to sell the cabin. Weldon resisted. He was fighting the good fight, he felt. But why? History. Tradition. You couldn't just get rid of that. Just turn it into money for a new damn car. Money wasn't history. It was nothing. It was transience. Faceless. The cabin was a place you could go to and sit in. You could smell the smells of it, and touch the wood.

The children scattered—Perry and the twins to the loft, Presley to the dock to text the friends she'd gone minutes without texting. Weldon wiped his brow and looked around. There were two loaves of bread on the counter from Ben's last visit. And next to that were three rows of four cans, neatly tucked together. Weldon went over to have a look. Four cans of baked beans—nice. Four cans of creamed corn—excellent. Four cans of green beans—meh.

Deb gave him a peck on the cheek and headed outside, with Perry and the twins in tow. Weldon stayed behind to fill the larders, then went to the window and exhaled happily and proudly. The lake. The dock. The dock was straight and flat and made of planks, a couple of which Ben had replaced with newer synthetic material. Those synthetic planks stuck out. They were a bummer, really, Weldon thought. They weren't in keeping with the feel of it. The dock was kept in place by two pilings, which were attached to the planking with D-shaped pile guides. He used to hide his beer in the cold water of the lake, chained to the underside of the dock. He'd been taught to drive a boat at a very early age, but he'd never really liked it. He preferred the shore. The little beach they had. The patch of grass.

The kids were running back and forth along the beach, tossing rocks, scrawling things into the sand— even Perry. The sun was getting low. The days were getting shorter.

With all the food now tucked away and ready for a weekend's worth of grubbing, Weldon got to work on starting a fire in the cabin's old stone fireplace. Fires were an area of expertise for Weldon. You started with a little pile of dry shavings, bedded down on strips of newspaper. Then you lit that and blew on it and placed a few small pieces of kindling. You built the heat up, in this way, from small to medium to big to blazing, and once it was blazing, you could add just about anything to the fire and the fire would burn it. Amazing. Once, as a child, Weldon had thrown a bunch of rotten bananas onto the blaze. Not the best idea he'd ever had. But not the worst.

He added a log to the burgeoning blaze, then took hold of a wooden paddle that was leaning against the mantel and used the end of it to shove the log into place.

"What's that?" said Perry, who seemed always to arrive on the scene just in time to puncture Weldon's peace and quiet.

Peace and quiet: fuck. That was his father's phrase.

"This," said Weldon, presenting the paddle to Perry as if it were a gem-encrusted sword, "is a family heirloom."

"What's an heirloom?" said Perry.

The twins had joined him by the fire.

"It's something very old, passed along from generation to generation. My grandfather made this, from a tree in his yard."

"It's a paddle," Danny said.

"What's it for?" said Perry.

"I'll show you!" said Reese.

"No, hold on," said Weldon. But it was too late. The twins were leading curious worried Perry boundingly outside and down the stairs of the deck to the place where the canoe was kept under a brown tarp. By the time Weldon caught up, they'd peeled back the tarp to reveal the smooth dark hull of that old boat.

Weldon's father had often taken them out in the canoe when they were kids. They'd bring fishing poles and cast about—pointlessly, it now occurred to Weldon, since they had no bait and zero skill. His father was furnishing them, young Weldon and Ben, with a sense of endeavor without having to provide the things that were necessary to achieve their ends. But they didn't really care. The weather would be nice. They'd cast and cast.

Their dad would read a book. Luther Tines. He'd always hand the paddle to Ben for the paddle home; never Weldon. Not once. Ben was older and stronger and smart enough to be entrusted with a paddle. Weldon had to make do with his flimsy child's fishing pole. But he really didn't mind. He'd never had much interest in paddling. On occasion he'd lie down in the bottom of the canoe, with a life jacket for a pillow, and look up at the sky. The sky was endless and timeless. It never changed, and it couldn't be owned or touched or even named.

"Can we take it out?" said Perry.

"No," said Weldon.

"Why not?"

"We just can't."

"Come on, Dad," said Reese. "Last time you said next time."

"Come on, let's go inside," said Weldon.

"But we want to go in the *canoe*," said Danny.

"Not today."

"What about tomorrow?"

"We'll see," Weldon said. (This had to be among a father's choicest phrases: *we'll see.* You committed to nothing. You simply deferred.)

"Can we have WiFi time?" said Perry.

"There's no WiFi here," said Weldon.

Perry's eyes went wide in panic.

"Can we watch a movie?" Danny said.

Fuck. This was the cabin. Did their screens have to infest every corner of every space of every trip? Still, it was getting dark, and they *had* played outside.

"One hour," Weldon said.

The kids flocked to the loft. Deb settled into the couch beside the fire. Weldon took his brother's binoculars from the shelf. Guys like Ben had binoculars and knew how to use them and knew what to look for through them. Knew what to look at, and for how long, and knew what to say about what they were seeing. Ernest Hemingway was one of those guys. He would hold them up and say something terse and good about what he was looking at. Or just hand them over without saying anything and pick up a shotgun. But whenever Weldon tried to use binoculars, he had a hard time getting the circles to come together just right. It always seemed the image was out of focus. And when he did, at last, on certain rare occasions, manage to bring the image into focus, it always gave him a slight headache. But he got them fired up, well enough, and held them to his eyes and scanned the lake. The lake was calm. There were a few boats out there, a couple of jet skis. A big yacht-type deal was cruising from right to left. A Pike Glazier kind of vessel. Pike, Ben: they would also know the names of the parts of that boat. Maritime terms. Starboard. Aft. Gunwale. Jib-Sheet. Mainsail. Topmast. Fizzle. Fuck.

I could get a boat. I could dig a moat. I could mainsail jib-sheet schooner skiff and sloop.

Whenever Weldon saw gatherings of boats—whenever he considered the people who used the word *boat* as a verb—he was reminded of Deb's father, Pedro. He was an incredibly conservative Mexican immigrant. He'd been a pilot for Aeromexico in the '60s and '70s and then moved to Orange County after marrying Deb's American mother. He flew for United for several years before retiring to Scottsdale—because, Weldon surmised, Orange County wasn't conservative enough. (To Weldon, greater Phoenix was a palpable sign that the world was about to end. Phoenix had happened. And the fact that Phoenix had happened meant that the world was almost over.) Pedro Alvarez formed a lump or node in Weldon's consciousness, an inevitable fact or feature of his world. Because—let's admit it (as Pedro liked to say)—he'd never been much of a fan of Weldon, and harbored a long-festering set of grievances regarding his swishy son-in-law. To wit: 1) he didn't have a job; 2) he was a Democrat; and 3) he didn't have a job. Which meant that a) he wasn't really a man because b) he didn't make any money, and therefore c) he was undeserving of their daughter, which meant that d) he was—let's admit it—kind of a piece of shit.

Like Pike Glazier, it now occurred to Weldon, Pedro had a boat that wasn't a yacht—Pedro made sure to make sure that Weldon knew it wasn't *technically* a yacht—but it seemed pretty damn yacht-like to Weldon. Mini-bar. Leather seats. One of those big-ass dome-shaped compasses. The kids loved it. And Weldon probably would have loved it too, if Pedro hadn't been either a) grilling him constantly about his lack of job, or b) trying to teach him how to drive that fucking Jaguar of a boat. Once, he'd left Weldon at the helm in a pretty crowded harbor on Lake Havasu. He'd gone down below to make some drinks. So there was Weldon, at the helm of this god-penis of a sportscraft, screaming across the choppy waters of a marina full of other drunken boats. Quickly Weldon became so flustered and bewildered that he simply killed the engine—which was actually way *more* dangerous, it turned out—and then Pedro emerged with the preposterously elaborate cocktails to ask him what the hell was going on.

You had to have some conflict in your life.

They ate a dinner of hot dogs and creamed corn and chips and a salad and then the kids, with Deb's backing, got Weldon to give them another hour of screen time. Presley, who had graced them with more than a handful of sentences at dinner, was in her room, on her phone. Deb lay reading her book, another trashy crime novel. (This was another thing that Weldon, a recovering English major, loved about Deb: her truly shitty taste in books.) Weldon tended the fire and flipped through some months-old issues of *The Atlantic.*

"All right everyone," he pronounced, soon after the clock above the mantel had struck eight, "time for electronic lockdown."

Perry and the twins were huddled around Perry's iPad on the big black leather couch.

"What's electronic lockdown?" inquired worried Perry.

"Everyone's stuff goes in that cabinet," said Danny.

The cabinet in question was a good old wood thing, built by someone many years ago, which stood against a wall in the living room.

"But it's only eight o'clock," said Perry.

Weldon dared not ask him how late he got to stay up playing iPad at his house, for fear of hearing his response.

Deb, swooping in from the kitchen, added the spin

of diplomatic lightness which Weldon so often struggled to find when talking to other people's kids: "We'll have more screen time tomorrow."

The truth was that she thought Weldon's insistence on *electronic lockdown* was silly. Why not, she'd asked him, on multiple occasions, just have them put their screens away? What Weldon didn't tell her—what he hadn't even really told himself—was that electronic lockdown was as much for *him* as it was for them. When his phone was locked away in that cabinet, it couldn't tempt him with its siren song of solitaire.

With no small measure of communal whining and dilation and digression, Weldon got the devices locked away and pocketed the key. As Deb read to the twins in the loft, Perry stayed behind to sharpen his teeth on Weldon's bones.

"Now what do we do?" said Perry.

"You don't want to hear the story?"

"That book is boring."

Did he even know what book it was?

"How about brushing your teeth?"

"Can we go in the canoe tomorrow?"

"We'll see."

"That's what you said before."

This kid. Weldon sized him up. So worried. So wronged. So bent on gnawing Weldon's bones to dust.

"I'll tell you what," said Weldon. "Let's get some rest and talk about it tomorrow."

Perry nodded, worried, wronged.

Weldon led him to the bathroom sink.

At last there was peace in the Valley of the Tines. The kids were all asleep, and Weldon and Deb were alone in the old log four-poster that filled the cabin's biggest bedroom.

"Some kid, huh?" said Weldon. He felt that Perry had swallowed up their whole damn day, and was threatening to swallow up the entire weekend. Again he reflected with dismay on his swift capitulation to Pike Glazier. The blackberries: somehow the blackberries were to blame. A confluence of bad conditions, of exhaustion and sweating and the cut on his hand. Weldon had finally gotten Deb to agree to go to the cabin, and that one brief moment of despair might tank their trip.

Deb shook her head and laughed. "Do you think he's just starved for attention?"

"It's called Asshole Father Syndrome," Weldon said.

"But you said he was nice."

"Yes. No. Yes. Asshole isn't the right word. And neither is nice. He's nice in a way that's nicer than nice. And he's an asshole in a much more comprehensive way. He's an asshole in a way he doesn't even know about. In like a way that would come as a complete surprise to him. In a way he'd never agree with." Now Weldon broke into Godfather Voice: "A man who doesn't spend time with his family can never truly be a man."

Deb laughed. Weldon felt warm and good.

"What do you want to do tomorrow?" he said.

She gave him a look—a look he'd seen a thousand times before.

"You're kidding," he said.

"I'm sorry, Wel. There's an agreement I have to review."

Agreements: Deb worked in the world of *agreements*. The kind of agreements that had to be *worked on*. The kind of agreements that caused endless disagreement. He laughed. "Man, you're really throwing me to the wolves."

"I'll try to make it back for lunch."

Weldon knew what that meant: see you at dinner. He sighed and stared at the ceiling and let his body sort of jelly down into the sheets.

David Costabile. That's who it was. The guy on *The Wire* and *Breaking Bad*. David Costabile.

"I miss the kids," he said.

Deb propped herself up on an elbow. "They're in the next room."

"That's not what I mean," he said.

She lay back and pulled the blanket tight over her chest and stared where Weldon was staring.

"I do too," she said.

He took her hand. She turned to face him. "I don't have all night."

Weldon slid the blanket off and went to work.

The knock on Deb and Weldon's door came at 6:30 A.M., which, even on a non-vacation day, would have been far too early for comfort. Weldon got up with a loud father-grunt and shuffled to the door and opened it. Perry.

"What's for breakfast?"

"What time is it?" said Weldon, pinching the sleep from the corners of his eyes.

"I'm hungry," said Perry. "That bed is too soft."

"Try the couch."

"The couch is scratchy."

Damn right it is. Scratchiest couch this side of Scratchville, little Perry.

Weldon waffled out of the bedroom and into the kitchen to make coffee. Coffee-making at the cabin was kind of delightful. You had to pour the water directly into the filter from a kettle. You had to be patient. It took time. Perry installed himself atop one of three stools at the counter.

"What's for breakfast?"

"You, my friend," said Weldon, "are in for a treat."

Weekend Breakfast was Weldon's domain. It was, in fact, one of the few areas where he felt his expertise was truly elite. Bacon, pancakes, french toast, eggs. Eggs however you wanted them. Toast. Hash browns. Fresh fruit. Milk, juice, coffee. The works. Sausage. Candied pecan pancakes. Anything. He could flip pancakes with a flick of his wrist. He could make an omelet out of anything. He could make the perfect crepe. He was the Breakfast King, capable even of navigating the maelstrom of modifiers used to describe the groceries that Deb made him buy. Organic berries. Organic, lactose-free milk. Even the bacon had to be bought in a package slathered with modifiers (uncured, nitrate-free, free-range, Harvard-educated). They led the league in modifiers.

"But first," Weldon, weary, added, "coffee."

"I don't drink coffee."

"It's for the chef."

"Can I have some OJ?"

Weldon poured the orange juice and slid the glass across the counter to Perry. Perry gulped it greedily.

"What are we doing today?"

"Coffee."

"It's dark in here."

"It's a cabin."

"We stay in hotels."

"I bet you do."

One of Weldon's signature dishes was a thing he called the toasturrito. A breakfast burrito—on toast. The secret was to *grill* the toast, but only on one side. And then fold the toast toasted side in and soft side out, with all of the burrito stuff inside. Delicious.

Weldon poured himself some coffee and inhaled deeply and sipped. Hell yes. He set down his mug—brown, chipped—and brought down one of the pans. All of the pans at the cabin were cast iron. Seasoned, heavy, clanking things.

"I'm hungry," said Perry.

"I know," said Weldon. His reserves of patience were relatively high—as they were most mornings—but draining rapidly. "You see," he said, "there's an order to things."

First you got the bacon going. This would fill the cabin with delicate yearning. Weldon's bacon method was simple: Chaos Bacon. You just dumped a package—the whole damn thing—into the pan and let it all get cooking in a solid lump. Then, in the calm warm minutes that you had before it started to really sizzle and spatter, you separated out the strips with tongs.

Next you got the griddle warming. With the bacon now starting to sizzle, and several lovely gulps of coffee down the hatch, Weldon brought out the electric griddle and unwound the cord and plugged it in.

"Is that thing clean?"

"Yes," said Weldon.

"It has scratches on it."

"It's been well loved."

"When you get scratches on a non-stick surface, you're supposed to get rid of it."

"I'll take that under advisement."

"You're not going to cook on that, are you?" worried worried Perry. Weldon stared at him. "When it's scratched like that, you're supposed to throw it away."

"You said that."

"You'll get cancer."

We all have to die.

"Here," said Weldon, shoving a stack of plastic plates—the kind you'd find at summer camps and college dining halls—into the kid's hands. "Make yourself useful."

"You don't have regular china?"

"It's called *cabinware*," said Weldon. "It's exactly what it's supposed to be."

"We have two sets," said Perry.

"Two sets, huh?"

"Plus the day set. Pike prefers the day set. But Maureen prefers the ones we got at Nordstrom's. Pike keeps his locked up in the dining room. And that's what he eats from. And Maureen eats from hers. But she doesn't lock it up. Because no one else wants to use those. And I get mine from the day set."

Weldon looked at Perry with puzzlement, but decided against probing the matter any further. The bacon was starting to dazzle the air. Deb emerged in running gear, her hair up in a ponytail, hugging her laptop to her chest. With her was Presley, phone in hand.

"We're off," said Deb, then pecked Weldon on the cheek.

"You're going too?" he said to Presley.

"I have homework," Presley said.

"On your phone?" Weldon raised an eyebrow.

"Yeah dad," said Presley, brandishing a notebook, "on my phone." She kissed him on the cheek and made for the door.

"Where are you guys going?" Perry said.

Deb stopped in her tracks. She and Weldon shared a look.

"She has to work," said Weldon.

"Can I go too?" said Perry. "I need WiFi."

"And miss out on all the fun here?" said Deb, with a wink at Weldon and then a beeline for the door.

Weldon envied her this power· the power to flee at a moment's notice, borne on the warm winds of *agreements*. The power to offer something highly desirable to Presley. Through the window of the kitchen he watched them back out of the driveway, then turned back to his boney little patron.

"How do you like your eggs, Perry?"

"Basted."

Basted?

"Basted?"

"Yeah."

"I don't do basted," Weldon said.

"Maureen bastes my eggs and brings them to my room."

"What room?"

"My bedroom."

"You eat breakfast in your room?"

"I eat every meal in there."

"You guys don't eat together?"

"Not really."

Weldon nodded, slowly. This seemed unimaginable. Seemed almost criminal. Suddenly he felt very badly for this kid. All those lonely meals alone.

"You know what?" he said. "I'm the Breakfast King. Basted it is!"

Weldon got down another pan and slapped a pad of butter in it. Basted: of course. Basted.

He cracked the eggs into the pan and watched them sizzle and then took a little silver spoon and scooped up the foaming butter and drizzled it over the face of the eggs, then did it again, and again, and again and again, until the eggs looked basted to perfection, if he did say so himself. He slid them out of the pan and onto a plate and tonged the most-done strips of bacon from the bacon pan and put them on the plate as well and slid the plate across to Perry.

"Where's the toast?"

"Of course!" said Weldon. Rookie mistake. The basting had thrown him off. He shoved two slices of Organic Wheat into the toaster.

"You'll have to have the protein first."

"I'll wait."

As Perry ate his breakfast, Weldon got going on the pancakes. He was in the zone now, a fugue state of flipping and pouring and singing aloud.

The Breakfast King was the only nickname he'd ever given himself. It had kind of stuck. It was his way of displacing the nickname he'd been given at the cabin as a kid, in the days when his standard response to questions from grown-ups, questions of almost any bent or slant, was *nothing much*, a phrase that had been etched into the walls of eternity by his Uncle Bert. *The King of Nothing Much.* That nickname was one of the few things Weldon kept from Deb. It could die a cold and lonely death, as far as he was concerned. And holy hell, you didn't want that phrase in the mouth of Captain Pedro Alvarez. Not ever.

"Let me tell you something, Perry," Weldon said, rolling the rolling dishwasher over toward the sink to hook up the hose. "This place has a certain magic to it. Good things happen here. Magical things."

"Like what?" said Perry.

"Well," said Weldon, stalling. "Once, when I was a kid—a little older than you—we saw a black bear swimming in the lake."

"So?"

"*So*? How many bears have *you* seen swimming in a lake?"

Perry shrugged. "Pike is getting me a puppy."

Pike Pike Pike Pike Pike.

"Pancakes!"—Reese, magically, mercifully burst into the room and flung herself into her dad.

After breakfast, as the twins and Perry carpet-bombed the floor of the living room with Legos, Weldon availed himself of a congratulatory round of solitaire in the can. When he emerged from the bathroom, Perry was standing at the sliding glass door, with the binoculars—Ben's binoculars—held to his face.

"Whoa whoa whoa," said Weldon, trotting toward him.

The binoculars were way too big for Perry. Comically big. He had to squeeze them all the way into an inverted V to get them to conform to the space between his eyes.

Put down the goddamn binoculars, Weldon stopped himself from saying. There had always been a strict regulatory framework surrounding the handling of Ben's binoculars. That was just the way it was. But the kid ate every meal alone, alone in his room, on his own damn plates.

"Hey," said Perry. "Is that a water slide?"

"Did you wash your hands?" said Weldon. This was as close as he could come to his father's time-worn *Put those down*.

"That's a slide!"

"Give me those," said Weldon, wiping his hands on his pants. He seized the binocs from little Perry and held them to his face. They were upside down. He righted them and then focused them and then, in time, located the slide in question, if only to confirm exactly what he already knew. But even though he knew what he was going to see, he also knew that part of the masculine act of hoisting binoculars to your face was to confirm what you already knew. Was to see the thing you could already see, but closer.

What Perry was looking at across the lake were the shaggy grounds of Belvedere State Park, where there was indeed a water slide, achy and creaking, a lighter blue hue with every passing year, in the shadow of a great white water tower. Weldon used to go there as a kid. That's how long that slide had been there. Too long. Now it was to Perry as that green light on the dock at East Egg was to Gatsby. His downward-coiling Daisy.

"Can we go to that slide?" said Perry.

"Yeah Dad," said Reese, who had wormed her way between Weldon and the window. Her back was against his knees, her face pressed against the glass.

"What about Spout'z?" said Danny, joining Reese and Perry at whiningside.

Spout'z was the local water park. "Maybe later," Weldon said. "If you're good." Nice: a little bit of leverage. The Ace of Spout'z, tucked up his sleeve. "Now go get your swimsuits on," he said. "Let's go baste ourselves in that lake!"

He opened the sliding glass door and stepped onto

the deck and took in the lake and the hills and, past the hills, the ragged, rugged mountains. These were the kind of mountains, Weldon imagined, which guys like Pike would see and want to climb, and then climb, and then come back down and talk about having climbed them. *Summit*: that was the verb for it. You summited.

I could join a climbing gym. I could learn to fly a plane. I could do some stretches.

It was a fine day—*a fine day*, his grandfather used to say, on that same deck, on that same lake, in the 1980s. Weldon now understood the elementary truth of that statement. There were few clouds, and it was warm. Not hot—not the kind of heat that would launch you into the lake unbidden—but warm, pleasant. *Fine.* There wasn't much wind, and the clouds were few and far between.

At that time of year—after the high season was over and all of the people who could afford to visit during the high season had left—the temperature of the lake started to dip. But the kids never seemed to mind. Somehow all water everywhere was warm to them.

"You need to wrap my finger."

Weldon looked down. Perry, finger extended. His swimming shorts were an absurdity, half a foot too long and cinched up tight around his tiny waist.

"Maureen says it needs to be wrapped when I go swimming."

The little metal brace embracing the kid's finger. White padding on the inside. Poor kid: couldn't pick his goddamn nose. Had to go off-hand with the nose-picking. Weldon told the twins to hang fire and took Perry inside and got a Ziploc bag and some packing tape and wrapped the finger. "There."

Weldon enjoyed the better part of a quarter hour of peace, sitting in a lounge chair on the deck, watching as the twins and Perry jumped into the shallows of the lake from the dock.

The cabin was kind of his version of church, it occurred to Weldon. The Tines family place of worship, where you worshipped old wood and deep water and the presence of mountains on the far shore. Not too shabby. Especially if you remembered to bring good coffee from the wet side of the mountains, which he had. It steamed from the mug—his Bonus Cup of coffee—which was perched atop his belly between his hands.

Moments such as these, with the kids entertained and Weldon sitting down and doing nothing, never lasted long. As soon as you committed the crime of sitting down, and tried to get comfortable, your wife or kids would, within a matter of seconds, want something from you. But this time it wasn't the twins that burst Weldon's little bubble of bliss.

"I'm bored," said Perry, shivering his way into Weldon's airspace. "I'm tired of swimming. And I'm cold. And my finger wrap is coming off."

"Why don't you go inside and play with Legos?"

"I'm bored of Legos."

Weldon tossed him a towel. "Dry off, go in, and find something to do. I know you can."

"How come you don't have a slide?"

"We just don't."

"Why not?"

Weldon shrugged, and gestured meaningful-ly-meaninglessly at the lake and mountains.

"It would be way better if you had a slide."

"I bet it would."

"There's nothing to do."

"Not true, my friend!"

"Can we go to Spout'z now?"

Weldon shook his head slowly, lips pursed. Miraculously, Perry draped the towel over his shoulders and went inside.

Weldon watched the twins. Goddamn. They really were good swimmers now. And they *loved* it. Just get them near a body of water, and all would be well. Weldon could watch them swim for hours on end, and, after so many hundreds of hours spent doing jumps and dives with them and carrying them around hotel swimming pools and letting them ride him as a surf board, he felt that he'd earned a well-deserved respite from entering the water himself.

When Perry came out of the house, the paddle of the canoe was perched perilously on his bony little shoulder.

"Whoa there, mister. Where you think you're going with that?"

Perry, worried, answered: "I want to go canoeing."

"Sorry," said Weldon. "Not today." He got up and commandeered the paddle and went inside to return it to its spot by the mantel, with Perry at his heels. "See that?" he said, pointing in an overly overt fashion at the paddle. "That stays there."

"But you said we could do it today."

"That's not what I said."

"But I'm bored. I want to go canoeing."

"You know what?" said Weldon. "I have an idea."

Weldon's idea was, as far as he was concerned, brilliant. Why hadn't he thought of it before? He led Perry to the shed, a spare wooden structure that stood across a small square yard from the cabin, and flung the doors open. That shed had been a truly glorious part of Weldon's childhood. Despite its routine encounters with Weldon, it was still laid out in just the way his father had laid it out, way back in the early '70s. A wall for tools, with nails tacked in for hanging. A wall for screws and nails and other kinds of fasteners and hinges, all of them tucked into little labeled drawers. Magnificent. And, on the third wall, your bigger tools—your shovels and rakes and weed whacker and whatnot. But these were not what Weldon had come for. What he'd come for was the crumpled mess of yellow rubber in the corner. An inflatable kayak.

"It smells in here," said Perry, plugging his nose.

"I know," said Weldon. "Ain't it beautiful?"

Weldon waded into the musty eons of the shed and grabbed the kayak and lifted it to the light for inspection. Dirty, yes, and long sad with disuse—Weldon could relate—but it could be recovered. The paddles were in decent shape.

"What's that?" said Perry.

"This," said Weldon, "is your ticket to adventure. Let's go blow 'er up!"

Weldon carried the disconsolate kayak to the dock. It was scuffed and kind of dark with various substances, the layer of stuff that accumulates when something festers in a shed for many months or years. He hooked up the foot pump, a round plastic accordion-type thing with a hose that screwed into the place provided on the shoulder of the kayak—starboard? bowsprit? gunwale?—and started pumping with his foot. At first, nothing. Then the kayak began slowly to swell, reaching with its pouchy frame toward the heavens. The rubber vessel whistled softly, inhaling the air, rising and falling with each breath. *Ssshi, ssshi, ssshi.* It looked a little bit like a dead animal coming back to life. Or a baked good starting to rise. A pie, maybe. No: a loaf of bread. Weldon's grandmother used to bake bread, regularly. And little Weldon would be there, by her side—maybe only once, but it seemed like it had happened over and over—and could tear off a hunk of the bread right when it came out of the oven, and the pale dough inside would be exquisitely soft, and the steam would rise toward the ceiling, and there was no better smell in the world. Throw a little square of butter in the middle and watch it dissolve. And then the eating: ecstasy. What else in life had been as good as that?

"Will that thing float?" said Perry.

"We're going to find out."

"Why is it taking so long?"

"Here," said Weldon, shoving the key to the cabinet into Perry's porcelain hand. "Go play with your iPad."

Perry went inside. Outside, the kayak, filling languidly, began to take shape, big and yellow and nice, really, despite that layer of gunk. The fuller it got, felt Weldon, the less that gunk would matter. It would just be a crappy little side-dish, and the yellow puffy body of the kayak would be the big buffet and good. He kept on stomping the accordion, switching from leg to leg with greater and greater frequency. He took a break to wipe his sweaty brow. It was getting there. He started again. Once it was almost all the way full—full enough to get into and paddle around in, if you wanted, though not quite firm to the touch—he took a step back. His heart was going. He was tired. He was sweating. He felt good. He wiped his brow again. He decided to leave the kayak there for a little while, see if it stayed inflated.

It didn't. When Weldon came back, about 25 minutes later—with the twins now horribly, wonderfully installed inside with Perry and his iPad—the thing was starting to sag, pathetically, depressingly. Weldon sighed. But he wasn't done. He wasn't quitting yet.

Soap, maybe: he saw that once, at a tire place in a rural area. The guy put soapy water all over the tire and where it bubbled was where the hole was. He would re-inflate the kayak and then douse it in dish soap and look for bubbles. He did that. And lo: there were bubbles! The culprit? A little slit, about as long as a dime is tall, and not especially mizzenfizzle of the starboard (?) fore-protrusion (?) of the kayak. *Fo'c'sle. Davenport. Sloop.* Now he knew what had to be patched. It looked eminently patchable. He huffed back over to the shed. Ben had an easy time maintaining the strict and sturdy order of the implements established by their father. For Weldon it was harder—harder either to remember to put things back, or not, say, to get distracted by subpoint (B) before you'd closed the file on subpoint (A). But where was he? Yes: the patch. The fucking patch. There was a patch kit in here somewhere, he was sure of it. He liked the idea of that: a patch kit. A discrete problem, a tangible hole you could patch. And be good as new again, at least for a while. Where would his dad have set up camp for patches? In the glue and tape region of the shed, Weldon wagered. Jackpot. *Patch Kit*, read the label on the baggie that contained the patch kit. The little booklet of directions was still in the bag, a Ziploc bag that wasn't made by Ziploc, a bag that was a little bit heavier duty than a Ziploc but still coming apart at the edge where every Ziploc always did. The band at the top was red. That was a nice little touch. He fished out the instructions. The pages were curled from the damp of the shed. He unfolded them gingerly and studied their soothing counsel for several breaths of depthless shed-time.

Leaving the patch-kit on the work bench in the shed, Weldon went back to the dock and knelt on the gray planks, bright in the glorious high sun, to inspect again the humbled kayak. He needed a towel. He went inside and got a towel and toweled off the area around that little slit. *You shitty little slit*, he thought to himself, *I'm coming for you*. Scissors, now: he needed scissors.

It was never just one thing. You always needed the thing you needed *plus some other fucking thing*. In this case scissors. The scissors in the shed were kind of disastrous: old and rusty and thick with the rage of passing time. But they worked well enough. The yellow rubber of that kayak was like the yellow rubber of the structures at JumpFest. Culled from the same scraps of Weldon's derelict manhood.

What was the point of kayaks? Why this odd compulsion to propel yourself? They had friends who lived on an island and had kayaks. *Come on out some time*, the man would say. *We'll take the kayaks out.* Weldon always wanted to reply by saying, *Then what?* Kayaking was, to him, a hilariously futile endeavor. Windmill your arms around a bunch. Shoot a second body through the water. But he never said *then what?* Instead he made vague promises to come on out and take the kayaks out (and use the word *out* a bunch—people who had kayaks liked to use the word *out*, maybe). He had gotten used to this facet of life: the constant making of vague plans which weren't really plans at all. You had to tell people—and be told by people—that you were going to do things, at some point, so as to keep that tiny fire alive between you. If you didn't make plans you had no intention of following through on, you might not make any plans at all. Then what?

That couple had no kids. There was an equation there, perhaps: you either had kids or kayaks. A Honda Odyssey or a kayak rack atop your Subaru. Crusted-over milkshake runoff in the wells of the seats, or neoprene booties. Diapers or dry-bags. Stubble from camping or stubble from not having shaved because you're just too fucking tired.

Work hard, play hard.

How perfect a job did he have to do in order to get the kayak to float? This was a problem for Weldon in general: he assumed—probably falsely—that he had to do a thing perfectly if he was going to do it at all. That if, say, you imperfectly repaired a kayak, you'd done something worse than not repairing it at all. But other people—other men in particular, maybe—seemed to get away with imperfectly executed jobs all the time. Angles on barns. Rooflines. Everything, seemingly.

Weldon wiped his brow. The day was hot. The lake was starting to get choppy.

My life is over halfway over.

The sliding door slid open to reveal the freckled face of Danny. "Dad," he said, "can we do some jumps?"

"Hell yes," said Weldon, sweating, kneeling, hands on thighs. Good call.

This was another time-worn tradition of trips to the lake: the doing of jumps. Leaving the semi-inflated kayak where it lay, Weldon went inside to boom the others out.

"Ladies and gentlemen," he boomed into the living room, "it's time for jumps!"

He led the kids down to the dock—Danny, then Reese, then that little worried Perry—and took up a position at water's edge. Reese—illimitable Reese—went first.

It is my job, Weldon said, to Reese, in his head, watching as she ran toward the end of the dock to do her jump, *to protect you.*

"Ladies and gentlemen," he boomed, "Reese Tines on deck. Will she do her patented Angel Firecracker? She will!"

Reese's arms and legs were a chaos of whirling as she plunged into the lake.

Danny went next and executed his signature move—the Perfect Side Dive—to perfection.

As Perry stepped to the edge of the dock, Weldon let out an anticipatory sigh. What kind of horseshit would he pull now? But no—the kid came through. "Cannonball!" he yelled, then leapt.

"The Glazier cannonball!" Weldon boomed. "The splash heard round the world!" He made it sound good, but it was a pretty spiritless cannonball, if truth be told. Perry didn't really tuck his legs up to his chest, and didn't perform the maneuver with anything like gusto. He just sort of gestured toward his shins with his hands, and then jumped, halfheartedly, into the water. The splash was not a splash heard round the world. It was more a quiet plish. But still.

"Your turn, Daddy!"—Reese.

"No," said Weldon. "I'm the announcer."

"Come *on*," said Danny. "We want to see the Wellyflop!"

In college, at parties, at his fraternity—really just a group of dudes who didn't know where else to live— Weldon had a trick he did. More of a maneuver, really. After a certain number of drinks, he'd clear the hot tub. "Clear the hot tub!" he would yell (or, once the trick became famous, someone else would yell it, and then Weldon would know that it was show time). Then Weldon would stand at the edge of the hot tub, fully clothed, and do a catastrophic belly-flop into the foamy waters of the tub. Anyone standing nearby got drenched. Weldon got drenched. Drunk and drenched. And then—for the second part of the trick, which was pretty frightening to people who hadn't seen it before—he *stayed under* the water for a really long time. For whatever reason—singing to himself in the car?—Weldon could hold his breath for a prodigiously long time. He could stay down for over two minutes. And almost inevitably someone would try to rescue him. But he was too heavy, even then, to lift out of the tub with ease. They'd pull at him and, depending on who it was, his frat half-brothers would let the thing play out—would not, like, tell the person that Weldon was OK and in on the joke and all. And just as the newcomers were starting to freak out in earnest, Weldon would burst back through the surface, gasping, yelling. What he yelled was different every time, and always spontaneous. The maneuver—the whole thing, from that cataclysmic leap to his delayed resurfacing—had become known, to Weldon and his circle, as a *Wellyflop*.

"Well-y-FLOP," chanted Danny. "Well-y-FLOP." Reese joined him, then Perry.

Weldon knew he had to heed the call. He took off his shirt, kicked off his flip-flops, and tested his back. Could it withstand the impact of a Wellyflop? He cracked his knuckles and sauntered down the dock and looked down into his own dark reflection. The kids had gone silent. Weldon leapt.

"Okay guys," said Weldon, wet, standing at the kitchen counter, sandwich in hand. Chips on a plate. A Diet Barq's. "I want to try something a little different."

Just then, the front door burst open—Deb.

"Hey," said Weldon. "You're back."

She gave him a kiss and turned to the kids. "Who wants to go to Spout'z?"

This was one of the things about Deb—admittedly, a delightful thing, if looked at from a different angle—that annoyed Weldon to no end. He called it The Flurry. The Flurry was his term for Deb's tendency to take a perfectly comfortable and acceptable and seemingly agreed-upon plan or situation and heap something completely superfluous onto it. You're playing Legos with Danny and Reese and everyone's fine and having fun? *Let's go get ice cream!* You just gave them some food that's pretty healthy and they're actually eating it? *Who wants some juice?* You're almost done cleaning off the goddamn kitchen table for the four hundredth time this week? *Let's make finger puppets!* So yeah, delightful, but also a complete and total situational wrecking-ball. Today, it appeared, The Flurry would take the form of Spout'z.

The kids flew into a frenzy. "Danny Danny Danny!" shouted Reese, sprinting across the cabin toward the stairs of the loft, which they'd turned into a FEMA cleanup site with Legos and stuffies. "We're going to Spout'z!"

Presley lifted her into the air, then swung her around in wild glee. "We're going to Spout'z!"

Weldon sighed, then polished off his sandwich in one leviathan swallow.

Spout'z was called Spout'z because of the first feature that greeted its visitors, an expansive textured rubber surface that was blue and flaking in places and pocked with little fountains that shot water—i.e., spouted—randomly and without cease. The kids—his kids, and all kids under a certain age, it seemed—could run endlessly among the randomly spouting spouts, getting sprayed and splashed. Holding their forehead over the spout and getting thunked with water. The place made Weldon think of enemas. This giant field of enema-spouts. It had been there since he was a teenager. Just late enough for Weldon to have been able to go only after he would have been most excited about going. When he was just cresting fully into the self-consciousness of having a body with hair on it and a voice that was completely unreliable. It hadn't changed very much, which Weldon appreciated. Not everything had to be redone. Some things could stay the way they were.

This, Weldon could see, from the moment they got to the ticket line, was a terrible idea. The throng of desperate parents and their squealing, writhing kids. And the sunscreen: so much sunscreen to apply. Holy hell.

Before they entered, Deb called a Family Meeting and laid out The Rules.

Danny wasn't a flight risk—Danny was well trained and well tethered. But Reese was a wildcard. You never knew when something might catch her eye, and ignite that mind so full of butterflies and bright things that were only in that mind, and send her dashing toward them. She was a wanderer. You had to look out for her because she didn't have that machinery—not yet, anyway—which told you that you had to look out for yourself. Weldon knew this better than anyone.

I am here to protect you.

Once, at last, they got beyond the opening spouts of Spout'z and put their stuff in lockers and administered what seemed like a gallon of sunscreen, their next stop was the wave pool. Because, Weldon thought, who *doesn't* want to be bobbing up and down and up and down and up? Here Presley detached herself from her parents and the younger kids and headed for the Afterburner, a hellion of a slide that was Spout'z's only truly worthwhile feature. Pro move, Press.

From there they made the rounds, with Deb somehow in charge of the twins, which left Weldon to shepherd worried inquisitive Perry from feature to feature.

I could write another play. I could start directing. I could get the mole on my shoulder looked at.

At last they found their way to the sanctuary of the Snack Shack. The paint on the trim of the Snack Shack—a faded waterslide-blue, chipping and bubbling—was symbolic of something. The menu was written out by hand on a whiteboard leaning up against the wall.

Reese went with a corn dog. Good call, Reese. A

burger for Danny, some nuggets for Perry. A truly dole-ful salad for Deb. Weldon got a foot-long. Damn. Who knew a lousy piece of meat could taste so good? A bag of chips. A little swig of Diet Coke to wash it down. You could do worse.

Maybe some nachos to share for dessert? Why not? Weldon was feeling good. The sun was out but not too hot. The outing was going surprisingly well.

With the wreckage of their second lunch arrayed before them, and still no sign of Presley, Weldon picked up his phone and texted her. *Where you at?*

He would have thought that it was unlike her not to have shown up where and when she was supposed to, but these days it might, in fact, have been like her.

"I'm going to take a little walk," said Weldon, shoving off from the table. "See if I can't find our fugitive daughter."

He started at the Afterburner. People came and went—no sign of Presley. Weldon was beginning to wor-ry. But what about? Presley was old enough to take care of herself, wasn't she? Was she old, or young? He didn't even know anymore. She was old enough to have a phone, but young enough to still refer to him as *daddy*, here and there. Youngly old and oldly young. Where was she now? The same kids he'd seen come down the slide before were coming down again. Weldon's worriedness intensified. He made his way over to the wave pool and scanned the crowd of bobbing heads. No Presley. He went to the lazy river and the Waffle Shed and even the little kiddo pirate cove, but couldn't find her. Then, on a whim, he lumbered up the hill behind the changing rooms. And there she was, his eldest child, Presley, sitting on that grassy slope. With a boy. The boy had his arm around her. Their heads were pressed together, dangerously close. *Holy shit.*

Weldon coughed a long, dramatic cough. They looked up. Presley: mortified. The boy all wadded up in dumb and awkward struggle. A couple years older than Presley, maybe. Weldon fixed his eyes on this boy. Where the hell had he come from? How had he found his, Weldon's, daughter at a goddamn water park?

"You should probably go back where you came from," he said.

The boy nodded, and slunk away, leaving Weldon with his mortified daughter.

"Can we talk?" said Weldon.

"No," said Presley.

Weldon approached her.

"Get away from me."

Weldon sat beside her.

"Listen."

Presley got up and moved away from him and sat again ten steps away. Weldon got up and went to her, but didn't sit.

"I just want you to remember one thing," he said.

"Stop talking."

"No," he said. "This is important. I'm going to say it, and then I'll stop talking."

She did not look at him.

"This is what I want you to remember," he said, placing a fatherly hand on her shoulder. "You have all the power, okay? These little shits"—he waved his arm in the direction of all the little shits who'd be trying to sleep with his daughter for years and years to come— "they don't know what they're doing. They're terrified of you. And if they're not, then you don't want anything to do with them. Because—"

"I get it, Dad."

"Just remember that: you have power. You're in charge. Okay?"

For a long while Presley didn't move a muscle and neither—to his credit, Weldon felt—did Weldon.

"Dad," she said, at long damn last. "Please don't tell Mom."

Weldon lit up inside. "Okay," he said, nodding solemnly. Hell yes.

The trip to Spout'z paid dividends. Everyone was worn out, in a mellow, pleasant way. Waterpark afterglow. They went out to dinner at Darby's Resort, a place across the lake with a big, Family-Friendly deck and heat-lamps and a generous selection of brewskies. Weldon had a large pork chop with sautéed apples, a pile of garlicky spinach, and a towering glop of mashed potatoes. A beer. Another beer. A glass of wine for Deb. Another glass. Nothing wrong with that. Everyone ate well and talked and there wasn't any bickering or bitching—not even from Perry.

Deb, though: something. Weldon made a joke, part of the way through dinner, which he thought would leave her in stitches—it was a poop joke, her weakness, and a good one, he felt, the kind of joke that was almost always a home run. But she hadn't laughed. Or she had, but it seemed a little forced. A little too something. Something at work, perhaps, still gnawed at her. Some lingering disagreement amid that shimmering panoply of corporate agreements. So, as they lay there in the four-poster, with the kids asleep and the cabin as silent as a lake, he felt that it was time to Ask a Question.

This was a thing with them: Ask a Question. Any time you felt that things weren't right—that something was weighing on the marriage—your job, as spouse, was to Ask a Question. To tap gently on that sheet of ice with a simple inquiry. The ice usually wasn't very thick. And by Asking a Question, you got the other person talking, and by talking he or she would feel better.

"Something on your mind?" he said.

(It didn't really matter, Weldon had learned over time, what the question was. The main thing was to Ask It.)

"I cheated on you," said Deb.

"What?"

What had she just said? Weldon felt like his stomach was swallowing itself. A stomach devouring a stomach.

"Years ago. Before we got married."

Weldon was silent, and then a question came frothing to his lips—a question he probably didn't really want to know the answer to, but he found himself asking it anyway: "Where?"

"I was so uncertain, Wel. I was scared. It was stupid. It was an act of self-destruction."

Unbidden, the image of an inflatable banana, pulled by a boat, came careening into Weldon's mind. This pissed him off. This wasn't what he was supposed to be thinking about. Get out of here, banana boat. But it just got bigger, and more obscene. Now the Mariner Moose was riding on it, waving to the shore. The things you thought.

"Where did this happen?"

He couldn't find the right tone of voice. He couldn't figure out what to say. He couldn't identify the thing or things he was feeling.

"Here. At the cabin. New Year's Eve."

"The lawyer," Weldon uttered, barely.

Deb began to cry.

Weldon's memory of that man was vague, blurry. A friend of Ben's from college.

"We'd been drinking," she said.

"Yes," he said. "I remember."

Someone had brought a bottle of Boodles gin. They'd all had way too much. It was one of the few times Weldon had seen Deb get drunk beyond control. Contentious, drifting. Utterly schnockered. No wonder, then, maybe, that she didn't like to drink. Or never seemed to have more than one or two glasses of wine, and never more than once or twice a week. No wonder, then. And yet.

They'd been fighting. Weldon didn't want to move to Connecticut. He'd been an asshole. He'd done some things to sabotage the relationship. This was her way, maybe.

"It was sudden, Weldon. It wasn't planned."

Bad news came in chunks, he'd heard someone say. Maybe. But everything came in chunks. It was all a chaos of information, streaming or thrumming or clattering through the workings of your brain.

"Did he rape you?" Saying this stirred Weldon's numbness to anger.

"Oh God, no. No."

Unbidden, the image of Pike Glazier came gliding into his mind. *Text me. Fifty-two-FUCKHEAD.*

"I'm getting up," he said. He got up.

"Where are you going?" she said.

"I don't know."

"Please stay," she said.

Weldon walked out of the room and out the lakeside door and walked down to the dock.

The air was cold. The lake was still. Its blue-gray surface seemed almost bright against the deeper, darker blue of the far shore. He stood in the middle of the dock, arms folded, casting himself back into that time in their lives, to all of Deb's roiling uncertainty. To the nights when he thought he had lost her for good, and the mornings after when everything seemed right and whole again. To the time he told her, on the sunny balcony of a restaurant at a brunch he couldn't really afford, knowing just how uncertain she'd become, that he'd be good to her. "I'll be good to you," he had said. She'd looked up at him probingly, searchingly, seeking something in him that he wasn't sure was there, though he felt then—and still felt—that it was.

He stood there, in the middle of the dock, for quite

some time, then walked to the end of it and sat with his legs hanging over the edge and his feet in the water. The moon was just past half full. He half expected to hear footsteps behind him, the footsteps of Deb, coming to try to make amends, but he knew that she knew him well enough to let him have this time to himself. He began to weep softly, but the weeping wasn't the weeping of sadness only, not the weeping of self-pity or of felt betrayal, but a fuller weeping, maybe, a weeping that filled you as it emptied you, that made you feel like you were alive and in the picture, as vivid as the moonlight on the lake.

Weldon wept, and then stopped weeping, and stood.

He went inside. He couldn't understand just what it was he felt. He couldn't un-unmoor himself. He couldn't foresee a night of decent sleep. What could you do, what could you do with news like this, which didn't fit but wouldn't go away?

Solitaire. He approached the cabinet, rifling through his pockets for the key. Perry. Fucking Perry. Weldon shuffled over to the kitchen and yanked the Junk Drawer open and tossed the junk around until he found what he wanted: a paper clip. He bent the clip into a kind of miniature dagger and went over to the cabinet and jammed the end of it into the lock and wiggled it around. He tried the knob. No play. He wiggled some more and tried the knob again. Nothing. His father had built that cabinet, maybe. His father was dead. You could, while battling a cabinet, feel the presence of your late father in the warmth of the wood on the wall and the oval braided carpet on the floor. The crisscrossing patterns of fabric in that carpet: his father was in them. Literally there.

Was it pronounced *Coast-uh-BEEL-ay* or *COST-uh-bile?*

He wiggled the paper clip again and tried to turn it but it bent so he jerked it out and flung it to the floor and lay his head against the cabinet and wept. He tried to sob silently, but silent sobbing wasn't something Weldon did. He scrunched his face against the great loud gasp he knew was coming, but he could only hold on so long before that big blubbering exhale came, and come it did, and then it was out. Would the kids wake up?

A hand alighted on his shoulder. Weldon peered up through a blur of tears. Deb.

"What's going on?" Perry.

Deb, firmly: "Perry, go back to bed."

Perry went back to bed, and Deb led Weldon by the shoulder into their bedroom.

Weldon woke in the dead of the night, flakes of his dream still drifting softly down his mind. Little pallid chunks of it. In the dream he'd been inside a massive confessional booth in the shape of a canoe. (Was he Catholic? No. But he'd seen movies.) The booth was massive and Weldon was tiny. Up in the confessional window he could see the outline of a woman, a woman whom he knew to be, in dream-logic, which is infallible because unarticulated, his wife. Deb. Up there, glowing down on him. Not glowing, though: a shadow. A glowing shadow, somehow (dream-logic). Weldon knelt before her—the floor was composed of flower petals and parking tickets—and began to confess. *Forgive me Father—Mother, Brother, Daughter, Daughter, Son—for I have sinned. I yelled too much. I yelled on many occasions. I was impatient. I drank a glass of Kahlua with milk at an odd hour. I drank another one. I didn't make any money. I wore Doc Martens to a funeral. I ate ice cream in bed watching TV. I finished the carton. I said I'd give up sweets but didn't. I yanked Reese's jacket off her arm when she was whirling in play. I lost my patience. I lost my grounding. I listened to Radiohead. I turned up the volume. I didn't read any of the books I bought at the book sale.* And on and on it went, with his wife-mother-daughter glowing down on him, shadowly. Sighing. Gentle. Unreproachful. A soft rain began to fall. A warm dream rain. Weldon (dream-Weldon) raised his head and opened his eyes and let the rain fall into them. He knelt there, silently weeping, his tears themselves the raindrops, warm and red and blue. And then a hand was on his shoulder. He looked up. It was Art McGinn (it took a dream to dislodge his name from memory). His beard grown out. His eyes wide and vacant. His expression blank but somehow brimming. The clouds—there were bright white clouds in the confession booth now— were racing behind him across a blinding cyan sky. Art was holding a large crucifix—but no, it wasn't a crucifix. It was the giant dick-and-balls which Weldon's friend Dell had made as a gag gift for Weldon many years ago. He was holding a giant penis.

And now he realized that he'd woken weeping. A splotch of tears upon his cheek. He wiped it with his sleeve and fixed his gaze on the ceiling.

Of what was Weldon certain, wondered Weldon. *Of what am I certain?* He was certain that he loved his kids. He was certain that the carpet in the living room of the Glazier residence was softer than the carpet in the living room of the Tines residence. He was certain that green was green.

But he wasn't certain that it was important to be certain. What was wrong with uncertainty? False certainty was far worse. False certainty was, in a way, the worse attitude there was. *The best lack all conviction, while the worse are filled with passionate intensity.* Yes: the best were clueless, and the worst too full of clues. Someone (UC Davis) had said that that was a poem—written by whom? Eliot? Pound? Yeats?—that encapsulated modernity. But Weldon felt that it had probably always been true. If you were an asshole, you yelled; if you weren't, you cowered in uncertainty. To be certain, Weldon often felt, was to be an asshole.

He spent too much time in the bathroom. He played too much solitaire. He didn't sit down with Presley enough to help her with her homework. And there had been a period of time when Deb had read the twins their books at bedtime, while he sat in the living room drinking beer and watching Netflix, feeling guilty and uncertain.

He had dwelt in self-pity. He'd welcomed it too readily. It had been a kind of salve. He'd been willing to trick himself into thinking that he had to pity himself because no one else would.

Deb woke, and turned to him.

"I lose my cool sometimes," he said to her, through brimming tears. "With the kids. When they need to get their socks on."

She placed her hand on his forehead and started slowly stroking his hair.

And he didn't do the laundry. He should help her with the laundry.

And he got mad, sometimes, when Danny wouldn't wear a jacket. Pointlessly furious. Fury might have been pointless no matter what. What was anger for? What purpose did it serve? And shoes: shoes could become, suddenly, an area of contention. Like the time that Danny had left his favorite shoes—his fairly new white high tops—at a friend's house and was therefore left with an array of unappealing options, including the blue sneakers which had preceded the white high tops as Danny's go-to pair of shoes, but which Danny claimed were now too small, even though, to Weldon's untrained eye—and to the eye of any reasonable fucking person, as far as Weldon was concerned—they clearly still fit fine. But Danny disagreed, and wouldn't put them on. So Weldon said *Danny* sternly, and Danny put on the shoes, reluctantly. And then they went outside in silence to trudge out to the bus stop. But halfway there Danny started complaining about the smallness of the shoes. *Then let's go change them*, Weldon said. But it wasn't what he said, it was what he did: he grabbed Danny by the arm. Not especially hard, but still too hard. This took Danny by surprise, and brought Weldon back to Level 0 as a parent. You worked your way up, through wise decisions and good counsel and cheerful interactions with your kids, level by level, toward a higher level of parenting—slowly, painstakingly, you raised your level of parenting, one good or decent or malformed but still well-intentioned deed at a time—and then you came crashing back to Level 0 at the stroke of one dumb angry move, like grabbing the arm of your innocent son in the driveway on the way out to the bus stop.

And when Reese wanted crayons for the bus in the morning—crayons; merciless, baleful, malevolent crayons—he said no. *No crayons on the bus.* Would it have killed him to slide a few damn crayons into a Ziploc? No. It wouldn't have. Children were endlessly forgiving. Holy hell.

And he wasn't trying hard enough with Presley. He wasn't gently carefully considerately providing openings for engagement with her. He could give her more, more of himself, more of a chance to come to him on her own terms.

And Danny: there was really never any reason to get mad at Danny. And when you yelled- -when anyone yelled—it might have been nothing more than an expression of helplessness. That's what it was when a baby or a kid did it, probably, and that was probably what it was when Weldon did it too. A desperate grasping at some shred of control. A grasping for a grasp. Was there ever any point in yelling?

And Danny the one at night sometimes, scared and wandering down to their bedroom. Presley.

And once, when Danny was a baby, and wouldn't sleep, and wouldn't lie down, Weldon shoved him down, forcibly, and held him there, against the mattress, and Danny screamed.

His sobs took fulsome shape again, and Deb too began to sob. They held each other very, very tightly.

"I'm so sorry, Weldon."

"They're growing up, Deb," Weldon blubbered. "They're streaming away."

Each moment with them, he felt, sometimes, was powerful. And the more trivial or banal the interaction, the more emotional it made him. Just meeting them at the bus stop every day was an exercise in self-control.

"And in the morning, when it takes them forever to get their jackets on, I snap at them. I lose it, Deb."

She was rubbing his head.

"And when Reese was young," he said. "When Reese was a baby. Once she learned to walk. I couldn't keep her safe."

You had to scoop up Danny, then—Danny would be near—and go running after Reese. And once, at a mini-mall, she'd gone running off toward the parking lot, and a truck was coming, and Weldon ditched his frozen yogurt and scooped up Danny and ran after her and scooped her up with the opposite arm, at feverish last, just as she was about to run screaming with delight into the parking spot that Weldon could see that massive truck was about to pull into. He caught her just as she was about to lurch so blissfully into that space, which probably looked to her, to one-year-old Reese, like a great expanse of wild place to run, and as soon as he lifted her into the air she started screaming in the other way, the way that was an expression of horror, the horror of having been deprived a thing—the wild freedom of that open space to run—she wanted so badly. And she writhed: she writhed, then and other times, so violently that Weldon could barely hold her, all the while also struggling to contain Danny with the other arm. And then she went into her plunge, her screaming plunge, thrusting her arms straight up into the air in an attempt to slide down through his grip. Which only made him grasp her harder. Too hard: really fucking hard: hard enough to make her scream in yet another way, a scream of pain, the pain of his too-tight grip against her shoulders, and how had it come to that, and what the hell was he supposed to do. And now everyone was looking at them. And Reese was wailing, wailing and writhing, and trying to run away, and he had to hold her arm because he didn't know where she might run.

"And Presley," he said. "I've already lost her."

"No," Deb whispered.

"I let her go. It's all my fault. I got wrapped up in the twins."

She kissed him on the forehead.

"I caught her with a boy today," he said. But *caught* didn't seem like the right word. "I sort of found her, I guess."

"Really?" Deb propped herself up on her elbow. "Where?"

Only now did it occur to Weldon that Presley's little meet-up with that boy might very well—might almost certainly?—have been prearranged. The things you could do on a phone.

"At Spout'z. Behind the changing rooms."

"Huh." Deb seemed incredulous, more amused than alarmed.

Weldon laughed. "Yeah. Like in that song, you know? Van Morrison."

"Wait a minute," said Deb. "They weren't—"

"No no," said Weldon. "They weren't *making love in the green green grass, behind the stay-dee-um.*" He sang these last words deliberately poorly, in a way that he knew would make Deb laugh. It did. Then a sudden panic shot through him.

"Shoot, I wasn't supposed to tell you about that." He'd breached Presley's confidence.

"Marital privilege," said Deb.

"Don't tell her that I told you. Seriously."

"I won't say a thing."

They both lay back and gazed at the planks of the ceiling.

"Was it worth it?" Weldon said.

"No," said Deb. "It wasn't. Not at all."

But she hadn't answered the question in the way he'd meant it. But what did he mean? What he really meant, he supposed, was something like this: was it worth marrying me? Was all of this worth it? Am I, Weldon Tines, the Breakfast King, the King of Nothing Much, worth it to you, Deborah Alvarez, the Queen of All that is Good?

"It was just—a dalliance. A lapse, Weldon. It was stupid. I'm sorry. I can't say that enough."

A dalliance. A lapse.

"You don't need to," he said.

The sheet was all the way up to his chin, he noticed.

His hands on it, one atop the other. Pressing down without pressing down. She put her hands on them. Pancake-stack of hands. The things you thought.

"No one gets out unscathed. You know?" He tilted his head, raised his eyebrows, laughed a little.

Deb smoothed the sheet against his chest.

Weldon woke with his head in the crook of Deb's arm. As if he were a child seeking his mother. As if what? As if where? As if when? The day's first light was streaming through the fissures in the blinds. Deb was lying there, awake.

"Can I tell you about this idea I had?"

"Of course," said Deb. She took his hand.

"I wanted to stage a play."

"A play?"

"Yeah. Out here. At the lake. With the kids. Even Perry."

"He really isn't such a bad kid."

"No," said Weldon, "he isn't. He's a good kid with crappy parents." And then, with half a smirk, he added, "aren't we all?"

"I think the kids would love that."

"Do you think so? I don't know," he said. "I'm not sure they'd go along with it."

"Which play?"

"A play within a play," said Weldon. "There are all these plays within plays in Shakespeare. One of those. Have you ever read *A Midsummer Night's Dream*?"

"Yes."

"That is like the all-time great play within a play."

He had more to say about the matter, but didn't. He felt oddly good. Ready to tackle the bacon remaining.

He rose and went into the living room and stretched a Weldon stretch. Everyone was still asleep. The day before had done a job on all of them. The sun, the swimming, the bickering, the pancakes. A classic cabin Saturday. They were cashed. They needed rest. It was good that they were getting it. He shuffled over to the kitchen.

While the coffee was brewing, Weldon got started on a morning fire. He tore up some newspaper and then laid in the kindling and one piece of wood, then reached for the paddle. It wasn't in its spot. The paddle was gone. The paddle was fucking gone. Weldon's stomach dropped. He went to the ladder of the loft and climbed up to where he could see the beds. Danny was there. But Reese was not. And neither was Perry.

"Oh shit."

He scrambled down the ladder and over to the sliding door. Was that them out there, in the middle of the lake? He got the binoculars and put them on backwards and then flipped them around and looked out the window. Fuck. Yes. It was them, Reese and Perry, out in the canoe, in the middle of the lake, without life jackets.

"Where's Reese?" Danny called down from the loft. "Where's Perry? Where's Reese?"

Deb came out, tying the belt of her robe. "What's going on?"

"I'm going after them."

My job, my purpose on this earth, is to protect you.

"After who?"

"They're out there," said Weldon, pointing wildly.

"Where?" said Danny.

"Call 9-1-1," said Weldon. "I'm going after them."

"Weldon," said Deb. "Be sensible."

Weldon went outside and ran to the dock, stopping once to scan the surface of the lake. There they were, out there in the middle of those placid morning waters, paddling toward the far shore. He yelled. They didn't turn around. He yelled again.

He looked around in desperation. The kayak: it would have to be the fucking kayak. He flung it in the water. It began to drift away. Weldon retrieved it by its thin white cord. It rolled up on its side. Fuck. He pinned it with his foot, then lowered himself into the boat.

"Weldon," said Deb. She was running toward him. "What are you doing?"

"I told you," he said. "I'm going after them."

"You need a life jacket," she said.

Weldon got his legs into the kayak, which rose around him like a flower petal embracing a bumblebee, then flailed his way into the life jacket Deb handed him and set out.

"Daddy," screamed Danny, running toward the shore in tears. "Daddy! Let me go with you."

Weldon turned to him—that shrieking voice! But it simply wasn't an option. He continued.

"Daddy!" Danny shrieked. "Daddy!"

Weldon had to tune him out and go. He went.

The water was calm. No wind. The day was breaking nicely. The life jacket smelled bad.

As he paddled, a sense of calm came over Weldon. His purpose—yes, his purpose was clear. Catch the kids. But shit: where were they? And shit: he'd forgotten the binoculars. He scanned the surface of the lake. Yes, there they were, he felt. And there, beyond the dot that was the canoe, their object: the slide, the fucking slide at Belvedere State Park.

"Shit," he said again. He should have stashed the paddle out of reach. He should have put it where no kid anywhere might get to it. This was all his fault. He had to make it right.

He paddled. The white broad plastic paddle of the kayak sliced through the water with relative ease, one side, then the other, then the one. The boat would not go straight. It pointed one direction, then the other, so that Weldon had to try to average out the wobbling if he wanted to go straight ahead. But he could do that. Just dig hard on both sides and keep the boat moving. Just go.

His breath was getting heavy. Sweat streamed down his cheeks and neck. He could do this. They were far away, but getting closer.

In a matter of mere minutes, the kayak started having problems. Fuck: his patch job wasn't holding. Either that, or the kayak had other holes he hadn't seen. Either way, the thing was deflating, was starting to sag and recede under the weight of all that Weldon. He had to make a decision on the fly, and decided to abandon ship, just moments, probably, before the ship—such as it was—decided to abandon *him*. He flung the yak-paddle off to the left and then plugged his nose—absurdly did he plug his nose—and rolled from the shriveling remains of the kayak into the amniotic waters of the lake.

The water was shockingly cold. Painfully, spasmodically, exhilaratingly cold. So cold it clamped the upper half of him, his breast and heart and brain and skull. Everything became clenched in that coldness. He gasped for air, flailing his arms, his heart surging through his chest. He tried to breathe more slowly. He moved his arms and legs in several slow, swooping circles, then launched his head and arms toward the middle of the lake. He dog-paddled, instinctively, and then, a little less instinctively, broke into an improvised breast stroke. Frog-kicking. Yes, he could do this. Just keep the canoe in front of you. Don't lose sight of the canoe. *I am here*, he said to Reese, to himself, *to protect you.*

His breast stroke was garbage, and the life jacket wasn't helping matters. He tried a crawl. Wrong again: His face froze and he panic-surfaced and flailed about, seeking the canoe. He'd lost sight of it. Where the hell is that fucking canoe? He couldn't see it. It might be anywhere. But there was the slide. That's where the little shit was going—to the slide. He stopped to tread water—flailingly, flailingly—so as to do a quick recon of the far shore. There: there's that fucking slide. Still he couldn't see the canoe. And he couldn't be sure the kid would know how to get to the goddamn slide. But the slide was the closest thing to a beacon that you had out there, if you were Weldon, flailing and flabby and cold. He starting swimming again, sticking to the breast stroke. If he swam a few strokes and then stopped—flailingly; flailingly—to survey the far shore for the slide he could keep on course. But soon he was tired. He was not built for distance swimming, even in a smelly life jacket. Still, he went on, churning his arms and legs against the cold, and against those forces—from lake-deep within him—which were telling him he couldn't fucking do this. He got a mouthful of water and started coughing and thought he was going to puke. He stopped to flailingly tread water and clear his throat and get his bearings. Then he flipped over onto his back. Hell yes: *elementary backstroke, motherfuckers.* This he could do. The sky was above him. The sky: the goddamn sky. It was always there. It was the one thing that was timeless. Even among tall buildings in a crowded city you could pick out a wedge of sky and focus only on it and be doing something that humans had been doing for as long as humans had been humans. It was the quintessential human activity. You looked to the heavens. You looked up for guidance, or if not for guidance than for respite, respite from looking at everything else. This he could do. He could do this. He could make it across. He could keep on going forever. He could upthrust those gelid pallid arms and then drag them down to his pouchy sides and then thrust them up again. And bend his legs up into a diamond and then shoot them down into an I. He was a machine made for the purpose of elementary backstroking. The sky was bright and blue and high. Limitless; haze-free. He could keep going. He could do this. He could do this probably forever.

It is my job, Weldon said to Reese, to the sky, *to protect you.*

He felt a certain freedom, like he was a blob of substance coursing smoothly through the darkest, most distant reaches of interstellar space. His panic had given way to something bigger: *purpose*. Just keep going, Weldon. Just keep going.

There was a poem, once, assigned in that UC Davis English department, in a class which Weldon was auditing, briefly, called "Keeping Going." You just kept going. You went and went and went and went. He felt spent. He went. He was starting to lose the sense of having a head, a little.

And when Pete Carroll, the coach of the Seahawks, wanted to say that a player hadn't played very well, he would say, *he got through it*. Which was one of the most heroic things that Weldon could think of. Getting through it. Getting across. Making it through.

My life is more than halfway over.

A guitar came drifting into his head, a certain distant guitar line, somehow, somewhere, as he swam, and as he gasping stopped to flail his arms in a gesture of staying afloat and looked ahead to see that he was still heading toward the slide. The guitar line was in him—what was it? where had it come from?—an acoustic guitar just kind of drifting down in a line at the high end of the range of things. It was fast and mandolin-like, kind of. He'd heard it before, maybe, but he didn't know where. Or he hadn't heard it, or he would someday, and was forehearing it now. The lake was like a large cold womb. Then there was singing. Levels of singing, a main voice, in the front part of the song, and another in the back. Choral. Chorale. On he swam. The clouds in the sky were few and far between. But there were clouds. And they—what? They seemed to say something. The voice and the guitar. That was all that there was in the song. It was starkly beautiful. And it kept repeating. It would start—the high, fast mandolin-guitar of the opening bars, and then the voices—and then end and then start again. He swam. He was tired, maybe, but he didn't feel like anything.

Just get there, Weldon. All you have to do is get there. All you have to do is arrive.

There was a sense in him, maybe, not of what it *meant* to be in the middle of things, but how it *felt*. It felt cold, and languid, and aqueous, and free. It wasn't freeing in itself, perhaps, but in the feeling that you felt it. That you were flailing and frog-kicking your way directly into the experience of the experience. You were in it. Everything was middle of the lake.

And then—but no. But no, but no: he could feel his eyes grow wide, and a warmth rising, orgasmically, through his torso, a warmth to wash away the coldness of the lake. He had it. He had it. Shooting forward, like a flabby white torpedo in the dark green blue lake. He had it. He had it. He knew what he was going to do. It was like a wave washing over his brain, or—no. No. It was like a liquid lightning bolt. There was such a thing, and it was this idea, striking him hard in the core of his heart, so hard and cool and pure and bright that he knew, instantly, that it was exactly the thing that he should do. He had it. He knew what he was going to do. He had it.

And then there was a noise, and then a yell. And everything went dark.

Weldon woke sputtering and coughing up water. His head was in a vise of ice, his chest shot through with burning cold and coughing. And his head, his fucking head. Oh god my head. He was in a boat, the bottom of a metal boat. He looked around through shards of head. Not far off, there were some trees. He slid down to his back. But where was Perry? Where was Reese? The canoe. Someone pounded on his chest. He puked.

Where was Perry? Shit. There was that. Oh shit my head hurts. But there was something else. There was something else. What was it? Yes: his idea. He'd had an idea. Something had come to him, just before he'd been knocked out, as he was gliding across the lake. What was it?

There was the smell of something metallic, maybe. And lake-smells. Smells of rotting life jackets. Beer, perhaps. Sloshy beerinated lakewater, sloshing. His head was a smashed pumpkin.

A man was speaking to him. The man was in the boat, and so was he.

"Where am I?" said Weldon. His head was a vortex. The lake was bright. "Where's my daughter?"

The man answered. Said something.

"I don't remember getting here," said Weldon.

The man replied.

"How did I get here? Where's my daughter?"

The light on the water was way too bright. The sky was wide. The mountains were like the haunches of lions bearing down on them. The mountains were toppling down toward them out of the sky and into the too-bright sunlight on the water.

"What was it?" he said. Yes: the sky. And the water. There had been something, before he got salvaged.

"I had something," he said. "An idea," he said. "I had an idea."

"You're lucky to be alive, man."

"I had an idea," he murmured.

The vision he knew he'd just had, the idea which had come to him so clearly and crisply at some point in the immediate past, now loomed up darkly like the inside of a cave, massive and obscure and impossible to apprehend.

What was it?

The walls of Weldon's hospital room were white. The floor was white. The ceiling was white. The lights were off. An artificial twilight. The next bed over was empty, the curtain between the beds drawn back. A small television was bolted to a wall in the corner. It was off.

It felt like everything in the room was oozing slowly up from the floor.

He could have sunk. He could have drowned. He could be dead.

The kneeboarder had told him, if he remembered correctly, that he was sorry. That he hadn't seen him. That he was just trying to catch a little air. He'd caught some air, and Weldon's head—burgeoning, as it was, at that moment, with his beautiful idea—had been his landing pad.

His little bitty budlet of a bald-spot the target. Kneeboard Guy had nailed it. Had probably ripped free some extra hairs too, to speed up the balding process. Sigh.

Presley was the first one back from dinner. She was carrying a box of food for Weldon. When was the last time he had eaten? Was he hungry?

She sat at his bedside.

"How's your boyfriend?" he said. He was speaking through something like a fog, a fog of head pain and pain-killers. But he felt consciously lucky—lucky to be alive.

"You could have died, dad," she said, and then broke down, shuddering and sobbing, and leaning into him. He held her gently to his chest. Her hair smelled good. They were alone again, as they'd been on so many occasions in a distant past that wasn't all that distant. And yet. Presley as a toddler, toddling around the playgrounds of greater Manhattan Beach while Deb was at work. Weldon and Presley, alone together all day long. It was the hardest thing he'd ever done. He didn't know how he would get through those days, at times, at the start of those days—would almost physically panic when Deb left for work—but he had. They had. And they'd streamed away, those days. They lived on only in photos, accessed only intermittently, the most vivid of which were the ones you hung in the walls of your mind. Because those had multiple dimensions. Sound and pain and feeling. Those were always present, in the way that the ever-reconstructed versions of your past were always present. Now she had a phone and wore a bra and made out with random boys behind the changing room at Spout'z. My baby.

Presley climbed onto the bed and curled herself into

a ball beside him. There was a photo of Weldon with Press when she was a baby. She was sleeping against him. He was reading a book by J.M. Coetzee. One hand on his belly. The other holding the book in the air. And Presley sleeping against him.

"Can I spend the night in here?" she murmured.

Weldon laughed. "Maybe not in this bed." Waves of pain shot through his head. "And by the way," he said. "What city am I in?"

Deb came in with the rest of the kids. Everyone was happy to see Weldon wide awake.

"All that bacon," Weldon said, pinching a center-cut glob of his belly, "saved my life."

They laughed.

"It's dark in here," he said to Deb. Her hand was on his wrist.

"No light yet," she said. "Doctor's orders."

"Reese," he said. It was Reese.

"Daddy," she said. "We went down the waterslide in our PJs!"

"Did you tie up the canoe?"

"I slid down a bunch of times!"

Weldon smiled. "Where's the canoe?"

No one seemed to know. This clearly wasn't something Reese had thought to consider. But no matter. So much, in fact, the better. Reese doubly, triply, always Reese.

Weldon could not help but laugh. "Please," he said. "Don't ever do that again."

Don't ever leave me again. Don't ever disappear on me like that. Be, please, where we think you are.

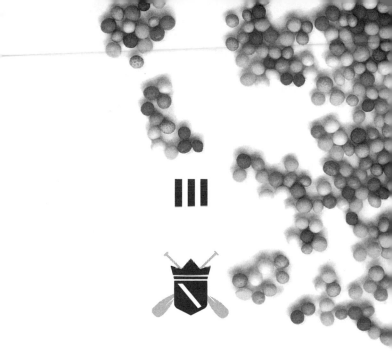

III

All throughout the ride home, with Deb driving, Weldon's mind kept circling back to that dark abyss beyond which lay the embers of the idea he knew he'd had. It was like a dream you couldn't quite remember beyond its general shape and form and feeling. *What was it?*

"It will come back to you," Deb said. "Just give it some time."

But what if it didn't?

By the time they'd dropped off Perry and his suitcases and gotten home, it was late. The kids went straight to bed. Weldon spent a short time wandering the dark environs of the house. It was good to be home. The familiar smells; the known placement of light switches and bathrooms. The click that the thermostat made when you cranked it back up, followed by the roaring-to-life of the gas in the furnace, then the whining of the blower. Home.

Weldon lay awake long after Deb was asleep. Her hand on his chest. The house was silent. The bed was warm. He placed his hand on Deb's. *You saved my life.*

A fog had descended on the Sound, which was only a few miles from their house, and the low moans of intermittent foghorns filled the air. They seemed to form a part of Weldon's consciousness as he tossed back and forth, his body itself a kind of small ship in the ocean of his bed, trying to navigate into a state of sleep that wouldn't come, that didn't come, that wouldn't come.

What was it?

At last he gave up and went down to the alcove in the kitchen where they kept the family computer. The screen glowed to life at the swipe of his fingers. In the search bar of the browser, he typed, *arthur mcginn.*

He was probably running his own business, or working for a law firm. He was probably in great shape, running marathons and things like that. Or no, maybe not. Maybe he was just the same as all of them, getting older, getting fatter, losing hair. Chasing his kids from arrival to arrival. Eating junk food. Staring at his phone. Maybe he'd amounted to nothing much at all.

There were many hits, all of them generic and banal. Weldon narrowed the search to *arthur mcginn berkeley law.* Then his heart dropped: the first hit was an obituary. Weldon clicked the link. There was a picture of the deceased. It was him. Undeniably. Older, yes, like all of them, but still quite handsome. Sandy blond hair, a victorious smile. Weldon read the obituary, then stared at his picture. He wasn't running his own business. He wasn't running marathons. He wasn't staring at his phone. He was dead.

Weldon picked up his phone and called Ben.

"What time is it?" Ben said. His voice sounded murky.

"It's almost midnight," Weldon said.

"So what's the emergency?"

"We just got back from the lake," said Weldon.

"You want me to call the cops or something?"

Art McGinn was dead. He had been killed in a car accident. Survived by his wife and two children.

"Ben," said Weldon, "I need to ask you something." But did he? Should he? Did he? "I was thinking," he said, scratching his cheek. "Maybe you're right about the cabin. Maybe we should find a listing agent. What do you think?"

What was it?

When they came back from the lake, Perry didn't want to go home. "Can't I just stay one more night with you?" (Nope!) He'd already been over to their house twice in the week since. And when he wasn't coming over, he was asking the twins to go over to his house. Always—at least as Danny reported it to Weldon—there was a promise of something special involved, a toy that only Perry had, a snack that only Perry's mom could make. At last, on Saturday morning, the twins agreed to go to Perry's house, and Weldon agreed to take them. This would be his first time out of the house since getting back.

Everything at the Glazier residence was as it had been the first time Weldon went there, except that a white BMW sedan was parked on the pavement outside the garages. In the corner of the rear windshield, there was a For Sale sign. Weldon went up to it. $28,500. Lips pursed, hands in the pouch of his hoodie, he peered through the tinted windows of the car. The interior was immaculate. Black leather, futuristic dials.

At the house next door an elderly Latino man was blowing leaves out of the driveway with a leaf blower. There was no other life in sight.

Someone—possibly the same old man—had recently mowed and raked the Glazier lawn, but yet more leaves had fallen since that recent raking. At this time of year, you could rake your lawn every five minutes and it would still have leaves on it.

Weldon knocked with the knocker, then rang the doorbell. The twins were swinging themselves in circles around a tree behind him. He banged once more, then opened the door and went in. The entryway was clean and silent. A fake fire burned low in the broad sleek fireplace. No sign of a puppy.

As Weldon turned toward the hall, a door opened— the door to the *powder room*—and out spilled Sherry, Pike Glazier's personal assistant, buttoning her blouse. And behind her was Pike, straightening his belt.

You coward. Weldon's sneer, he felt, was cinematically pronounced.

"Weldon," said Pike. "You're early!"

No, I'm not. I'm right on time.

"Perry!" Pike shouted into the rafters.

With his kid in the house.

Perry came down, and the twins flocked to him, and the three of them, as if driven by a gust of wind, went cavorting out onto the deck and into the yard.

"I should go," said Sherry.

"I'll join you in a moment," Pike said to Weldon.

Weldon gave him a wary look and went out to the deck. It was a fine day. A few low clouds, but plenty of sunlight too. Not much wind. No boats on the lake. As he stood there, looking out at the water from that broad gray deck, his idea, he felt, was on the tip of his tongue, humming there, metallic, like a nine-volt battery. Just beyond his grasp. Barely not present. But what was it?

Pike came out. "Nice day," he said, with an awkward laugh. "We finally caught a break."

Weldon said nothing. The kids ran in and out of the trees, making noise.

"So the little brat didn't give you too much trouble?"

Weldon shook his head and, without removing his gaze from where the kids were playing, said, "He's a good kid."

A look came over Pike. For the first time in the many minutes Weldon had spent in his presence, he seemed to be at a loss for words.

But Weldon was not. "You cowardly rascal," he said.

Pike looked more confused than hurt.

"You're a knave," Weldon continued, crisply, bitingly. "A rogue. A varlet." These words had arisen from the depths of Weldon's memory, from his days spent hurling literary insults with his English-major friends. It felt good to air them out. Exhilarating, really, like riding a slide into a pit of plastic balls. "Thou art a boil."

Pike's look hardened. He knew he'd been insulted, but the terms of the insult remained unclear. He said nothing. His phone rescued him. "I have to take this."

Weldon followed Pike with his eyes, then turned to watch the kids. They were playing at the edge of the trees, and in and out of them, screenlessly.

Weldon stood there for a lingering moment, then went inside to make himself at home. *Mi casa es tu casa.* He went to the kitchen and opened the mammoth fridge and looked around.

He tore into the turkey leg as he trudged up the stairs. It was a nice staircase, U-shaped, extending from the entryway to a platform and then up to the upper floor. The first stretch of terrain to the right, as you got off the stairs, was a bridge with black metal railings. Weldon went to the middle of the bridge. It overlooked the dining room. You could make pronouncements from up there. You could stage a play. The dining room table was glass. There were flowers in the center—white, beautiful. In the corner there was a black wood piece of furniture. China in there, likely. Pike or Perry's personal set. Glassware that had to be dusted more often than it was used. Placemats. Through the windows over the doors to the deck he could see the kids in the distance, in the yard, doing something.

The turkey was delicious, cold, with a light gelatinous coating of fat, a little bit of which got stuck to Weldon's upper lip. He sleeved it away and continued along the bridge. At the end of the bridge there was a short hallway. At the end of the hallway there was a mirror in which Weldon saw himself approaching. To the left and right were doors. Black doors. Everything was black and white. He opened one of the doors and went in.

The master suite. A large made bed. A well-groomed carpet. The windows came almost all the way down to the floor. You could see everything, everywhere. The lawn, the lake. The kids running back and forth. At the base of the windows, there were two white slippers, lined up neatly. Weldon slipped off his shoes and slid his feet into the slippers. They were soft and nice but far too small for him. His feet overflowed them. This he kind of liked. He kept them on.

Weldon ate the turkey leg slowly, standing at the window of Pike Glazier's bedroom, then turned to his right to go into the master bathroom. An array of automatic lights—lights over the mirror, lights built tactfully into the ceiling—rose slowly to greet him. Two wide white sinks were set into a shiny black countertop, which ended at a large jetted tub that jutted out into the room. Opposite the sinks, illuminated by its own constellation of artificial stars, there was a closet like a small garage, with racks of shoes and endless coats and slacks. At the far end of the room, there was a door. A carefully curated fragrance filled the air.

Weldon regarded himself in the mirror. The half-eaten turkey leg. The oceans of his eyes. Behind him, hanging from a hook on the wall beside the entrance to that gaping closet, was a thick, plush robe. Dark gray with a purplish sheen. He lay the turkey leg on the counter and turned to feel the softness of the robe, then slid one arm into it, then the other. He tightened the belt and regarded himself again. The shimmer of the robe in all that light.

The turkey leg left a greasy blotch behind on the counter. Weldon took it to the far door, which he pushed open with his elbow. There it was: the toilet. And not just any toilet: a toilet with a view. A bright white toilet facing a wall of floor-to-ceiling windows. Weldon went to the windows. There were the kids, down by the shoreline, throwing sticks into the lake. Two boats, about a football field away, passed one another.

Weldon shuffled to the toilet and lowered himself onto the closed lid. He took a bite and chewed and looked outside. From this vantage, he couldn't see the kids. But there was the lake, and the tops of the trees, and the sky.

His phone rang. He fished it out of his pocket and swallowed and answered.

"Hey!" It was Deb. "How's it going?"

"It's going well," said Weldon. "I'm wearing a robe, and sitting on a toilet."

"Okay."

"And eating a turkey leg."

Deb laughed. "Where are you?"

"I'm eating it cold, straight out of the fridge. What's

up with you?"

The light grew brighter with the passing of a cloud.

"I had this idea," said Deb. She had that tone in her voice—that tone that held the world in it. Mischievous, glowing, portentous.

Weldon pressed his feet into the slippers—tight, warm—and looked out at the blossoming sky.

"You have my attention."

ABOUT THE AUTHOR

Jesse Edward Johnson is a writer and artist based in the Pacific Northwest. As a fiction writer, he has been described as "a master of the family dramedy." His debut novel, *Yearbook* (Paul Dry Books, 2017), addresses issues of sonhood and divorce. His latest work, *The King of Nothing Much*, responds indirectly by taking up questions of fatherhood and marriage.

When he is not writing fiction, Jesse makes images out of original text. His work as a visual poet has been exhibited in galleries throughout the Pacific Northwest. In 2016, he was commissioned to create a two-story mural of his text portrait of the Chilean poet Pablo Neruda for the Port Vashon building on Vashon Island.

Jesse received his B.A. in English from UC Berkeley, with an emphasis in creative writing and literary translation, and his Ph.D. in English from UCLA, where he taught literature for five years. He has also taught writing at Hugo House in Seattle and at San Quentin State Prison.

For more information about Jesse's work and ongoing projects, please visit jesseedwardjohnson.com.

TOMARE!

Manga is a completely different type of reading experience.

To start at the beginning, go to the end!

That's right! Authentic manga is read the traditional Japanese way—from right to left. Exactly the opposite of how American books are read. It's easy to follow: Just go to the other end of the book, and read each page—and each panel—from right side to left side, starting at the top right. Now you're experiencing manga as it was meant to be!

JUL 0 9

KN

Aibiki, page 172

In Japanese, the homophone *aibiki* can refer to either a secret romantic rendezvous or a combination of ground beef and pork, leading to this comical exchange between Lan-Lan and Issa. As with many phonetic puns, there is no exact equivalent in English, so the translator has chosen to use the word "grind" for both its literal relevance to the latter and its slang illusion to the former.

Rock-Paper-Scissors, pages 189 and 192

A children's hand game that merely requires two or more people and a prize to be won, rock-paper-scissors is known by many different names (i.e. *jan-ken-pon* in Japanese) but there's only one way to play. On the chanted count, contestants throw out one hand with their fingers either clenched in a fist (rock), splayed palm up (paper), or a sideways V-sign (scissors). Rock defeats scissors (because it can smash scissors), paper defeats rock (because it can wrap around a rock), and scissors defeat paper (because they can cut paper). The winners of each round continue on until only one person is left.

Engel coefficient and angels, page 196

The Engel coefficient is an economic indicator that is defined as the proportion of (family) income that is spent on food. German statistician Ernst Engel, after whom the term is named, found that the lower a family's income is, the greater proportion of it is spent on food. The more one earns, the lower the number. Issa, however, misunderstands the question, not being the intellectual sort who's familiar with the term. His answer is something of an inside joke, referring to a special contest Dragon Eye's Japanese publisher, Kodansha, held, in which contestants collected chocolate balls whose packaging was embossed with angels.

Non-edged weapons, page 72

Both regular VIUS training bouts and the exhibition tournament forbid the use of edged weapons and firearms. However, contestants may use their everyday bladed weapons as long as they are in their sheaths, or even if the edges have been covered.

Oshibori, page 93

Literally meaning "wrung out," *oshibori* are folded moistened hand towels (either hot or cold, usually the former in the winter and the latter in the summer) that Americans are most familiar with as something used to clean one's hands before eating at a Japanese restaurant. Here, Leila hands a damp towel to Issa for him to wipe off his sweat after his match against Lan-Lan, which at eating establishments is an etiquette no-no, although one is usually allowed to use like a napkin to wipe one's lips. (Hence, in Japan, you do not regularly see paper or cloth napkins except at a fast food chain or Western-style eatery.) Disposable non-cloth *oshibori* are gaining in popularity (and are considered more hygienic), and can be found not just in cafés and restaurants but also on airplanes, with take-out *bento* boxes, and even sold in packs and in bulk to the general public at drug stores.

Senpai, page 141

A term or title referring to someone more senior than oneself. Used most commonly in schools by lowerclassmen to refer to upperclassmen, it is also used in sport and club organizations, in the workplace, and, of course, by alumni, and also implies or acknowledges a mentoring or other close relationship. The word literally translates to "he who went before," and there is a mirror term, *kohai*, which means "he who goes after."

Mikuni, Fifth VIUS City, page 22

We find out in volume 8 that there are currently six cities that make up the VIUS Alliance and Mikuni is the fifth of these six cities. This probably also explains why the *kanji* for five appears on the side of the Central Hall (volume 1, page 6, panel 1). Interestingly, the Head Heavenly Elder's robe has the roman numeral VI emblazoned on it, perhaps making VIUS Central the sixth city...?

Tsuzumi hand drum, page 28

Emperor Jana of Kinshisen displays an object that looks like a *tsuzumi*, a Japanese hand drum. Consisting of an hourglasslike wooden frame with drum faces on either "base," or end, held taut by colorful braided cords that can be further tightened or loosened with one hand to change the pitch while the drum is being struck with the other hand, it is an instrument unique to Japan that is still used to this day in traditional Japanese music concerts and to accompany *Noh* and *Kabuki* plays. Curiously, Emperor Jana introduces his *tsuzumi*-like possession as his lady mother... and there are rumors he was born from the belly of a snake...

Kirin, page 50

The *kirin* is a mythological creature probably best known in modern times as the symbol of the Japanese brewery that also bears its name. It is commonly depicted as a horse-dragon hybrid, with dragon's head and scales standing on four hoofed legs with a horse's tail and either one or two horns. In the world of *Dragon Eye*, it appears that this fabulous beast has also been adopted as the symbol of the VIUS. Incidentally, back in volume 1, Fujiyama drew *kirin* on page 4.

Anadoren, page 63

A fictional energy drink invented by the author. Its name is a play on words, exploiting the similarity between the Japanese word meaning "despicable" and the hormone "adrenaline..."

TRANSLATION NOTES

Japanese is a tricky language for most Westerners, and translation is often more art than science. For your edification and reading pleasure, here are notes on some of the places where we could have gone in a different direction in our translation of the work, or where a Japanese cultural reference is used.

roop designation symbols, various pages

Most VIUS members wear their troop designations somewhere on their uniforms, and equipment and objects sometimes bear stamps as well. For example, on page 1, the sash ied to Sakuraba's sleeve depicts an archaic way of writing the number one, while Issa's eil bears an archaic character meaning the numeral zero.

hamber of the Horse, Chamber of the Sheep, pages 6 and 19

he rooms where the exhibition tournament preliminary rounds are held appear to be amed after the twelve Asian zodiac signs: Rat, Bull, Tiger, Rabbit, Dragon, Snake, orse, Sheep, Monkey, Rooster, Dog, Boar.

That dog... we just call him "Dog." Although sometimes I just use "Hey you"... I suppose we should give him a proper name?! The Elder Vice-Directors used to be fierce warriors! Now they are in charge of cultivating and training young soldiers. They're really scary if you get them mad. Oops, out of space. That's all for now, so see you next time!

Like I said, you're all so nitpicky...!! Masuo!!

Does Kajiyama-san have a girlfriend?? What is the name of the dog? Have the Elder Vice-Directors ever fought? (Do they still fight?) Masuo-san

That's amazing, Kanikama! You're on par with *Sirius*'s chief editor! Well then, let's get to our last question!

I wouldn't be able to come up with such huge inventions! But in response to you, my heart is endlessly bushy and expansive!

Same as before,

Seeking all questions and concerns about *Dragon Eye*! Keep them pouring in!

**Announcing new corner!!
Your ideas can become
4-panel manga!**

Send in the names of characters and scenarios you'd like to see. Fujiyama will turn interesting suggestions into 4-panel manga! What if Yukimura and the dog are put in a room together? What if Kajiyama and Iesa started ballroom dancing!? Fujiyama will decide the outcomes!

Seeking Correspondence!

Furthermore, please be aware that all submissions, including your personal information, will be handed over to the author, so send us your questions at your own risk.

What to submit

In addition to your question(s), please send us your address, name (and a pen name, if you have one), age, school year (or type of work), and phone number or e-mail address. If your submission is printed, we will send you a small present.

Mail to:
112-8001 Tokyo City
Bunkyô District
Otowa 2-12-21
Kôdansha
Monthly Shônen Sirius
Attn: "*Dragon Eye* Q&A Corner"
or "*Dragon Eye* 4-panel manga"
Email:
sirius@kodansha.co.jp

(If you are e-mailing us your question(s), please write the Q&A corner name in the subject line.)

Q

Why was Sōsei originally part of the spellcaster-heavy Squad Five? And what happened to the Squad Zero members before Leila?

Katô Kenji-san

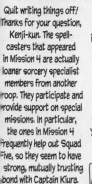

Quit writing things off! Thanks for your question, Kenji-kun. The spellcasters that appeared in Mission 4 are actually loaner sorcery specialist members from another group. They participate and provide support on special missions. In particular, the ones in Mission 4 frequently help out Squad Five, so they seem to have a strong, mutually trusting bond with Captain Kiura.

Aah! This question came with illustrations, thanks! Uhh... I'm sure they are currently with other squads. And what was that about Yukimura? Well, never mind. Waah!

(Five minutes later) All right, I went and asked! What? "I feel like there was a character I was looking forward to drawing, but I don't think this character is going to make an appearance for another one or two years. My memory might fade by then." What a negative fellow! Let's ignore him and move on. ...Wait, so it's not me!!?

Q

Hello. I have a lot of questions regarding Dragon Eye, but one in particular is bothering me. How much salary do Issa and the others get? I would also like to know Issa's Engel coefficient.

Cat's-Eye Amber-san

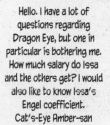

I believe my pay gets deposited every month into an account at the Niko-niko Bank in District One... but how much was it? I'm pretty sure squad captains are paid quite a bit, but it never accumulates. Why is that!!? Oh, and... Engel? What's that? Uh... hmm, if you mean Angels, I think I've got 4 Silver Angels. I'll earn a Gold Angel with just one more Silver Angel, but... it's still a long way off!

There you have it! Got that!?

Q

Hold it right there! Don't answer questions you don't know anything about, Kazuma-kun!? Hey, hey, if I kept obsessing about being bald, prematurely or not,

Huh? What a difficult question. Kanikama's been smooth-scalped since the time I first met him. So it's probably premature...

Is Kajiyama bald? Is it premature balding? Or does he have a bushy, full head of hair?

Morning Banana-san

Deliberate before spending, eh!!

Issa-kun, you spend without thinking too often! I am a new recruit, so I do not get paid much. However, headquarters covers the cost of weapons repair and battle uniforms, so I am not lacking for money.

Q

 A

 Q

 A

 A

 Q

 A

 Q

 A

Q — Hello. I am a *Dragon Eye* reader. After hearing about the Q & A corner, I decided to submit a question. How was the Dragon Eye transplanted? And where did the surgery take place? Matsucha-san

A — Whoa! Core questions from the get-go! My age, huh. I don't know my own birth date, so I've never counted... but I'm pretty sure it's more than what I can count with both hands! And regarding the man with the Dragon Eye, I befriended him many years before I came to Mikuni. It's a long story, so I think Fujiyama will cover it at some point. All right, next...

Q — Exactly how old is Issa? And how did Issa encounter the Dragon Eye-bearing man that Leila had also met?

A — Yo! We'll be starting with a question for me.

A — Oh yeah, I do, I do! I bathe with them on! And... civil what? What's that?

Q — Hello. Do you take baths with the spell fetters on, Issa? And are the VIUS civil servants? Fuku-san

A — Hmm!? Seems y'all are real curious about that Eye! Well, I guess since this series is named after it, it's inevitable! Just between you and me, not just anybody can transplant or receive the Dragon Eye. As far as I know, there is only one surgeon around who can do it. I wonder where that person is now...? Great questions! OK, moving on!

A — A question for Fujiyama, huh. What a bother... Well, I'm sure it's me, but...

Q — Hello. I like Hibiki, and my friend K likes Issa, but which character does Fujiyama-sensei enjoy drawing the most? Sakata-san

Q — Zzz. Oops, I was about to fall asleep! Next question!

A — Issa-kun, please don't give random answers! Uhh, the VIUS are soldiers attached to Central VIUS Headquarters, but their costs are defrayed using the taxes paid by that municipality's citizens. Mikuni City is a part of the larger organization known as the VIUS Alliance, and each member city has its own governing body. So as employees of that organization, I think the VIUS can be considered fine civil servants indeed!

再録！
Dragon Eye Q & A
Encore

This volume, we've got a second Q & A for you!! The following is a reprint of the Dragon Eye Q & A Corner that appeared in the September 2006 issue of *Monthly Shônen Sirius*, by popular demand!

I actually get this question a lot. I.e.: "Aoi-san has perfect abilities, personality, and beauty. What are her 3-sizes? Akimizu-san," "I would like to know all of the girls' 3-sizes. Please ask them, Issa. Kumako-san," "Please tell me Aoi-san's 3-sizes and if she currently has a lover. I can't die until I find out. Nashigoren-san"

You really said that?

Issa-kun, in volume 5's Q&A corner, you described Leila with "she's got big breasts." So now I'm obsessed with knowing Leila's "3-sizes" (bust, waist, and hip measurements). Also, please give me the stats for Aoi and other female characters too. Kanikama-san

Stop giving unnecessary details! Any VIUS member can apply to enter the dorms. They are located on headquarters grounds, near Center Hall. It's a homey, relaxing place.

I've got a dorm room! Although right now, I sleep in a secret little room that I really like. Shun'ichi used to commute from his private residence, but right now he crashes at headquarters, for certain reasons!

(Watch it!!)

Thanks for coming. You see, I want to take your measurements so that we can get your disguise for the next mission made. (measure) *click-click-click*

You really called her here!!?

What was it you wanted to discuss?

Yeah, yeah. You go ask.

All right, I'll go ask her!

They mostly ask about Aoi. And there's no way you'd know.

A

* Incidentally, in the July 2006 issue of Sirius, Leila's 3-sizes were listed as 32-22-32.

I forgot to ask if she had a lover or not...

We've been played. *(Ten minutes later)*

Rock-Paper-... Scissors!!

!!? U-Uh, sure.

Well then, if you win against me in a game of rock-paper-scissors, you may measure me. But if I win, you must do as I say, OK? And please join us, Sakuraba-san.

:
....
△△

(Ulp) Uh... very form-fitting, figure-flattering clothes.

Oh my, what kind of outfit is it?

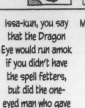

You love me? Aww, you make me blush... My spell fetters are Mikuni VIUS-issued loaners, so the one-eyed man definitely didn't have those. But he might have had something similar.

Issa-kun, you say that the Dragon Eye would run amok if you didn't have the spell fetters, but did the one-eyed man who gave you the Dragon Eye also need spell fetters? I-love-Issa-san

My parents named me!!

In terms of backstories, he also says, "I think I debated whether to call Sakuraba Kazushi or not." Aren't you glad it ended up as Shun'ichi!

Only a day...?

there are 3-second names, one-day names, and one-week names," he says. Incidentally Yukimura's, Aoi's, Hibiki's, and Hyûga's were 3-second names, Sakuraba's and Yume's were one-day names, and Leila's and mine were apparently one-week names. How long it took seems proportional to the profundity of that character!!

That's not a move.

Well then, yours is "Black Lanky"!

Those are just their special moves aimed at you. I know one of yours. It's "Secret Art: Extort and Run"!

What a difficult question! I'm pretty sure Leila was taught many moves directly by her scary teacher, Master Shimon of the Sacred Blade, Shimon School. I think Yukimura has developed ten or so moves using his father's sword design as his inspiration. With regard to favorite or special moves, I would say Leila's is throttling and Yukimura's is single-stroke assassination.

Everyone in VIUS has unique moves, but about how many of them do they have?? And what are each of their favorite or special moves?? Hara Yutô-san

Question! Do all VIUS live in dorms? What are the dorms like? Ayaka Aruto-san

Most of the time, the captain picks the design!

Mask veil design varies between each squad, but even within a single squad, there can be 2 or 3 different kinds. I think there are about 25 total styles among the nine squads?

I'll have Shun'ichi-kun answer this one!

How many different versions or types of mask veils are there? Some appear to be attached to visors, right? They're so fashionable I look forward to seeing new ones each volume. Sora-san

Nice question. That's classified information... but I do believe they have a few special powers.

Do the Igunido have any special abilities or battle skills? Gongen-san

Dragon Eye Q&A

Those were questions already answered last time! You don't get it at all!

I have work to do, fool. What, you want to know more about us? OK, I'll tell you. The biggest idiot here is Issa. His mental age is only 13. His specialty is shirking his duty. And if you want to join VIUS, get on my good side. That's it.

Hold up! Er, this is Shun'ichi-kun, who will be my assistant today. Sorry, but I haven't been able to catch either Leila or Yukimura all day.

Hey, what's going on? If you don't need me, I'm going to get going.

Wow, we're already up to our fourth Q&A corner! Thanks for all of your correspondence! We're going to hammer them out this time, including a bunch we couldn't cover in the last volume!

Yup, yup! Spell gadgets are weapons and protective gear that have been imbued with spells. My wrist guards contain Spell Shield power.

Aren't your wrist guards also spell gadgets?

A

I'll start with the first question! By "those square things," you must mean my wrist guards. They're like little shields.

Q

Dragon Eye is super-cool!!! So here are my questions!! (1) What are those square things strapped to Issa's arms? (2) That dog seems to possess incredible powers, so can't you enlist him? Or is that not allowed? Tako-san

You're more passionate about this than your real job...

A

I'm back! Uh... "I name things and people as they come to me. In general,

(He did *not* just say that...)

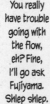

You really have trouble going with the flow, eh? Fine, I'll go ask Fujiyama. Shlep shlep.

Back-stories...? But you usually get named by your parents.

Q

Are there any back-stories to the names of any of the characters or weapons? Zukabu-san

I think they're still embedded in the walls of a sewer tunnel somewhere. Also, I don't know if the dog can enlist or not, but we're so accustomed to him that I feel like he's already one of us.

Now that you mention it, I haven't seen you wearing them lately.

Wow, we're already up to Volume 7!!
Thank you so much for supporting me for so long, everyone!

When the release month of each volume approaches,
I always start feeling the pressure of graphic novel production.
And each and every time, I engage in discussions
with my editor S.G. about what to draw on the cover.
The problem is that we almost always
have slightly differing opinions.
Now that I think of it, we subtly disagreed when I proffered
"What about Sakuraba and Issa?" for Volume 4's cover.
It was modest.
And my editor's opinion was also modest,
so it fittingly ended up being just Issa. Fittingly, huh...

Well, our opinions matched for the next two covers,
so all is well.
Please buy the next volume, too!!
Fujiyama

My Very Nice Staff
[Scissors] Uemura Erika
[Rock] Kamimura
[Paper] Ueda Satomi

Akira Ryoji
The most distinguished warrior of Squad One. His super-confident attitude is justified by his brilliant abilities. His asking Sakuraba to nominate him for captain-elect and his squabbling with Hibiki originate from his sense of VIUS spirit and pride... but that will be explained further in the next volume.

Hibiki Masamune
A former Squad One member who is currently with Squad Six. Has been on bad terms with Akira since his Squad One days, and even now their run-ins always end in trouble... or rather, he seems to have a personality that leads him to butt heads with everyone he encounters. In his battle skills, not only is he gifted, but he also adapts rapidly, has sharp instincts, and is very industrious.

She's just a young girl!

This year's top scorer is entering her second match in the Chamber of the Sheep.

Miscellaneous • The Gallery
Even in the midst of the open exhibition, the daily grind of Dracule elimination goes on for the VIUS. In other words, the only spectators in the gallery other than contestants are those who are off-duty. Incidentally, Hyûga is able to attend not because he is off-duty but because he apparently traded shifts so he could watch Issa's matches.

Dragon Eye 7 END

chatter
chatter
cheer
The match is just approaching its climax.
Lord Irié!
Yes, milord.
All is well.
...aah!
Irié, have you seen to your business?

...unh, his bad "habit" is coming out.

· · · · · ·

Oh? Is it not rare for someone to leave your squad?

Yes... quite so...

He... used to be part of my squad. He is currently with Squad Six...

What is he like?

That other child... h seems t have gri despite h youth.

Oh! You mean that Yukimura fellow and that little girl!

One of them is a contestant. I think the other one is probably lost.

What? Just let them come back on their own.

I think they might be getting their rind on somewhere.

I don't think they're lost.

?

Yeah, they might not come back.

Knowing you, Captain, they probably got disgusted with you and ran off somewhere together.

...grinding meat!!?

a-a-a

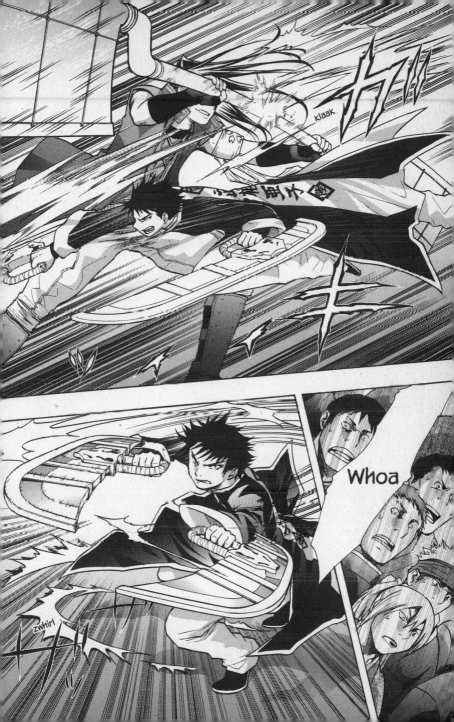

You think?

We seem to be running into each other a lot these days.

And it also seems neither of us can rise up...

without settling things between us first.

whoomp

loom...

For Captain Sakuraba has high expectations of both of them.

三国武相亜子 執行部代表 箕天組壱番

and currently the most highly anticipated VIUS in our city.

Yes. He is Akira Ryôji, a member of my squad,

三国武相 執行部代表

What excitement

Is it for that taller child?

And make no mistake, he'll probably become an important pillar supporting Mikuni, one day.

He is definitely talented.

And what is your opinion?

Yume Lan-Lan

Currently with Squad Three, Lan-Lan is a former Squad Zero member. She has a bright, cheery personality—and a great body that's muscular and yet still shapely. Not one to rely on weapons, she engages in direct physical attacks, specializing in underhanded moves like the one she used to trap Issa. Even so, she was still unable to defeat him.

Kazuma Issa

Exempt from the preliminaries, Issa enters the tournament in the finals. Acquaintances of old with Lan-Lan, he suffers her taunting at the start of the match, but then displays his captain's strength and defeats her in an instant. Back in the old Squad Zero days, they were apparently close as superior and subordinate... or rather, like tormented older brother and cheery younger sister.

Jin Kanjûrô

A member of the spellcaster-rife Squad Seven, he keeps his head covered with a scarf at all times, and seems expressionless except for his insolent attitude. In his match against Sudô, he cast spells without any spellcasting tools and defeated the Squad One powerhouse with a single blow, suggesting he is quite formidable himself. The secret to his power appears to lie in the tattoos peeking through...

Sudô Hajime

A warrior who is a unit head within Squad One. Squad One being a crack crew the fact that he has risen to the rank of unit head indicates he has at least captain-level strength. However, his lack of knowledge and experience against spells causes him to lose against Jin, proving that in Mikuni, spellcasters are a fearsome presence about whom information is scarce.

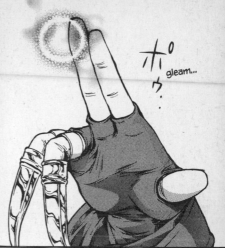

gleam...

most regular VIUS would be as helpless as newborn babies.

Before a High Master...

snag

Starting with Match Three, we will be switching referees.

The new referee is Squad Four Captain Madoka Marika.

pat...

fizz

And a pretty formidable one at that.

...He's a spellcaster.

What just happened?

Wha the...

Heh heh.

Just as I expected, other squads are ignorant about sorcery.

You muscle men of Squad One are especially easy to handle.

No way... You don' have any casting tools, sc how...!?

pant

pant

stomp

stomp

That he's a Squad One unit head means he's at least captain-level in strength, eh! You hardly ever get to see matches of this caliber!

Finally, one of the real candidates to win this, Sudô Hajime.

You're not going to watch? It has the looks of a spectacular...

whump

shiver...

You make it sound like it's already decided.

But that's where he's fearsome. He's unreadable.

Ha ha! I know he doesn't look it.

...Is he really that incredible...?

If anyone can take him down, I think it'll be someone other than Akira.

Nah.

Oh, and I need to speak to Sakuraba-kun about the referees.

H-Home-work? I can't believe he gave me homework, even after I've graduated...

mutter   mutter

peer

Excuse me.

you're fferent n front f your isciple.

Aah.

What is it?

Mission ◉ Twenty-Two
The Pitch-Black Voice

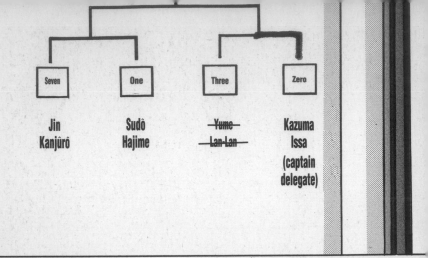

Seven	One	Three	Zero
Jin Kanjûrô	Sudô Hajime	~~Yume Lan-Lan~~	Kazuma Issa (captain delegate)

Wow, that was incredible!

Did you see that last exchange? Hey...

I told you the view's much better down here than up in the skyboxes! This is the best spot.

Data on Neighboring Nations

Kinshisen

Kinshisen is known as a nation advanced in sorcery, but it rarely interacts with other lands, and so is a great mystery. In addition, its current ruler, Emperor Jana, is also an enigmatic figure said to have been born from the belly of a snake. While many other nations live under the threat of Dracule attack, Kinshisen continues to defend itself with tight security. This is the first time they have shown interest in the VIUS and have paid a visit.

Rintôka

Ruled by Princess Suihi, Rintôka is a lush, verdant land steeped in history. While small in size, it fiercely defends itself with both martial arts and sorcery. Although her aide Takamaru is weak-kneed around beautiful women, the fact that he is her only guard speaks volumes about his true talents. One wonders what form the weapon at his back has...

Nashuan

Nashuan, which is to the south of Mikuni, is a beautiful country whose citizens are skilled in the arts. Having engaged in limited cultural exchange with Mikuni City before, its Minister of State is acquainted with Elder Kido, one of the Mikuni Three Heavenly Elders. The Minister has long led his government fairly and honestly, but seems to have injured legs and hips in his old age, and has arrived in a wheelchair with an aide. However, the true identity of his aide Irié is... Is the minister aware of it?

Head Heavenly Elder

The Head Heavenly Elder is the leader of VIUS Central, which joins all of the VIUS cities together. One could say he is the VIUS commander in chief. The current Head Heavenly Elder used to be the minister of state of a small nation that has been destroyed some time ago.

The VIUS Heavenly Elders

VIUS Central is an alliance of cities that were built specifically to resist Dracules. This year, the Heavenly Elders of Queen As Azel City, Shin City, and Elenabeth City are paying Mikuni a visit.

The plan has changed...

Took you a while.

But should be no more problems now.

Found it, here it is.

I'm going to send the signal that we're proceeding to Phase Two.

clatter

We can get to target location from here.

rip

slap

I'm back.

Includi[ng]
thes[e]
two.

Much
luck on
your two
remaining
matches!!

Good
job!!

Thank
you.

Elder
Vice-
Director,
the next
match is
about to
begin.

三國三天

shiver...

Yeah

And now begins the final rounds of the 29th Mikuni VIUS exhibition tournament!

The rules are identical to those of regular VIUS training bouts; that is, the use of any non-edged weapons other than firearms is permitted.

Keep in mind, however, that if you should happen to deal your opponent a mortal wound, you will be immediately disqualified and severely punished.

In addition, if your opponent yields or loses consciousness, you will also be declared the victor.

The match will end once you have scored a point against your opponent or are awarded the win by the referee.

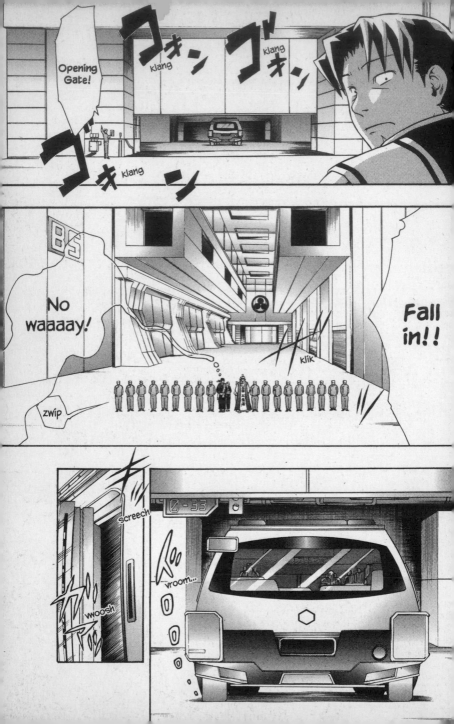

Blah blah

Center Hall B5

Tube Gate Floor

I told you, we'll discuss it later!!

ド' stomp ド' stomp

HH shup

shup HH

Gah, hurry, he's about to arrive.

Elder Vice-Director, sorry I'm late.

Don't let any further messages through.

Yes, sir.

Gah, shut up!

zwip

Would I still not put it though?

I-It's from Hitomi-san. First message in three months...

grimace

I am incommunicado from this moment on!!

S-Sakuraba-san.

No!

chatter

Zero	Eight	Six	One	Seven	One	Three	Zero
Yukimura Sōsei	Rin Kyoko	Hibiki Masamune	Akira Ryoji	Jin Kanjūrô	Sudô Hajime	Yume Lan-Lan	Kazuma Issa
							(captain delegate)

chatter

chatter

· · ·

Ha ha!

I'll get to fight Hibiki in the first round!!

Hey, hey, look at that...

What's he like?

The captain delegate is the Squad Zero captain.

It's just as I had heard.

There they are!

pop

Chatter

Chatter

Chatter

tread

tread

tread

Unit 3 is about to start escorting our guests of honor to the arena.

Shup

Shup

shup

shup

Sakuraba-san, we have word from Unit 2 that the Heavenly Elders from the other three cities have arrived.

Very well.

Good. And Unit 3?

Unit 1 reports that the Lord Head Heavenly Elder will be arriving momentarily.

Yeah, I'm on my way.

三國武相亜
執行部牧
天組定

blare

How dare you, Sakuraba!!

Huh? What could be so...

カチッ click

Sakuraba-san, we have an urgent incoming message from Queen City...

Mission o-Twenty-one
Despicable!

Kazuma Issa

As captain delegate, Issa does not have to participate in the preliminaries. Instead, he is sent to help greet dignitaries from other lands. The cape he is wearing over his usual uniform is one of the dress pieces that captain delegates traditionally wear. Incidentally, the symbol on the front of Leila and Yukimura's dress uniforms represents a *kirin*, the logo mark of the VIUS.

Yukimura Sôsei

In the preliminary rounds, he battles a robust Squad Three member with a shaven head, an imposing opponent one-and-a-half times his size—and who packs a powerful punch. But Yukimura slammed his elbow with the hilt of his sword right away! With his enemy momentarily immobilized by the pain, Yukimura deals a blow to the abdomen and easily knocks him out. Incidentally, he was awarded the dress uniform he is wearing for taking top score on the previous year's enlistment exam.

Mikami Leila

Easily won her first match of the preliminaries, then faces off against Rin Kyoko in the second round. Boldly attacks, hitting vital points, but is unable to inflict damage and is thwarted by Rin's "Palmar Spell Defense" and defeated. Leila regards her Shimon School teacher and one of Mikuni's Three Heavenly Elders, Elder Vice-Director Shimon, as her savior and father figure. He's looked after her since childhood.

VS

Rin Kyoko

A spellcaster and Squad Six member. In her match against Leila, she reveals a glimpse of her strength with powerful spells that stop and can even inflict damage on an opponent without touching them. She is also a former Squad Zero member, someone who knew Issa at the time the squad was disbanded, and seems to have a personal motive for participating in this exhibition tournament...

The final contestants have been decided!!

The preliminaries are concluded!!

Squad	One	Sudô Hajime
	Three	Yume Lan-Lan
	Eight	Rin Kyoko
	One	Akira Ryoji
	Seven	Jin Kanjûrô
	Zero	Yukimura Sôsei
	Six	Hibiki Masamune

The final rounds will commence at noon!!

Lost

...Master
Shimon...

I
lost...

roar

roar

roar

roar

Don't
lose
heart!

She's a
strong
child,
though.
And she
has plenty
of room to
grow.

Leila...

Bad
luck
of th
draw
huh.

三國

I didn't even touch her!!!

In fact...

...get stronger.

Lass...

waft...

Can't move...

Touch

And despite its air of tranquility...

it is first and foremost an anti-Dracule stronghold.

You must have some... formidable defenses.

Thank you.

Do not worry.

And for the duration of your stay, we have additional protections in place.

Yes, indeed.

!

whirl

Lady mother...? You mean...

In-deed!

Right here!

the Empress Dowager is here!!?

Per-vert.

Shh!

Many anks! lease, this way.

Aah, but I am not here for reasons of state, so please relay to him my fondest wishes for his recovery.

However, I have heard that your own esteemed prime minister is currently afflicted with an illness?

Ha ha, it is fine.

A-Aah... please forgive my great insolence for not noticing.

Y-Yes, Your Highness, he sends his most profound regrets for his absence.

Thank ye for the welcome.

I am Jana, emperor of Kinshisen.

We may be neighbors, but we had yet to set foot here.

My lady mother has been looking forward to this as well.

Not all! It is our great pleasure to have gathered here to greet you.

Yes, thank you.

Welcome, and please enjoy your stay.

And at least some of them will have a special interest in *you.*

Just letting you know... the VIPs are probably *really* here to inspect Mikuni VIUS City.

I'm positive some will try to suss out the rumored holder of the Dragon Eye.

However, it's highly probable that the leaders of rival nations know of its existence.

Technically, the Dragon Eye is a Mikuni state secret.

Fall in!!!

So be prepared to be exposed to ridicule.

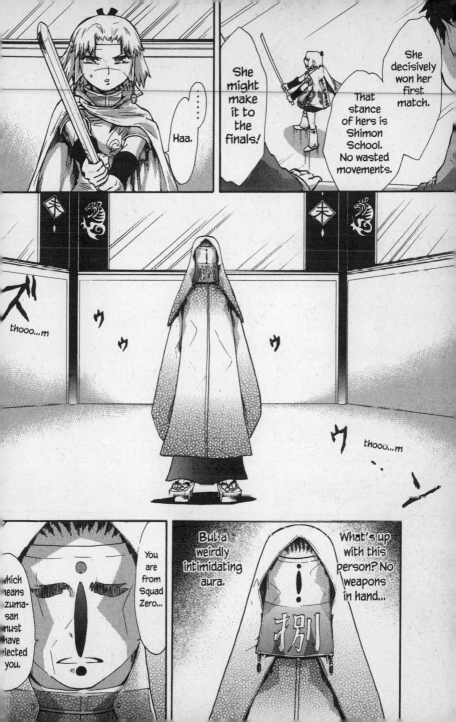

swish

thwap

He's not carrying his weapon. I guess he doesn't need it until the finals!

W-Wow, it only took a second!!

whoa

thud

I don't know that face. Who is he?!

Hey, look over here at the Chamber of the Horse!!

We are looking forward to battles that are worthy of the honorable Mikuni VIUS!!

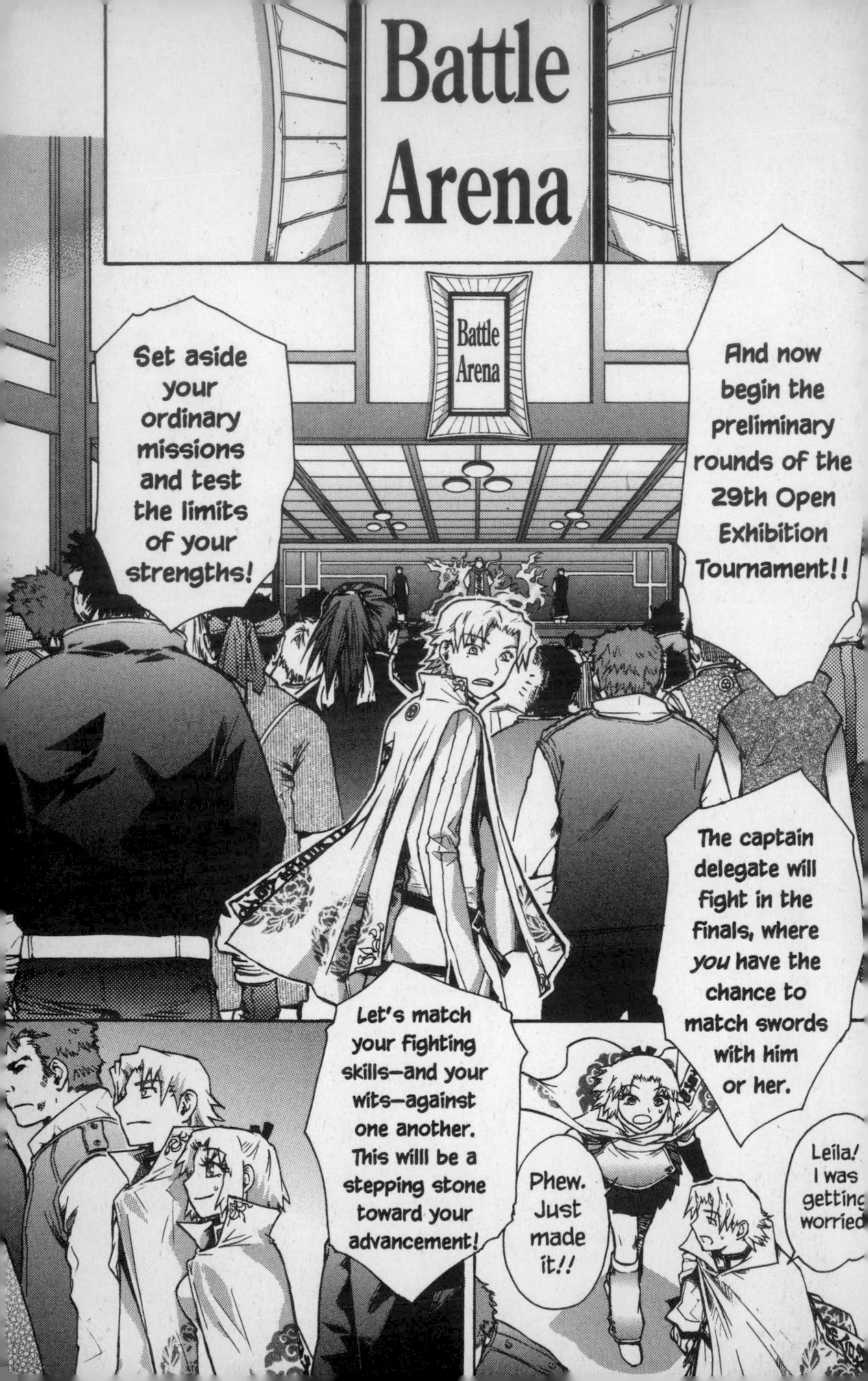

Mission • Twenty
Mikuni Entered

Aoi Shizue

Squad Six captain. Because Squad Six is a covert ops unit, is good at undercover investigations. She's also the most beautiful member of the Mikuni VIUS; everyone has a crush on her.

Sakuraba Shun'ichi

Said to be the sharpest and strongest Mikuni warrior, he is Squad One captain and a good friend of Issa's. Searching for a woman named Hitomi-san?

Akira Ryoji

Said to be the strongest Squad One member. Seems to have been on bad terms with Hibiki since they were squad mates.

Hibiki Masamune

A former Squad One member who is now with Squad Six. A young but brilliant and talented warrior. Wields two giant blades.

Hyūga Rokurô

Assigned to the Intelligence Corps. Idolizes Issa because his first mission was with Issa's squad. Likes Mikuni's pop star NATSUMI ★ chan.

Rin Kyoko

Was a member of the old Squad Zero, and is currently with Squad Eight. A spell caster who knows the reason the old Squad Zero was disbanded.

Daraku

A mysterious group that is trying to assault Mikuni by manipulating Dracules. They are also the ones who infected Yukimura's twin sister with the D Virus.

Mystery Man

A man who is trying to get Issa exiled from Mikuni by setting Hibiki on him. No one knows why he hates Issa so much. Seems to be a high-level official of some sort...

龍眼物語

It has been several decades since the D Virus, whose infected victims transform into murderous monsters known as Dracules, spread across the world. The human population plummeted severely and the world was approaching a crisis point....Those who emerged to protect people from the Dracules came to be called the VIUS.

VIUS Squad Zero captain Issa is a warrior who bears the Dragon Eye, a mysterious and powerful weapon, on his forehead. Together with his Squad Zero members Leila and Sôsei, he spends his days protecting Mikuni City from Dracules.

The exhibition tournament that displays Mikuni VIUS's strength through competition will soon be taking place. Issa, Leila, and Sôsei are selected to participate in the tournament, but unimaginable intrigue and wonder await!

Kazuma Issa

Squad Zero captain. Seems lackadaisical, but possesses a Dragon Eye and wields the broadsword Diamond Sacred Steel. Because his older sister, Ciara, was taken hostage by Dracules, has a history with them.

Yukimura Sôsei

A former Squad Five member who has transferred to Squad Zero. In search of the Daraku that killed his twin sister. Wields twin blades.

Mikami Leila

Newly inducted VIUS member. When she was little, both of her parents were killed by Dracules, and she alone survived. She is searching for a Dragon Eye in order to exterminate Dracules. Her weapon of choice is the *katana* blade.

-kun: This suffix is used at the end of boys' names to express familiarity or endearment. It is also sometimes used by men among friends, or when addressing someone younger or of a lower station.

-chan: This is used to express endearment, mostly toward girls. It is also used for little boys, pets, and even among lovers. It gives a sense of childish cuteness.

Bozu: This is an informal way to refer to a boy, similar to the English terms "kid" and "squirt."

Sempai/Senpai: This title suggests that the addressee is one's senior in a group or organization. It is most often used in a school setting, where underclassmen refer to their upperclassmen as "sempai." It can also be used in the workplace, such as when a newer employee addresses an employee who has seniority in the company.

Kohai: This is the opposite of "sempai" and is used toward underclassmen in school or newcomers in the workplace. It connotes that the addressee is of a lower station.

Sensei: Literally meaning "one who has come before," this title is used for teachers, doctors, or masters of any profession or art.

-[blank]: This is usually forgotten in these lists, but it is perhaps the most significant difference between Japanese and English. The lack of honorific is known as *yobisute*, and it means that the speaker has permission to address the person in a very intimate way. Usually, only family, spouses, or very close friends have this kind of permission. It can be gratifying when someone who has earned the intimacy starts to call one by one's name without an honorific. But when that intimacy hasn't been earned, it can be very insulting.

Honorifics Explained

Throughout the Del Rey Manga books, you will find Japanese honorifics left intact in the translations. For those not familiar with how the Japanese use honorifics and, more important, how they differ from American honorifics, we present this brief overview.

Politeness has always been a critical facet of Japanese culture. Ever since the feudal era, when Japan was a highly stratified society, use of honorifics—which can be defined as polite speech that indicates relationship or status—has played an essential role in the Japanese language. When you address someone in Japanese, an honorific usually takes the form of a suffix attached to one's name (example: "Asuna-san"), is used as a title at the end of one's name, or appears in place of the name itself (example: "Negi-sensei," or simply "Sensei!").

Honorifics can be expressions of respect or endearment. In the context of manga and anime, honorifics give insight into the nature of the relationship between characters. Many English translations leave out these important honorifics and therefore distort the feel of the original Japanese. Because Japanese honorifics contain nuances that English honorifics lack, it is our policy at Del Rey not to translate them. Here, instead, is a guide to some of the honorifics you may encounter in Del Rey Manga.

-*san:* This is the most common honorific and is equivalent to Mr., Miss, Ms., or Mrs. It is the all-purpose honorific and can be used in any situation where politeness is required.

-*sama:* This is one level higher than "-san" and is used to confer great respect.

-*dono:* This comes from the word "tono," which means "lord." It is an even higher level than "-sama" and confers utmost respect.

A new story arc has begun!
During these chapters, someone
will mature, and a certain
mystery will be cleared up. But
more than anything else, this
author just can't wait to actually
draw the upcoming pages!

—Kairi Fujiyama

Contents

A Del Rey Manga/Kodansha Trade Paperback Original

Dragon Eye volume 7 copyright © 2007 by Kairi Fujiyama
English translation copyright © 2008 by Kairi Fujiyama

Published in the United States by Del Rey Books, an imprint of The Random House Publishing Group, a division of Random House, Inc., New York.

DEL REY is a registered trademark and the Del Rey colophon is a trademark of Random House, Inc.

Publication rights arranged through Kodansha Ltd.

First published in Japan in 2007 by Kodansha Ltd., Tokyo

ISBN 978-0-345-50672-6

Printed in the United States of America

www.delreymanga.com

9 8 7 6 5 4 3 2 1

Translator/Adapter—Mari Morimoto
Lettering—NMSG

Dragon Eye
Volume 7

Kairi Fujiyama

Translated and adapted by Mari Morimoto

Lettered by North Market Street Graphics

Ballantine Books · New York

of faith. He saw his work as located at the *threshold* of faith. In a conversation with his friend and former pupil, Paul Ricoeur, he reflected: 'I consider myself as having always been a philosopher of the threshold, a philosopher who kept himself in rather uncomfortable fashion on a line midway between believers and non-believers so that he could somehow stand with believers, with the Christian religion, the Catholic religion, but also speak to non-believers, make himself understood by them and perhaps to help them.'[7]

Let me now introduce the other dialogical thinker, Martin Buber. He was born in Vienna in 1878. If Marcel defies easy categorisation as a thinker, this is even more true of Buber. Do we read him as a mystic, as a general theologian, as an existentialist, as a social theorist, or as a Hebrew humanist? These are just some of the categories which have been suggested. While there are those who associate him almost exclusively with the notion of the I-Thou relation, others will know him as a translator and exegete of the Hebrew Bible and as an interpreter of Hasidic wisdom. Indeed, Pamela Vermes concludes her long search for the 'real' Martin Buber with the suggestion that 'the Bible and Hasidism were the twin tabernacles of [his] soul during his lifetime'.[8] While this is no doubt true, I believe that Laurence Silberstein[9] is also saying something very important when he suggests that Buber should be understood as an 'edifying' philosopher (the term comes from Richard Rorty[10]). Indeed, Marcel should also be understood in this light. Whereas a conventional philosopher aims at an accurate mirroring of objective reality, the edifying thinker is intent on pointing up for his or her contemporaries the value systems, cognitive patterns and social structures which militate against real existence, against realisation of the self and of the community. The edifying philosopher provides his or her fellow travellers with a new vocabulary and grammar for interpreting life in the world. In this humanising vision, one is given the outlines of an authentic, life-enhancing presence to others.

Two key metaphors in the humanising vision offered by Marcel and Buber are *availability* and *confirmation*, respectively. *The whole of this book is structured around these important notions.* Availability involves both a *reception* of the other - her thoughts and feelings, her hopes and dreams, her pain and her fears - into one's personal centre, and a *belonging* to her in which one is prepared to substitute her freedom for one's own. Confirmation is a process in which one struggles with the other, sometimes against herself, as she endeavours to fulfil her God-endowed psychological, spiritual and moral potential. A genuinely loving presence, Buber holds, is one which aims at assisting the other in growing into her potential.

While, as was mentioned above, pastoral presence is often construed in terms of the Rogerian categories of acceptance, empathy and genuineness, Marcel and Buber, I suggest, offer us rich conceptualisations which, while being closely related to Rogers' relational keys, also take us beyond them. The argument that I will be attempting to develop in the first part of the book is that *in pastoral relationships availability is before skills and techniques and confirmation is beyond acceptance and empathy*. It is necessary to describe exactly what is meant by this formulation. Before getting to more substantive issues, I need to explain just what is intended by the term 'pastoral relationships'. It is used to refer to both the relationships developed in the course of local community ministry and in a specialised counselling ministry. On the whole, our interest is in the pastoral presence offered by parish or local community ministers as they exercise their ministry of care. At certain points, however, our discussions will be orientated more to the work that pastoral counselling specialists do. Even there, though, the understanding is that the ideas developed will have an application in the short-term, often informal, counselling ministers are called upon to offer.

Let me move now to an explanation of the claims in my main argument. It was the great achievement of Carl Rogers to shift the emphasis in psychotherapy from interventions and techniques to the quality of the therapeutic relationship. He identified the relational attitudes and skills in the therapist which he saw as 'necessary and sufficient' to create a healing and growth-promoting environment. However, the 'core conditions' can only be fully established - and this is something Rogers was keenly aware of - when the therapist is genuinely 'present'. In the absence of a personal capacity for disposability, I will be suggesting, even acceptance and empathy can be reduced to the level of techniques. The counsellor adopts an accepting attitude and reflects thoughts and feelings in a detached, mechanical way and thus fails to communicate empathy.

Therapists outside the client- or person-centred approach argue that it is necessary to go beyond the core conditions and make use of appropriate interventions and techniques. In recent times, we have witnessed a willingness by both theorists and practitioners in pastoral care to appropriate the techniques of the various schools of counselling (e.g. script analysis [TA], various Gestalt therapy techniques such as the empty chair and polarities exploration, re-framing and paradoxical intent [brief therapy], and reshaping of cognitions [cognitive therapy]). While it is acknowledged that techniques certainly have a place in pastoral care and may be used to good effect, I will argue that in the absence of giving of self, of real emotional availability, of genuine love and fidelity, they will be only minimally effective in facilitating healing and growth. Put differently, a person feels genuinely cared for not so much because she has received expert psychological assistance, important as this is, but rather because she has received a gift of self from her pastor or counsellor. To be sure, too many pastors suffer from a woeful lack of psychological and therapeutic knowledge. It is important that those offering care develop good counselling skills. My argument, however, is that in pastoral care availability is the *foundation* which supports skills and techniques. Without this solid base the edifice of care is very shaky indeed.

What initially led me to think that in Marcel's concept of *disponibilité* we have the foundation for pastoral care was the observation that it has a strong affinity with the biblical notion of compassion. For some, the biblical idea of compassion is captured by the Rogerian terms acceptance and empathy. No doubt, in being accepting and empathic we are showing compassion. I will argue, though, that beyond these core relational attitudes and skills is a more profound communication of self. Right at the heart of the biblical understanding of compassion is a commitment to dispose of oneself, to receive the other into one's 'home-space'. Marcel conceives of availability as a willingness to receive the other *chez soi*, at home. Here, it will be suggested, there are very strong connections with the biblical interpretation of compassionate love. The Old Testament writers understand compassion as an expression of an intimate attachment to the other. They identify the seat of this emotion as the womb or the heart. For Paul, compassion is more than the registering of emotion, it is an expression of one's total being at the deepest level. The Greek word he uses, *splánchnon*, originally referred to the 'inward parts of the body', or to the womb. These two terms, one's home-space and the womb/heart, both point to a deep level of receptivity. Both suggest that to be compassionate in the fullest sense is *deeply personal*; it involves the exercise of the virtue of love.

That disposability is foundational in the ministry of care was confirmed when I began to reflect on the covenantal dimension in the important Marcelian concepts of *belonging* and *substitution*. Marcel works with the concept of 'disposability as belonging'. To belong to the other involves substituting her freedom for one's own. 'Belonging' is also a rich biblical and theological term. Indeed, Marcel extends the idea of availability to include belonging to Christ - the key fact in a life of faith. For the Hebrew people, personhood was defined through the belonging established in a covenantal relationship. Using the theology of covenant as a framework, I will endeavour to extend our understanding of the foundational role availability plays in pastoral care and counselling. I will aim to show that the willingness to substitute the other's freedom for one's own is an important dimension in a covenantal relationship. Substitution is thus a fundamental attitude for the pastor and for the pastoral counsellor.

The above statement of the main argument in the first part also contains a reference to the necessity of going beyond acceptance and empathy. While Rogers advocated a non-directive approach to counselling, a commitment to confirmation involves a readiness for sensitive confrontation. We have already noted Buber's idea of helping a person against himself. This relates to his understanding of the polarities in the self. In each one of us there is a 'yes' and a 'no', refusal and acceptance. Sometimes we want to refuse our possibilities because the path onto which they are leading us looks dangerous, threatening. We need someone who is prepared to push us onto the path, so to speak. Now of course for someone committed to the Rogerian belief in a non-directive approach, this suggestion presents as a violation of the autonomy of the counsellee. Indeed, Buber and Rogers debated this issue at a conference on the former's thought organised by the University of Michigan in April of 1957.[11] In the course of the dialogue, Buber argued that every genuinely existential relationship begins with acceptance of the other, but moves on to an active engagement to help her realise her potential.[12] Included in the notion of confirmation is the need for acceptance, but there is also a recognition of the need for an active contribution to the other's growth.

The idea of confirmation will be applied both to psychological wholeness and to moral development. The two, of course, are interrelated and cannot be neatly separated. Sometimes, however, psychological issues are more to the forefront; and on other occasions moral concerns are more central. In relation to the quest for psychological integration, we will observe that most, if not all, people live with unacknowledged polarities. That is to say, there are 'sub-selves' which are disavowed because to recognise them is anxiety-producing. Growth towards psychological wholeness, it will be argued, involves recognising these disowned selves and integrating them into the community of the Self. In pastoral counselling, then, an important aim is a sensitive confrontation concerning a person's disavowed polarities and a facilitation of the process whereby they are integrated into her expression of her personhood.

Buber, however, also establishes an explicitly moral context for confirmation. He observes that persons sometimes act in ways which injure what he calls the social 'order-of-being'. When this happens there is an experience of *ontic* or *existential guilt*. Buber understands the *conscience* in terms of the inner place where one attends to one's existential guilt. In a paper delivered to a group of psychotherapists, he argued that the members of their profession often fail their clients because they, the therapists, tend to construe all guilt feelings as neurotic.[13] He urged them to recognise existential guilt and the constructive role of conscience. Under the demands of her conscience, a person feels a need to repair the damage she has inflicted on the order-of-being. This work of repair Buber calls *reconciliation*. Confirmation in the moral context consists of encouraging and sometimes challenging a person as she struggles to respond to the demands of her conscience.

While in recent times a number of theorists have argued for a rediscovery of the moral dimension in pastoral care, very few have addressed the role of conscience. The focus tends to be on method in ethical decision making. I accept that this is an important issue. I will be advocating, though, a greater stress on conscience, responsibility and reconciliation in the practice of pastoral care.

Availability and confirmation indicate *two fundamental moments in the ministry of care*. First, there is a disposing of self in entering into the pain of the other and in committing oneself to her support and growth. Second, there is sensitive challenge or confrontation aimed at helping the other realise her God-given psychological, spiritual[14] and moral possibilities. While both these moments are primarily oriented to the interpersonal realm, a concern with socio-economic and political realities and structures is not excluded. Behind the analyses of both Marcel and Buber is a keen awareness that contemporary cultural ideologies and social structures result in alienation and suffering and need to be challenged and reformed. In this sense, the interpersonal moments point to a third moment in pastoral care, namely, a commitment to socio-economic and political renewal. As important as this political dimension of the ministry of care is, we will only be able, given the focus of our research, to engage with it to a very limited extent.[15]

The first moment - the one defined by availability - is foundational. The willingness to be receptive at a deep level to the pain, confusion and fear of the other is a fundamental quality in the pastoral ministry. Another fundamental quality, as was indicated above, is a readiness to establish a relationship of belonging with those one serves. The second moment - defined by confirmation - involves an attempt to build on the first.

The two basic moments, then, are closely linked. Disposability is foundational in pastoral care. We need, however, to build on the foundation and work with the other to help her develop her God-endowed potential (confirmation). Confirmation is actually an extension of the idea of availability. To say to the other, 'I belong to you; I give myself to you' (Marcel) means for Buber, 'I am prepared to struggle with you, even to help you *against* yourself, as you grow into the person God created you to be'.

Up to this point, we have concerned ourselves with, on the one hand, what genuine presence looks like, and, on the other, how it functions in pastoral practice to assist a person towards healing, growth and wholeness. What happens, though, when pastoral presence is distorted. Ministers and counsellors can subvert their intention to heal and to help through defective modes of relating to those in their care. When this happens, it will be argued, both the person offering care and the person receiving it experience a sense of shame. The systematic theologian and ethicist, James McClendon, expresses the situation well. 'The primal defection from presence', he writes, 'is found in the experience of shame. In genuine presence I am with another and she or he with me, and there is a wholeness in the shared act or fact of our being there. But shame is a failed wholeness.'[16]

The first aim in the second part of the book is to describe the shame dynamics in *both the providers and the recipients of care* associated with pastoral non-availability and lack of confirmation. We are interested, first of all, in the harm done when pastors and counsellors fall from the ideals of availability and confirmation. Our attention will be directed especially to those persons in care who have a strong propensity for shame. They are, of course, particularly prone to be hurt when on the receiving end of dismissive or inattentive treatment.

While our major concern is the harm done to clients, we are also interested in the shame feelings pastors and counsellors suffer in causing that harm. When we, the providers of care, can get beyond our rationalisations and our other defences, we see the negative impact associated with our distorted way of relating. Face-to-face with this subversion of our intention to help, we feel ashamed. This brings us to a second aim in the reflections on shame and presence. I want to establish a positive role for shame. Shame feelings stimulate the reforming function of the conscience. The main argument in the second part of the book is that *the shame feelings a pastor or counsellor experiences as a result of his distorted way of being present have a potentially positive function, namely, moving him to a period of critical introspection in which he may grasp a vision of a higher capacity for genuine presence.*

Let me explain this argument. The main idea contained in it is that shame feelings may lead a care provider to a time of what Marcel calls *contemplation*. In contemplation, a person is faced with two modalities of being. On the one hand, there is the actual self: the self experienced as flawed and defective. On the other hand, there is the potential self: the new person one can become if one is prepared to make certain decisive changes. Looking squarely at his tendency to defective forms of presence, a pastor or counsellor may also see a vision of himself in which he is more available, more ready for the demands associated with confirming others. In a theological interpretation, the Holy Spirit has moved him to contemplation, and now empowers him for growth towards genuine presence.

We now have before us a sketch of Marcel and Buber as dialogical thinkers, and an indication of how their thought informs the theory and practice of pastoral care. In Part 1, we will fill out some of the outlines in an attempt to develop an adequate understanding of what it means to be authentically present in an act of care.

1 See H. Nouwen, *The Wounded Healer* (Garden City, NY: Doubleday, 1972). See also A. Campbell, *Rediscovering Pastoral Care*, 2nd ed. (London: Darton, Longman & Todd, 1986). Along with courage and integrity (the image of the shepherd), Campbell identifies both woundedness (Nouwen's image) and 'wise folly' as marks of a helping presence.

2 See D. Capps, *Hope: A Pastoral Psychology* (Minneapolis: Fortress, 1995).

3 See W. Avery, 'Toward an Understanding of Ministry of Presence', *The Journal of Pastoral Care* 40, no. 4 (December 1986), pp. 342-353.

4 See C. Gerkin, *Prophetic Pastoral Practice* (Nashville: Abingdon Press, 1991), chp. 4.

5 See 'Conversation with Paul Ricoeur', in Marcel, *The Participant Perspective: A Gabriel Marcel Reader*, T. Busch ed. (Lanham, MD: University Press of America, 1987), pp. 285-292, p. 285.

6 T. Busch in his introduction to *The Participant Perspective*, p. 1.

7 Marcel, 'Conversation with Paul Ricoeur', p. 288.

8 P. Vermes, *Buber on God and the Perfect Man* (London: Littman Library of Jewish Civilisation, 1994), p. 75.

9 See L. Silberstein, *Martin Buber's Social and Religious Thought* (New York: New York University Press, 1989), p. 10.

10 See R. Rorty, *Philosophy and the Mirror of Nature* (London: Basil Blackwell, 1980), chp. 8.

11 See M. Buber and C. Rogers, 'Dialogue Between Martin Buber and Carl R. Rogers', in M. Friedman and R. Gregor Smith trans., *The Knowledge of Man* (London: George Allen & Unwin Ltd., 1965), pp. 166-184.

12 See ibid., pp. 181-183.

13 See Buber, 'Guilt and Guilt Feelings', *Psychiatry* 20 (1957), pp. 114-129.

14 In every age, spiritual guidance has had a role to play in pastoral care. For most of the history of the Christian Church, this role has been a substantial one. However, in the fifties, sixties and seventies of this century there was a tendency for pastors - especially those with a therapeutic orientation - to downplay the role of spiritual guidance. The recent upsurge of interest in spirituality has led to something of a turnaround. Be that as it may, the reference here is not to spiritual direction *per se*. We will not be engaging with the literature on spirituality and spiritual guidance. Rather, the word 'spiritual' is used to indicate my conviction that the attempts persons make to overcome distortions and defects in both their psychological functioning and their moral character constitute spiritual growth.

15 The emphasis in pastoral care in the recent past has been largely on promoting healing, growth and self-realisation in the individual. Recently, however, writers in the field have been advocating a widening of the scope of the ministry of care to include a commitment to transform unjust, oppressive social structures. See, for example, P. Selby, *Liberating God: Private Care and Public Struggle* (London: SPCK, 1983); J. Poling, 'An Ethical Framework for Pastoral Care', *The Journal of Pastoral Care* 42, no. 4 (Winter 1988), pp. 299-306, and idem, *Deliver us From Evil* (Minneapolis: Fortress Press, 1996); S. Pattison, *A Critique of Pastoral Care* (London: SCM Press, 1988, 1993), chp. 5, and idem, *Pastoral Care and Liberation Theology* (Cambridge: Cambridge University Press, 1994); and P. Couture and R. Hunter eds, *Pastoral Care and Social Conflict* (Nashville: Abingdon Press, 1995). One of the main points these writers make is that since socio-economic and political ideologies and structures are very often potent factors in the symptomology of suffering individuals, holistic care involves action aimed at changing those oppressive ideologies and structures. A third moment in pastoral care is a joining in with God's work of redeeming the prevailing socio-economic and political structures. While my work is focused on the first two moments and the interpersonal dynamics captured in them, there is some overlap with the third moment. Buber's key idea of *responsibility* includes a concern for the well-being of the social 'order-of-being'. It follows that helping a person grow in moral character may mean confronting her with the need to act for social and political change. Indeed, this is precisely what I suggest in one of the case studies in chapter 5 (concerning a woman who has a guilty conscience over her involvement in corrupt business practices).

16 J. McClendon, *Systematic Theology: Ethics* (Nashville: Abingdon Press, 1986), p. 107.

Part 1

PRESENCE IN PASTORAL CARE AND COUNSELLING

The major aims in this first part are twofold. First, I want to develop an understanding of the nature of genuine presence through an exploration of the ideas of Marcel and Buber (chapters 1 and 2 respectively). The two key notions here, as we have already seen, are *availability* and *confirmation*. However, attention will be given to other important and related concepts. With reference to Marcel, these will include the ideas of presence as a grace, participation, and contemplation. Much of the thrust of Marcel's thought is captured by the term 'participation'. He calls for a whole-hearted, authentic sharing in being, in life, in the life of the other. It is not possible, though, to teach someone how to fully share herself: it is a grace. But if a person has the grace, moments of profound contemplation lead her into a deeper expression of presence.

The concepts related to confirmation are the I-Thou relation, inclusion and responsibility. Again, one thought flows into the next. Buber began his reflections on dialogue with the famous notion of the meeting between the I and the Thou. Even a wordless acknowledgement between two passing strangers can be confirming. At a deeper level, one listens for the claim the other is making on one and attempts to respond faithfully and courageously (responsibility). In order to really hear that call, to hear it in its fullness, one must be able to swing over into the inner world of the other, even as one remains firmly anchored in one's own experiencing (inclusion). From one's own inner universe of ideas, beliefs and values one reaches out to confirm the inner universe of the other.

The second major aim in this first part is to describe the two fundamental moments in pastoral care that we are working with. The foundational moment is the extension of oneself in the service of support and healing. In chapter 3, I will argue that the affinity *disponibilité* has with the biblical notion of compassion indicates its foundational role. Disposability, further, is expressed in acts of care through *belonging*. For Marcel, to belong to the other means that one is prepared to substitute her freedom for one's own. It will be argued that this chain of thought establishes a covenantal basis for pastoral care.

The second fundamental moment in pastoral care is a commitment to struggle with the other to help him realise his God-given psychological, spiritual and moral potentialities. In chapter 4, confirmation will be worked through as facilitating a process in which a counsellee reclaims disavowed polarities or sub-selves. A two-stage model will be proposed. In the first stage, the aim is to help the person acknowledge disowned selves. Facilitating an inner dialogue focused on positively integrating the rejected selves is the goal of the second stage.

Finally, the explicitly moral dimension in confirmation will be picked up in chapter 5. It will be argued that a greater emphasis on stimulation of conscience is required in the theory and practice of pastoral care. The link between conscience and responsibility will be established. Here, the notion of what I will call *first-* and *second-order* responsibility will be developed. First-order responsibility refers to those responses which are commonly embraced, by convention, in the family, the church, and the society. Creativity and conscientiousness define second-order responsibility. Pastors and counsellors, it will be suggested, need to promote both as they each have a role to play.

In chapter 5, I will also give attention to the need persons feel for what Buber calls *reconciliation*. The pangs of conscience result in a feeling that one should do something to repair the damage one has done to the social order-of-being. An important role for the pastor or counsellor, I will suggest, is helping a person find appropriate ways to heal the wounds he has inflicted.

Hopefully, the broad outlines of my argumentation are now clear. In filling in the detail, I will begin with Marcel's interesting and challenging contribution to our understanding of what it means to be fully present to the other.

Chapter 1
PRESENCE AS GRACE AND AVAILABILITY:
The Contribution of Gabriel Marcel

Presence is fundamentally a gift of the self. Gabriel Marcel has observed that it is not so much the content of the communication of a person that is stimulating and revelatory, as the fact that she gives herself through that communication. For Marcel, presence is not a skill one learns, but rather a grace.

What one brings to a genuine encounter is not first and foremost an ensemble of communication techniques but one's-self[1] and, to be more precise, the depth one has to share. The depth in the self develops through a whole-hearted engagement with others, with life, with God. The whole of Marcel's philosophy can be understood as an attempt to describe what a genuine participation in being really means. At first, Marcel contrasted participation with being a spectator. He came, however, to see that this bipolar understanding of engagement is inadequate because it fails to take account of *contemplation*. Contemplation is one of participation's 'most intimate modes'.[2] Without inwardness there is no possibility of establishing the self in depth. And where there is no depth there is no possibility of a meeting in the full sense of the term. For Marcel, then, there are indissoluble links between engagement, contemplation, depth and encounter. Engagement with one's-self in contemplation is orientated to engagement with the other. The depth that I am, the grace that I am, ultimately only has meaning in the context of my capacity to give of myself to the other. This receptivity or permeability to the claim of the other Marcel calls *disponibilité*. There is no exact equivalent in English, however it is translated as availability or disposability.

This engagement with the other characterised by availability, Marcel came to understand in terms of *belonging*. When I commit myself to be available to the other, it can be said that I belong to her. This relationship of belonging is constituted through a free substitution of the other's will for my own. Far from entering into a relationship of bondage, in belonging to a person one is set free. In freely disposing of myself for the other I am liberated.

His investigation into belonging is part of his project of understanding the real meaning of *fidelity*. The problem of committing oneself to the other first exercised Marcel's mind when he wrote the entries to the continuation of his journal of metaphysical reflections (published in *Being and Having*). He was attempting to understand how one can genuinely make a promise to the other when one's disposition towards him may change. For example, one visits a sick friend and one feels filled with compassion. A second visit is promised. However, when the time appointed for the subsequent visit comes one finds that the feeling of compassion one felt so strongly earlier is now gone. One is now in the unhappy position of being reduced to a kind of play-acting.

Later, Marcel reflected on the authenticity of commitment by contrasting fidelity with *constancy*. Constancy is a counterfeit form of fidelity in which one is driven by one's own sense of honour and obligation rather than by a spontaneous desire to dispose of one's-self for the sake of the other.

The aim of this chapter is to use these metaphors developed by Marcel, namely grace, inwardness, openness, belonging, and fidelity (along with its counterpart, constancy), to begin building our understanding of genuine presence. Our discussion of Marcel's teaching on presence and availability is structured as follows. The idea of participation opens our description and sets the scene for what follows. A presentation of the notion of presence as grace is followed by a discussion of availability. Availability is described in terms of openness, fidelity and belonging.

ENGAGEMENT WITH LIFE: PARTICIPATION

The notion of engagement with being, with life - what Marcel calls *participatio* — is absolutely central in his philosophy. While existentialists such as Sartre and Heidegger connect engagement with the individual's struggle to bear the burden of her personal freedom, responsibility and choice, Marcel interprets it in an inter-subjective or relational framework. He sees participation as *the discovery of depth through togetherness*. Marcel recognises that *contemplation*, 'one of participation's most intimate modes', is essential if one is to reach the depth dimension of life. Further, without this inwardness, there can be no genuine meeting. At the heart of an encounter is the discovery of depth together, and how can two people who live on the surface ever hope to descend to the inner meaning of their existence?

In his earliest exploration of participation (in the continuation of his journal of metaphysical reflections), Marcel works with the idea of being present at a dramatic improvisation.[3] He wants to contrast participation with being a spectator by referring to the self-commitment that characterises the former modality. The concept that he works with in his reflections is the *totum simul*, the intelligible whole. The idea is often used in textual analysis (scriptural interpretation, for example). One must be able to assemble the meanings of the parts into an intelligible whole in order to grasp the text's meaning. Marcel begins by observing that if one is able to recognise the unity of the improvisation one is in fact participating. The only way to constitute the various individual actions as a whole is to in some way get 'on the inside'. He goes a step further and suggests that it is not inconceivable that the participation contributes in some way to the improvisation itself. The more effective the participation the more one is actively involved in the improvisation, and the less one is able to treat it as an object of study. One is not a detached, analytical observer but a person who is fully immersed in the drama.

He observes, on the other hand, that one can turn oneself into a pure spectator. The risk here is that the *totum simul* will appear as a pure spectacle, even a spectacle without meaning. The meaning in the improvisation is only available when one is actively engaged with it, when one participates in 'the creative intention that quickens the whole'.[4] For the spectator, there is a rift between him and the *totum simul*, and more seriously, within himself.

In the first series of his Gifford Lectures of 1949-1950, Marcel again takes up the idea of participation.[5] He suggests that one begins to grasp the idea of 'sharing, taking part in, partaking of' by looking at the lower end of a graduated scale of participation. Consider the cake that is brought in at a birthday party. I claim my share of it; I participate through consumption. There are other forms of consumption. I can, for example, claim my share of a collection of photographs through 'consuming' them visually.

Participation need not of course, Marcel observes, have the meaning of ownership. If we think of participation in a service or ceremony, it is a mental engagement. Rather than grasp objects, one participates in an idea. In worship, says Marcel, this would be God (although he thinks of God as much more than an idea). We are beginning to move to a deeper form of participation, what Marcel calls 'submerged' participation.[6] He is referring to that participation with a reality, idea or value that is so intimate and all-involving that one's very being is defined by the participation. Marcel points to the relationship between a peasant and the soil.[7] The peasant's soil is linked to his inner being. The expression of his inner self through his relationship with the soil involves both his acts and his sufferings. 'Effective participation transcends the traditional opposition between activity and passivity; participation can be considered now as active, now as passive, according to the point of view at which we place ourselves.'[8] What I take Marcel to mean at this point is that while sometimes the peasant will act upon the soil - with tilling implements for example - at other times he will simply enjoy the feel of it under foot, or the smell that reminds him that he belongs to the earth.

Participation, then, involves receptivity. For Marcel, however, receptivity is not equivalent to passivity. Receptivity involves a certain prior ordering of one's feelings and mind. Here we are reminded of the fact that one receives a guest in a room, in a house, in a garden, but not out in the woods. That is, one extends hospitality in a space representing one's centre, one's own proper place. Marcel suggests that participation is closely associated with the idea conveyed in the French language by *chez*, as in the expression *chez soi*.[9] It does not come over so clearly in English, but 'when one says "at Smith's", for instance, that does imply that Smith is at his own centre, and that I can be aware of him as being at his own centre, not at mine, and also that Smith, to be Smith adequately, does need his own proper place that he can be at.'[10] It is this sense of welcoming, of inviting others into one's own prepared place of reception (to receive *chez soi*) that leads Marcel to suggest that the receptivity associated with participation is not something passive but rather constitutes an act.

A spectator, on the other hand, does not so much act as exercise her curiosity.[11] Consider a member of the audience at a play. She feels none of the anxiety, still less the anguish, that is associated with self-commitment. To be sure, there is a certain emotional engagement with the actors and the story they present. Her emotions are superficially similar to those of the people really committed to the story, but she is aware that there is no practical outcome for those emotions. She 'makes as if to participate without really participating' and thus enters into a 'half-serious voluntary self-deception'.[12]

Marcel's purpose in contrasting *homo particeps* with *homo spectans* is to highlight the importance of the self-commitment that is lacking in the latter mode of being. He realises, though, that the inadequacy in this bipolar typology of the modalities of human existence is that it fails to take account of *contemplation*. Contemplation is one of 'participation's most intimate modes'. Contemplation is 'a turning inwards of our awareness of the outer world'.[13] There can be no contemplation 'without a kind of inward regrouping of one's resources, or a kind of ingatheredness; to contemplate is to ingather oneself in the presence of whatever is being contemplated, and this in such a fashion that the reality, confronting which one ingathers oneself, itself becomes a factor in the ingathering.'[14]

It is not possible to effect this inner regrouping when the reality that is confronting me is interpreted as a mere spectacle. All one sees in this case is an outer show; there is no desire to penetrate to an inner meaning. But it is true, observes Marcel, that a spectator (as a member of an audience at a play) can be emotionally engaged.[15] There is in this case a level of participation. He may reflect on the inner meaning of the drama that is unfolding before him. That is, he allows the story to act as a stimulus for contemplation. Marcel uses the prepositions *in front of* and *inside* to tease out the distinction between being a spectator and contemplating. A spectacle is in front of me, facing me, before me. But to the extent that the reality confronting me is something more than a spectacle for me, it must also be within me, inside me.

To get at the full meaning of contemplation, though, we must go beyond the spatial imagery - external/internal, outside/inside - to the notion of *togetherness*.[16] Marcel uses the example of the contemplation of a landscape. As I make spiritual contact with the landscape, there is a certain togetherness established between us. There is an inner regrouping of my resources, and the contact I have made with the landscape is a factor in this ingatheredness. Through my contemplative act the opposition between inner and outer worlds has been overcome.

It is through contemplation that one reaches the depth dimension in human existence. Since Marcel understands the ultimate meaning of inter-subjectivity as discovering depth together, it is to be expected that he would say that 'there cannot be an encounter or a meeting in the fullest sense of the word except between beings endowed with a certain inwardness'.[17] The blind cannot lead the blind to safety and neither can those who live on the surface of life find the way down to its inner meaning. Discovering depth together means, says Marcel, that there is a *shared secret*.[18]

In order to develop the idea of the shared secret, Marcel uses the example of a shy young man at a fashionable cocktail party.[19] The young man is concentrating on himself, gripped by an inner tension that separates him from others. We may imagine, says Marcel, that a man comes up to him to put him at ease. At first, the young man does not engage with the other fellow in a direct way, does not relate to him as a *you* but rather as a *him*. 'Why is *he* talking to me? What is *he* after?' The young man is on his guard and so he cannot really be *with* the other guest. It is 'the relationship expressed by the preposition *with* that is eminently inter-subjective'.[20] Contrast this with the world of objects. A chair is beside or under the table, but it is not *with* the table.

In any case, let us now suppose, suggests Marcel, that the ice has been broken. The other guest says, 'I knew your parents.' A bond has been established and there is a relaxation of the tension in the young man. 'It is as if something gripped tight together inside him were able to loosen up. He is lifted out of that stifling here-and-nowness in which.... his ego was sticking to him as an adhesive plaster sticks to a small cut.'[21] Now the two men are on a journey. They are linked together by a shared secret.

There is a unity in intimate relationships forged through a shared secret. On a mundane level, there are shared experiences, jokes, understandings which others are not privy to. On a deeper level, there may be 'a really incommunicable experience.... about which the initiated feel that others, who did not share it in the flesh, have no right to speak'.[22]

In this way, Marcel arrives at the conclusion that the ultimate significance of the notion of the secret is *discovering depth together*.[23] Depth, he suggests, can be understood in terms of both spatial and temporal images. When two people begin to move into the region of the depths of human existence, they catch a glimpse of a vast expanse that cannot be grasped by the mind. (Here we see a theological turn in Marcel's reflections.) It is as though one is standing at the mouth of the ocean and one 'catches a sudden bewildering glimpse of the whole broad dazzle of the sea'.[24] One senses that a promise is being made, a promise of the revelation that awaits, but one can only now catch a glimpse of it. Paradoxically, however, this 'dazzling *yonder*' is not felt to be elsewhere, but within reach. 'We should have to describe it as a distance, yet we also feel it is intimately near us - "Near, and hard to catch hold of", says Hölderlin, "is God"....'[25]

In terms of time, the deep thought, or the profound notion, is one that 'pushes well ahead'.[26] It takes time to reach the depths. Just as in the previous image we gazed out onto the vast expanse of ocean before us, now we project into a revelatory future. A deep thought unfolds according to its own temporal rhythm; it cannot be forced. It is not just futurity, however, that is determinative of depth. Past and future are indissolubly linked in the discovery of profundity. Reaching back into the past and out into the future, gazing into the yonder which promises so much - here we find ourselves within grasp of the eternal.

> In the dimension of depth the past and the future firmly grasp hands; and that they do so in a region which, from the relative points of view of all my heres-and-nows, and all your heres-and-nows, would have to be described as the absolute Here-and-Now, and this region where the *now* and the *then* tend to merge, as the *near* and the *far* did in our previous illustration, would and could be nothing other than Eternity....[27]

Participation in being, in life, is the discovery of depth in togetherness. Ultimately, it is a participation in Being-Itself, in God.

PRESENCE AS A GRACE

As we have just seen, the depth dimension in life emerges through communion. Communion is more profound than communication. In an important passage from the first volume of *The Mystery of Being*, Marcel distinguishes these two forms of being present to another. He refers to the situation where one is sitting in a room with another person, but somehow the other fails to make his presence felt. While one can communicate with him, there is no communion. There is, though, the opposite experience. A person really does make his presence felt, and it is stimulating and revelatory. I discover something in myself that I had not seen before. It is worth quoting Marcel's analysis at some length:

> We can.... have a very strong feeling that somebody who is sitting in the same room as ourselves, sitting quite near us, someone whom we can look at and listen to and whom we could touch if we wanted to make a final test of his reality, is nevertheless far further away from us than some loved one who is perhaps thousands of miles away or perhaps, even, no longer among the living. We could say that the man sitting beside us was in the same room as ourselves, but that he was not really *present* there, that his *presence* did not make itself felt. But what do I mean by presence, here? It is not that we could not communicate with this man....Yet something essential is lacking. One might say that what we have with this person, who is in the room, but somehow not really present to us, is communication without communion: unreal communication, in a word. He understands what I say to him, but he does not understand *me*... By a very singular phenomenon indeed, this stranger interposes himself between me and my own reality, he makes me in some sense also a stranger to myself; I am not really myself while I am with him.
>
> The opposite phenomenon, however, can also take place. When somebody's presence really does make itself felt, it can refresh my inner being; it reveals me to myself, it makes me more fully myself than I should be if I were not exposed to its impact.[28]

It is not possible, Marcel observes, to teach someone how to make her presence felt. It would be like attempting to teach a person to be charming. We should not regard charm and presence as simply identical.[29] Charm, nonetheless, is one of the ways in which a person makes her presence felt. Marcel reflects systematically on the nature of charm in his *Metaphysical Journal*.[30] It is a grace; it 'appears to decline with the decline of the gratuitous element in behaviour, or when a person's attention is more and more taken up with precise and specifiable ends'.[31] If one tries to will charm, the result is a tension that militates against one's attempt to be charming. It cannot be forced or manufactured; it is 'the presence of the person round what he does and what he says'.[32] It is not possible to isolate the quality or qualities which constitute a charming person. Charm is beyond conceptualisation; it is that elusive factor that makes for what Marcel elsewhere refers to as a *lively* person.[33] (This latter term probably captures Marcel's intention better for contemporary readers; we tend to think of a 'charming' person as somewhat false.) The really alive person has a 'taste for life' and showers it around him; so that quite apart from any talents possessed or achievements recorded his presence is creative. For Marcel, charm cannot be considered as merely incidental to human existence. He makes the bold claim that charm can be linked 'with all that is most metaphysical in the personality, with the quality which is irreducible and incapable of being objectivised - the quality which is doubtless only another facet of what we call existence'.[34]

Charm is one way a person makes her presence felt, one way in which communion is facilitated. While the experience of communion is real and is easily identified when it happens, it is very difficult to conceptualise. It is not possible through an analysis of an experience of communion to isolate the words, phrases and gestures that produced it. The revelatory and stimulating qualities of communion, observes Marcel, come not so much from the content of the words, from the style of the gestures, of the other, but from he himself who says the words, who makes the gestures.[35] Ultimately, communion, and the presence that is associated with it, is *a grace*. Presence is beyond knowledge, beyond teachable techniques. 'It would be obviously utopian to hope that one can teach a man the art of making himself present to the other. One can teach only gestures and grins. This art is truly a grace; and inversely not to possess it is a disgrace.'[36] The non-objective character of presence does not mean, though, that it is simply a subjective reality. It is, in fact, more appropriate to speak of inter-subjectivity. And inter-subjectivity is 'essentially an openness'.[37] An openness to the claims of the other is what Marcel calls *disponibilité* or availability.

PRESENCE AS AVAILABILITY

As Otto Friedrich Bollnow has observed, Marcel's identification of availability as a virtue constitutes a genuine discovery in the field of ethics.[38] Availability, however, does have close links with *agape*, a virtue which has of course received a great deal of attention in theological ethics. Thinkers such as Søren Kierkegaard, Anders Nygren, Reinhold Neibuhr and Gene Outka have all provided in-depth ethical analyses of *agape*.[39] However, they focus on issues such as equal regard - the ethical requirement that love be impartial - and the relationship between self-love and self-giving (or, as some insist, self-sacrifice). Marcel approaches the giving of one's-self from a quite different perspective. He asks questions such as: What does it mean to promise to be there for the other? (the question of fidelity) and, What does it mean to say to the other, 'I belong to you'? Fidelity and belonging are grounded in openness, being permeable to the call of the other.

Availability as Openness

Marcel develops the link between receptivity and disposability in an essay in *Creative Fidelity* entitled 'Phenomenological Notes on Being in a Situation'.[40] To exist with others, he observes, is to be exposed to influences. It is not possible to be human without to some extent being permeable to those influences. Permeability, in its broadest sense, is associated with a certain lack of cohesion or density. Thus, the fact of being exposed to external influences is linked with a kind of *in-cohesion*. I am 'porous', open to a reality which seeks to communicate with me. 'I must somehow make room', writes Marcel, 'for the other in myself; if I am completely absorbed in myself, concentrated on my sensations, feelings, anxieties, it will obviously be impossible for me to receive, to incorporate in myself, the message of the other. What I called incohesion a moment ago here assumes the form of disposability...'[41]

Disposability, then, is closely associated with receptivity. As we saw above, receptivity involves a readiness to make available one's personal centre, one's innermost domain. We receive others in a room, in a house, or in a garden, but not on unknown ground or in the woods. Receptivity means that I invite the other to 'be at home' with me. A home receives the imprint of one's personality; something of myself is infused into the way my home-space is constructed. Contrast this with 'the nameless sadness' associated with a hotel room; this is no-one's home. To share one's home-space is disposability or availability because 'to provide hospitality is truly to communicate something of oneself to the other'.[42]

The meaning of hospitality can also be broadened to include receiving into one's-self the appeal of another for understanding and compassion.[43] When I open myself to the call of the other to be with her in her pain and confusion, I am able to spontaneously feel with her. The intonation of my words, my facial expressions, perhaps my tears, say to her that I am with her in her suffering. Contrasted to this responsiveness, however, there is an indisposability which Marcel refers to as an 'inner inertia' or 'spiritual asthenia'.[44] The distress of the other is experienced as something alien; I simply cannot receive it into my innermost sphere. To illustrate this fundamental lack of responsiveness, Marcel contrasts the mundane scenario of a person asking for information which is not at one's disposal with the case of a person appealing to one's sympathy.[45] In the first case,

I must respond to a concrete question such as, What is the population of Rome? I go through my 'file' of information and find that there is nothing available in relation to this question. Marcel then moves to the appeal for understanding.

> Here again I must furnish a response but it will be of a completely different kind; it could turn out that this response which involves my feeling is not within my power to draw out of myself. I do not succeed in summoning forth the sympathy which is entreated. I would have wished it to be otherwise and it is painful to deceive my questioner, but what can I do? I can only utter certain formulas I have in mind which are part of my repertory and seem to suit the present circumstances; perhaps I can find it possible to give them a sympathetic intonation, but in any case I am only reading something out of a catalogue; this reaction is relevant only to having as in the case of the file above; it has nothing in common with that positive human sympathy to which the other person appeals and which I really do not feel. The suffering of the other person is alien to me and I do not succeed in making it my own.[46]

The only way to break out of this 'self-obsession', according to Marcel, is by 'submerging oneself suddenly in the life of another person and being forced to see things through his eyes'.[47] One cannot break out of this 'inner inertia' on one's own; it is through the presence of another person that this 'miracle' is accomplished. The miracle does not, of course, happen automatically; one must be open, responsive, to the appeal of the other.

We are, however, still left with the questions, Why am I non-responsive to the suffering of the other? Why do I feel opaque, non-permeable?[48] Marcel believes that non-availability is associated with the tendency to see one's existence in terms of possession. I will treat myself as indisposable 'just so far as I construe my life or being as a having which is somehow quantifiable, hence as something capable of being wasted, exhausted or dissipated'.[49] In this attitude, I become like a person who knows that his small sum of money must last a very long time. I become afflicted with an anxiety and a concern which discourage self-giving. These negative affects are 'reabsorbed into a state of inner inertia'.[50]

If I think of my emotional resources in terms of having, in terms of a non-renewable resource to be jealously guarded, I will find it almost impossible to promise myself to the other. Marcel is very interested in the problem of making a commitment to be there for the other. He wants to establish the metaphysical base for fidelity. Here, though, his focus is not so much on the issue of emotional 'stinginess' as on the change in feeling states which is so often associated with the lapse of time between promising and delivering the promise.

Availability as Fidelity

In the continuation of his journal, Marcel concerns himself with the metaphysical problem of committing one's future.[51] He notes, first, that all promises are 'partly unconditional'.[52] I cannot make a commitment to another person without setting aside certain variables. Suppose I promise to go and see a person tomorrow. I cannot commit myself to a continued experience of the desire I feel now, nor can I guarantee that I will not be attracted by a rival opportunity. Marcel believes that there is an important distinction to be made between the committal in itself and one's future feeling state. To highlight these considerations, Marcel presents the case of a promise to re-visit an invalid friend. It is a

> promise moved by a wave of pity: he is doomed, he knows it, he knows I know it. Several days have gone by since my visit. The circumstances which dictated my promise are changed; I have no room for self-deception about that. I should be able to say - yes, I even dare assert - that he still inspires the same compassion in me. How could I justify a change in the state of my feelings, since nothing has happened since which could have the power to alter them? And yet I must in honesty admit that the pity I *felt* the other day, is today no more than a theoretical pity. I still judge that he is unhappy and that it is right to be sorry for him, but this is a judgment I should not have dreamed of formulating the other day. There was no need. My whole being was concentrated into an irresistible impulse towards him, a wild longing to help him, to show him that I was on his side, that his sufferings were mine. I have to recognise that this impulse no longer exists, and it is no longer in my power to do more than imitate it by a pretence which some part of me refuses to swallow.[53]

There seems to be here an inescapable dilemma. The self I am today feels compassion, but the self I will be tomorrow may not. Thus, all commitment to being there for the other seems to depend on committing the self-I-am-not. Here one is reminded of Sartre's gloomy interpretation of commitment, according to which there can never be any certainty associated with the making of promises. Any faith in the power of commitment to the other is misguided because of the constant threat that tomorrow will bring the annihilation of my promise. Indeed, Marcel seems to be thinking of Sartre when he says that 'a consistent phenomenalism... asserting that the ego coincided with its immediate present, ought to exclude even the possibility of commitment; for indeed, how could I bind someone else, a someone whom, by definition, I cannot know because he does not yet exist?'[54] But rather than go along with this 'consistent phenomenalism' and declare any faith in commitment as 'bad faith', Marcel wants to locate it 'at the very core of [one's] promise' and see it as giving the promise 'its peculiar weight and worth'.[55] Marcel rejects the idea of the basic fidelity being fidelity to myself. If this is the case, I betray myself through a self-deception. I deny myself, 'not my being but my becoming; not what I am today but what I shall perhaps be tomorrow'.[56] He points to the fact that the way to overcome the problems associated with splitting the 'I' into present-I and future-I is to focus on fidelity to a *unity*.

> This unity is just me; it is a single unvarying principle.... which insists on its own continuity. The fidelity is no longer to a life-process, a 'becoming', for this is meaningless, but to a *being* which I can see no possibility of distinguishing from myself. And so I escape from the mirage of a tomorrow which loses its colour as it sharpens its outlines.[57]

For Marcel, this line of thought provides the way out of what seems to be the impossibility of being sincere and faithful at the same time. The supra-temporal identity of the subject is the basis for making it a point of honour to fulfil a commitment. Creative fidelity means the capacity to relegate the possibility of breaking a promise to the status of *temptation*.[58] When I commit myself, I 'grant in principle that the commitment will not again be put in question'.[59] To adopt this point of view is not to fall into self-deception or bad faith, but rather to engage with one's integrity as a person.

Fidelity, Marcel suggests, should be contrasted with *constancy*.[60] Constancy may be thought of as 'the rational skeleton of fidelity'.[61] Being constant is a way of relating which can be defined in terms of 'perseverance in a certain goal', in terms of 'immutability'.[62] While these elements also enter into fidelity, there is another all-important factor in being faithful, namely, *presence*. Presence casts off 'the feeling of *staleness*, of *rancidity*' which taints a purely formal adherence to the obligations of a promise.[63] As we have seen, it not easy to objectify the meaning of a presence which is stimulating and life-giving. The best way to describe it is to say that the other makes me feel as if he is really *with* me.

Constancy is oriented to one's-self. *I* need to feel satisfied that *I* have been a trustworthy, reliable friend. I want to feel as if my conscience is clear. There is in my mind an ideal of what a good friend is, and I wish to avoid the distress, the shame, that comes with a sense of falling short of that ideal. Marcel gets right to the core of the distinction between constancy and fidelity when he says, 'I am constant for myself, in my own regard, for my purpose - whereas I am *present* for the other, and more precisely: for *thou*.'[64]

Consider this scenario. I am careful to fulfil all my obligations and I may feel justified in making the judgement that I have been a faithful friend to X. But how can I really think that I can give myself the title, 'faithful friend'? The real question, Marcel points out, is, How does the situation seem to X?

> Assuming that X learns in some way or other that I have behaved towards him in a *conscientious* way, it is likely that he will release me from this obligation at least in his conscience; there is then the possibility that he will say to me with an intonation that can have infinite variations: "Don't think you are obligated to me..." To be sure, he knows that my conduct has been irreproachable; however, or rather because of this very thing, something has been shattered within him; we can even say that in his view a certain value has been lost and that what remains is only straw and it is here that we see the problem of fidelity dawn, strictly speaking.[65]

A formal commitment to obligations, a doing-for without the spontaneity and spark of being-with, is only the empty shell of fidelity. The genuinely faithful person says in her heart not the soulless words 'I will do for you what honour requires', but rather the fully committed, 'I belong to you'.

Availability as Belonging

We seem to be on dangerous ground in speaking about *belonging* to another person. It seems as if I must disenfranchise myself in giving myself away. Do I not in this act give up my personal autonomy? Marcel is acutely aware of the pit-falls associated with conceiving of disposability in terms of belonging. He begins his analysis[66] with the case of servanthood. If I assert, he says, of a servant 'he belongs to me', I treat him as a thing acquired, as something to be disposed of as I wish.[67] Everything changes, though, if I declare to another person, 'I belong to you'. 'Jack, I belong to you', means 'I am opening an unlimited credit account in your name, you can do what you want with me, I give myself to you'.[68] As Robert Gibbs observes, the use of the name, 'Jack', is important here.[69] I am speaking to a unique person, to a *thou*. The claims associated with belonging can only be communicated in the first person.

The fact that I give myself to you does not mean that I am your slave. I establish my freedom in the very act of freely giving myself to you. 'The best use I can make of my freedom is to place it in your hands; it is as though I freely substituted your freedom for my own; or paradoxically, it is by that very substitution that I realise my freedom.'[70] (This is like Jesus' teaching on gain through loss - cf. Mk 8:35; Mk 9:35; Jn 12:24.)

Though Marcel can assert that to give oneself freely to the other is to be free indeed, he feels the need to establish how it is possible that one can substitute the freedom of another for one's own without a disenfranchisement. In order to freely give one's-self, one must have some authority over the self that is given. That is to say, if I am to dispose of myself I must belong to myself.[71] In an attempt to understand what this means, Marcel develops the highly original notion of the self as constituted by an older and a younger brother.[72] He begins with the (inadequate) idea that I treat myself as an object belonging to the subject which I at the same time am. The difficulty here is that 'I' is the very negation of objectivity. In adopting the formulation 'object belonging to the subject which I at the same time am', one is really saying that the 'I' can be treated as a 'him', which is meaningless in this context. It is evident, then, that the 'I belong to myself' must be *personalised*. In this way, I can say that 'I have custody over myself or I am a trustee of myself'.[73] Belonging to myself means that I am responsible for myself, and this seems to suggest that I am two persons. It is as if I am at once the older and the younger brother of myself. Marcel has in mind two orphaned brothers; the older one being responsible for the younger one. When one begins to think this way, it is possible to construct a relational triad in which mutual availability and personal autonomy can co-exist. The components in this triad are these: *I belong to you; you belong to me; I belong to myself*.[74]

In a more conventional fashion, the theologian, Alistair McFadyen, arrives at the same conclusion in his Christian theory of personhood and relationships.[75] Crucial to the formation of personhood is what McFadyen calls 'being centred'. The centring of one's experience in the self is what constitutes autonomy. Being centred is defined as the 'achievement of organising one's life from an organisational locus within oneself; the ability to refer the features of the world to oneself and one's own location, so that the possibilities for action may be focussed on as they relate to oneself and so be self-ascribed'.[76] I refer my experience of the world to my personal centre and thereby ensure that my actions are self-ascribed. This is another way of stating Marcel's idea that 'I belong to myself'. The normative pattern for dialogue, in McFadyen's schema, is built on the understanding that 'we are properly centred as persons only by being directed towards the true reality of other personal centres: we become truly ourselves when we are truly for others'.[77] In Marcel's language, I avoid the self-constricting egoism potentially associated with the 'I belong to myself' when I simultaneously assert that 'I belong to you' and 'You belong to me'.

McFadyen points to the fact that in a Christian understanding mutual giving in a relationship is grounded in the presence and power of Christ. It is our faith in Christ and the grace of his sustaining love which allows us to risk ourselves with others: 'The otherness of other people, including their brokenness, does not pose a threat of disintegration for those who live in the knowledge that they are upheld as integral beings

in the presence of Christ, the indwelling of the Holy Spirit and in the love
and acceptance of God and/or others: who are, in other words, empowered
by the Spirit, conformed to Christ and called into responsibility before
God and others.'[78] In Marcel's terminology, belonging to others is
grounded in a belonging to Christ.[79] He acknowledges that there may be
an initial revolt against Christ's claim that I belong to him. It seems as if
Christ is exerting a tyranny over me. But, says Marcel, what frees this
claim from any possibility of tyranny is the fact that, in a sense, Christ
is not really someone else but 'more internal to me than myself'.[80] His
right is exercised not in terms of power but of love. If I can but overcome
my unproductive resistance to what seems a tyrannical claim, I am set free
from the strangulating grip of egoism.

> Who am I to pretend that I do not belong to You? The point really
> is that if I belong to You, this doesn't mean: I am Your possession; this
> mysterious relation does not exist on the level of having as would be
> the case if You were an infinite power. Not only are You freedom, but
> You also will me, You arouse me too as freedom, You invite me to
> create myself, You are this very invitation. And if I reject it, i.e. Thou,
> if I persist in maintaining that I belong only to myself, it is as though
> I walled myself up; as though I strove to strangle with my own hands
> that reality in whose name I believed I was resisting You.[81]

I belong to myself; I belong to Christ; I belong to you; you belong to me.
With these statements, Marcel creatively constructs an understanding of
availability which holds together personal freedom on the one hand, and
genuine self-giving to others and to Christ on the other. Christ is the ground
of the free act in which I substitute your freedom for mine, just as you
substitute mine for yours. If this is a slightly clumsy way of putting it, one
might prefer to say that in Christ we come to realise that we cease to belong
to ourselves and so we 'transcend one another in the very heart of *our love*'.[82]

A FLAW IN THE NOTION OF AVAILABILITY?

It may seem on the surface that associated with the idea of disposability
is a necessary failure in self-love. As we have seen, Marcel occasionally
makes extravagant statements such as, 'I am opening an unlimited credit
account in your name; you can do what you want with me; I give myself
to you.' It seems that he is here asking us to open ourselves to be 'used
up' by others. This, of course, has no place in a constructive Christian
love ethic. Feminist writers have made us especially aware of this fact.
They have highlighted for us the damage that has been done in the past
to untold Christian women as they have sacrificed themselves to their
families and to others in living out the distorted interpretation of *agape*

promoted so freely in many of our churches. In recent times, we have witnessed a concerted effort by moral theologians and by pastoral theologians such as Don Browning to replace the older notion of Christian love as self-sacrifice with the idea of 'equal-regard'.[83] In living by the principle of equal-regard, a person seeks to integrate a healthy love of self with her love of neighbour. One has an equal regard for self and for others. The theological rationale is as follows. One is called to love each and every person without exception because each one is created in the image and likeness of God and is someone Christ died for; one is called to love oneself for precisely the same reason. Now because one values self and others equally, one will consider the needs of the other, but one will not submit to his attempts at exploitation.

Marcel, in his statement that in belonging to the other one gives him the right to do what he wants, seems to be advocating a submission to exploitation. However, the statement must be taken in the context of a mutual commitment to belonging. The unreserved offering of self - 'I belong to you; do with me as you will' - assumes an identical intention from the other. Further, Marcel does include a discussion on the role of self-love within his reflections on disposability as belonging. His treatment ends with a statement which is clearly, I believe, in support of the principle of equal-regard. To begin with, he defines self-love as a 'charity towards oneself'.[84] The self is to be thought of as 'a seed which must be cultivated, as a ground which must be readied for the spiritual or even the divine in this world'.[85] This nurturing requires patience. Harshness towards the self stunts growth. But in being patient one is also 'lucid' in relation to the self. That is, self-love does not come with a licence to overlook one's moral failings and defects. Self-love, properly understood, incorporates both 'distance from and nearness to the self'.[86] In maintaining distance from ourselves we are able to see clearly the areas we need to work on to strengthen our capacity for love. Nearness to ourselves means that we have a 'contact with ourselves that we should always have with our fellow-men'.[87] That is, we should show the same charity to ourselves as we do to our neighbours. It seems to me that this is precisely the notion contained in the principle of equal-regard.

Despite his occasional extravagant statement *vis-à-vis* self-giving, Marcel does not advocate self-sacrifice. He understands, I suggest, the importance of self-valuing and of rejecting attempts by others to make use of one.

We have seen how Marcel uses notions such as grace, fidelity, availability, and belonging to describe genuine presence. In the next chapter, we will use the quite different conceptualisations of Martin Buber to expand our understanding of genuine attentiveness.

[1] 'One's-self' is the term Marcel uses to refer to the self of the individual. We will follow his usage.

[2] Marcel, *The Mystery of Being*, vol. I (London: The Harvill Press, 1950), p. 120.

[3] See Marcel, *Being and Having*, trans. by K. Farrer (London: Dacre Press, 1949), pp. 16-20.

[4] Ibid., p. 18.

[5] See Marcel, *The Mystery of Being*, vol. I, pp. 111-139.

[6] See ibid., p. 114.

[7] See ibid., p. 115ff.

[8] Ibid., p. 117.

[9] See ibid., p. 118.

[10] Ibid., p. 118.

[11] See ibid., p 121.

[12] Ibid., p. 122.

[13] Ibid., p. 126.

[14] Ibid., p. 126.

[15] See ibid., p. 127.

[16] See ibid., p. 128.

[17] Ibid., p. 136.

[18] See ibid., p. 192.

[19] See ibid., p. 176ff.

[20] Ibid., p. 177.

[21] Ibid., p. 178.

[22] Ibid., p. 181.

[23] See ibid., p. 192.

[24] Ibid., p. 192.

[25] Ibid., p. 192.

[26] See ibid., p. 193.

[27] Ibid., p. 194.

[28] Ibid., p. 205.

[29] See ibid., p. 207.

[30] See Marcel, *Metaphysical Journal*, trans. by B. Wall (London: Rockliff, 1952), pp. 300-301.

[31] Ibid., p. 300.

[32] Ibid., p. 301.

[33] See Marcel, *The Mystery of Being*, I, p. 139.

[34] Marcel, *Metaphysical Journal*, p. 301.

[35] See Marcel, 'Presence and Immortality', in T. Busch ed., *The Participant Perspective: A Gabriel Marcel Reader* (Lanham, MD.: University Press of America, 1987), pp. 245-264, p. 256.

[36] Ibid., p. 256.

[37] Ibid., p. 257.

[38] Cf. O. Bollnow, 'Marcel's Concept of Availability', p. 182.

[39] See G. Outka, *Agape: An Ethical Analysis* (New Haven: Yale University Press, 1972) for an overview of the various ethical treatments of *agape*.

[40] See Marcel, 'Phenomenological Notes on Being in A Situation', in *Creative Fidelity*, trans. by R. Rosthal (New York: The Noonday Press, 1964), pp. 82-103, p. 87ff.

[41] Ibid., p. 88.

[42] Ibid., p. 91.

[43] It is interesting to observe that Henri Nouwen also thinks of hospitality as a healing power (see his *The Wounded Healer* [New York: Doubleday, 1972], p. 91ff.) Hospitality in a ministry of pastoral care, suggests Nouwen, involves *concentration* and *community*. Thus, one needs, first, to be able to pay attention to one's guest without intention. That is, one disposes one's-self (to use Marcelian language) through refusing to entertain thoughts of what one can get from the other. And secondly, one offers community by sharing in the common human struggle with fear, loneliness, anxiety and confusion (woundedness as a resource in healing).

[44] See Marcel, 'Belonging and Disposability', in *Creative Fidelity*, pp. 38-57, p. 50.

[45] See ibid., pp. 50-51.

[46] Ibid., pp. 50-51.

[47] Ibid., p. 51.

[48] Ibid., p. 51.

[49] Ibid., p. 54.

[50] Ibid., p. 54.

[51] See *Being and Having*, pp. 41-54.

[52] See ibid., p. 42.

[53] Ibid., pp. 47-48.

[54] Ibid., p. 42.

[55] Ibid., p. 49.

[56] Ibid., p. 51.

[57] Ibid., p. 52.

[58] See Marcel, 'Creative Fidelity', in *Creative Fidelity*, pp. 147-174, p. 162.

[59] See ibid., p. 162.

[60] Ibid., pp. 153-156.

[61] Ibid., p. 153. We encounter here what I think is a terminological difficulty. To be constant in a relationship is actually a virtue. However, Marcel uses the term in a pejorative sense. A term such as 'counterfeit fidelity' conveys his meaning more accurately.

[62] Ibid., p. 153.

[63] Ibid., p. 153.

[64] Ibid., p. 154.

[65] Ibid., p. 155.

[66] See Marcel, 'Belonging and Disposability', in *Creative Fidelity*, pp. 39-57.

[67] Ibid., p. 39.

[68] Ibid., p. 40.

[69] See R. Gibbs, 'Substitution: Marcel and Levinas', *Philosophy and Theology* 4 (Winter 1989), pp. 171-185, p. 174.

[70] Marcel, 'Belonging and Disposability', p. 40.

[71] See Marcel, 'Belonging and Disposability', p. 41.

[72] See ibid., pp 42-46.

[73] Ibid., p. 42.

[74] Ibid., p. 42.

[75] See A. McFadyen, *The Call to Personhood: A Christian Theory of the Individual in Social Relationships* (Cambridge: Cambridge University Press, 1990), chapter 5.

[76] Ibid., p. 312.

[77] Ibid., p. 151.

[78] Ibid., p. 157.

[79] See Marcel, 'Phenomenological Notes on Being in A Situation', pp. 99-101.

[80] Ibid., p. 100.

[81] Ibid., p. 100.

[82] Ibid., p. 99.

[83] See G. Outka, *Agape: An Ethical Analysis* (New Haven: Yale University Press, 1972), esp. pp. 9-16 and 290-291; L. Janssens, 'Norms and Priorities in a Love Ethics', *Louvain Studies* 6 (Spring 1977), pp. 207-238; D. Browning, *Religious Thought and the Modern Psychologies* (Philadelphia: Fortress Press, 1987), pp. 150-160, and idem, 'Altruism and Christian Love', *Zygon* 27, no. 4 (Dec. 1992), pp. 421-436; and S. Post, 'Communion and True Self-Love', *Journal of Religious Ethics* 16 (Fall 1988), pp. 345-362.

[84] See Marcel, 'Belonging and Disposability', in *Creative Fidelity*, p. 46.

[85] Ibid., p. 46.

[86] Ibid., p. 46.

[87] Ibid., p. 47.

Chapter 2

PRESENCE AS I-THOU RELATION AND CONFIRMATION:

The Contribution of Martin Buber

In what follows, we will be using Martin Buber's dialogical philosophy to add to our understanding of what constitutes genuine presence. A philosophical analysis of the other can either start with subjectivity or with relationality. While existentialist thinkers such as Sartre and Heidegger locate authentic existence in self-being, in communication with the self, Buber orientates his thinking around the sphere of the 'between'. It is out of the I-You relation that real life emerges. A person's deepest identity is to be found in the need, the urge, for dialogue. The innate You reaches out for its realisation in the meeting with the other.

In endeavouring to understand Buber's description of meeting in *I and Thou*, one is, on the one hand, captivated by the power of the vision, and on the other, frustrated by the abstract nature of the language. Where, one asks, is the concrete guidance for the person wishing to learn the way of genuine presence? During the twenties and thirties Buber began, in fact, to flesh out the bare bones of his philosophy of the inter-human. It was during this period that he developed his thought on the nature of genuine dialogue. He identified confirmation as one of the key elements in dialogue. Confirmation is grounded in an acknowledgement of otherness. As I enter into dialogue with the other, I accept her uniqueness and particularity and struggle with her in the release of her potential as a person.

Confirmation depends on a capacity for *inclusion*. Inclusion, or 'imagining the real', is the attempt to grasp the thoughts, feelings, and wishes of the other while maintaining one's own concreteness and particularity. Through inclusion one is able to catch hold of otherness. This grasp of the particularity of the other is the first step in confirmation.

Confirmation is closely related to *responsibility*. Responsibility refers to a readiness to listen for the call of the other and to follow through on it. The responsible person is the one who, first of all, tunes in to the claim the other is making, and then, aware of what is being asked, applies her resources to the task of responding. Confirmation refers to a particular kind of claim, namely, a call for help in the realisation of inner potential.

Anyone familiar with person-centred therapy will immediately see in Buber's formulations of inclusion and confirmation close connections with Carl Rogers' concepts of empathy and acceptance (or unconditional positive regard) respectively. In fact, the two entered into a dialogue over their respective theories during an American Midwest conference on Buber in April of 1957.[1] Below we will attempt to fix points of convergence and divergence in the thought of Buber and Rogers in order to identify the unique contribution the former makes to psychological thought and therapeutic practice.

THE I-THOU RELATION

A person sits in quiet, contemplative mood gazing at a lake surrounded by snow-capped mountains. Two strangers seated beside each other on a busy commuter train exchange glances in a moment of mutual confirmation. A person shares with her friend thoughts and feelings which are deep and intimate. It is in moments such as these that the I-You world is constituted. In these 'peak' experiences there has been a genuine meeting. Surrounding these fleeting moments of communion is a sea of ordinary, mundane, everyday reality. It may seem, as one interpreter suggests,[2] that Buber establishes a contrast between the extraordinary, 'spiritual' world of the I-You and the ordinary, routine, drab world of the I-It. The polarity, though, that Buber is really interested in is, on the one hand, the actualising power of immediacy and, on the other, the depersonalising effect of an instrumentalist ethos. A direct relation is humanising; objectification produces a soul-destroying sense of alienation.[3]

Tönnies had already located the fundamental problem of modern life in the shift from organic, voluntary communities (*Gemeinschaft* or community) to depersonalised, contract-oriented social structures (*Gesellschaft* or association).[4] The modern capitalist and industrial society is founded on the canons of efficiency, production, and goal-setting. Not only material goods but persons also become objectified; they become things which can be used to achieve a purpose. This instrumentalist ethos and its alienating effects must be countered, Buber believes, through the actualising power of communion. In *Daniel*, Buber contrasts *orientation* with *realisation*.[5] The former describes the rational, technocratic, goal-oriented mode of consciousness rampant in the modern industrialised society. Realisation refers to the pure life experience in which two persons come to each other with their whole being. In genuine community it is 'immediacy which... makes it possible to live the realising as real'.[6] Buber is under no illusions about the extent of the problem facing his society. In an early essay entitled 'Productivity and Existence'[7] (1914), he laments the fact that the technological, production-oriented ethos has permeated even the sphere of human creativity. There is no longer any immediacy between author and reader. A sense that the author is holding back her essential being is disturbing for the reader. The former seems only intent on producing more and more books. 'The overvaluation of productivity that is afflicting our age has so thrived and its par-technical glance has set up a senseless exclusiveness of its own that even genuinely creative men allow their organic skills to degenerate into an autonomous growth to satisfy the demands of the day.'[8] Buber's teaching on the I-You world needs to be set in the context of his deep concern over the alienating effect of an instrumentalist mentality.

I and Thou

In the utilitarian ethos of the modern society, life with others is construed in terms of a subject-object split. The other is viewed as an object, a thing, to be used and manipulated. Buber, however, imagines a new way of speaking in an attempt to reshape modern consciousness. In place of the language of atomisation - I, You, It, She, He - he offers the word-pairs I-You and I-It.[9] A word-pair is immediately suggestive of communion. The one who speaks the word 'You' appears as a *person*, a person-in-relation.[10] He is aware of his subjectivity, but he does not think of himself as an subject over against an object. Only *egos* construct themselves in terms of the over-against. Setting apart, possession, experience and use - these are the categories the ego uses to shape her life in the world. She lives in the sphere of goal-directed activity.[11] She wants, perceives, feels, uses something. The person, on the other hand, is conscious of himself as being-with, as participating in being. Being-with is unmediated.[12] In the relation nothing is allowed to get in the way. Preconceptions, purposes, and goals prevent communion; they have no place in the world of the You.

There are persons and there are egos. Indeed, we all partake to a greater or lesser extent in both poles of existence. In virtually every encounter with another person, there is a mix of immediacy and distance, of personalism and objectification. While one may intend to simply 'be there' for the other, to cast aside any thought of how the other can be useful to one, any thought of what one can get out of the encounter, very quickly these negative intentions begin to intrude.

The I of humanity is twofold. The I of the I-You is different from the
I of the I-It.[13] Apart from the relation, the I does not exist. 'There is no
I as such but only the I of the basic word I-You and the I of the basic word
I-It.'[14] It is my attitude to the other which establishes her as either a You
or an It. Anyone or anything can become an object. There is nothing that
cannot become a You. My comportment to the other will either generate
presence or objectivity. It is my attitude which constitutes either a You-
world or an It-world.

Intending something, having a purpose in mind, analysing and
evaluating - the mindset characteristic of the It-world - objectifies the
other. You-saying, on the other hand, creates a relation. 'Whoever says
You does not have something for his object. For wherever there is
something there is also another something... Whoever says You does not
have something; he has nothing. But he stands in relation.'[15] In the
relation no thing, no object is intended or constituted. No purposes,
perceptions, imaginings are allowed to come between the I and the You.
There is simply the immediacy of presence. As soon as one contemplates
using the other in some way, however, the immediacy of the moment has
been lost and now all I have are representations. The person with whom
I shared a moment of presence and wholeness is now split apart in analysis
and judgement. I constitute her as a bundle of predicates.[16] She is the
woman with the lively face, a liking for stylish clothes, and a quick wit.
The person I was speaking *to* a moment ago I now speak *about*.

The reader may at this point be put off by this tendency to construct
human relations in an either-or fashion. Either we live in the personalism
of the I-You world, or we fall into the objectifications of the I-It world.
Surely human relations in fact range over a continuum between the two
poles. This concern is valid and will be discussed more fully below.

We address others directly on the one hand, and we talk about them
on the other. Language establishes the interpersonal sphere. This becomes
clear when we contrast relations with other persons with relations in two
other spheres. Buber refers, first, to a relation with *nature*, but this
operates on the 'threshold of language'.[17] When I talk to a dog, for
example, I may receive a response but never a reply. Second, in the
relation with '*spiritual beings*' (the immaterial entities of art, knowledge
and example) there is a 'demanding silence'.[18] The form 'calls out'
demandingly to the artist - to use that example - to be actualised. It is
through the relation between the form and the artistic mind that a work
is generated. Relations in the inter-human sphere, in contrast, are
distinguished by the capacity of language to create address and response.
In the interpersonal domain 'language is perfected as a sequence and

becomes speech and reply. Only here does the word, formed in language, encounter its reply. Only here does the basic word go back and forth in the same shape; that of the address and that of the reply are alive in the same tongue...'[19] Language enables reciprocity. There is in the human relation an essential similarity between asking and answering, assertion and counter-assertion, loving and being loved. 'My You acts on me as I act on it.'[20]

While Buber uses language to set the inter-human apart from the other two spheres, he also stresses the power of silence in the I-You relation. He refers often, for example, to the glance silently exchanged between strangers. 'Speech can renounce all the media of sense, and it is still speech.'[21] In fact, Buber is somewhat ambivalent about the role of language. It is possible, he observes, to say You with one's lips while treating the other as an It.[22] The spoken word can so easily be distorted and misused. Almost without realising it, one utters the word which objectifies the other. It is difficult to address the other in such a way that his freedom is absolutely guaranteed. Marcel expresses the matter well: 'Only silence... leaves the Thou its freedom, and subsists with it in unobtrusiveness; then, spirit no longer announces itself, but *is*.'[23]

The moment in which the spirit simply 'is' never lasts long. Speaking-to inevitably passes over into speaking-about. There is always and necessarily a swing between presence and objectivity. 'The human being who but now was unique and devoid of qualities, not at hand but only present, not able to be experienced, only touchable, has again become a He or She, an aggregate of qualities, a quantum without shape.'[24] Buber does not, however, use the concept of the It-world in a pejorative sense. The swing from actuality to latency is inevitable, as it should be. The world of the It is an ordered one. It is reliable; it has 'density and duration'; one can turn again and again to that which has been analysed, catalogued and stored away.[25] It is only when the sphere of objectivity is allowed to assume a mastery, thereby pushing immediacy and communion to the margins of human co-existence, that it becomes a demonic force.

Buber characterises this movement from presence to objectivity as a swing from the present to the past. 'Insofar as a human being makes do with the things that he experiences and uses, he lives in the past, and his moment has no presence. He has nothing but objects; but objects consist in having been.'[26] In the directness of the encounter with the other the partners are caught up in a moment of actuality of being. It is not a point in time that is experienced but the 'actual and fulfilled present'.[27] In order to describe, analyse, or use something I must be able to 'look back on it', so to speak. I need some temporal distance in order to be able to formulate descriptive terms and categories.

The I of the I-You relation is not only released from temporality in the immediacy of presence, but also from the system of spatial co-ordinates we use to locate the elements in the physical world. It is only the world of the It which is set in a spatio-temporal-causal context.[28] A You measured, analysed, described and catalogued is transformed into an It. It becomes a thing which can be integrated into a space-time grid. The You also appears in space, but only in the context of a direct encounter in which everything else becomes a background rather than a means of measurement. The You appears in time, but only as a fulfilled, actualised presence, not as part of an organised sequence.

If a major aim for Buber is to offer a way beyond the alienation generated through the instrumentalist ethos dominant in the modern age, it is also a significant purpose of his to show that in every encounter with a You there is an orientation to the absolute You. In the meeting between persons there is also a meeting with God. Extended, the lines of all relationships intersect in eternity. 'Every single You is a glimpse of [God]. Through every single You the basic word addresses the eternal You.' [29]

Every genuine encounter, those in which God is an explicit theme and those in which it is not, orients a person to God. Though a person may repudiate the idea of God, when he addresses with the whole of his being the You given to him he addresses God.[30] In the relation to God, there is both an unconditional exclusiveness and an unconditional inclusiveness.[31] On the one hand, nothing in heaven or on earth, no particular thing or being, retains any importance in the context of this relation. And yet, on the other, everything is included in it. Entering into a relationship with God does not involve cutting oneself off from the things of this world, but rather locating them in the context of the absolute You. 'Looking away from the world is no help toward God; staring at the world is no help either; but whoever beholds the world in him stands in his presence.'[32] A 'worldly' life cannot separate us from God. Only life in the It-world, in the world of experience and use, is alienating. Whenever we live in the world in truth we live in God.

Buber's vision is the actualisation of God in the world through the community of persons who actualise being through the I-You relation. It is not appropriate or even possible to banish the It-relation from the world. Rather, we are to sound the 'holy basic word' in order to humanise the world of the It. In this vision, all I-You encounters are the radii which lead from all I-points to the centre of a circle.[33] It is this common relation to the centre, to God, which assures genuine community and actualisation of the real in the world.

Clearly, Buber's language for the I-You relation is abstract and difficult. It may be helpful at this point to present some concrete examples of inter-subjectivity. Indeed, Buber himself offered some. Responding to just this criticism, he referred to the confirming glance shared between two strangers on a bus or a train. We have all had the experience of being 'looked up and down' by a fellow commuter. That he is making some observation or judgement is evident. He thinks, 'He's a funny looking character.' Or perhaps he is trying to decide what line of work one is in. One is for him no more than an object of passing interest. On other occasions though, we experience a look which is warm and encouraging. Through the smile or the nod of the other there is a sense of being recognised as a person. Buber also refers this experience of confirmation to the factory floor. As two workers labour at their machines, battling with monotony and boredom, they validate and encourage each other through a warm glance.

Think, too, of the experience of shopping for a gift for a loved one. The shop assistant who engages fully with you in the project of finding the 'right' present establishes an I-You relation. Her warmth, her genuine interest, 'personalises' the experience. She could have constructed it in terms of a 'customer' making a 'purchase', thereby entering the world of the I-It. Instead, she chooses to focus on you as a person, as a caring husband or wife, who wants to find a nice gift for his or her beloved.

Distance and Relation

More than thirty years after the publication of *I and Thou*, Buber investigated a new problem in the idea of relation. In an important essay entitled 'Distance and Relation',[34] he inquired into the condition of the possibility of the encounter between the I and the You. In other words, he was searching for the anthropological foundation of meeting.

Buber refers to the twofold nature of the principle of human life.[35] Human existence involves a twofold movement such that one movement is the presupposition of the other. The 'primal setting at a distance' is the presupposition for entering into relation. That is to say, it is only possible to establish a relation with a being which has been set at a distance, has become 'an independent opposite'.

That this is in fact the case becomes clear when human life is contrasted with life in the animal world. Animals exist in an environment (understood in the sense used in biology). Only those things which immediately concern them, with which they are directly engaged through their needs, constitute their environment. Out of the elements they utilise to meet their requirements, animals construct their realm or 'world'. An animal is totally immersed in its realm of existence. Only the human can imagine a unity which is existing in and for itself. The animal lives only in a segment of the world which exists without an horizon; the human adopts a perspective which allows her to 'grasp a totality'.[36] 'An animal in the realm of its perceptions is like a fruit in its skin; man is, or can be, in the world as a dweller in an enormous building which is always being added to, and to whose limits he can never penetrate, but which he can nevertheless know as one does know a house in which one lives - for he is capable of grasping the wholeness of the building as such.'[37] The human is able to detach 'what is', beings in the world, from herself and so establish them as independent realities. This setting at a distance establishes a world.

In the second movement, the human turns to 'the withdrawn structure of being'[38] and enters into a relation with it. It is only possible to relate to that which is set apart from oneself, existing in and of itself. This view of reality is not obtained simply from the action of 'setting at a distance'. Establishing the independence of the world simply means that objectivity is constituted. It is only when I am fully present in the world, relating to it with my whole being, that I experience the world as whole and one. Buber is quick to point out, however, that the idea of establishing other entities as independent opposites is not the same as the idealist conception of the I who establishes the world[39] (as in Husserl's philosophy of the transcendental subject who projects her world). Rather, he means to say only that the human can cut the world away from himself and make it an independent whole; the animal, on the other hand, lives immersed in a realm constituted by things it needs and uses. It is the act of establishing the other as independent opposite which conditions the possibility of entering into relationship. The fact of distance grounds the possibility of human existence. The realisation of the human person is founded in the movement of relation. 'Distance provides the human situation, relation provides man's becoming in that situation.'[40] The movement which creates distance is the fundamental act which makes us human - beings who are able to enter into relation.

Objections to 'I and Thou'

Over the past eighty years, countless thousands of readers have warmly welcomed Buber's vision of the overcoming of the instrumentalist ethos through the actualisation of the real in relation. A positive evaluation has also been the response of many to his articulation of the encounter with

God through encounters between persons. There are, however, a number of quite obvious problems with the way the concept of relation is developed in *I and Thou*.

One such problem is the seeming impermanence of the I-You world. K. Plant observes that as the sphere of the I-You covers the 'extraordinary and the fleeting... we are left with a large residue of the I-It...'[41] Consequently, he thinks, the world of encounter is 'at the periphery and not at the centre of our lives'.[42] Plant, however, finds permanency in Buber's later formulation of the community of the We.[43] The We is the fellowship of those who are capable of truly saying You. It is a community shaped by the dynamic of call and response. This, says Buber, may be found, for example, in revolutionary groups working to conscientise and liberate the oppressed, and in religious groups committed to each other and to service.[44] While it is no doubt true that sharing in the joys and struggles of the on-going life of a community gives to the inter-human sphere the continuity that is absent from the fleeting I-You encounter, it is important to recognise that Buber sees already in the concept of relation a possibility of permanency. That is to say, he differentiates between encounter or meeting, on the one hand, and relation or relationship on the other. Relation is the primary category; there must be a relation before any encounter can take place.[45] Two people must be somehow connected, or at least aware of each other, before the event that is encounter can take place. This becomes clear when one studies Buber's reply to Marcel's suggestion that encounter or meeting (*Begegnung*) conveys more accurately the meaning he, Buber, has in mind than relation (*Beziehung*).[46] For Marcel, relation (the French word which matches *Beziehung* most closely) has a mathematical connotation, suggesting as it does a connection between data or arithmetical terms. Buber, however, believes that both relation and encounter should be retained in the description of the sphere of the between:

> ...."*Begegnung*" signifies only something actual. He who remains with a person whom he has just met when this event is past, now meets him no more. The concept of relationship (*Beziehung*), in contrast, opens the possibility - only the possibility, but this really - of the latency. Two friends, two lovers must, to be sure, experience ever again how the I-Thou is succeeded by an I-He or I-She; but is it not often as though the little bird whose wings are crippled in this moment secretly seeks its soaring? And does not an incomprehensible, as it were vibrating, connection manifest itself at times between the moments of Thou?...

One can only try to overcome the lack of an adequate designation through using the "skeleton word" relationship (*Beziehung*), always according to the context, next to the other, at once more concrete and more limited terms, such as meeting (*Begegnung*), contact, communication; none of them can be replaced by any of them.[47]

While an encounter (*Begegnung*) is necessarily a passing experience, permanency is a possibility in the relationship (*Beziehung*). Some relations, to be sure, are only temporary, but others are ongoing. This is the case with friendships and love relationships. They are characterised over time by latency and actuality. These relations continue in the possibility of the actualisation of being in the partners. The I-She is the chrysalis; the I-You the butterfly.[48]

Emmanuel Levinas points to what is a second potential problem in Buber's treatment of relation. He is concerned that the theory has little or nothing to say about meeting the other in his physical suffering. 'It may be conjectured', he writes, 'that clothing those who go hungry [sic] is a more authentic way of finding access to the other than the rarefied ether of a spiritual friendship.'[49] Obviously there is some force in Levinas' objection. Before dealing with it directly, however, I must point out that it is not actually correct to say that Buber's thought lives in the 'rarefied ether of a spiritual friendship'. He is not addressing through his dialogical reflections only those persons who by inclination and through circumstance have the luxury of deep and meaningful conversations. Rather, he wants to reach those also whom each day must contend with the monotony and depersonalisation of life in the factory or the office. It is here that genuine encounters - it may be only a confirming glance - actualise the real and humanise daily existence. 'Dialogue', writes Buber, 'is not an affair of spiritual luxury and spiritual luxuriousness, it is a matter of creation, of the creature, and he is that, the man of whom I speak, he is a creature, trivial and irreplaceable.'[50] And again, '....I am not concerned with the pure; I am concerned with the turbid, the repressed, the pedestrian, with toil and dull contrariness and with the breakthrough.'[51]

It is still possible to argue, of course, that there is a greater degree of authenticity attached to meeting the other in the misery of physical deprivation than in the meaninglessness of monotonous, dehumanising toil. There is no doubt that the satisfaction of physical needs is more basic, more urgent, than experiencing communion with others. A hungry person does not have the luxury of reflecting on existential problems; he is driven by a desperate need to fill his belly and to survive. Nonetheless, rather than attempt to establish a hierarchy of authenticity, I am content to say - as I think Buber perhaps would have - that whether one meets the other in the guise of poverty or of alienation, what is ultimately important is that one responds to her call with the whole of one's being. In the case of hunger and deprivation, naturally the most basic fact is that material help must be offered. If, however, the person helped is to maintain her dignity, the physical offering must be accompanied by the spiritual gift of You-saying.

Perhaps the most obvious objection to *I and Thou,* as was noted above, is that the complexity of human relations cannot be captured through the I-It and I-You polarity.[52] According to Buber, one either says You or It; there are no other possibilities. This seems to oversimplify, and thus distort, the reality of the meeting between persons. In a relationship there are many shades in between presence and objectification.

Equally obvious, is the fact that Buber fails to give specific guidance *vis-à-vis* relationships.[53] *I and Thou* is filled with rather abstract depictions of the I-You relation. Buber refers, for example, to entering the relation 'with the whole of one's being'. It is characterised by 'immediacy' and 'directness'. The other is encountered as a 'unity' rather than as a multiplicity of characteristics. And so on. But what, one may ask, do these terms tell us in a concrete sense about how one is to act in a relationship?

In fact, Buber himself dealt with these last two objections. During the twenties and thirties, Buber shifted his emphasis from relation to dialogue. In his description of the latter, he overcomes some of the limitations associated with *I and Thou.* First, he incorporates into his thinking on the inter-human realm various gradations.[54] 'Reflexion', the tendency to view the other only as an extension of oneself, appears in a variety of guises: self-concern, self-pity, enjoyment of the self, and even self-worship.[55] When speaking about the various forms of perception in the inter-human sphere, Buber presents three possibilities.[56] One can approach the other as a collection of traits (as a scientist), or as a communicative existence (as an artist), or as a word calling for a response (as a partner in dialogue).

We also find in his reflections on dialogue specific guidance *vis-à-vis* genuine relationships. In concepts such as inclusion, responsibility, and confirmation we see the concreteness not found in *I and Thou.*

BECOMING AWARE: THE START OF DIALOGUE

How one relates to the other is conditioned by the way one perceives her. One can observe or study the other, or one can listen for the claim she makes. The one stance is characterised by keeping-at-a-distance, the alternative by opening-one's-being-to-the-other. For Buber, all dialogue starts with a fundamental awareness of the word the other is speaking.

Observing, Looking On, and Becoming Aware

Buber suggests that there are three basic modalities in the perception of the other.[57] The *observer* operates with a quasi-scientific mindset. She is interested in a careful, analytical study of the other. Her aim is to compile a comprehensive list of traits. For the purposes of observation, the other person is nothing but a bundle of characteristics.

The *onlooker* is not at all interested in traits. Focusing on traits, he thinks, leads one away from one's real purpose. Looking on - the artistic perspective - involves trusting one's intuitive powers. That which is really significant about the other will show itself if only one is attentive and receptive.

Neither in observing or in looking on, however, do we find the possibility of being addressed directly by the other. The observer perceives a bundle of traits, the onlooker an existence, but the one who is *aware* perceives a call to action, feels the weight of destiny falling on him:

> In a receptive hour of my personal life a man meets me about whom there is something, which I cannot grasp in any objective way at all, that "says something" to me. That does not mean, says to me what manner of man this is, what is going on in him, and the like. But it means, says something *to me*, addresses something to me, speaks something that enters my own life.[58]

In becoming aware of the claims the other is making, one has a moral obligation to respond with all one's being.

RESPONSIBILITY

In hearing a word spoken which carries with it the urgent demand for an answer, one is called to responsibility.[59] One has the feeling of being claimed and, consequently, that one ought to respond.[60] The claim is characterised on the one side by trust and on the other by loyalty (or disloyalty).[61] The other addresses me from a position of trust, and I can either respond in loyalty or fall into disloyalty. A loyal turning to the other, given the weightiness of the claim, will probably not receive a clear articulation. It is not realistic to expect oneself to be totally composed, ready with a well-rounded reply, able to smoothly commit oneself. And yet it happens that one really does want to let this challenging word penetrate the armour of one's defences. An answer is required; ignoring the claim is not an option. One gropes for words to frame one's response.

'But it is an honest stammering; as when sense and throat are united about what is to be said, but the throat is too horrified at it to utter purely that already composed sense.'[62]

To respond to the other is to confirm her as a person. However, when Buber uses the term 'confirmation' he has a specific response in mind. One must respond to the call from the other to accept her as she is and, beyond that, to help her grow into her potential. The process begins with an attempt to include oneself in her inner world.

CONFIRMING THE OTHER

Inclusion

In order to become aware of the other and her claim on oneself it is necessary, observes Buber, to include oneself in her inner world. Inclusion is the process of 'imagining the real'.[63] One attempts to imagine what at this moment the other person is thinking, feeling, wishing, perceiving. This can only be achieved through a 'bold swinging, demanding the most intensive stirring of one's being, into the life of the other'.[64]

Inclusion can also be thought of as 'experiencing the other side'.[65] This can be illustrated through somatic references. A man caresses a woman. He feels the touch from two sides - with the palm of his hand and with her skin.[66] I attempt to experience the pain of the other. As I attempt to imagine her pain - her particular pain and not simply physical discomfort in general - the two of us are embraced by a common existential situation.[67]

Through imagining the real one endeavours to move over into the inner world of the other - his physical experiences, his emotional state, his hopes and fears. To anyone familiar with psychotherapy, this sounds very much like empathy. Carl Rogers was one of a number of psychotherapists to show an interest in Buber's ideas on the interpersonal. For Rogers, empathy is one of the core conditions of therapy. In an early attempt (1957) to define it, he wrote:

> To sense the client's private world as if it were your own, but without ever losing the "as if" quality - this is empathy, and this seems essential to therapy. To sense the client's anger, fear, or confusion as if it were your own, yet without your own anger, fear, or confusion getting bound up with it, is the condition we are endeavouring to describe.[68]

Despite the fact that inclusion and empathy may seem to be almost identical concepts, Buber is quick to say that there are in fact important differences between the two. He sees empathy as a process in which one 'transposes' oneself over to the place of the other. This transposition 'means the exclusion of one's own concreteness, the extinguishing of the actual situation of life'.[69] In inclusion, on the other hand, a person does not forfeit 'anything of the felt reality of his activity, [and] at the same time lives through the common event from the standpoint of the other'.[70]

The 'as if' quality Rogers stresses puts, I think, his understanding of empathy very close to Buber's idea of inclusion. Thinking and feeling herself into the inner world of the client, the therapist is careful not to identify with it. She goes over in her imagination to the other side, but nevertheless maintains her own boundary, her own personal concreteness. In a later (1980) definition of empathy, though, Rogers shows himself to be much less concerned about the possibility of identification. To enter the private world of the client

> means that for the time being, you lay aside your own views and values.....In some sense it means that you lay aside yourself; this can only be done by persons who are secure enough in themselves that they know they will not get lost in what may turn out to be the strange and bizarre world of the other, and that they can comfortably return to their own world when they wish.[71]

A clear distinction can be drawn between this definition of the empathic way of being, containing as it does the idea of laying oneself aside, and Buber's description of imaging the real. As we have seen, Buber insists on the importance of maintaining the actual situation of one's life when attempting to enter the experience of the other. For him, there is an important difference between empathy and inclusion. It is not simply a desire for terminological precision which motivates him here. The reason he insists on the maintenance of one's own concreteness is that this is absolutely necessary if one is going to confirm the other in his concreteness.[72] I can only confirm the other in his particularity from my own particular life situation. It is not possible to affirm the other while 'lost' in his world. Rogers also stresses the importance of affirmation or, as he calls it, *acceptance*. He would, of course, agree that in order to communicate unconditional positive regard one must first return to one's own world. Nevertheless, it is not the case, as we are about to see, that confirmation and acceptance can simply be equated.

Confirmation as a Step Beyond Acceptance

For Buber, dialogue is founded on the confirmation of otherness. Maurice Friedman rightly points out that an affirmation of the uniqueness of another person rests on the human capacity to both establish distance and enter into relation.[73] Buber's notion of confirmation is indissolubly linked to his understanding of the two ontological movements that make us human in distinction to other animals. I can only confirm the uniqueness of the other through first establishing her in her concrete, particular existence. Setting at a distance necessarily precedes affirming uniqueness in relation.

Particularity implies *difference*. To acknowledge the particularity of others I must be able to grasp the breath of potential difference. I become aware 'that this one or that one does not have merely a different mind, or way of thinking or feeling, or a different conviction or attitude, but has also a different perception of the world, a different recognition and order of meaning, a different touch from the regions of existence, a different faith, a different soil...'[74] The challenge is to live in genuine openness to alternative opinions and worldviews without losing the seriousness of the struggle for truth and justice. A debate can go in one of two ways.[75] If I fail to acknowledge the independence and individuality of the other, I engage not in dialogue but in propaganda, manipulation and self-promotion. The desire to influence is expressed through an injection of what I take to be right and true. My aim, whether or not I am fully conscious of it, is to deceive the other into thinking that this view I inject is really something coming from within her, and needing only my assistance to allow it to rise into full awareness.[76] My partner, rather than being allowed the freedom and dignity of otherness, is constituted simply as an extension of my existence. This Buber terms *reflexion*, and it happens

> when a man withdraws from accepting with his essential being another person in his particularity - a particularity which is by no means to be circumscribed by the circle of his own self, and though it substantially touches and moves his soul is in no way immanent in it - and lets the other exist only as his own experience, only as a "part of myself."[77]

Opposed to this imposition of self, there is what Buber calls *unfolding*.[78] If I confirm the other in her uniqueness I naturally seek for that truth which lies in her as potentiality. Through my sharing of myself and my views I hope for an opening out of this latent truth.

Rogers saw in Buber's understanding of confirmation something quite close to his own view of acceptance. During their dialogue at the Midwest Conference in 1957, he wanted to establish just how Buber saw the relationship between the two concepts. He began by explaining how acceptance works in the therapeutic relationship:

> I feel a real willingness for this other person to be *what he is*. I call this "acceptance"... I am willing for him to possess the feelings he possesses, to hold the attitudes he holds, to be the person he is.[79]

Buber responded by commenting that all genuine relationships must begin with acceptance, with communicating to the other that 'I take you just as you are'.[80] But he also felt compelled to point out that confirmation is actually a step beyond acceptance. Buber shared his conviction that it is possible to see in the other his God-given *potential*: 'I can recognise in him, know in him, more or less, the person he has been (I can say it only in this word) *created* to become.'[81] Seeing the potential is a movement beyond acceptance, and it implies the need to *act* with the other: 'And now I not only accept the other as he is, but I confirm him, in myself, and then in him, in relation to this potentiality that is meant by him and it can now be developed... He can do more or less to this scope but *I can, too, do something*' [emphasis added].[82] Imagining the potential of the other and helping in the realisation of that potential constitute for Buber the critical points of distinction between acceptance and confirmation.

Rogers reacted by asserting that in therapy he accepts not only the individual in his current emotional state but also his potentiality.[83] This unconditional positive regard is the 'strongest factor' in promoting change. Buber found himself unable to find the same level of confidence as his discussion partner in the power of acceptance alone to produce growth. His experience is that often one must struggle with the other *against* himself. The other knows the direction he should take, but for some reason he finds himself moving in another direction, or not moving at all. For Buber, the human can best be understood as a polar reality.

> The poles are not good and evil, but rather yes and no, rather acceptance and refusal. And we can strengthen, or we can help him strengthen, the one positive pole. And perhaps we can strengthen the force of the direction in him because this polarity is very often directionless.[84]

It is only possible, according to Buber, to help the other move through his ambivalence on the basis of a distinction between accepting and confirming.[85] This seems right. Given the fact that there is often this struggle between 'yes' and 'no' in the other, a more active approach than acceptance is required. Here Buber's image of 'unfolding' comes into play. I struggle with the other against herself not to impose a direction, but to facilitate a release of that which is latent in her. Friedman captures well the nature of this wrestling with the other while respecting her autonomy and independence:

> You'll never be confirmed by me simply by my putting myself aside and being nothing but a mirror reflecting you. Confirming you may mean that I do *not* confirm you in some things, precisely because you are not taking a direction. It is not just that you are wrestling with

yourself; I am wrestling with you. There is an added factor here that is not what one calls being *empathic*, which strictly speaking means temporarily leaving my ground to enter into yours. It is not just that I am watching you wrestle with yourself; I am also entering into the wrestling... I may not, of course, impose myself on you and say, "I know better than you." It is only insofar as you share with me and as we struggle together that I can glimpse the person you are called to become.[86]

The Moral Context of Confirmation

Confirmation, as we have seen, is the process of helping another realise his potential. The realisation of the self has psychological, spiritual and moral dimensions. In one place, Buber establishes the moral context for confirmation. In a reflection aimed at mental health professionals, he offers his view that when genuine or 'existential' guilt is overlooked in therapy an opportunity to help the client grow into the person she was created to be is missed.[87] We will look at this side of confirmation in more detail in chapter 5. At this point, it is sufficient to simply note that, first, Buber encourages therapists and counsellors to help their clients to work through their ontic guilt constructively, and that second, he identifies this as a confirming act.

In the last two chapters, the aim has been to use the dialogical thought of Marcel and Buber to help us interpret what it means to be genuinely present to the other. Applying the insights we have gained to the practice of pastoral care is the task that will occupy us in the following three chapters.

1 See M. Buber and C. Rogers, 'Dialogue Between Martin Buber and Carl R. Rogers', in M. Buber, *The Knowledge of Man*, trans. by M. Friedman and R. Gregor Smith (London: George Allen & Unwin Ltd., 1965), pp. 166-184.

2 See K. Plant, 'The Two Worlds of Martin Buber', *Theology* 88, no. 2 (July 1985), pp. 282-287. Plant suggests that the I-Thou world 'could plausibly be regarded as an escapist world, with religious belief forming an escape from everyday hardships, drudgery and drabness' (p. 285). It is this 'residue' of the ordinary and the mundane which makes up the I-It world (p. 284).

3 Cf. L. Silberstein, *Martin Buber's Social and Religious Thought: Alienation and the Quest for Meaning* (New York: New York University Press, 1989), pp. 104-122. Silberstein traces the theme of actualisation vs. alienation through a wide selection of Buber's early writings.

4 See F. Tönnies, *Community and Association*, trans. by C. Loomis (London: Routledge & Kegan Paul, 1955), pp. 37-116, esp. pp. 37-41. First published as *Gemeinschaft und Gesellschaft* in 1887.

5 See Buber, *Daniel: Dialogues on Realization*, trans. by M. Friedman (New York: Holt, Rinehart and Winston, 1964), pp. 74-78.

6 Ibid., p. 78.

7 See Buber, *Pointing the Way*, trans. by M. Friedman (London: Routledge & Kegan Paul, 1957), pp. 5-10.

8 Buber, ibid., p. 8.

9 Cf. Silberstein, *Martin Buber's Social and Religious Thought*, p. 127.

10 See Buber, *I and Thou*, trans. by W. Kaufmann (Edinburgh: T.&T. Clark, 1970), p.112.

11 See ibid., p. 54.

12 See ibid., pp. 62-63.

13 See ibid., p. 53.

14 Ibid., p. 54.

15 Ibid., p. 55.

16 See ibid., p. 59.

17 Ibid., p. 57.

18 Ibid., p. 150.

19 Ibid., p. 151.

20 Ibid., p. 67.

21 Buber, 'Dialogue', in *Between Man and Man*, pp. 1-39, p. 3.

22 See *I and Thou*, p. 85.

23 G. Marcel, 'I and Thou', in *The Philosophy of Martin Buber*, pp. 41-48, p. 46.

24 *I and Thou*, p. 69.

25 See ibid., p. 82.

26 Ibid., pp. 63-64.

27 Ibid., p. 63.

28 See ibid., p. 81.

29 Ibid., p. 123.

30 See ibid., p. 124.

31 See ibid., p. 127.

32 Ibid., p. 127.

33 See ibid., p. 163.

34 See Buber, 'Distance and Relation', *Psychiatry* 20 (1957), pp. 97-104.

35 See ibid., p. 97.

36 Ibid., p. 97.

37 Ibid., p. 98.

38 Ibid., p. 99.

39 See ibid., p. 99.

40 Ibid., p. 99.

41 K. Plant, 'The Two Worlds of Martin Buber', p. 284.

42 Ibid., p. 284.

43 See ibid., pp. 285-286; and also Buber, 'What is Man', in *Between Man and Man*, pp. 175-176.

44 See Buber, 'What is Man', p. 178.

45 Cf. P.Vermes, *Buber on God and the Perfect Man* (London: Littman Library of Jewish Civilization, 1994), p. 197.

46 See G. Marcel, 'I and Thou', pp. 44-45.

47 Buber, 'Replies to My Critics', p. 705.

48 See *I and Thou*, p. 69.

49 E. Levinas, 'Martin Buber and the Theory of Knowledge', p. 148.

50 Buber, 'Dialogue', in *Between Man and Man*, p. 35.

51 Ibid., p. 36.

52 Cf. Silberstein, *Martin Buber's Social and Religious Thought*, p. 142.

53 Cf. Siberstein, op. cit., p. 142.

54 Cf. Silberstein, op. cit., p. 144.

55 See Buber, 'Dialogue', p. 23.

56 See ibid., pp. 8-10.

57 See ibid., pp. 8-10.

58 Ibid., p. 9.

59 *Responsibility* is also an important concept in the thought of another major figure in dialogical philosophy, Emmanuel Levinas (see his 'Diachrony and Representation', in *Time and the Other*, trans. by R. Cohen [Pittsburgh: Duquesne University Press, 1987], pp. 97-120, and idem, *Otherwise Than Being or Beyond Essence*, trans. by A. Lingis [The Hague: Martinus Nijhoff, 1981]). What is different about the two treatments, however, is that while Buber locates responsibility in the present of dialogue, Levinas situates it in the 'immemorial past'. According to Levinas' interpretation, the human is *elected* by God (or the Good) to live *for-the-other*. Responsibility is prior to choice and deliberation. The Good has a 'pre original hold' on the human. This election by God, however, does not reduce the human to slave status. The call is 'indeclinable' but it nevertheless comes from an authority which refuses compulsion. In our freedom, we can reject the call, but not without losing our essential humanity. The responsibility described by Levinas constitutes the ontological ground of Buber's 'answerability'. For Levinas, responsibility 'is prior to dialogue, to the exchange of questions and answers' (*Otherwise Than Being*, p. 111). Prior to the claim and the answer is the election to the for-the-other.

60 See Buber, 'Dialogue', p. 14.

61 See Buber, 'The Question to the Single One', in *Between Man and Man*, pp. 40-82, p. 45.

62 Buber, 'Dialogue', p. 17.

50

63 See Buber, 'Distance and Relation', p. 103; and idem, 'Elements of the Inter-human', *Psychiatry* 20 (1957), pp. 105-113, p. 110.

64 Buber, 'Elements of the Inter-human', p. 110.

65 See Buber, 'Education', in *Between Man and Man*, pp. 83-103, p. 96.

66 See ibid., p. 96.

67 See 'Distance and Relation', p. 103.

68 C. Rogers, 'The Necessary and Sufficient Conditions of Therapeutic Personality Change', in H. Kirschenbaum and V. Land Henderson eds., *The Carl Rogers Reader* (London: Constable, 1990), pp. 219-235, p. 226.

69 Buber, 'Education', p. 97.

70 Ibid., p. 97.

71 C. Rogers, *A Way of Being* (Boston: Houghton Mifflin Co., 1980), p. 143.

72 Cf. M. Friedman, *Dialogue and the Human Image: Beyond Humanistic Psychology* (London: Sage Publications, 1992), p. 52.

73 See M. Friedman, 'Reflections on the Buber-Rogers Dialogue', *Journal of Humanistic Psychology* 34, no. 1 (Winter 1994), pp. 46-65, p. 58.

74 Buber, 'Question to the Single One', pp. 61-62.

75 See Buber, 'Distance and Relation', p. 102.

76 See Buber, 'Elements of the Inter-human', p. 110.

77 Buber, 'Dialogue', pp. 23-24.

78 See Buber, 'Elements of the Inter-human', p. 110.

79 C. Rogers, 'Dialogue Between Martin Buber and Carl R. Rogers', in M. Buber, *The Knowledge of Man*, trans. by M. Friedman & R. Gregor Smith (London: George Allen & Unwin Ltd., 1965), pp. 166-184, pp. 169-170.

80 Buber, ibid., p. 181.

81 Buber, ibid., p. 182.

82 Buber, ibid., p. 182.

83 See ibid., p. 182.

84 Ibid., p. 180.

85 See ibid., p. 183.

86 M. Friedman, 'Reflections on the Buber-Rogers Dialogue', pp. 63-64.

87 See Buber, 'Guilt and Guilt Feelings', *Psychiatry* 20 (1957), pp. 114-129

Chapter 3
PASTORAL AVAILABILITY:
The Foundation For Care

In this chapter, we are concerned with the first, the basic, moment in pastoral care, namely the pastor's capacity for compassion and self-giving. An important question in pastoral theology is this: What is foundational in the ministry of care? Is it the interpersonal skills and counselling techniques that receive so much emphasis today? Or is it something else, something more fundamental? Here I aim to demonstrate that availability is the personal quality which is foundational in pastoral care and counselling. The arts and skills of care need a solid base. Without it, the edifice of pastoral care will be very shaky indeed. The base is a disposability which can be described, first, as a deep receptivity to the other's pain and, secondly, as a willingness to substitute the other's freedom for one's own.

Recall that Marcel describes receptivity to the other in terms of permeability or 'in-cohesion'. He uses the suggestive image of hosting a person *chez soi* to indicate that receptivity involves a communication of something of oneself. To receive a person *chez soi* is to bring her into one's innermost sphere, into that home-space where everything has the stamp of one's personality.

Marcel broadens the notion of hospitality to the other to include receiving into oneself the other's appeal for compassion and understanding. This spontaneous, genuine, deep receptivity is set beside an 'inner inertia', a 'spiritual asthenia', which makes feeling with the other all but impossible. Where there is only a limited capacity for compassion there is clearly no basis for effective pastoral care.

The Old Testament writers understand compassion as an expression of an intimate attachment to the other. They identify the seat of this emotion as the womb or the heart. For Paul, compassion is more than the registering of emotion, it is an expression of one's total being at the deepest level. The Greek word he uses, *splánchnon*, originally referred to the 'inward parts of the body', or to the womb.

These two terms from Marcel and from the scriptures, one's home-space and the womb/heart respectively, both point to a deep level of receptivity. In what follows, an attempt will be made to demonstrate the close correlation between the receptive dimension of availability and the biblical understanding of compassion. This is our first step in establishing availability as the foundational quality in pastoral care.

For Marcel, as we have seen, receptivity is just one dimension in disposability. He also uses the concepts of *belonging* and *substitution* (intimately related to each other) to develop his key idea. 'Belonging' is a rich biblical and theological term. Marcel refers to belonging to Christ - the key fact in a life of faith. For the Hebrew people, personhood was defined through the belonging established in a covenantal relationship. Using the theology of covenant as a framework, we will attempt to extend our understanding of the foundational role availability plays in pastoral care and counselling. This will be achieved through showing how the willingness to substitute the other's freedom for one's own is an important dimension in a covenantal relationship. Moreover, we will be endeavouring to demonstrate that substitution is a foundational quality in pastoral care. This task will involve a discussion of four closely related concepts, namely generosity of spirit, trust, mutuality and servanthood.

While qualities such as empathy, acceptance and compassion are clearly fundamental in pastoral care, I will be arguing that availability is a rich, comprehensive concept which on the one hand embraces these basic qualities, and on the other adds it own distinctive and unique ideas. We begin our discussion with an exploration of the relationship between receptivity and biblical compassion.

COMPASSIONATE AVAILABILITY AS FOUNDATIONAL IN PASTORAL CARE AND COUNSELLING

Pastoral counsellors have tended to identify acceptance and empathy as the corner-stones of their work. If pressed for a biblical and theological rationale, they quickly point to the central themes of love and compassion in the Christian tradition. I want to argue here that the foundation of pastoral care and counselling is to be found in a quality which includes but which also goes beyond acceptance and empathy, namely compassionate availability.

Availability involves receiving the other and her hopes and fears, her joys and sorrows, *chez soi*. In the case of compassionate understanding, one draws the pain and distress of the other into one's innermost sphere. The biblical writers, in describing compassion, use different images - *viz.*, the womb, the bowels, the heart - but the idea is very similar. They also identify a deeply personal act in which the hurt the other suffers is experienced in that space which is most intimately one's own. It is this very close link between *disponibilité* and the biblical notion of compassion which, I believe, identifies the former as foundational in pastoral care.

The Biblical Understanding of Compassion

Dianne Bergant observes that in the cluster of Hebrew words for compassion, *rhm* is the most prominent.[1] It has the primary meaning of 'cherishing', 'soothing', or 'a gentle attitude of mind'. It refers to a tender parental love. The word *rehem*, meaning womb, is also derived from this root. Hence, Bergant concludes that this Hebrew word-group indicates a bond like that between a mother and the child of her womb.[2]

Xavier Leon-Dufour describes the Hebrew notion of compassion, as we would expect, in a very similar way. He suggests that *rhm* 'expresses the instinctive attachment of one person for another'.[3] He observes that this feeling has its seat in the maternal bosom or in the bowels (we would say, heart) of the father. It is a tenderness which drives a person to action on behalf of those in distress.

The New Testament writers often use *éleos* (mercy) when speaking of compassion.[4] A form of the verb *oiktiro* (connoting sympathy) also appears. However, when reference is made to the compassion of Jesus, *splánchnon* is always used. In early Greek usage, the word denotes the 'inward parts' of a sacrifice.[5] Later, it was used to refer to the 'inward parts of the body', and finally to the womb. We also find the noun form used in the *Testaments of the Twelve Patriarchs*. There it denotes 'the centre of feelings' or 'noble feelings'. Once the verb is used to indicate mere emotion, but it generally refers to the inner disposition which generates acts of mercy. The adjective, *eúsplanchnos* (tender-hearted), denotes human virtue and the disposition of 'pity'.

The noun appears in three of Jesus' parables: the Good Samaritan, the Prodigal Son and the Unmerciful Servant. Of particular interest for our discussion is the way Paul describes compassion. Only the noun occurs in his writings. He uses *splánchna* not merely to express natural emotions but as 'a very forceful term to signify an expression of the total personality at the deepest level'.[6] It occurs twice in Philemon (vv. 7, 20); reference is made to the refreshing of the *splánchna*. In v. 12 of that letter, Paul says that in Onesimus he is, in effect, coming in person with a claim for Philemon's love. Phil. 1:8 contains a unique phrase. Paul declares that 'God can testify how I long for all of you with the affection (*splánchna*) of Jesus Christ.' The reference is to 'the love or affection which, gripping or moving the whole personality, is possible only in Christ...'[7]

In these various uses of the word *compassion* by the writers of the scriptures, there are a number of key features. First, the idea of tenderness comes out in a number of places. Secondly, compassion is associated with an instinctive, intimate relationship: it is like the loving, soothing action of a mother or father. Finally, it refers (most clearly in Pauline usage) not just to an emotion, but to the deepest part of one's personality. This depth dimension is indicated by the cluster of inner parts identifying the seat of the emotion, namely the womb, the bowels and the heart. We moderns naturally take these organismic references as metaphorical. It seems, however, that the Semite view of emotion was very definitely psychosomatic.

Biblical scholar, Terrence Collins, has carried out a very careful study of a number of Old Testament references to emotional disturbances and concluded that they are not distinguished from physical disturbances.[8] He describes how the Hebrew person views distressing circumstances as producing a physiological reaction in a person, which starts in his intestines and then proceeds to affect the whole body, especially the heart. This physical disturbance is thought of as actually altering the tone of the organ; there is a general 'softening up'. Thus, when a person changes his mind or experiences an alteration in his emotional disposition, there is an associated change in the physical composition of the heart.[9] In Hosea 11:8, for example, the change of heart is characterised by strong emotional overtones of compassion, along with the physical reaction connected with 'becoming hot'. In concluding his investigations, Collins states that the way the Old Testament writers describe the tears associated with both compassion and personal distress is 'expressive of a whole anthropology which is essentially psychosomatic, and which allows no distinction between physiological and emotional disturbances. In the biblical view, "sickness of heart" and "a broken heart" mean exactly what they say.'[10]

This psychosomatic view of emotion, of course, seems odd to us today. We naturally think of the organismic descriptions of emotional reactions in the Old Testament as metaphorical. What these striking somatic references indicate very clearly, nonetheless, is the depth of compassion in the Hebrew people. When a kinsperson was suffering, the empathic reaction was so strong it felt like the very composition of the heart was changing, was 'softening up'.

Availability, Tenderness and Biblical Compassion

In a study of the foundational role of compassion in pastoral care, the pastoral theologian, Arthur Becker, identifies both the intensity of emotion and the somatic base we have been discussing. For the writers of the scriptures, he observes, compassion entails 'a perception of another's pain, hurt, sorrow, longing, so intense and vivid and organismic that "you feel it in your guts"'.[11] Becker goes on to suggest that empathy and acceptance are 'modern therapeutic correlates of the biblical word'.[12] While it is clear that compassion is a strong component in empathy, it is much less clear that this is the case with acceptance. The distinction between compassion and acceptance I want to draw is grounded in the fact that whereas the former indicates a *personal quality*, the latter refers to an *attitude*. Thus, it may be that a person who manifests only a moderate capacity for tolerance and understanding outside the therapeutic setting may nevertheless be able to be highly acceptant within it. Very simply, in the controlled, limited environment of the 50 minute hour, he can allow himself the luxury of being accepting. After all, he does not have to live with the client!

James Dittes is right, I believe, in his observation that acceptance is 'built in, not a personal achievement'.[13] Acceptance is a fundamental characteristic of therapy, it is not an emotional response on the part of the therapist. In communicating unconditional positive regard, the therapist does not have to express love or affection (although this may be the case). The act of prizing is not necessarily an indication that the therapist feels a strong affinity with the client. In fact, quite often he will not feel strongly 'connected'. Acceptance is not a personal response but 'the much starker experience of being fully known and trusted and shared with. In emotional tone, it may be more like the relationship at the end of fifty years of a good marriage, rather than at the beginning'.[14] Acceptance is an attitude built-in to therapy rather than a personal quality.

If acceptance denotes an attitude, empathy involves the use of a *skill* or an *art*. Person-centred therapists suggest that of the three core conditions, empathy is the one which is most trainable.[15] Obviously some people have a greater aptitude for this way of being with another person than others. In order to have the potential to reach a high level of empathic in-tuneness, a person needs the personal attributes of perceptivity, imagination and sensitivity. Equipped with these qualities, a therapist is able to hone her skill of moving into the client's inner world of feeling and cognition. Being empathic, says Rogers, 'means entering the private perceptual world of the other and becoming thoroughly at home in it. It involves being sensitive, moment by moment, to the changing felt meanings which flow in this other person....'[16] The capacity to imaginatively get inside another person's inner world of perception is an art or a skill one develops. However, one needs to go beyond imagination and cognition to the level of experiencing. Sensing what the other is thinking and feeling, one shares this experience - although in an attenuated way. It is here that one's capacity for compassion comes into play.

The key question is this: In seeking to be accepting and empathic, to what extent does the therapist allow herself to engage personally with the client? It is possible to adopt an acceptant attitude and to accurately reflect feelings and thoughts with only a minimum of emotional availability. In this case, acceptance and empathy are reduced to the level of techniques. A genuine commitment to unconditional positive regard and to feeling-with the other, I suggest, is grounded in disposability.

Person-centred counsellors sometimes refer to an experience of self-giving which is beyond empathy and acceptance. Rogers himself talks about a highly personal, one would say almost mystical, dimension in the healing process. In an article written late in his life (it was published in 1986), he says:

> When I am at my best, as a group facilitator or a therapist, I discover another characteristic. I find that when I am closest to my inner, intuitive self, when I am somehow in touch with the unknown in me, when perhaps I am in a slightly altered state of consciousness in the relationship, then whatever I do seems to be full of healing. Then simply my *presence* is refreshing and helpful. There is nothing I can do to force this experience, but when I relax and be close to the transcendental core of me, then I may behave in strange and impulsive ways in the relationship, ways which I cannot justify rationally, which have nothing to do with my thought processes. But these strange behaviours turn out to be *right*, in some odd way. At those moments it seems that my inner spirit has reached out and touched the inner spirit of the other.[17]

This extra dimension in the therapeutic process was not something that Rogers emphasised. He was more interested in those relational attitudes and skills which could be clearly defined and rationally discussed. However, another proponent of the person-centred approach, Brian Thorne, describes how he found himself repeatedly caught up in a similar kind of experience and considered that it was important to describe as closely as possible the nature of this added dimension.[18] He did not want to contradict Rogers' dictum concerning the necessity and sufficiency of the core conditions, but he did want to say that when a fourth quality is present, which he called *tenderness*, something 'qualitatively different' may occur. He was unsure about exactly which word to use to denote this fourth dimension; 'tenderness' was the closest he could get. It is a word 'which means both vulnerable and warmly affectionate, easily crushed and merciful, not tough and sympathetic. It seems to incorporate both weakness and gentle strength, great fragility and great constancy'.[19] The connections with the biblical understanding of compassion, I think, are obvious. We saw above how the Hebrew word group denotes the love in the maternal bosom and in the father's heart. Healthy parental love is gentle and soothing when required, and firm and strong when it needs to be. Parental love also renders a person vulnerable. While one's children sometimes act and speak in ways which fill one with joy and pride, on other occasions their deeds and utterances cut, hurt, and disappoint.

Recall that for Paul compassion is an expression of the whole personality at the heart of one's being. We saw the same element of depth in discussing the Hebrew understanding of the role of the heart or bowels in emotion. In discussing what it means for a person to possess the quality of tenderness, Thorne begins with the involvement of the whole person. To emphasise the point, he covers virtually the whole gamut of bodily expression, personal attitudes and ethical commitments: '[Tenderness] is a quality which irradiates the total person - it is evident in voice, the eyes, the hands, the thoughts, the feelings, the beliefs, the moral stance, the attitude to things animate and inanimate, seen and unseen.'[20] He goes on to specify the other personal characteristics associated with an experience of tenderness:

> Secondly, [this quality] communicates through its responsive vulnerability that suffering and healing are interwoven. Thirdly, it demonstrates a preparedness and an ability to move between the worlds of the physical, the emotional, the cognitive and the mystical without strain. Fourthly, it is without shame because it is experienced as the joyful embracing of the desire to love and is therefore a law unto itself. Fifthly, it is a quality which transcends the male and female but is nevertheless nourished by the attraction of the one for the other in the quest for wholeness.[21]

One of the most striking and touching illustrations of Jesus' compassionate nature is his response to the ministrations of the 'sinful' woman who anointed him (Lk. 7:36-50). Implicit in the narrative is a previous experience of forgiveness. The woman comes with a deep feeling of gratitude moving her whole being. Her thankful heart is bursting as she kneels behind Jesus, weeping. A chain-reaction is set in train. Some of her tears fall onto Jesus' feet. Having nothing to hand to wipe the tears, she uses her hair. Spontaneously, her affection and gratitude is expressed through a shower of kisses on the freshly cleaned feet. Finally, the perfume intended for the head, given her proximity to Jesus' feet, is poured out there.

It is interesting to note the parallels with Thorne's description of tenderness. Contrary to the expectations of his host, Jesus graciously receives the intimate, affectionate contact from this 'sinful' woman. He knows what it is to be misunderstood and rejected. Those in his own town failed to accept his prophetic words and deeds (Lk. 4:14-30). Even the members of his own family thought he was mad and needed to be reined in (Mk 3: 31-34). A person who has been cut and struck down by the pain of misunderstanding and rejection tends to look for the goodness in the other. Jesus is not preoccupied with this woman's sinful past, but instead is deeply moved by her beautiful display of thankful affection. A heart which has suffered reaches out in love to a heart full to the brim with the joy and gratitude of liberation from past hurt and exploitation (Thorne's second descriptor).

This intimate meeting takes place on a number of levels: the emotional, the spiritual and the physical (cf. Thorne's third descriptor). First, the woman's tears are not simply the tears of joy of a person liberated from a past of degradation and exploitation. Certainly it is the case that her experience of a new life in which she is able to treat her body respectfully has elevated her mood. But it is divine forgiveness which is uppermost in her mind when she comes to express her gratitude. The spiritual dimension of the encounter is primary. Finally, there is the physical dimension. The joy, the relief, the sense of liberation and forgiveness are all gathered together in a bodily expression of gratitude and affection.

This bodily expression of gratitude is perhaps the most striking feature in the story. Wiping a man's feet with one's hair and smothering them with kisses are very intimate, sensuous actions. Alastair Campbell suggests that the reason the sensuous aspect of the anointing is often not fully explored is the result of a tendency to confuse sensuousness with sensuality.[22] 'Sensuousness', he writes, 'is an acceptance and celebration of our senses: sensuality the exploitation of them. Anointing is sensuous, but not necessarily sensual...'[23] Jesus and the woman, I believe, were enjoying an altogether appropriate physical expression of love. Their tactile centres were alive in a celebration of togetherness. For this reason, neither felt any embarrassment or shame (Thorne's fourth descriptor).

Enough has been said, perhaps, to demonstrate the close connection between the biblical understanding of compassion and this fourth quality in the therapeutic relationship, tenderness. I suggest that *availability embraces both tenderness and biblical compassion.* In identifying a dimension in the healing relationship which can be distinguished from the core conditions, Thorne goes beyond attitudes and skills and into the area of *personal qualities*. Tenderness describes the capacity of the therapist to manifest vulnerability, affection and gentle strength. These capacities cannot be learned. Marcel describes the ability to makes one's presence felt in this intimate way as a grace. Availability is the grace which shapes every thought, word and action in one's interpersonal encounters. It is the capacity to relate at depth with the other. It describes the integrity and gentleness capable of handling sensitively a 'shared secret', 'a really incommunicable experience'. On some occasions, the shared secret involves a more mundane experience. This is the case in Marcel's illustration of the shy young man at the cocktail party. The young man is caught in the misery of intense self-consciousness; he is stuck in 'a stifling here-and-now in which... his ego [is] sticking to him as an adhesive plaster sticks to a small cut'. A fellow guest, sensing his deep uneasiness, wants to release some of the tension that is within him. In a tender concern for the poor young fellow, he searches for an opening line which will put him at ease. It must be carefully chosen; he could so easily make matters worse. For example, a question, even an innocuous one, may cause the young man to feel threatened. The fellow guest is sensitive enough to find just the right comment: 'I knew your parents'. A bond is established through a shared secret. The tension within the young man is released and the two men can begin a journey together.

This very ordinary, but nonetheless important, moment in which there is a sense of togetherness is identified by Thorne in the more intense setting of therapy. He observes that when tenderness is present in a relationship, there is a profound sense of liberation and wholeness. 'At such a moment', he writes, 'I have no hesitation in saying that my client and I are caught up in a stream of love.'[24] In different words, Thorne is describing what it means to make one's presence felt. For Marcel, a real presence 'refreshes my inner being; it reveals me to myself, it makes me more fully myself than I should be if I were not exposed to its impact'. Here we have two different labels, tenderness and presence/availability, but the experience being described is fundamentally the same. Two people moving in the stream of love: refreshed, liberated, made whole.

This experience of another's presence, I suggest, is grounded in the kind of compassion described by the biblical writers. As we have seen, in the biblical understanding to feel compassion means to take the sorrow and distress of the other into the core of oneself. The seat of the emotion is identified as the womb or the heart. Marcel uses a different image in an attempt to describe this absolute openness to the other's appeal for understanding. To receive the hurt and sorrow of the other is to meet her *chez soi*. If I am to truly be open to the other in her pain, I must take her into my home-space. The heart, the home-space - these are the places which represent the core of one's being.

Availability is a richly comprehensive concept which describes a radical openness to the other which results in a full giving of the self for him. It captures the essence of Thorne's important notion of tenderness, which is itself a correlate of biblical compassion. There seems to be good reason to posit availability as foundational for pastoral care and counselling.

The centrality of availability in pastoral care distinguishes it from most (but not all) forms of psychotherapy. The core conditions are built-in to the structure of the therapy hour. It is usually and appropriately the case that the therapist does not put his emotional equilibrium at serious risk by entering into a counselling relationship. This is not to say that therapists are on the whole uncaring, or that they are untouched by the vicissitudes in the emotional lives of their clients. The point being made is simply that the relationship between therapist and client is unique in that it is highly structured and carefully delineated. In a parish setting on the other hand, the relationship of care is neither usually nor appropriately so controlled and contained. A pastor meets her people in a variety of settings: in the home, in worship, in bible study, in church meetings, on youth nights, on week-end fellowship camps, and so on. Together they share in a community of faith. They belong together as brothers and sisters in Christ. Over time, deep bonds of fellowship and friendship often develop. In offering care to her parishioners, a pastor will frequently, though not always of course, find herself taking their hurt and sorrow deep into her heart. This is not an act of the imagination alone; the pain is felt 'in the guts'.

I am aware that in speaking this way, it may appear that I am expecting too much from pastors. Sometimes in offering care to a suffering parishioner a pastor will not feel the loving tenderness and deep compassion I have been describing. There may be all kinds of reasons for this. For example, he may be feeling tired or emotionally 'out of sorts'. Or it may be that he does not feel particularly close to the person (it may even be that there is a serious 'block' in their relationship). And so on. It is unreasonable and unrealistic to expect that a pastor will be profoundly available in each and every pastoral encounter. There will be times when he simply has to offer the best care he can, in view of the mitigating circumstances. The aim in our reflections to this point is not to project an image of the effective caregiver as the person with a genius for self-giving. Rather, it is to identify a disposition, a virtue, which relatively ordinary persons have and which allows them to care well for others, namely a receptivity to the pain and distress of the other. The virtue need not and cannot be fully functional, so to speak, on each and every occasion, but it does need to be there. The pastor needs to have a capacity, as the biblical reflections on compassion indicate, to feel the hurt of others 'in his guts' if he is to have a foundation for his practice of care.

In working with the biblical understanding of compassion, a communal setting is implied. The biblical authors reflected on love and mercy in the context of the household of faith (although of course compassion extends beyond it). When two people belong together in community, the hurt of one is taken in by the other. Marcel is acutely aware of this reality; for him, as we have seen, to be available to the other involves belonging to him.

BELONGING AND SUBSTITUTION AS FOUNDATIONAL IN PASTORAL CARE AND COUNSELLING

We are attempting to build an argument for availability as the foundation of pastoral care and counselling. A solid start has been made by demonstrating the close correlation with the biblical notion of compassion. In what follows, we will look at another dimension of availability, namely substitution. The willingness to take the hurt and sorrow of the other into one's home-space is one cornerstone of care. Another, I will argue, is the willingness to *substitute* the other's freedom for one's own. Disposability, understood in this light, means a generosity of spirit in which one gives according to the need of the other.

Marcel conceived of his philosophical reflections as situated at the threshold of faith. That is to say, he did not attempt to be a theologian, and neither did he wish to limit his work to those of the household of faith. He wanted to make his thought available to believer and non-believer alike. Occasionally, though, he overtly declares his faith commitment. He says, for example, that 'I belong to you' has a counterpart in 'I belong to Christ'. Here he points to that which is central in the Christian faith, namely living *in Christ*. To live in Christ is to live in the new family he established. The New Testament writers construct the life of faith within a communitarian framework. Here they reflected their religious and national heritage. For the people of Israel, belonging to the community of God was indissolubly linked to the covenant God had established. An exploration of key themes in the biblical notion of covenant will provide a theological orientation for our discussion of the foundational role of substitution in pastoral care.

Israel's Experience of Belonging

'I will be your God, and you will be my people' is fundamentally a declaration of belonging. For the Hebrew, his very personhood was established through the covenant. As Walter Brueggemann expresses it: 'The act of claiming is the act of giving life and identity to that person. Before being called and belonging to, the person was not. In the Bible, "person" means to belong with and belong to and belong for.'[25]

There is no doubt that in the Pentateuch the view is that God is sovereign, takes the initiative, in the covenantal process. What is debatable is whether or not the stress is on *obligation* or on *fellowship with God*. Some Old Testament scholars argue that *berit* always means an obligation or a duty.[26] Thus, the covenant involves on the one hand Yahweh's promise to Israel, and on the other Israel's duty to fulfil the commandments laid down by Yahweh. There are two dimensions in God's dealings with God's people. First, there is God's graciousness expressed through the divine promises. And secondly, there is God's call to be faithful to the divine law. In such a view, there is no room for the idea of a bilateral relationship between God and God's people. This view seems to be somewhat idiosyncratic. Most biblical scholars point to the two-sided nature of the covenant. In a recent study, Ellen Juhl Christiansen carefully follows the horizontal or ecclesiological thread of the covenant through the writings of Judaism and of Paul.[27] She rejects as one-sided the view of the covenant which stresses the duty of keeping the law. The horizontal relationship established by God is founded on an understanding of promises and obligations as 'juxtaposed aspects, as marks of a mutually binding relationship'.[28] Ernest Nicholson makes a similar point in his study of the theology of the covenant. The bilateral nature of the covenant is manifested through two basic facts. First, Israel expressed her response to Yahweh's graciousness through *choice* and *decision*.[29] At Sinai, Israel chose to become a covenant partner with God. Twice over the people gave their commitment to the covenant in response to Moses' reading of the commandments (Ex. 24:3-8). On the plains of Moab, a subsequent generation made their decision and declared that on 'this day' Yahweh had become its God (Deut. 26:19).

Second, there is the fact that not only was the covenant established on God's initiative, but God in fact is a *partner* to it.[30] This means that it is wrong to think that the covenant was viewed as merely the observance, under the threat of curse, of divinely decreed laws. 'Rather, life for Israel was understood as fellowship with Yahweh who had entered a covenant with this people, and the fulfilment of Yahweh's commandments was to be an expression of this fellowship.'[31] It is obviously outside the scope of this work to attempt any resolution of this debate. A categorical rejection, however, of any notion of a two-sided relationship does seem to constitute a radical position. A conservative approach to the theology of the covenant would suggest that the programmatic statement 'I will be your God; you will be my people' does in fact indicate a partnership. On this view, Yahweh called Israel into a mutually binding relationship characterised by the divine promises on one side and by the people's obligations on the other.

Covenant and Substitution

While the word *berit* is most often used in the Old Testament with reference to this vertical relationship, it is sometimes used in the context of horizontal relations. We see this is the special friendship between Jonathan and David: 'And Jonathan made a *berit* with David because he loved him as himself. Jonathan took off the robe he was wearing and gave it to David, along with his tunic, and even his sword, his bow and his belt' (I Sam. 18:3). Under serious threat from Saul, David calls upon the promise made by his friend: 'As for you, show kindness to your servant, for you have brought him into a *berit* with you before the Lord' (I Sam 20:8). Jonathan replies thus, 'Whatever you want me to do, I'll do for you.' Marcel identifies the essence of belonging as the commitment to *substitute* the other's freedom for one's own. Here we see the depth of Jonathan's commitment to his friend: he is prepared to substitute David's will for his own.

There was in the action of making the covenant, a symbolic act of substitution. Jonathan hands over to his friend his robe and his armour. Here he is effectively giving over his right to claim the throne.[32] In this way, he indicates the depth of his love and respect for his friend.[33]

Substitution: A Case Study

In his book entitled *Prophetic Pastoral Care*, Charles Gerkin presents the report of Edith L., a student training in hospital chaplaincy.[34] Edith received a call to be with the lover of a homosexual white male in his late 20's who had died of AIDS. No other friends or relatives were at the hospital. Even though the man had a terminal illness, his death had not seemed imminent. The lover was deeply upset with grief and with a sense of guilt. He was himself an AIDS victim.

Edith looked in both the patient's room and 'the quiet room' for the man. Finally, he was noticed walking out of the men's toilet and the administrative nurse introduced them:

N. J., this is the chaplain.

E. Hi, J. I'm Edith L., one of the ministers in the hospital. I understand that you have had a great loss.

J. Hi. Will you talk to me?

'Will you talk to me?' reveals a certain apprehension and tentativeness. Gerkin refers to it as 'the cry of the outcast who both desires someone, even a stranger, to share his time of grief and expects to be rebuffed'.[35] A fully available presence is needed if there is to be any genuine sharing in his grief. In endeavouring to be that presence, Edith has to struggle against two powerful pulls. She could be pulled away, first, by her fear of being infected with the virus. Second, she has to overcome the repelling force of being close to a person with 'the smell of a sick body'.

In her report, Edith acknowledges her tentativeness about establishing communion:

> I noticed that his face was swollen due to the crying. I placed a chair almost directly in front of him, very close. I remembered that the nurse had told me over the phone that he had AIDS and she thought I should know. So as I placed the chair in front of him I remembered that he was an AIDS victim and that I should take every precaution necessary. I did not, however, change the position of the chair, because I felt that he needed someone to be close. The thought occurred to me that if he had been a woman, I would probably have simply sat beside him on the sofa in the room.[36]

She also shows through her verbatim the intensity of J's distress:

J. Is he dead; is he really dead? (with great sobs and tears)

E. Yes, he is really dead (embracing him).

J. I should have been with him more time. But I was afraid. I could not hold him as he wanted. I should of known. He told me he felt like on a roller-coaster and that he wanted to get off.

E. He did get off.

J. Yes he did. And he died alone. I missed him by two minutes. (Now he began to cry and speak very loudly in his cry.) I don't want to die alone![37]

Edith comments on her instinctive reaction at this point of holding him. She also notes her urge to let him go when his nasal discharge falls on her arm:

> Now he was crying so hard I couldn't resist embracing him, trying to hold him in order to give some comfort. He was not only crying for his loss, but for his own death he was foreseeing would be as lonely

> as his lover's death. As he cried, tears fell on my arms and some mucus too when he moved. I felt like letting him go to dry myself up, but feared for his well-being. I could smell the smell of a sick body. As I write this I can still smell it.[38]

J. straightens up now and dries both his tears and the mucus on her arm. Edith continues to talk with J. She moves to his fear of dying alone and his sense of having failed his lover. She also allows J. to talk about the relationship that was shared. And then a male friend arrives. Edith decides to leave them alone and she says goodbye. In noting her reflections on her farewell, it is evident both how much J. appreciated her ministry and how scared Edith was of the risk of infection.

> I said my farewells; they said their thank yous and I left. I searched for the bathroom and washed my arms and hands. I looked for the administrative nurse to let her know that I was leaving. She told me they had expressed their thanks to her for my being there with them. I thanked her and was on my way. I didn't want to touch anyone. I walked into the office and as soon as possible went to the apartment to wash my hands and face again. I feared for my health and the health of others and I prayed for continued health and the hope of not having tempted God with the risk of being with this young man. Perhaps I will never forget his eyes of gratitude and his smile for me when I left him, but I probably will also never forget the fear over my health being in jeopardy, either.[39]

Edith offered J. a real presence. She stood with him in a fully committed way; she made herself emotionally and physically disposable. It is not absolutely clear from medical evidence whether or not Edith was taking any real risk by embracing an AIDS sufferer. It is generally accepted that infection does not occur in this manner; but the infection of health workers who do not seem to have been exposed to contaminated blood casts some doubt on this consensus view. In any case, the salient point is that Edith perceived a very real risk. One could understand her opting for a less committed contact with J. By placing a hand on a shoulder, and offering trained empathic responses she would establish a 'professional' presence. All the while she would hold herself at a safe distance from this body oozing the smell of a potentially lethal sickness. She would be able in this way to save herself from deep fear and anxiety. Edith wanted to withdraw; she felt a strong urge to clean herself up. But she didn't.

Edith substituted J's need for care for her desire for emotional equilibrium. This was a costly substitution for her. As soon as she opened herself to J's need for solidarity and community, she gave up her freedom to pursue her own security, safety and comfort. Edith and J. shared in a real presence. For a brief time, they belonged together. J's 'eyes of gratitude and his smile' on leaving testified to that fleeting, but nonetheless rich, experience of communion. It is this willingness to substitute the needs of the other for one's own desires that is foundational in pastoral care.

Covenant Versus Contract

One of the key elements in substitution is the radical openness characterising its commitments. When Edith first made her decision to be a chaplain, she had only a generalised conception of what may lie ahead. Implicit in her original commitment was a readiness to embrace a man who smelt of death, who may have been dripping death. From a theological perspective, a covenant is a promise binding two people or two parties in a relationship of unconditional love. It is the open, trusting, unconditional nature of a covenant which differentiates it from a contract. The latter term refers to a *legal* relationship in which conditions are clearly stated and agreed to so as to promote and protect the interests of both parties. James Torrance points out that the sin of late Judaism was to attempt to turn God's covenant of promise, grace and unconditional love into a contract.[40] As he indicates, the offer of grace is always prior to the duty of fulfilling the law. Judaism, however, wanted to turn things around. It sought to secure God's gracious action on the basis of fulfilment of the obligations of the law. God's promise of posterity and land began with Abraham. Four centuries later, the obligations of the law were spelled out at Sinai. This act did not, however, constitute the introduction of conditions on divine grace. 'It did not', writes Torrance, 'turn the covenant into a contract. To introduce conditions would be to break a promise. Love always brings its obligations. But the obligations of love are not the conditions of love... *The God of the Bible is a Covenant-God not a contract-god....*' [emphasis in the original].[41]

A good contract is one in which all possible loop-holes are closed. The parties to a contract will act quickly to alter any conditions which are not tightly specified. What is striking about the covenant God made with Abraham is its radical openness. Abraham is called upon to place a very high degree of trust in God. God simply says to Abraham, 'Leave your country, your people and your father's household and go to the land I will show you' (Gen. 12:1). Nothing is clearly specified; the issue for Abraham is one of faith and trust. With this aspect of the distinction between covenant and contract in mind, Jewish authors Kalman Kaplan and Moriah Markus-Kaplan distinguish two basic forms of relationship.[42] In the 'Hebrew Humanist-Ecclesiastic' mode of relationship, one sees the other as an end and feels able to trust her.

> To the extent that one sees the other as an end, for Buber (I-thou), one becomes able to make commitments on intuitive faith before all the evidence is in. In other words, one is *able* to form a covenant relationship based on trust... Being freed from the contractual demands of outlining evidence in advance, one is able to attempt to know the other directly rather than through a cognitive screen and as a whole person rather than as a set of behaviours.[43]

A person who tends to relate in the 'European Humanist/Stoic' mode, on the other hand, will see the other person as a means, and consequently will define the relationship in terms of furthering his own interests.

> To the extent that one sees the other as means [sic] for Buber (I-it), one is preoccupied with aspects of control and manipulation. This tendency toward suspicion makes it impossible for a person to engage with another unless all aspects of the situation are laid out in advance.[44]

Here, then, are two fundamental orientations to relationship. One is based on openness and trust, the other on control and suspicion. In terms of pastoral care, it is obvious which relational mode is to be preferred.

Substitution, Contract and the Covenant of Care

Let us take as the starting point for our reflections the situation for a particular minister - a fictitious one - at the beginning of a parish settlement. We will suppose that this minister values precision, clarity and order. We will further suppose that she is quite generous with her time and energy. In a previous parish, however, she felt that her parishioners had taken advantage of her willingness to make herself available for their care. She considers that she needs to do something this time to protect herself. The idea comes to her of a 'charter of care'. In this charter, her duties and responsibilities will be clearly specified on the one hand, and on the other, the responsibility of her parishioners to ask appropriately for care. With regard to the latter, this will mean, in particular, refraining from making calls over trivial matters and from contacting her on days off when it is not absolutely necessary. Initially she is quite excited about the idea; but later she finds herself having second thoughts. She feels uneasy about the notion of a charter of care. In reflecting on why she feels this way, it occurs to her that the mainspring of pastoral care is openness and trust. A formal statement of duties and responsibilities would introduce undesirable elements of suspicion and over-control.

Substitution is grounded in the radical openness associated with the Abrahamic covenant. To say to someone 'I belong to you' means, says Marcel, 'I am opening an unlimited credit account in your name, you can do what you want with me, I give myself to you'. There is an almost outrageous level of trust associated with this declaration. Given that there will be those who will abuse the privilege extended to them, is it really possible to establish substitution as foundational in pastoral care? I contend that it is. It is precisely this deep generosity of spirit and this radical openness in the relationship which constitute the essential nature of pastoral care.

There will be, as has just been indicated, those who will betray the trust in the relationship of care. Consider the case of the parishioner who makes unreasonable demands on the availability of the minister. He is constantly requesting the presence of his pastor for help in dealing with relatively unimportant matters. From the minister's point of view, a relationship which began in a spirit of joy and with a sense of the privilege of offering care is now being coloured by disappointment, anger, frustration and a feeling of alienation. She will feel the need to negotiate with the unreasonable parishioner over what constitutes an acceptable demand on her time. The whole complexion of the relationship of care has changed. Openness, spontaneity and trust has been superseded by negotiation and the spelling out of expectations. There has been *a movement from a covenantal to a contractual basis*.

It may be, of course, that the pastor is the one who weakens the bond of trust in the relationship. Here, I think, Marcel's concept of *constancy* is especially relevant. A constant presence is one which is driven by a sense of obligation rather than by a genuine desire to be with the other in her need. Most people can quite easily sense through observation of verbal and non-verbal signals whether or not a pastor is really present. When a person becomes aware of a duty-driven act of care, her faith in her minister's commitment to her is eroded. There is a rupture in the covenant of care. It is likely, unless the person is particularly bold, that she will not raise with the pastor her feelings of disappointment. In this case, future contacts will be characterised by formality and inauthenticity. Here is the tragic situation of two people simply 'going through the motions' of a care event.

Mutuality in the Covenant of Care

We have identified above two common failures in the project of maintaining the joy and trust in the covenant of care. It is a project which can only be optimally maintained, I suggest, when there is *mutuality* in the relationship. In identifying substitution as foundational in pastoral care, it is important to note that Marcel's concept implies reciprocity. He is able to make his extravagant declaration of an unlimited credit account because there is within the concept of substitution a central place for reciprocity. Substitution assigns primacy to giving, but it also acknowledges the importance of receiving. 'Since I cease to belong to myself', Marcel writes, 'it is not literally true to say that you belong to me; we transcend one another in the very heart of *our love*' [emphasis in the original].[45]

Marcel, as we saw in chapter 1, sets the concept of availability within the context of a healthy self-love. The decision to declare to the other 'I belong to you' does not indicate, he insists, the presence of some kind of self-hatred.[46] One loves the other while at the same time displaying a certain 'charity towards oneself'.[47] Appropriate self-love he defines in terms of 'distance from and nearness to the self'.[48] The distance pole indicates a certain objectivity, a capacity to overcome the urge to rationalise one's behaviour. In this way, one can see it for what it really is. Nearness refers to the 'contact with ourselves that we should always have to our fellow-men' (*viz.*, a loving contact).[49]

The radical openness in the covenant of care which I am arguing is foundational does not carry with it an elevation of self-sacrifice, as if this is closer to the spirit of Christ than is reciprocal love. There are times, of course, when a pastor is called upon to give without receiving. Indeed, giving is primary in pastoral care. The ideal for the act of care, nonetheless, is mutuality. Moral theologian, Stephen Post, arguing in a vein very similar to Marcel, writes that it is *communion* rather than a one-sided giving which constitutes the ideal for Christian love.[50] He observes that a love which is heedless of self is commonly thought to be ethically superior to a love which is grounded in both giving and receiving. It is possible, though, to give communion a central place in the act of love without falling into egoism:

> The equilibrium of communion that allows each participant to find fulfilment through the process of mutuality is set aside to make room for the rare genius of selflessness. However, in our view, a 'true' or proper self-love defined as the pursuit of one's own good... can be distinguished from both selfishness (the pursuit of one's own separate interests) and self-infatuation.[51]

In the covenant of care, giving is a primary concern. There are, nevertheless, certain contexts in which the act of care is greatly enriched through communion. A person who is highly neurotic, it is true, will probably be unable to contribute much to the pastor's sense of fulfilment. He will greatly stretch the minister's capacity to give of herself. There are many other cases, though, when the person offering care actually feels as though more is received than is given. Consider the case of the care of the sick. There are those people who in sickness are gracious and long-suffering. Marcel refers to a lively, creative presence. Some people are able to make their presence felt even under the duress of serious illness. In such a situation, the minister will find himself giving at his best. His acts of care will have a spontaneous, even joyful, quality about them. Though he feels sorrow, he finds his spirit also lifted. All acts of care require emotional and spiritual exertion. Care is the extending of oneself for the sake of the other. Where there is communion, however, the minister finds the exertion relatively effortless.

> Irene was dying of cancer. She was a person who lacked both a formal education and the social graces. She possessed neither sophistication nor wit. Irene was, however, a beautiful human being. Her battle with cancer was not the dominating factor in her life. She did not constantly complain; neither did she lapse into a deep depression. It is perfectly understandable when a cancer patient does manifest these traits. However there was something in Irene, her deep faith and her indomitable spirit, which allowed her to cope well with her illness. What struck me most was her genuine concern for, and interest in, the lives of others. Our conversations would usually start with me asking her how she was getting on. I would ask her, for instance, about the great discomfort she was experiencing as a result of nuclear therapy. After a time, she would ask me how things were going at the church. She would ask me about my family. I remember telling her once that my daughter, Louise, had just started piano lessons and was loving it. She seemed genuinely interested and pleased. I looked into her eyes and I noticed that they were sparkling. Her pleasure was real. I always left Irene's place feeling uplifted. Moreover, as a result of the communion established between us, I believe I was able to care for her at my best. I was alive to her and to every word she said, every concern she expressed. It was not an effort but rather a joy and a privilege to be with her.

There are other care situations, of course, when it really is a struggle to be with the person. One simply must substitute the other's needs for one's own at that point. One extends oneself for the sake of the other, even though he is giving very little. The ideal, though, is when there is a mutuality in the relationship. Then one is able to care at one's best. To be fully available to the other when he is contributing almost nothing to one's own fulfilment requires, in Post's words, a 'rare genius'. In general, it is the case that the giving of the other draws out the best the pastor has to give.

Jesus and Belonging to his Family

Jesus was, of course, one of those rare geniuses. There is perhaps no better indication of his deep capacity for care and concern than his last act from the Cross (Jn. 19:26-27). Jesus says to his mother, 'Dear woman here is your son', and to the disciple, 'Here is your mother.' And the narrator adds, 'At that hour, this disciple took her into his home.' Given the fact that on the one hand the references to 'woman' and 'that hour' suggest an intended link with the events at Cana, and on the other that the scene is climactic, a number of commentators argue that some symbolic meaning is intended.[52] However, other scholars argue that the naturalness of this scene gives a depth to the last action of Jesus, and that the drawing out of symbolic meanings tends to obscure this important fact.[53] It is indeed important not to lose sight of the reality of Jesus' profound act of compassion and care. Nonetheless, with this aspect of the scene firmly in mind, one may still search for some deeper level of meaning. There is no consensus amongst biblical scholars as to what that meaning might be. Yet, there is one interpretation which is favoured by a number of scholars and which has the merit of staying close to the setting of the scene. This is a *family* scene.[54] Jesus gives his mother to the beloved disciple, and the beloved disciple takes her into his home. The evangelist, it seems, is seeking to confirm the testimony of the beloved disciple by portraying him as a member of the family of Jesus on the basis of Jesus' own words. In the Synoptic tradition, Jesus declares that his disciples are indeed members of his household. When his mother and his brothers (and sisters) came looking for him, he said, 'Who are my mother and my brothers?' And looking at those who sat around him, he said, 'Here are my mother and my brothers! Whoever does the will of God is my brother and sister and mother' (Mk. 3:31-35). At the Cross, in this climactic moment in Jesus' life and ministry, the beneficiary of this 'adoption' is the beloved disciple.

New Testament scholar, Gerhard Lohfink, observes that great demands were made of the disciples called into the new family established by Jesus.[55] They were to leave behind brothers and sisters, fathers and mothers, children and fields. Jesus called them to a costly act of substitution, namely, the old life and all that it meant for a new life under the coming reign of God. However, in leaving behind everything they had, everything that was precious to them, they received back a hundredfold (Mk. 10:29-30). Lohfink expresses the situation well:

> They left their families, but then found new brothers and sisters among the disciples. They left their parental home, but found new mothers throughout the country where they received hospitality.

They left their children, but new people whom they had not previously known, all filled with something new, constantly stream to them. They left their fields, but found a firm and supportive community as a 'new land'.[56]

It is significant, argues Lohfink, that although in Mk 10:29-30 Jesus promises that those who follow him will be blessed with homes, brothers, sisters and mothers, there is no reference to fathers. The exclusion is deliberate; in the new family there are to be no 'fathers'. The 'father' is too symbolic of patriarchal domination.[57] I find this a very interesting observation. Of course, it may be that Lohfink is making too much of the omission in the text. However that may be, his point about Christ ushering in a new age in which control and oppression have no place is surely right.

Resistance to domination is important in relation to the notion of substitution. Marcel begins his reflections on belonging and substitution with the case of a master-servant relationship. He points out that in this context to say, 'You belong to me' is abhorrent. Everything changes, however, when one says, 'Jack, I belong to you'. Implied in this declaration is its counterpart, 'You belong to me'. This mutuality is expressed through a transcendence of each person in the bond of reciprocal love. A patriarchal father, far from substituting the other's freedom for his own, takes that freedom from her.

The fact that there are to be no 'fathers' in the new family, Lohfink points out, is reiterated by Jesus in Mt 23:8-12:

But you are not to be called rabbi, for you have one teacher, and you are all brethren. And call no man your father on earth, for you have one Father, who is in heaven. Neither be called masters, for you have one master, the Christ. He who is greatest among you shall be your servant; whoever exalts himself will be humbled, and whoever humbles himself will be exalted.

Jesus declares that there is no place for honorific titles. He also addresses the issue of proper official conduct. He advocates a servant heart. Though Jesus did, in general, tolerate being addressed as 'rabbi', here he challenges the rabbinic custom of being served by one's students.[58] At the Last Supper, Jesus blocked what would have been a normal, expected act from students (Jn 13:1-20). Here was one who did not come to be served, but to serve (Mk 10:45).

Though Marcel does not specifically refer to service in his description of belonging (except in the negative sense of being treated as a slave), it is obvious that the former is implied. The declaration 'I belong to you; I substitute your freedom for mine' is grounded in deep humility. 'You can do whatever you want with me' is another way of saying 'I am at your service'. The possession of a servant-heart underpins disposability and is at the core of Jesus' ethical teaching. It is foundational in pastoral care.

Mark, a teacher, had recently come to faith in Christ. His attendance at worship was regular. He was attempting to bring up two small children on his own, and the strain was showing. Mark came to see me because his drinking and gambling were getting out of control. The way in which we attempted to address these problems is not relevant in this context. What is salient is the fact that Mark appeared to be tense and somewhat suspicious of me. Understandably, he felt some shame over his lapses in self-control and the negative impact this was having on his children and on his work. I attempted to reassure him by acknowledging his courage in coming to see me and by declaring my respect for him. Despite these attempts at confirmation, he continued to be uneasy and on edge during our conversations.

Mark went away on holiday for a number of weeks. After his return, he came neither to worship nor to my study. I received a 'phone call from his boss at the school, also a member of my congregation. He indicated that Mark's performance at school had seriously deteriorated and that his job was in jeopardy. I decided to call on Mark at his home. We had not been speaking for long when we heard a disturbance from his children in the upstairs bedroom. He excused himself and went to settle them for sleep. It was obvious that he was going to be away for quite a while. I looked around and noticed that he was not keeping up with his domestic duties. It occurred to me that perhaps I could assist in some way. I thought I would begin with some ironing. For a few moments I hesitated, wondering if Mark might construe such an act as patronising. In the end, I decided to take the risk and began work. By the time he returned I had finished the whole basket. I was pleased to observe that Mark did in fact receive the work I had done positively. It was a small thing, and yet it had a marked effect on our relationship. I was no longer 'the minister'; now I was a friend. Mark visibly relaxed in my presence. Our conversations were more open and honest.

A servant-heart, along with trust, mutuality and a generosity of spirit, are the qualities which are intimately associated with substitution. It is the willingness to substitute the other's freedom for one's own which is foundational in pastoral care.

BEFORE SKILLS AND TECHNIQUES THERE IS AVAILABILITY

In counselling and psychotherapy, there is often a significant commitment to, and emphasis on, particular theories and interventions. What I believe the discussion above points to is the notion that there is a personal quality, availability, which is more important in care-giving and in counselling than any skill or technique. This is not, of course, an original idea. A number of counsellors and psychotherapists shape their healing work around this conviction.[59] As we have already seen, Brian Thorne has discovered the healing power in a personal quality, 'tenderness', which is beyond the conventional skills and arts of the counsellor. When he finds himself neglecting his best wisdom, Irvin Yalom uses his 'therapist's prayer' to put himself back on track. 'It's the relationship that heals, the relationship that heals, the relationship that heals - my professional rosary.'[60] James Bugental finds it hard to believe that he could have neglected the fundamental importance of presence for so long. And he is aware that others continue to do so. 'All too often', he writes, 'therapists seem to be so attentive to the content of what is being said and to their prior conceptions about client dynamics and needs that they don't notice the distance that exists between themselves and their partners.'[61]

The conviction that availability is the cornerstone of effective care and counselling is beautifully illustrated in a story told by the pastoral psychotherapist, James Jones.[62]

Sylvia's parents immigrated to the U.S. when she was five and settled in an Eastern European Pentecostal ghetto. She had a long history of childhood sexual abuse and incest. Jones tells us that the major struggle for Sylvia was over acceptance. During the termination phase she tells her therapist that:

'For hours and hours you struggled with me, fighting with me, battling my defences against your acceptance. Finally I had to say to myself, you must care or you wouldn't fight so hard. Fighting you made me realise how I repel others' acceptance....

The most helpful thing in therapy was the experience of having someone hanging in there with me, of caring enough to stick with me... I could understand and accept what had happened to me because you understood and accepted what happened.'[63]

Jones then asked Sylvia, 'Did God's love help you to accept yourself with your mistakes and guilt?'[64] To which she replied, 'No it was the other way around. Only after I accepted myself could I accept that God and others cared.'

Jones struggled with Sylvia; he battled against her defences; he fought hard. It is this willingness to engage in emotional and mental toil for the other that expresses genuine availability. Though she does not use the word, it is evident that Sylvia had a profound experience of belonging in this therapeutic relationship. No doubt Jones from time to time - probably often - verbally encouraged and affirmed his client; the really potent source of prizing, however, was Jones' willingness to dispose of himself for her. It was this experience of belonging which helped Sylvia to accept herself, and ultimately recapture a feeling of belonging to God.

Even experienced pastors and counsellors can allow themselves to become so focused on content, skills, techniques and interpretations that they fail to notice that they are no longer making their presence felt in the therapeutic relationship. The really gifted and graced helper knows, however, that when she allows herself to enter heart-and-soul into the relationship, it is not so much words or techniques which are healing and renewing but her very presence.

CONCLUSION

In this chapter, we have been attempting to spell out what it means to refer to availability as foundational in pastoral care and counselling. With the thought in mind that compassion is absolutely fundamental in any form of care, we began our task by showing that there is a close correlation between availability and the biblical notion of compassion. Marcel works with the metaphor of *chez soi*, while the biblical writers use the images of the womb and the heart. However, both are referring, it was argued, to the same reality, namely, the capacity to feel the pain and distress of the other in the depths of one's being.

The second stage in the task was an exploration of the role of substitution in pastoral care. Noting the close link between belonging and the idea of the covenant, we used the framework of covenantal theology for our reflections. In discussing a number of concepts which are intimately related to the notion of substitution - generosity of spirit, trust, mutuality and servanthood - we identified the foundational qualities in effective care. In this way, we were able to demonstrate what it means to say that the capacity to substitute the other's freedom for one's own is a cornerstone of the pastoral care project.

It is common amongst those who practice and/or theorise about pastoral care and counselling to identify empathy, acceptance and compassion as foundational. Clearly, these qualities *are* basic in pastoral care. The burden of our argument has been, however, that availability is a rich and comprehensive concept which on the one hand embraces these qualities, and on the other adds its own distinctive and unique meanings.

Finally, it was suggested that what these pastoral reflections on compassionate self-giving lead to is the notion that presence is ultimately more important in care-giving and counselling than any skill or technique. A technically competent caregiver who lacks compassion and a capacity for self-communication will be only minimally helpful. The tools only become powerful when they are placed in the hands of a person who is personally available. While this may seem obvious, it is the case that a surprisingly large number of counsellors and care-givers have lost sight of this fact.

1 See D. Bergant, 'Compassion', in C. Stuhlmueller ed., *The Collegeville Pastoral Dictionary of Biblical Theology* (Collegeville, Minnesota: The Liturgical Press, 1996), pp. 154-157, p. 154.

2 See ibid., p. 154.

3 X. Leon-Dufour, 'Mercy', in *Dictionary of Biblical Theology* 2nd edit., updated, trans. by P. Cahill & E. Stewart (London: Geoffrey Chapman, 1988), pp. 351-354, p. 351.

4 See D. Bergant, 'Compassion', p. 156.

5 This discussion of *splánchnon* in pre-NT and NT usage is informed by H. Köster, '*splánchnon*' in G. Kittel & G. Friedrich eds., *Theological Dictionary of the New Testament*, one vol. edit., trans. by G. Bromiley (Grand Rapids: Eerdmans, 1985), pp. 1067-1069.

6 Ibid., p. 1068.

7 Ibid., p. 1068.

8 See T. Collins, 'The Physiology of Tears in the Old Testament: Part I', *Catholic Biblical Quarterly* 33 (1971), pp. 18-38.

9 See ibid., pp. 30-31.

10 Ibid., p. 38.

11 A. Becker, 'Compassion: A Foundation for Pastoral Care', *Religion in Life* 48 (Summer 1979), pp. 143-152, p. 145.

12 Ibid., p. 146.

13 J. Dittes, *The Church In the Way* (New York: Charles Scribner's Sons, 1967), p. 100.

14 Ibid., p. 102.

15 See B. Thorne, *Person-Centred Counselling: Therapeutic and Spiritual Dimensions* (London: Whurr Publishers, 1991), p. 40.

16 C. Rogers, *A Way of Being* (Boston: Houghton Mifflin Co., 1980), p. 142.

17 C. Rogers, *The Carl Rogers Reader*, H. Kirschenbaum and V. Land Henderson eds., (London: Constable and Co., 1990), p. 137.

18 See B. Thorne, *Person-Centred Counselling*, p. 41.

19 Ibid., p. 75.

20 Ibid., p. 76.

21 Ibid., p. 76.

22 See A. Campbell, *Moderated Love: A Theology of Professional Care* (London: SPCK, 1984), p. 108.

23 Ibid., p. 108.

24 Thorne, *Person-Centred Counselling*, p. 77.

25 W. Brueggemann, 'Covenanting as Human Vocation', *Interpretation* 33 (April 1979), pp. 115-129, p. 120.

26 This is the view promoted by E. Kutsch. For a summary of this approach to the theology of covenant, see E. Nicholson, *God and His People: Covenant and Theology in the Old Testament* (Oxford: Claredon Press, 1986), pp. 89-94.

27 See E. J. Christiansen, *The Covenant in Judaism and Paul: A Study of Ritual Boundaries as Identity Markers* (Leiden: E.J. Brill, 1995).

28 Ibid., p. 26.

29 See Nicholson, *God and His People*, p. 214.

30 See ibid., p. 215.

31 Ibid., p. 215.

32 Cf. R. Gordon, *I & II Samuel: A Commentary* (Grand Rapids: Zondervan, 1986), p. 159; and W. Brueggemann, *First and Second Samuel, Interpretation Series* (Louiseville: John Knox Press, 1990), p. 136.

33 Some have argued, however, that Jonathan's love reflects a political commitment rather than an emotional attraction. That what we have here is in fact an example of loving substitution is evident when one bears in mind that 'in this chapter everyone — apart from Saul, that is — loves David (vv. 16, 20, 22)!' (R. Gordon, op. cit., p. 159). The love these others have is not that of the relatively cold and calculating commitment associated with a political alliance, and neither is Jonathan's.

34 See C. Gerkin, *Prophetic Pastoral Care* (Nashville: Abingdon Press, 1990), pp. 126-132.

35 Ibid., p. 127.

36 Ibid., pp. 127-128.

37 Ibid., p. 128.

38 Ibid., p. 128.

39 Ibid., p. 131.

40 See J.B. Torrance, 'Covenant or Contract', *Scottish Journal of Theology* 23 (1970), pp. 51-71, p. 56.

41 Ibid., p. 56.

42 See K. Kaplan & M. Markus-Kaplan, 'Covenant Versus Contract as Two Modes of Relationship Orientation', *Journal of Psychology and Judaism* 4, no. 2 (Winter 1979), pp. 100-116, p. 110.

43 Ibid., p. 110.

44 Ibid., p. 110.

45 Marcel, 'Phenomenological Notes on Being in a Situation', in *Creative Fidelity*, p. 99.

46 See Marcel, 'Belonging and Disposability', in *Creative Fidelity*, p. 46.

47 Ibid., p. 46.

48 Ibid., p. 46.

49 Ibid., p. 47.

50 See S. Post, 'Communion and True Self-Love', *Journal of Religious Ethics* 16 (Fall 1988), pp. 345-362.

51 Ibid., p. 345.

52 See, for example, R. Brown, *The Gospel According to John XIII-XXI*, Anchor Bible Series (New York: Doubleday, 1970), p. 922 ff; D. Senior, *The Passion of Jesus in the Gospel of John* (Collegeville, Minnesota: The Liturgical Press, 1991), p 108 ff.; and G. O'Day, *The New Interpreter's Bible*, vol IX (Nashville: Abingdon Press, 1995), pp. 831-832.

53 See G. Beasley-Murray, *Word Biblical Commentary* 36 (Waco, Texas; Word, 1987), p. 350.

54 For symbolic interpretations which pick up the idea of family, see D. Senior, *The Passion of Jesus*, p. 110; and G. O'Day, *NIB* IX, p. 832.

55 See G. Lohfink, *Jesus and Community* (London: SPCK, 1985), p. 41.

56 Ibid., p. 41.

57 See ibid., p. 45.

58 See ibid., p. 46.

59 Maurice Friedman and Richard Hycner suggest that there is a loose school of psychotherapy, spanning the various approaches, which posits dialogue as primary in healing. See M. Friedman, *The Healing Dialogue in Psychotherapy* (New York: Jason Aronson, 1985), and idem,'Buber's Philosophy as the Basis for Dialogical Psychotherapy and Contextual Therapy', *Journal of Humanistic Psychology* 38, no. 1 (Winter 1998), pp. 25-40; and R. Hycner, *Between Person and Person: Toward a Dialogical Psychotherapy* (Highland, NY: The Gestalt Journal, 1991).

60 I. Yalom, *Love's Executioner and Other Tales of Psychotherapy* (London: Penguin Books, 1987), pp. 91-92.

61 J. Bugental, *The Art of the Psychotherapist* (New York: Norton, 1987), p. 46.

62 See J. Jones, *Contemporary Psychoanalysis and Religion: Transference and Transcendence* (New Haven: Yale University Press, 1991), pp. 71-73.

63 Ibid., p. 71.

64 Ibid., p. 73.

Chapter 4

PASTORAL CONFIRMATION I

Integration in the Community of the Self

In the last chapter, we attempted to establish availability as foundational in pastoral care and counselling. The first and basic moment in pastoral care is the capacity for deep being-with the other in her pain and distress. Buber's dialogical thought takes us into the second moment. As we have seen, he understands confirmation to mean helping another person, sometimes against herself, to become the person she was created to be. From this perspective, we are describing the second moment in pastoral care and counselling as helping in the realisation of God-endowed potential. Here we focus on the first aspect of this process, namely, the facilitation of growth towards psychological wholeness. In the next chapter we shall discuss the other dimension, confirmation in relation to ethical confrontation. In seeking to describe the way in which confirmation functions in pastoral care, we will shift our attention from the general practice of providing care to a more concentrated treatment of the specialised function of counselling.

A basic feature of the counselling process is the attempt to help the counsellee enter into a dialogue on a feeling level. In using the word 'feeling', I have in mind the model of counselling developed by the British psychotherapist, Robert Hobson. For Hobson the healing dialogue revolves around 'feeling-images'. The expression of feeling is more, however, than the release of pent-up emotion. As we shall see below, a feeling-language also incorporates cognition, choice, will and action. I will suggest, moreover, that when a person relates on the level of feeling, she encounters the polarities in her personhood. As Buber notes, there is in a person a 'yes' and a 'no', acceptance and refusal. Feeling-images, one might say, are bipolar.

Now recall that Buber distinguishes confirmation from acceptance. Confirmation begins with acceptance, but it also includes wrestling with the other against himself as he grows into his potential. Buber's insight into the need for this struggle with the other is founded on his understanding of the polar nature of the self. The philosopher, Herbert Fingarette, has developed an understanding of the almost universal tendency to self-deception in terms of avowal and disavowal within the community of the Self.[1][2] A sub-self (the 'angry self', for example) which is considered unacceptable is disclaimed and isolated from the other selves. I will attempt to develop the links between Buber's idea of the polarities in the Self and Fingarette's model of avowal/disavowal of sub-selves. If there is in fact a close association of ideas here, it is possible to understand *confirmation in the context of counselling as helping the counsellee reclaim disavowed selves*. Struggling with the counsellee against herself means, in part, helping her discover the person she actually is, her real self. In other words, it is a process of moving her to the point where she can accept the rejected members in the family of the Self. This is an essential first step in the journey towards psychological wholeness.

However, there is obviously a need to go further. The person who, for example, reclaims an angry self she has split-off, now must learn how to appropriately deal with anger when she feels it. I will be suggesting that it is helpful to think of the healing process as *facilitating a dialogue within the community of selves*. Buber refers to helping the other strengthen positive polarities in the Self. He also indicates the value in changing the relationship between the polarities. An 'internal dialogue' can achieve these goals. I want to show how in this inner dialogue Buber's concepts of inclusion, confirmation and responsibility can be usefully applied.

In sum, I will endeavour to develop a two-stage model for helping the counsellee deal with his inner polarities. The first stage involves helping the counsellee reclaim disavowed selves. In the second stage, the counsellor facilitates a process of dialogue within the community of selves.

Some may consider that this focus on psychological wholeness is really an encouragement of self-centred introspection. Instead of wasting time and energy on attempting to integrate disavowed selves, persons should be devoting themselves to doing good to others. Of course we must make time for service and social action. However, I will argue that reclaiming the dark side of the personality is also a moral imperative. To live as if these polarities do not exist is a dangerous self-deception. Dangerous because not only will one suffer from a fragmented, disordered psyche, but others will also suffer from the destructive outworking of that psyche.

It is interesting to observe, finally, that the key dynamics described above - a feeling-dialogue and the avowal/disavowal of polarities - seem to be operating in certain sections of the Bible. In the psalms of lament, first, image is piled upon image as the psalmists pour out their anguish and distress before God. I will offer the view, following Walter Brueggemann, that they regress into a language of the 'pit' in an attempt to call God into the action which will bring transformation and reorientation.

I will also suggest that the dialogue between God and Jonah in the final scene of the novella can be construed as a 'confirmation game'. God is 'playfully' (it is serious play) endeavouring to help Jonah to be honest by reclaiming the egoistic self he has disavowed.

COUNSELLING AND THE LANGUAGE OF THE HEART

It is a contradiction in terms to talk about a surface dialogue. Any real meeting between two people is a meeting at depth. In Marcelian language, the mainspring of dialogue is the 'shared secret'. When the other shares something from his heart, something which is precious and makes him vulnerable to me, and I receive it sensitively and graciously I have confirmed him as a person who is unique, valuable. In a counselling context, the shared secret forms the basis for challenging personal work. Not everyone, however, is prepared for the demands this kind of work makes.

Tom came to see me because he was distressed over disturbances in his home environment. He is not the sort of man who would naturally think of counselling as an option. He came with a reticent, apprehensive attitude. 'The wife seems to think talking to you will help', he said. Tom is an intensely practical man, currently working as a carpenter. He began our conversation with the comment, 'Well what do we do? I tell you what the problem is and you tell me how to solve it. Is that what it's about?' I of course told him that that was not what it was about. 'I'm not the fount of all wisdom', I said. 'What I can do is work through with you some of the things that are concerning you at the moment. Let's start by you telling me what has brought you here.' (I was aware of the key details in relation to Tom's home situation. His partner, Anne, attended my church. She had a son, Michael, with a man whom she subsequently divorced. Michael, aged 12, suffers from Attention Deficit Disorder. Tom and Anne have two small children of their own.) 'Well', said Tom, 'Michael's driving me crazy with his strange behaviour. The kid is often up 'till after midnight. He's just as likely to be prowling around in the middle of the night. At meal-times he's throwing food at the little ones. Or he's eating some strange concoction that makes me want to throw up. I love Anne and the kids, but I don't think I can stand it for too much longer.'

As we explored the frustration and anger Tom was feeling, he spoke of his years in the Navy and how good it was. He loved the order, the precision, the neatness. There was routine, everyone knew what was expected of them, and there was discipline. He also mentioned his love of his current work. I had seen some of Tom's carpentry work. I was greatly impressed by the neatness and precision in his work.

I realised that in a subsequent session we would need to look at some practical strategies for coping with his family situation. It was also evident, however, that Michael's bizarre, chaotic behaviour was going to continue; concrete coping strategies would never be the whole answer. Tom would have to reshape his attitude to the behaviours he found so distressing. I decided to begin by pointing up the stark differences between what brought him a sense of peace and fulfilment and the situation in his home environment. Life in the navy was characterised by order, routine, discipline. He loved that milieu. In his current work situation he enjoyed the neatness and precision he achieved in putting together structures. Contrast this with the home situation. The family was continually thrown into confusion by Michael's unpredictable and strange behaviour. I wanted to help Tom work with two sets of contrasting and conflicting sets of images. On the one hand, there was the *order, neatness, precision* and *discipline* characterising the life he cherished; on the other hand, the *disorder, unpredictability* and *messiness* of the home environment he found so deeply disturbing. Working with this conflict would take Tom to the heart of his personhood. It would require him to rework his characteristic emotional and cognitive patterns. Sadly, he was not ready for that kind of demanding personal work. Tom simply wanted a few quick pointers that would help him transform his family life into the neat, ordered existence he wanted and, he thought, deserved. He did not return for a second conversation.[3]

Hobson's Notion of a 'Feeling-Language'

At the heart of the counselling process is two people sharing in a conversation on a feeling level. This was something Tom was not prepared for. I am using the word *feeling* here in the sense developed by Robert Hobson. He construes the healing relationship as a dialogue between two persons aimed at developing a 'feeling-language'. A central feature of this dialogue is *aloneness-togetherness*.

To understand Hobson's notion of aloneness-togetherness, one must recognise the distinction between on the one hand, aloneness and isolation, and on the other, between togetherness and fusion.[4] With this concept, he refers to 'an individual-in-relationship'.[5] The aloneness pole indicates distinction, autonomy and personal identity; whereas the togetherness pole refers to mutuality, reciprocity and sharing.[6] Aloneness-in-relationship means that there is an inner dialogue taking place within the therapeutic conversation (something we will explore in developing our two-stage model of confirmation in counselling): 'To be alone means being together in an open dialogue, but it also means an inner dialogue: a conversation with many "selves" in a society of "myself".'[7]

Though Hobson does not make this connection, the idea of aloneness-togetherness is clearly an expression of Buber's understanding of distance and relation. Before one can enter into a relation, the other must be set at a distance. That is, the establishment of independence and otherness (aloneness) is the pre-condition of coming together in relation.

Hobson's choice of the word 'feeling' to describe the therapeutic conversation is perhaps a little unfortunate. When one thinks of 'feeling', the natural association is with affect or emotion. Hobson, however, understands the term to incorporate a much wider range of human experience than the emotional. The term 'heart-language' may be more helpful, although it also has its limitations (e.g. the word 'heart' has for some the connotation of sentimentality).

Hobson observes that in everyday speech we use the word 'feeling' in a variety of ways.[8] It can mean the following: (a) examining by touching (the 'feel' of a piece of cloth), (b) bodily sensation ('I feel light-headed'), (c) tenderness for others ('I feel for you'), and (d) ethical assessment ('It feels the right thing to do'). He incorporates all of these connotations, along with others, into his understanding of a feeling-language.

> 'Feeling'... is a growing 'family' or 'society' of meanings which range from elementary physical sensations, perceptions, and emotions, metaphors of touch, and groping exploration, to organised, vivid, and heart-felt artistic shapes. It expresses personal knowledge with a growing self-awareness in sympathetic ('feeling-with') conversations between persons. The meanings, as it were, 'ascend' from the literal body and yet remain firmly tied to it (especially the sense of touch)....
>
> A personal feeling-language means a progressive increase in mutual understanding and its form must be such as to promote that creative process within a relationship. It is not a mere matter of discharging affect....[9]

This last statement by Hobson is particularly important. It would be to gravely misunderstand his intention to think of the feeling dimension in counselling as simply a 'blowing off' of pent-up emotion. Obviously emotion is involved in a feeling-conversation, but other elements are also important.

While it is usual to distinguish cognition and emotion, Hobson joins the two together in his understanding of feeling. 'When I speak of feeling', he writes, 'I do not mean a faculty of emotion *plus* cognition. It is a kind of "emotional knowing" or, as Mill [John Stuart Mill] puts it, an "imaginative emotion" related to an "idea"...'[10]

Feeling also involves choice, will and directedness.[11] Through feeling, experiences are assigned a value. As a result of the likes and dislikes, desires and fears, attaching to them, we make certain choices about what we will do with our experiences. Feeling plays an important role in shaping our attitudes and behaviours. To a large degree, the actions we choose are determined by feeling.

Hobson recounts an early experience in therapy in which he struggles to develop a feeling-language with an adolescent.[12] At the time, Sam was 14 and had been referred because of disturbed behaviour at home and at school. He was previously a mannerly and obedient son to his widowed mother. In the year before entering therapy, however, he had become aggressive and had manifested various inappropriate behaviours. At school he was rude and uncooperative. He was caught passing around papers containing erotic stories.

At first, Sam was surly and disinterested in therapy, 'a picture of dumb insolence', as Hobson puts it. Hobson attempted to show an interest in his life. He tried to explore his attitudes to his teachers, schoolmates, and his mother. An attempt was made to engage him in talk about what might have been interests - films, games, and girls. 'All he gave me', recalls Hobson, 'was a surly frown and the very occasional favour of a short, grudging answer.' This attitude of non-cooperation persisted for weeks. Finally, Hobson felt he could no longer stand it. In desperation, he began talking about cricket. He discovered that he and Sam shared a love for the game. Here was the turning point in the therapy. Now Sam smiled and responded with some enthusiasm. For the first time, they were talking together.

Hobson goes on to report that one day Sam entered the room with a strange expression on his face. They sat together in silence for a while. This, though, was different to the tense, disengaged silences that had dominated the therapy previously. When Sam finally spoke, it was to tell his therapist about a dream.

> I was by a dark pool. It was filthy and there were all sorts of horrible monsters in it. I was scared but I dived in and at the bottom was a great big oyster and in it a terrific pearl. I got it and swam up again.[13]

Hobson responded with: 'That's good. Brave, too. You've got it though, and pearls are pretty valuable.'

Nothing more was said about the dream. Importantly though, the interview was followed by another significant step. Sam began to share his feelings and thoughts, his hopes and fears. He told Hobson how he hated himself for becoming violently angry when his mother treated him like a child. And yet, he feared she did not really love him, and he was terrified at the thought of being separated from her. When he shared how he felt about the loss of his father, he wept with grief and rage.

In sharing his ideas, wishes and impulses and finding that his therapist still liked and accepted him, he lost much of his hate for himself. A new self emerged. He had a much more positive attitude to both home and school.

Only once did Sam refer to the dream; it was many months later. He shared with Hobson a beautiful insight: 'Its queer about that pearl. I suppose it's me in a *sort of way*.' The pearl is an example of what Hobson calls a *feeling-image*. For Freda,[14] it was emptiness. She revealed to Hobson that 'there's this terrible empty feeling I've got inside'. Joe Smith[15] spoke of feeling 'hollow' and like 'a wobbly child learning to walk'. The images are used in therapy to 'carry experience forward' and 'disclose a meaning which is beyond, or prior to conceptual thoughts and formulated words'.[16]

While a good deal of time and energy is devoted in the therapeutic process to helping a person overcome the blocking associated with various defences in order to get to this level of immediate experiencing, it seems that many of the people of the Old Testament quite naturally and spontaneously poured out the pain felt deep within. Job and his cries of anguish comes immediately to mind. On her return from a disastrous stay in Moab, Naomi, overcome with distress, responds to the greeting of her friends by telling them that the name 'Mara' (meaning bitter) suits her better: 'I went away full, but the Lord has brought me back empty' (Ruth 1: 20-21). In the psalms of lament we find image piled upon image as those who suffer pour out their agonies before God.

The Language of Feeling in the Psalms of Lament

In reading the psalms of protest, one is immediately struck by both the rawness of emotion displayed and the vivid imagery used to communicate it. Those in distress have reached a point of extremity; the old certainties, along with the feelings of serenity and joy associated with them, have been swept away. In this limit experience, it is impossible to hold on to a restrained, domesticated way of communicating with God. There is now no slippage between the agonies of the heart and the primitive, aggressive articulations before God. The images of distress and anguish coming tumbling out in prayer.

> Because of all my enemies, I am the utter contempt of my neighbours;
> I am a dread to my friends - those who see me on the street flee from me.

I am forgotten by them as though I were dead;
I have become like *broken pottery*. (Ps. 31: 11-12)

[My enemies] spread a net for my feet - I was *bowed down* in distress.
They dug a *pit* in my path - but they have fallen into it themselves.
(Ps. 57:6)

How long will you assault a man?
Would all of you throw him down - this *leaning wall*, this *tottering fence*?
(Ps. 62:3)

Your wrath has *swept over* me: your terrors have destroyed me.
All day long they surround me *like a flood*; they have completely *engulfed* me. (Ps. 88:16)

These ejaculations of anguish do not, however, simply represent a release of emotion. They are, in Hobson's terms, manifestations of an 'emotional knowing'. Behind the metaphors is an understanding of the dynamics of the distress. 'Enemies' of various kinds are being allowed by God to press in and wreak havoc. The modern person feeling something of the same agonies of the soul will easily be able to put her own names on the enemies.

We note, too, that those who cry out to God in these psalms are not lost in a whirl of emotion. They are not paralysed by their distressing circumstances. Associated with their cries from the heart are will and directedness. The note sounded is not so much lament as *protest*. There is a very clear expectation that God should intervene in the current turmoil to bring order, freedom and peace.

Walter Brueggemann characterises the experience of casting off the niceties and the serene language of better times and of unleashing a torrent of anguish and anger as regression: 'The *lament as plea and petition regresses* to the oldest fears, the censored questions, the deepest hates, the unknown and unadmitted venom...' [emphasis in the original].[17] Following Ricoeur, he sees in the life-experience three movements, namely, orientation, disorientation and reorientation.[18] When one is experiencing the shattering effects of a period of dislocation, joy and newness of life are not to be found in simply getting back to the old order. There is no way back. One's life-experience has been radically transformed; the old perspectives have lost their power. The way forward is to find fresh hopes, a different vision, a new order - reorientation. In order to get there, however, there must first be a regression, a fall down into the depths. One must learn to speak the language of the 'pit'.

Until the reality of the 'pit' is spoken about with all its hatred of enemies, its mistrust of God, its fear of 'beasts', its painful yearning for old, better times, its daring questions of dangerous edges - until all that is brought to speech - it is likely that one will continue to assume the old now-discredited, dysfunctional equilibrium which is in fact powerless.[19]

A Feeling-Language and The Polar Self

In the healing dialogue, there is also a regression in the service of reorientation. Counsellee and counsellor, alone and together, need to discover a language in which the images of the 'pit' emerge. These images penetrate the experience of the person as it really is. A new self is constructed through a re-shaping, a re-ordering, of this experience. Sam went down into the depths and confronted his 'monsters' in search of his pearl. He had to learn how to talk about his hatred for himself in becoming violently angry toward his mother, about his terror that she would leave him, about his grief and rage over the loss of his father, before he could find a new self, the pearl 'that's me in a sort of way'.

When a person moves to this level of experiencing, he encounters the polarities in his personality. As Buber puts it, there is in a person a 'yes' and a 'no', acceptance and refusal. In the counselling context, the 'yes' stands for all those tendencies, traits, fantasies, emotions, and actions which are considered acceptable and owned; the 'no' refers to those that are unacceptable and disclaimed. In Sam's case, he had to work through the negative pole - his self-hatred over his ambivalent feelings toward his mother and his father - before reaching the vision of himself as something precious and rare.

The art of the counsellor is in paring back the protective layers of the counsellee in order to make present to her the heart of her personhood. There are almost endless possibilities for a counsellor in learning with the person a language of the heart. Some will use P A C theory (Transactional Analysis). The counsellee is invited to play with images of authority and control, rationality, and emotion respectively. Others find the Empty Chair technique of Gestalt therapy useful. In the chair opposite, the counsellee fixes an image of the person (he or she may even be deceased) primarily associated with the current distress. He is invited to carry on a 'dialogue' with that person, raising and working through key issues. The particular technique a counsellor might use is not of primary interest here. Behind all of the available interventions is the art of the counsellor. It is an art requiring intuition, playfulness, and a willingness to take risks.

In trying to get beyond the superficiality and pretence of jolliness of a client he calls Betty, Irvin Yalom used two 'playful' interventions.[20]

Bored with her endless meaningless chatter, Yalom asked her to rate her level of self-disclosure on a scale of one to ten. To his amazement, she gave herself a 'ten'. When he told her that he would have given her a 'two' or a 'three', they began a dialogue about her pride in her ability to entertain others. An obese person, Betty saw herself as the jolly fat woman.

> "I'm really interested in what you said about being, or rather pretending to be, jolly. I think you are determined, absolutely committed, to be jolly with me."
>
> "Hmmm, interesting theory, Dr. Watson."
>
> "You've done this since our first meeting. You tell me about a life that is full of despair, but you do it in a bouncy, 'aren't-we-having-a-good-time?' way."
>
> "That's the way I am."
>
> "When you stay jolly like that, I lose sight of how much pain you're having."
>
> "That's better than wallowing in it."
>
> "But you come here for help. Why is it so necessary to entertain me?"
>
> Betty flushed. She seemed staggered by my confrontation and retreated by sinking into her body. Wiping her brow with a tiny handkerchief, she stalled for time.
>
> "Zee suspect takes zee fifth."
>
> "Betty, I'm going to be persistent today. What would happen if you stopped trying to entertain me?"
>
> "I don't see anything wrong with having some fun. Why take everything so.....so.....I don't know - You're always so serious. Besides, this is me, this is the way I am. I'm not sure what you're talking about. What do you mean by my entertaining you?"
>
> "Betty, this is important, the most important stuff we've got into so far. But you're right. First, you've got to know exactly what I mean. Would it be O.K. with you if, from now on in our future sessions, I interrupt and point out when you're entertaining me - the moment it occurs?"[21]

This option of immediately interrupting Betty's superficial jolliness is the second playful device used by Yalom. He comments, 'Within three or four sessions, her "entertaining" behaviour disappeared as she, for the first time, began to speak of her life with the seriousness it deserved.'[22] Yalom's confirmation of Betty allowed her to get in touch with her serious side. As he did so, she was able to own a feeling-image, 'emptiness'.

> She reflected that she had to be entertaining to keep others interested in her. I commented that, in the office, the opposite was true: the more she tried to entertain me, the more distant and less interested I felt.

> But Betty said she didn't know how else to be: I was asking her to
> dump her entire social repertoire. Reveal herself? If she were to reveal
> herself, what would she show? There was nothing inside. She was
> empty. (The word *empty* was to arise more and more frequently as
> therapy proceeded...)[23]

Later, Betty would own other heart-images, namely isolation and hunger
for closeness. She could now speak authentically out of her serious self.

When Betty began to relate on the level of feeling-language, she
discovered the polarities in her personhood. She had disclaimed her
serious self and was living in bad faith through the false self of the 'jolly
fat lady'. Speaking out of the serious self, she was able to own the
emptiness, isolation, and hunger for closeness she felt. A movement
towards psychological wholeness begins when a person gets in touch
with her feeling-images. These images will be bipolar. Confirmation in
counselling, I suggest, is a process in which one helps the counsellee move
to the point where she can own and integrate disclaimed polarities.

CONFIRMATION AND RECLAIMING SPLIT-OFF SELVES

Recall that in his dialogue with Carl Rogers over the difference between
confirmation and acceptance, Buber argued that in order to help the
other grow into his potential one must 'help him against himself'. This
need to move beyond acceptance he related to a polar understanding of
the self. We have seen these polarities at work in Sam and in Betty. It is
interesting to note that the person-centred therapist, Ralph Quinn, also
attests to the reality of the polar nature of the self, although he does not
refer to the Buber-Rogers debate. In an article entitled 'Confronting Carl
Rogers', he points up the limitations in an 'acceptance-only' policy and
cites his own clinical experience:

> In the last year I have worked with a man who claimed he *desperately*
> *needed* to be more assertive in his life, with a lonely woman who
> *wanted* to quit spending all her evenings alone at home, with a student
> who *would do practically anything* to stop using marijuana, and with
> a husband and wife whose constant fighting was "ruining their
> marriage."
>
> With all of these clients at some point in the course of therapy I
> spent a good deal of time confronting their (largely unconscious)
> desires to *not be* assertive, to *not be* with other people, *to keep smoking*
> marijuana, and *to maintain the same dysfunctional patterns* of fighting
> [emphasis added].[24]

The theorist who has done the most to relate Buber's ideas to counselling
is Maurice Friedman. In an article co-authored with Tamar Kron on the

role of confirmation in counselling, the need affirmed by Quinn to go
beyond acceptance to confrontation is related to the polar self: 'It is not
enough to reflect back to you what you are and affirm it. I have to
confront you with your unacknowledged polarity so that you will be
ready to take responsibility for it.'[25] The authors illustrate their convictions
through a case study involving a young doctoral student who came to
Kron for counselling in order to work through the difficulties created by
his low self-esteem and lack of confidence in his intellectual capabilities.

> The client is one of seven children of a North-African, low socio-
> economic multi-problem family who grew up in a non-encouraging
> environment. Overcoming all his hardships, the talented youngster
> succeeded in his studies and became a doctoral student in a highly
> valued natural sciences program.

> Listening carefully to the client's way of describing himself, the
> therapist sensed, concealed within his self-deprecation, a tone of
> arrogance. She verified her impression during the next few sessions.
> When the client once again expressed his feelings of inferiority and
> despair at his inability to go on with his somewhat pretentious
> project, she stopped him and said, "But you know, actually you are
> arrogant and presumptuous."

> The client was taken aback and responded with surprise, "Arrogant?
> I never thought of myself as arrogant, for I usually feel so inferior."

> The therapist told the client that side by side with his feelings of
> inadequacy, he does feel proud of his high achievements in the face of
> his low background and his hardships. "You can be justly proud of
> yourself for all your achievements," she added, "but you are also
> arrogant for being the only child in your family who made it and
> climbed high up into the academic world."

> The client became quiet and reflective. In the next session, he came
> in and said, "Last time I felt hit as though you had sent a missile at me.
> I was confused and bewildered the whole week. I feel as if my whole
> self-image is being turned upside down." He then continued by telling
> a dream he had. In the dream, he sees himself standing precariously on
> a hill of stones. He looks down the hill and feels afraid that the stones
> will start rolling down and he will fall and get himself hit hard. He
> then starts to descend the hill very slowly and cautiously, holding on
> to the more solid-looking stones with his hands and feet until he
> succeeds in going down all the way and standing on firm ground.

> Both the client and the therapist understood the dream to be about
> the patient's ego inflation, his fear of failure, and the acknowledged
> need to go slower and adapt his work to his present abilities.[26]

Within this student there are both acknowledged and unacknowledged polarities. He claims his sense of inferiority and low self-esteem, but disclaims arrogance and pride. Above we saw similar dynamics in Betty. Betty lives out of a false self - the jolly fat lady - in a misguided attempt to entertain and keep others interested. It is the disclaimed serious self, however, which is authentic and most likely to engage others. 'Yes' and 'no', acceptance and refusal - these are the dynamics the counsellor must reckon with; she must wrestle with her client against himself.

In this section, I offer the view that *confirmation in counselling means helping the counsellee reclaim disowned selves within the society of the Self.*[27] Confirming the other as the unique person she is obviously means more than simply reflecting back to her what she appears to be. It involves struggling with the person to help her discover the selves which she has lost contact with. Confirmation in counselling, I will argue, means, as a first step, affirming the particularity and uniqueness of the person by re-acquainting her with some of the isolated members in the family of the Self.

This is obviously only a first step. Confirmation is also about helping a person grow into her potential. To refer to the case study presented above involving the North African student, Tamar Kron has not done her work in simply confronting him with his disclaimed arrogance. Certainly, it is a crucial step in the direction of growth to acknowledge a proud self. The next step for the student, though, is to integrate the inferior and arrogant selves so that he can reach a point of healthy self-esteem and appropriate confidence in relation to his research. I will offer a view of the second stage of the confirming process as the facilitation of a dialogue within the community of selves. Further, I intend to show the value in using some of Buber's key concepts - namely inclusion, confirmation and responsibility - in understanding this inner dialogical process.

It seems likely that in his reference to the polarities in the self Buber had in mind the almost universal tendency to self-deception. Even if he did not, there appears to be a very close connection between the two concepts. We have already seen how Friedman and Kron interpret confirmation in counselling as helping the other recognise unacknowledged polarities. The 'no' in a person is manifested in the production of clever cover-stories aimed at the avoidance of the real Self. To acknowledge the Self as it really is would result in deep anxiety and distress; hence the deception. The philosopher, Herbert Fingarette, has developed an understanding of self-deception in terms of avowal and disavowal within the community of the Self. When selves are split-off, there is confusion and alienation of the Self from itself. It is the over-coming of this disorder and self-alienation - the conflict between the 'yes' and the 'no' polarities - which confirmation is aimed at.

Self-Deception and Disavowal of Selves

Fingarette develops a new understanding of consciousness in order to construct his model of self-deception. In place of a passive registration and reflection to the mind of what the eyes see in the world, a 'mental mirror' model, he posits consciousness as the exercise of the skill of 'spelling-out' (making explicit) an aspect of one's way of being engaged with the world.[28] Engagement is Fingarette's short-hand for the complex ways a person lives in the world. It covers 'the activities he engages in, the projects he takes on, the way the world presents itself to him to be seen, heard, felt, enjoyed, feared, or otherwise "experienced" by him'.[29] A person is involved in self-deception when there is a compelling reason *not* to spell-out a particular engagement. He avoids becoming explicitly conscious of his engagement, and he avoids becoming explicitly conscious that he is avoiding it.[30] Thus in self-deception there is a 'purposeful discrepancy between the way the individual really is engaged in the world and the story he tells himself'.[31]

All this raises the question, Why bother to hide from oneself what is really there? For Fingarette, the answer lies in the need to disavow certain engagements to avoid anxiety and to maintain self-esteem. There are three chief dimensions of disavowal, namely, isolation, non-responsibility and the incapacity to spell-out.[32] A disavowed engagement is cut-off from the influence of the Self. In this way, the Self no longer takes responsibility for it. Since this feature of a person's way of being in the world has been split-off, she would not, if asked, be able to make explicit what she is doing in a situation in which that feature comes into play.

In developing this idea of avowal/disavowal of engagements, Fingarette uses the idea of the Self as an achievement, a synthesis. Avowal of engagements in the developing Self produces a synthesis; self-deception contributes to a failure of this synthesis. The model of the Self Fingarette uses is a *community*. In the growing child, the members of this community are the 'various originally independent forms of engagement, the rudimentary but unified complexes of reasons-motive-feeling-aim-means-and-moralistic reaction'.[33] Thus, within the developing community which is the Self, there are angry selves, shameful selves, creative selves, aggressive selves, righteous selves, dishonest selves, logical selves and so on. When a self is avowed it is claimed as part of one's personal identity. If a self is unacceptable, on the other hand, it is isolated, split-off. It is this process of disavowal which leads to confusion, disorder and a sense of alienation of the Self from itself. 'Disavowed desires that in fact continue to exist are experienced as "alien," as "forces" that press us, drive us, or overcome us.'[34] Disavowal contributes to a failure in the synthetic processes within the community of the Self. If the coherence is weak, there will be great inner distress, anxiety, shame, guilt and self-hatred.[35]

The literature on self-deception is immense, and there are, of course, authors who are critical of Fingarette's approach. David Jones, for example, believes that the introduction of the notion of a community of selves, along with disavowal of sub-selves, needlessly complicates the matter.[36] He contends that in self-deception there is only one self and that this self uses a 'biased cognitive style' and 'motivated excusing strategies' to maintain the cover story. In order to hide the truth from herself, a person develops a cognitive style which is selective in regard to attention, memory and judgement. Put differently, a person sees what she wants to see, remembers what suits her purposes, and makes biased judgements. Along with these selective thought processes, there is a tendency to make excuses for behaviour which is unacceptable. A person is able to rationalise her actions in such a way that the blame is always laid elsewhere.

There is no doubt that self-deceivers use these strategies to maintain their cover stories. But a description of these ploys does not in itself prove that it is illegitimate to talk in terms of disavowal of unacceptable selves; the two approaches are not incompatible. In any case, my purpose in introducing Fingarette's model is not to enter the complex and controversial debate over the processes involved with self-deception. Rather, I am using it because it has a close affinity with what is a central concern in psychotherapy, namely defence mechanisms, and, moreover, because it sheds light on some of the cases we have been discussing. Sam had repressed his ambivalent feelings toward his mother and father because they were too painful and frightening to face. Betty had disavowed her serious self because she believed that she needed a jolly self to keep others interested in her. And finally, the young doctoral student had disclaimed his arrogant self. He was happy to own an inferior self; he found it acceptable to spell-out to others his problems with his studies in terms of low self-esteem and lack of confidence. What he could not make explicit was his tendency to look upon the under-achievers in his family with disdain.

As we have seen, a key element in Fingarette's model is the notion of the Self as a community. This idea has also become important in contemporary psychological theories of the Self. In order to continue laying the foundation for a view of confirmation in counselling as helping the counsellee re-claim isolated selves, it is necessary to discuss further this theory of the Self.

The Self as a Community

Marie Hoskins and Johanna Leseho argue that there has been within psychological theorising on the Self a dramatic shift from a focus on the unitary Self to an exploration of the Self in terms of sub-personalities.[37] While older theories worked with the metaphors of cohesive self, core self and authentic self, postmodern theories throw up images of sub-selves, possible selves and a community of selves. It is true that there has been a shift in the way the Self is theoretically constructed, but I contend that it is a mistake to over-emphasise the differences in approach between older and more recent theorists. In my view, psychological theorists have always worked with the community model of the Self.

Hoskins and Loseho present Heinz Kohut's notion of the 'cohesive self' as paradigmatic of the traditional approach.[38] Kohut certainly understands the Self in terms of a personal core; it is 'a center of productive initiative'.[39] This Self is superordinate to the psychic agencies (id, ego, and superego).[40] Nevertheless, the Self is also understood by Kohut as a community. The smallest form of community is a couple. What Kohut calls the 'bipolar self' accounts for two basic psychological functions: healthy self-assertiveness in relation to the 'mirroring' (approving and admiring) self-object and healthy admiration for the idealised self-object.[41] (*Self-object* is the term Kohut uses to indicate the infant's tendency to merge with her parents. The self of the child and the parent, an 'object' for the child, are perceived as a unity).Thus it is possible, theorises Kohut, to identify a *grandiose self* which seeks admiration and approval, and an *idealising self* which desires merger with an admired other. When the two basic psychological needs are fulfilled in infantile development, a *cohesive self* emerges.

It is also possible to identify a communitarian element in Freud's construction of the Self. Id, ego and superego may be construed as metaphors for an instinctual self (itself composed of a loving self and an aggressive self), an executive self and a moralising/civilising self, respectively.

The P-A-C conceptualisation of the Self developed by Eric Berne likewise contains a reference to sub-selves. The Parent is the image of authority, control, strictness. Playfulness and spontaneity, along with irrational fear, are the metaphors we associate with childhood. And the Adult carries with it connotations of maturity and rationality. Persons grow up under the influence of a whole host of parental injunctions, rules, values and taboos. They carry a 'Parent-self' around inside them. They also live with a 'Child-self'. Dysfunctional emotional reactions developed in childhood break out in current stressful situations. The 'Adult-self' represents the rational faculty which is able to challenge parental injunctions and modify dysfunctional emotional patterns.

Freud, Berne and Kohut, then, all have a communitarian dimension in their constructions of the Self. The idea of a community of selves is not a new one. It is, however, true that contemporary psychological theorists make explicit reference to the existence of multiple selves within the Self.

Hazel Markus and Paula Nurius, for example, have developed a theory of 'possible selves'.[42] They refer to a type of self-knowledge which refers to how individuals imaginatively construct their future existence. Caught up in a vision of potential selves are the hopes and dreams, along with the fears and anxieties, of a person. A possible self is the ideal self a person dreams of. It can, nonetheless, be a self she is afraid of becoming. 'The possible selves that are hoped for might include the successful self, the creative self, the rich self, the thin self, or the loved and admired self, whereas the dreaded possible selves could be the alone self, the depressed self, the incompetent self, the alcoholic self, the unemployed self, or the bag lady self.'[43]

J.M.M. Mair has exploited the therapeutic potential in the metaphor of a community of selves.[44] He begins his discussion with a reference to the smallest form of community, namely a community of two persons. It is common to refer to being 'in two minds'. There is part of one tending in a certain direction, but another part is pulling in the opposite direction. It is like having to do battle with oneself. The community of two can be expanded to three, four or more selves. Some of these selves will persist over time, others will play a role for only a time. Sub-selves may be 'loners', or they may be 'team-players'. Some will be powerful and dominant, others will be docile and agreeable.

Mair encourages his clients to reflect on their psychic conflicts in terms of their internal selves. He suggests that they may find it helpful to work with the 'characters' provided by communities they are familiar with. These will be political groups, business communities, sporting clubs, and the like. His experience in working with 'John' illustrates his approach.[45]

John came to Mair because he wanted to give up smoking but was unable to. As they talked together, it became evident that there were a variety of personal issues impacting on the presenting problem. In his attempt to establish a healthy relationship both with himself and with others, John was experiencing a good deal of conflict. Mair suggested to him that it might be helpful to think of his contradictory feelings, desires and concerns as different 'selves' constituting his personal 'community'.

As John began this therapeutic experiment, he was able to identify the most powerful person in his 'community' as his 'Foreign Secretary'. The Foreign Secretary spent very little time at home. He was continually travelling in order to visit other 'communities' (other people) to provide assistance. The Foreign Secretary was trying to impress others at the cost of his own 'community' (his family). He wouldn't refuse calls for assistance because he needed to be needed and he wanted to be popular. Sadly, the neglect of the home community left its members feeling neglected and stressed. As a consequence, they were resentful.

At the next interview, John presented a typewritten page detailing further insights into his personal community, which he had called 'The Home Team'. John had used in his reflections the fact that Britain was at the time deciding whether or not it should enter the Common Market of the E.E.C. He identified two major groups, namely 'The Wise Ones' and 'The Common Marketeers'. The positions and policies of both the 'Home Secretary' and 'The Chancellor of the Exchequer' were outlined. He decided to sack the Home Secretary because of his weakness of will and to replace him with a stronger one. The powers of the Foreign Secretary were curbed. Now all requests for help from other communities had to be discussed 'in Cabinet'; no longer could the Foreign Secretary engage in unilateral decision-making.

John shared with his therapist that for the first time he had been able to say 'no' to a request for assistance, recognising that he was over-committing himself. In the past he had always felt too lonely to be alone even for a few minutes. But now he felt that recognising the diversity of 'characters' in his personal community allowed him to feel comfortable in his own company. In addressing his inner conflict, John was able also to reduce his cigarette smoking to just a few a day. Mair reflects that John's use of the metaphor of a personal community 'seemed to provide him with the beginning of a personal "language" within which to conceive and begin to control aspects of his ways of dealing with himself, others and the world'.[46]

While the idea of a community of selves has been around in the world of psychology for some time, there is no doubt that increasingly theorists and therapists are exploring its potential. It is an important element in our attempt to identify the role of confirmation in counselling.

Confirmation as The Process of Reclaiming Isolated Selves

Confirmation means making the other present in her uniqueness and particularity. In counselling, as we have seen, a person will often present just some of the selves in her personal community. Selves which are unacceptable remain unacknowledged. They are split-off in an attempt to avoid anxiety and a lowering of self-esteem. The particularity of the person, however, is constituted through both avowed and disavowed selves. To help a person re-claim rejected selves is to confirm her. The first step in a movement towards wholeness is always an awareness of the real Self; the person must be able to discover the Self that she actually is.[47] In the terms we are using, there needs to be an acknowledgement of disowned sub-selves in the society of the Self. While it is not possible, or even necessary, to get in touch with all disavowed selves, it is critical that the repressed self (it may be selves) which is most closely associated with the person's psychological dysfunction is acknowledged.

Confirming the counsellee through a re-claiming of disavowed selves requires artistry from the counsellor. It is not possible to precisely identify a series of steps which will lead a person to the point of being able to acknowledge disclaimed polarities. What can be identified, as we have already noted, is the need for the counsellor and the counsellee to engage in serious play. The British psychotherapist, Donald Winnicott, suggests that we view playing as a form of communication in psychotherapy.[48] Play is universal and belongs to health. It is the natural reality; the sophisticated modern version of it takes place in the therapist's office.

> Psychotherapy takes place in the overlap of two areas of playing, that of the patient and that of the therapist. Psychotherapy has to do with two people playing together. The corollary of this is that where playing is not possible then the work done by the therapist is directed towards bringing the patient from a state of not being able to play into a state of being able to play.[49]

In Winnicott's description of the dynamics of play, an important concept is that of the *potential space*.[50] Play is not located in inner psychic reality; nor is it to be found in external reality; it is something which takes place in the space between, in the first instance, the mother and the baby. In the context of counselling, it is located in the 'overlap of two areas of playing'. As Buber stresses time and again, dialogue is an event in the sphere of the 'between'. If the counsellor cannot establish with the counsellee a potential space where they can creatively explore the latter's psychic conflict, no healing is possible.

Winnicott also draws attention to the central place in play for the element of *surprise*.[51] If a child knows exactly what is going to happen at every stage of the game, the joy of play is lost. Similarly, in the therapeutic context it is the moments when the client surprises himself that are the significant ones.

> My description amounts to a plea to every therapist to allow for the
> patient's capacity to play, that is, to be creative in the analytic work.
> The patient's creativity can be only too easily stolen by a therapist
> who knows too much. It does not really matter, of course, how much
> the therapist knows provided he can hide this knowledge, or refrain
> from advertising what he knows.[52]

For Winnicott, then, it is not the insightful interpretations of the
therapist which are turning points in the healing process, but rather the
creative connections, the surprising insights, which come to the client.
With this in mind, it is interesting to review the way in which Tamar
Kron chose to expose the student's arrogant self. In reading the report of
the case, one is immediately struck by the bluntness of Kron's approach.
She simply says, 'But you know, actually you are arrogant and
presumptuous.' He feels like she has 'sent a missile' at him. In this case,
it seemed to work; it led to a very significant dream related to the
disclaimed self. The danger, of course, is that such a direct approach can
create so much anxiety that the client begins a blocking strategy. He then
moves further away from a recognition of the self he has disowned. It
seems to me that Winnicott's guiding principle that the counsellor create
the space in which the person comes to his own insights is to be preferred.
Sensing the possibility of a disclaimed self, the counsellor seeks for ways
to lead the counsellee to the point where he can acknowledge it. It may
be, for example, that in playing with the idea of a community of selves
(Mair's strategy) the counsellee discovers a self that he has split-off. Mair's
suggestion that a framework from politics, business, sports or the arts be
used is an important factor in the process. In looking at his inner
dynamics from a different perspective, the counsellee may be helped to
recognise a polarity that he has been blocking out. The new frame for his
self-examination may provide the key in breaking through some of his
defences.

A Biblical Game of Confirmation: God and Jonah

It seems to me that the two key insights offered by Winnicott, namely
that therapy is play and that the moments when the client surprises
herself are the really significant ones, are valuable guiding principles for
helping a person reclaim a disavowed self. Interestingly, there seems to
be a parallel with the way God is presented as working in the book of
Jonah. These two principles are in evidence, I suggest, in God's dialogue
with the prophet in the last scene of the novella.

    Why was Jonah so unwilling to carry out the Lord's commission to
go to Nineveh and call the citizens to repentance? James Limburg

outlines a series of proposed answers.[53] Josephus suggests that it was fear
that was behind Jonah's flight towards Tarshish. In the first century A.D.
book, *Lives of the Prophets*, the suggestion is made that if Jonah prophesied
against Nineveh and it was not destroyed, then Jonah would be made to
look like a false prophet. The ninth century A.D. *Pirke de Rabbi Eliezer*
offers the view that motivating Jonah's flight was a desire to protect Israel
and his own reputation. He suspected Nineveh might repent and God
would relent. Then the Lord would be angry with his Chosen People for
being so slow to repent and Jonah, who had announced impending doom
for Nineveh, would be seen as a lying prophet.

The answer to the question of why the flight becomes clear in the
dialogue between God and Jonah in chapter 4. H.W. Wolff describes this
interplay between the two as playful: 'The Creator of all things begins a
game with him, just as Wisdom, God's delight, plays a game before the
Creator on the inhabited globe... Just as in 1:17 God "appointed" the
great fish... so he now appoints a castor oil plant.'[54] The focus for this
playful dialogue is Jonah's anger. On the surface, it may seem that the
prophet is angry because he is distressed that God failed to honour the
demands of his own system of justice. Jonah upholds the ancient
tradition that sin must be punished; there should be no relenting on
God's part. Certainly a number of interpreters take this line.[55] I contend,
though, following Wolff, that the real concern is not theodicy but
Jonah's self-assertion.[56] The reason for the prophet's self-pity may be
described as follows.[57] Jonah subscribes to a view that when a message of
God is authentically received and faithfully proclaimed it is bound to be
fulfilled. The corollary is that if such a message is not fulfilled the
reputation of the prophet is destroyed. It is the fact that God, through his
act of mercy, has allowed him to fall into disrepute that causes Jonah to
be enraged.

Chapter 4 opens this way:

> But Jonah was greatly displeased and became angry. He prayed to the
> Lord, "O Lord, is this not what I said when I was still at home? That
> is why I was so quick to flee to Tarshish. I knew that you are a gracious
> and compassionate God, slow to anger and abounding in love, a God
> who relents from sending calamity. Now, O Lord, take away my life,
> for it is better for me to die than to live."

Jonah uses what appears to be a celebration of God's grace and mercy as
a reproach against God. In this way he seeks to cast the problem of his
anger in terms of theodicy. He is asking God to justify his decision to have
mercy on the merciless Ninevites. I suggest, however, that this is simply
a cover story. What Jonah is hiding from himself is his own egoism and

exaggerated self-concern. He avows an identity as an upholder of the ancient view of divine justice; he disavows his own egoism and self-pity.

God can see through the cover story, though. Reflecting Winnicott's insight that the significant moment in a therapeutic dialogue is when the client surprises himself, God does not directly confront Jonah over his self-deception. The Lord does not say, for instance, 'You think you can convince me that you are concerned about divine justice, but I can see that the real issue is your arrogance and egoism.' Instead he begins a game with the prophet. He asks, 'Have you any right to be angry?' (v.4). God begins to nudge Jonah towards self-examination.

Jonah, however, forcefully resists God's lead. He heads off to the east of the city and builds himself a shelter as he waits to see if there will be a reversal (v.5). Perhaps, he muses, the Ninevites will relapse into their old ways and God will punish them as they deserve. This wordless response constitutes a defiant reply. His self-concern and arrogance are displayed in the way he directs his focus away from God's question and onto the fate of the city.[58]

God continues his game as he provides a plant for shelter from the burning sun (v.6). When he sends a worm to eat it and a hot east wind to heighten the effects of the loss of shelter (vv.7-8), Jonah's cover story is all but in tatters. His death-wish says it all. Wolff comments:

> Earlier Jonah was indignant because Yahweh took pity on Nineveh. Now it is self-pity that incites his indignation. By showing Jonah as ready to die because there is no more shade, the satirist exposes the fact that his first expression of unwillingness was also *deeply rooted in self-pity, not in genuine concern about the validity of God's word and his justice* [emphasis added].[59]

God, meanwhile, is patient and continues to push the prophet to honest self-reflection. He asks, 'Do you have a right to be angry about the vine?' (v.9). God still has the hope that Jonah will re-claim the egoistic self he has isolated and is refusing to take responsibility for. In the end, Jonah fails to reach that point. We are left with God contrasting Jonah's compassion for the plant (here, as Wolff[60] observes, there is a note of irony) with his own compassion for the city (vv.10-11). Helping a person see what he desperately does not want to see is no easy task, not even for Almighty God!

Integration Through a Dialogue in the Community of the Self

Buber's understanding of confirmation extends beyond affirming the other in her uniqueness. He also sees the need to help her against herself as she grows into her potential. Confirmation begins with acceptance of a person as she is, and moves to helping her become the person she is potentially. In the context of counselling, there is a need to move from the recognition of the disfavoured selves in the society of the Self to a point of relative integration in the functioning of that society. A turning point for Betty came when she was able to own her serious self, but she still needed to learn how to utilise her capacity for thoughtful, profound reflection to deal with her over-eating, her sense of emptiness, and her experience of social isolation.

Buber suggests that in order to help the other achieve a higher level of personal integration, it is necessary to work with her to strengthen a polarity, and to change the relationship between the polarities. This points, I believe, to the need for an internal dialogue. In this second stage of the model of confirmation being developed here, I offer the view that a genuine internal dialogue works according to the same principles Buber develops for an interpersonal dialogue. As the selves within the community learn how to relate more constructively, the synthesising function of the Self facilitates a dialogue oriented around *inclusion, confirmation* and *responsibility*.

It is essential that the selves understand the needs, fears and hopes each of them have. This involves a bold swinging into the life of the particular self being considered. In *inclusion*, or 'imagining the real', there is an attempt to think and feel from the other side. This is precisely the process which is required in this internal dialogue. Let us take the case of John's 'Foreign Secretary'. What are his needs, his fears, his hopes? The Foreign Secretary has a need to be needed. Behind the readiness to provide his services to everyone he can is a need to be praised: 'John's such a good fellow; always ready to lend a helping hand'. His self-esteem is flagging; the affirmations that regularly come his way as a result of his helpfulness provide him with the boost he needs. What about his fears? He is clearly afraid of being alone. Is it the case that a frenzy of activity means that he never has to sit still long enough to think his own thoughts, face his own short-comings? Or is it simply the case that he is bored when he is by himself? Finally, we consider his hopes. He can see the distress his family is suffering; it hurts him to observe the resentment that is building up in them due to his neglect. He wants to cut down on his trips away in order to be fair to the members of his family and to enhance the quality of their life together.

Confirmation means valuing the uniqueness of the other person. It involves understanding the differences between oneself and the other through inclusion and then learning to appreciate those differences. The generic reason behind a disavowal of a sub-self is that it is considered to be unacceptable. Learning the way of confirmation is learning to appreciate the gifts such a self possesses. It will also have serious short-comings; but this must not lead to a failure to value its positive contribution to the society of the Self. With his vision of the Christian community as the Body of Christ, Paul is very aware of the important role played by the 'weaker' members. 'The eye', he writes, 'cannot say to the hand, "I don't need you!" On the contrary, those parts of the body that seem to be weaker are indispensable, and the parts that we think are less honourable we treat with special honour' (I Cor. 12:21-22). The Foreign Secretary is busy for all the wrong reasons. He neglects his family and causes them unnecessary distress. There are clearly areas he needs to grow in. However, he also possesses significant gifts. The Foreign Secretary has a generous spirit. Despite being motivated by a need to be needed, he nevertheless makes himself available to people when they require assistance. An abundant source of energy, a healthy vitality, are also assets. It is simply the case that the generosity and the vitality need to be channelled appropriately.

Responsibility means a willingness to allow the address of the other to penetrate one's defences and to act accordingly. It means the capacity to live in 'the receptive hour'. A word calling for a response has been spoken. What will one do with it? That is the crucial question guiding Buber's reflections on responsibility. What will the Foreign Secretary do with the 'motion' that has been put that all requests for outside assistance must go before the 'Cabinet'. He is being asked to give up his practice of unilateral decision-making. The positive changes in John's life came because he was able to respond to that call. Now, for the first time he could say 'no' when he was over-committed.

The final stage in the process of confirming a person in counselling is the facilitation of an inner dialogue. It will be of value, I am suggesting, to structure this dialogue between sub-selves around the principles of inclusion, confirmation and responsibility. It is not, of course, important or even desirable that the counsellor use these rubrics in her facilitation. What is essential is that she helps the counsellee to incorporate the dynamics described by the rubrics into his internal dialogue.

EGOISTIC INTROSPECTION OR GROWTH IN HOLINESS?

There may be some who consider that this focus on psychological wholeness is really an encouragement of self-centred introspection.

Instead of wasting time and energy on attempting to integrate disavowed selves, some will say, persons should be devoting themselves to serving others. Rather than joining in the rampant individualism plaguing our modern industrialised societies, we should broaden our interests to include the well-being of the local community and of the society as a whole. Of course we must devote ourselves to doing good to others. It goes without saying that we must have a communitarian commitment. I argue, though, that reclaiming the less attractive side of one's personality is also a moral imperative. To live as if these polarities do not exist is a dangerous self-deception. Dangerous because not only will one suffer from a fragmented, disordered psyche, but others will also suffer from the destructive outworking of that psyche. In some of the cases we have studied, the pain inflicted is relatively minor. For example, one may have to suffer Betty's boring, annoying 'entertainment'. Other cases, though, pointed to more serious harm. Untold damage is done in the church and in the world by 'good' people who are not nearly as good as they would like to think they are. Cut off from their tendencies to hate, power and control, they unleash their dark forces in subtle, covert ways. Others pay the price for their repression.

Growing in the way of Christ involves acknowledging and integrating the rejected members in the family of the Self in order that we may relate to others more constructively. This process takes effort and it requires courage and honesty. It is not something, fortunately, that we have to do in our own strength. In Romans chapters 7 and 8, Paul emphasises the need to rely on the resources of the Spirit in conforming oneself to Christ. Gerald Borchert, a scholar with an interest in both the New Testament and pastoral care, helpfully links integrating one's shadow side with Paul's exhortations in these chapters:

> Christians who seek to achieve holy living by depending upon their own resources - namely by living *kata sarka* - will discover again and again their helplessness. They may well perceive the way of God, as the Jews did through the law, but hope does not spring from the self-made person, even the self-made perceptive person! Indeed, the life which relies on its own resources - *kata sarka* - will suffer ruination (8:6). The alternative for the Christian is reliance on the Spirit - namely a life which is lived *kata pneuma*. Such a life is the life of faith about which Paul spoke earlier. It is, in psychological terms, the acceptance of the dark side of the human personality and the learning of how to live with it positively.[61]

These reflections by Borchert remind us of the importance of grounding all attempts at psychological transformation in the power of the Holy

Spirit. Further, they point to the link between the integration of the shadow side and sanctification. They tie in, I suggest, with the case of God and Jonah analysed above. God was attempting to help the prophet grow in holiness through confronting his tendency to self-assertion. Working towards integration within the community of the Self should be construed as part of the process of sanctification.

CONCLUSION

We began with a discussion of Hobson's notion of feeling-images. It was suggested that when a person relates on the level of feeling she encounters the polarities in her personhood. As Buber says, there is in a person a 'yes' and a 'no', acceptance and refusal. Feeling-images are bipolar.

That confirmation in the context of counselling means helping a person to reclaim disavowed selves was another important notion in our reflections. We attempted to develop a two-stage model for helping the counsellee deal with his inner polarities. The first stage involves assisting the counsellee reclaim disavowed selves. In the second stage, the counsellor facilitates a process of dialogue within the community of selves. This dialogue is shaped around inclusion, confirmation and responsibility.

Finally, it was argued that seeking to achieve integration within the Self, far from constituting self-centredness, is a moral imperative. To live as if disavowed polarities do not exist is dangerous. Dangerous because not only will one suffer from a fragmented, disordered psyche, but others will also suffer from the destructive outworking of that psyche.

1 See H. Fingarette, *Self-Deception* (London: Routledge & Kegan Paul, 1969); and idem, 'Alcoholism and Self-Deception', in M. Martin ed., *Self-Deception and Self-Understanding* (Lawrence, K.A.: The University Press of Kansas, 1985), pp. 52-67.
2 In order to avoid confusion, I will use a capital 'S' to distinguish between the personal entity which is a unity, the Self, and the various sub-personalities, selves.
3 In reflecting back on this case, I am aware that I would now choose to handle it somewhat differently. Certainly, I needed to confront his basic premise: 'If only the others in my family would change, life would be just fine.' However, in beginning to explore his psychological patterns, perhaps I scared him. Or perhaps I was signalling a task which seemed to him to be much too difficult, namely becoming more tolerant of messiness and disorder. It may have been better to raise the issue of his *interpretation* of his family situation. Michael's behaviour was unlikely to improve significantly. The home scene would always be more chaotic than he, Tom, would want it to be. If he wants to stay with the family and, also, to find an acceptable level of inner peace, he needs to reframe his situation, to change the meaning the

chaos in his domestic environment has for him. Whatever approach I took, I needed to make it plainer for Tom that the counselling process would require something *from him*. It could not simply be about me giving some good advice that would get the problem fixed. He may have still decided to discontinue counselling, but at least he would have been more in touch with both the reality of his situation and what counselling could realistically offer him.

4 See Hobson, *Forms of Feeling* (London: Tavistock Publications, 1985), p. 194.

5 Ibid., p. 19.

6 See ibid., p. 19.

7 Ibid., pp. 194-195.

8 See ibid., p. 89.

9 Ibid., p. 89.

10 Ibid., pp. 89-90.

11 See ibid., p. 90.

12 See ibid., pp. 3-8.

13 Ibid., p. 5.

14 See ibid., p. 23.

15 See ibid., p. 34.

16 Ibid., p. 81.

17 W. Brueggemann, 'Psalms and the Life of Faith: A Suggested Typology of Function', in D. Clines ed., *The Poetical Books* (Sheffield: Academic Press, 1995), pp. 35-66, p. 58.

18 See ibid., p. 40.

19 Ibid., p. 61.

20 See I. Yalom, *Love's Executioner and Other Tales of Psychotherapy* (London: Penguin Books, 1987), pp. 87-99.

21 Ibid., pp. 97-98.

22 Ibid., p. 98.

23 Ibid., pp. 98-99.

24 R. Quinn, 'Confronting Carl Rogers: A Developmental-Interactional Approach to Person-Centered Therapy', *Journal of Humanistic Psychology* 33, no. 1 (Winter 1993), pp. 6-23, p. 12.

25 T. Kron & M. Friedman, 'Problems of Confirmation in Psychotherapy', *Journal of Humanistic Psychology* 34, no. 1 (Winter 1994), pp. 66-83, p. 81.

26 Ibid., pp. 81-82.

27 The idea that a central aim of psychotherapy is the re-integration of isolated sub-selves is not novel. Jung highlighted the destructive consequences associated with disavowal of the shadow. The gentle, peace-loving person, for example, represses his tendency to hatred and aggression. Jung also pointed to the fact that males tend to disavow their female side, and vice versa. Psychological integration involves the reconciliation of opposites. 'The conscious mind is on top, the shadow underneath', writes Jung, 'and just as high always longs for low and hot for cold, so all consciousness, perhaps without being aware of it, seeks its unconscious opposite, lacking which it is doomed to stagnation, congestion, and ossification' ('The Problem of the Attitude-Type', in *Two Essays on Analytical Psychology*, Vol. 7 of *The Collected Works*, Bollingen Series XX, 2nd edit. [Princeton: Princeton University Press, 1977], p. 54). The idea is also found in the Gestalt therapy school. There is a recognition that persons have a tendency to reject parts of themselves which they consider unworthy. Acknowledgement of the disowned parts as a first step is advocated. This is followed by a facilitation of a process of integration into the Self (see M. Korb et al, *Gestalt Therapy: Practice and Theory*, 2nd edit [New York: Pergamon Press, 1989], p. 15). What is different in our analysis is, first, the linking of this process of repression to the concept of self-deception (Herbert Fingarette's contribution) and, second, the association of the lifting of the repression with Buber's notion of confirmation.

28 See Fingarette, *Self-Deception*, p. 39.

29 Ibid., p. 40.

106

30 See ibid., p. 43.

31 Ibid., p. 63.

32 See ibid., p. 74.

33 Ibid., p. 82.

34 Fingarette, 'Alcoholism and Self-Deception', p. 53.

35 See ibid., p. 54.

36 See D. Jones, 'Pervasive Self-Deception', *The Southern Journal of Philosophy* 27, no. 2 (1989), pp. 217-237.

37 See M. Hoskins & J. Loseho, 'Changing Metaphors of the Self: Implications for Counselling', *Journal of Counselling and Development* 74, no. 3 (Jan-Feb 1996), pp. 243-252.

38 See ibid., p. 243.

39 H. Kohut, *The Restoration of the Self* (New York: International Universities Press, 1977), p. 18.

40 See Kohut, 'Remarks About the Formation of the Self: Letter to a Student Regarding Some Principles of Psychoanalytic Research', in P. Orstein ed., *The Search for the Self*, vol. 2 (New York: International Universities Press, 1978), pp. 737-770, p. 757.

41 See Kohut, *The Restoration of the Self*, p. 171.

42 See H. Markus & P. Nurius, 'Possible Selves', *American Psychologist* 41, no. 9 (Sept. 1986), pp. 954-969.

43 Ibid., p. 954.

44 See J.M.M. Mair, 'The Community of Self', in D. Bannister ed., *New Perspectives in Personal Construct Theory* (London: Academic Press, 1977), pp. 125-149.

45 See ibid., p. 131ff.

46 Ibid., p. 132.

47 Social psychologists, Roy Baumeister and Dianne Tice, refer to four selves: the public self, the self-concept, the actual or behavioural self, and the ideal self (see their 'Four Selves, Two Motives, and a Substitution Process Self-Regulation Model', in R. Baumeister ed., *Public Self and Private Self* [New York: Springer-Verlage, 1986], pp. 63-74). The public self refers to how one is known and experienced by others. The self-concept differs from the public self because of secrecy and a tendency to present oneself in a distorted or falsified way. The actual self is defined by what one really thinks and what one really does. Finally, the ideal self is the person one aspires to be. The gap between the self-concept and both the actual and public selves, they point out, is partly due to self-deception (see op. cit., p. 66).

48 See D. Winnicott, *Playing and Reality* (London: Tavistock Publications, 1971), p. 41.

49 Ibid., p. 38.

50 See ibid., pp. 47, 52-53.

51 See ibid., p. 51.

52 Ibid., p. 57.

53 See J. Limburg, *Jonah* (London: SCM Press, 1993), pp. 42-43.

54 H. W. Wolff, *Obadiah and Jonah: A Commentary*, trans. by M. Kohl (Minneapolis: Augsburg Publishing House, 1986), p. 169.

55 R. B. Salters provides a convenient summary of such views. See his *Jonah and Lamentations* (Sheffield: Academic Press, 1994), pp. 56-57.

56 See Wolff, *Obadiah and Jonah*, p. 176.

57 See Salters, *Jonah*, pp. 59-60.

58 Cf. Wolff, *Obadiah and Jonah*, p. 169.

59 Ibid., p. 172.

60 See ibid., p. 173.

61 G. Borchert, 'Romans, Pastoral Counseling, and the Introspective Conscience of the West', *Review and Expositor* 83, no. 1 (1986), pp. 81-92, p. 87.

Chapter 5

PASTORAL CONFIRMATION II:
The Role of Conscience

Confirmation in a helping relationship involves moving with a person towards integration within the community of the Self. It also entails, it will be argued here, ethical challenge and stimulation of conscience. While Buber speaks generally about confirming the other as helping him 'against himself' to grow and develop as a person, in one place he sets confirmation in an explicitly moral context. We find this development in a lecture he delivered in the mid-fifties to a group of psychotherapists and psychiatrists.[1] In this address, Buber challenges the tendency amongst therapists to focus exclusively on neurotic guilt and to ignore real or 'existential' guilt. He argues that mental health professionals should be concerned about conscience and the demands it places on those in their care.

While a number of theorists in the pastoral care field have advocated a greater emphasis on ethics, very few have paid attention to the role of conscience.[2] Attention tends to be directed at establishing an effective method for use by pastoral counsellors in dealing with the various ethical issues which crop up in the counselling context. To be sure, the methodological aspect of moral guidance is an important issue; it needs further development. The burden of this chapter, however, is to demonstrate that attention to conscience and its demands should have a central place in pastoral counselling.

Buber argues that human beings have a responsibility to promote the health of the social 'order-of-being'. When a person injures the order-of-being, the result is an experience of ontic guilt. In the depths of conscience she experiences the pangs of that guilt. An appropriate response is what Buber calls *reconciliation*: action aimed at healing the wound that one has inflicted. In what follows, an attempt will be made to develop the link between responsibility and conscience. It will be argued that calling others to responsibility and moving with them towards reconciliation are key functions in pastoral care. An understanding of the difference between two different orders of responsibility, I will suggest, is important and helpful in this task. What we will call *first-order* responsibility refers to those responses which are commonly embraced, conventional responses in the family, in the church, and in society. Creativity and conscientiousness define *second-order* responsibility. Pastoral counsellors, I will argue, need to promote both as they each have a role to play.

The chapter will begin with a discussion of Buber's understanding of the relationship between guilt, conscience and confirmation. Since we are following Buber's lead into the area of the moral context of pastoral care, it will be necessary to contrast our approach with existing ones. The next task is the development of the important link between responsibility and conscience. Finally, we will focus on the practical issues of the stimulation of conscience and of encouraging reconciliation in the pastoral context.

THE ETHICAL DIMENSION IN CONFIRMATION

In an article in *The Journal of Pastoral Care* Kenneth Potts uses Buber's dialogical philosophy to interpret his marital therapy with a couple made known to us as Tom and Mary.[3] We will be particularly interested in the way Potts uses the concept of confirmation in his discussion.

He worked for some time with Mary in individual therapy before commencing conjoint work. At Mary's request, he continued with the individual sessions after the marital therapy had begun.

Tom suffers from chronic diabetes and requires regular dialysis treatment. As a result of his illness, he is sexually impotent. Mary sees in her husband a fear of intimacy and a concomitant tendency to be emotionally distant. She also indicates that he is dependent on her, expecting her to assume responsibility for tasks he could quite easily do himself. For example, she makes the arrangements for his dialysis.

In relation to herself, Mary describes the sense of fulfilment and the boost to self-esteem she receives through the caretaker role. This need to take on the care role has been with her all her life. As a child, she felt that her father had not really wanted her; he communicated to her that she was an 'after-thought'. In what seemed like a form of punishment to Mary, he was cold and distant. Her mother was busy with her paid employment and in taking care of her rather large family. 'In response to these dynamics', recounts Potts, 'Mary attempted to become not only assertively self-sufficient, but a caretaker of others as well. In such caretaking, she recalls she at least found acceptance and approval within her family and other social systems.'[4]

Mary felt that she was giving much and receiving only a little in return. Potts' work with her in individual therapy focused on her struggle over whether or not to continue in the marriage. He raised with her in this context the need to express the anger which had long been building up inside her. They agreed that if a sense of guilt over abandoning Tom in his time of need was her main reason for staying, continuing in the marriage would prove to be destructive for both of them in the long-term. Potts has this to say about Mary's unacknowledged anger:

> Though initially resistent [sic] to the depth of her pain and rage, especially its roots in her family of origin experience, Mary was eventually able to recognise these feelings and her related behaviours. This led to an awareness of the pervasiveness of her role as caregiver and the underlying attempt to gain acceptance and security in this role. Issues of self-worth, competency, and eventually meaning were all raised when this basic dynamic of Mary's personality was brought into question.[5]

It is in this context that Potts introduces the idea of confirmation:

> Though every dialogical relationship begins with acceptance, therapy also requires confirmation. Sometimes in helping a client to move toward her potential, the therapist is required to help a client "against herself." With Mary, this meant confronting her on the unacknowledged depth of her anger which shaded her perceptions of her relational life. I worked to convince her that she must first see clearly if she were to assess the potential for dialogue in her relationship with Tom.[6]

Potts construes confirmation in his therapeutic relationship with Mary entirely in psychodynamic terms. I agree that it was important to challenge her concerning her unacknowledged anger. However, it is possible, and indeed necessary, I contend, to establish in this case the moral context of confirmation. In a marriage relationship (or in any close relationship) a fundamental ethical question is: What does my partner require of me for the promotion of his well-being? Put in terms of Buber's language of responsibility: What are the claims associated with his good that he makes on me and to which I must respond? The claim Tom makes on Mary is not one which he would recognise or articulate. What he needs for his own personal development, and what is required for the health of the marriage, is for him to take a greater responsibility for his care and for his life in general. Mary uses her caretaker role to establish her sense of worth. From a *psychological* point of view, as Potts observes, this is not healthy for her. Self-worth needs to grounded in being rather than in doing. In terms of the *ethical* requirements of the relationship, she needs to decide to do less for Tom and to encourage him to become more responsible. Confirmation here means challenging Mary in relation to what her husband, and their marriage, needs from her.

On the other hand, Mary's desire for and need of emotional intimacy constitutes a moral claim on Tom. He needs to be challenged over his tendency to withdraw into himself. (When Tom was referred to another counsellor for individual work, he was in fact confronted concerning the destructive effects of his propensity for isolation.[7]) Not only is this tendency psychologically unhealthy for him, it causes his wife a good deal of emotional pain. He has a moral responsibility to overcome the blocks to intimacy.

Though, to my knowledge, it has not been recognised in the literature on confirmation, Buber himself identifies - at least implicitly - a moral dimension in confirming the other.[8] In his article on guilt and guilt feelings, he comments on the case of an acquaintance made known to us as Melanie.[9] She was a woman

> of more intellectual than truly spiritual gifts, with a scientific education, but without the capacity for independent mastery of her knowledge. Melanie possessed a remarkable talent for good comradeship which expressed itself, at least from her side, in more or less erotically tinged friendships that left unsatisfied her more impetuous than passionate need for love. She made the acquaintance of a man who was on the point of marriage with another, strikingly ugly, but remarkable woman. Melanie succeeded without difficulty in breaking up the engagement and marrying the man. Her rival tried to kill herself. Melanie soon afterwards accused her, certainly unjustly, of feigning her attempt at suicide. After a few years Melanie herself was supplanted by another woman. Soon afterwards she fell ill with a neurosis linked with disturbances of the vision. To friends who took her in at the time, she confessed her guilt without glossing over the fact that it had arisen not out of passion, but out of a fixed will.[10]

Melanie subsequently went to see a psychoanalyst. He set out to free her from her feelings of guilt. He affirmed in her a 'genius of friendship', and suggested that here she would find her due compensation. Melanie, Buber tells us, involved herself in a rich and active social life. Here she established bonds of friendship. In contrast, her attitude towards her clients in her professional welfare work was instrumental rather than personal. She viewed her clients, Buber comments, 'not as persons needing her understanding and even her consolation, but as objects to be seen through and directed by her'.[11] The therapy was a 'success'. 'The guilt feelings were no longer in evidence; the apparatus that had been installed in place of the paining and admonishing heart functioned in model fashion.'[12] Buber, however, identifies a high cost for Melanie in failing to work through her existential guilt:

> With the silencing of the guilt feeling there disappeared for Melanie the possibility of reconciliation through a newly won genuine relationship to her environment in which her best qualities could at the same time unfold. The price paid for the annihilation of the sting was the final annihilation of *the chance to become the being that this created person was destined to become through her highest disposition* [emphasis added].[13]

Though he does not use the word 'confirmation' in this statement, it is clear that Buber is referring to the concept. We saw in chapter 2 that in his discussion with Rogers over the difference between confirmation and acceptance he refers to helping a person grow into the person he was created to become.

> Confirmation means first of all, accepting the whole potentiality of the other and making even a decisive difference in his potentiality, and of course we can be mistaken again and again in this, but it's just a chance between human beings. I can recognise in him, know in him, more or less, the person he has been (I can say it only in this word) *created* to become. In the simple factual language, we do not find the term for it because we don't find in it the term, the concept *being meant to become* [emphasis in the original].[14]

The contention that Buber is talking about confirmation in this discussion on working through real guilt receives added support when his comment immediately following his presentation of Melanie's case is taken into account. He argues that the psychotherapist needs to be concerned to help 'the essence' of his client thrive. He defines 'essence' as 'that for which a person is peculiarly intended, what he is called to become'.[15] In these statements, we see very clearly Buber's characteristic language for confirmation. Confirmation, we may say, needs to be referred to helping a person deal appropriately with her guilt and the associated pangs of conscience. We now turn our attention to the way in which Buber develops the links between real guilt, conscience and reconciliation with the order-of-being.

EXISTENTIAL GUILT, CONSCIENCE AND RECONCILIATION

In the article we have been referring to, Buber is concerned to point out to psychotherapists and psychoanalysts that they need to pay attention not only to neurotic guilt but also to real guilt. This latter form of guilt does exist and is 'fundamentally different from all the anxiety-induced bugbears that are generated in the cavern of the unconscious'.[16] There are normative principles which define the nature of right relations in the world. When a person acts against these principles harm is caused to others. In this case, the guilt one experiences has an ontic character; it cannot be reduced to the level of 'anxiety-induced bugbears' associated with trespass against parental and societal taboos. This genuine experience of guilt Buber refers to as *existential*, and the structure of being created through human relationships he calls *the human order-of-being*. When there is injury to the order-of-being, one is obligated to attempt healing.

> Each man stands in an objective relationship to others; the totality of this relationship constitutes his life as one that factually participates in the being of the world. It is this relationship, in fact, that first makes it at all possible for him to expand his environment (*Umwelt*) into a world (*Welt*). It is his share in the human order of being, the share for which he bears responsibility. An objective relationship in which two men stand to one another can rise, by means of the existential participation of the two, to a personal relation; it can be merely tolerated; it can be neglected; it can be injured. Injuring a relationship means that at this place the human order of being is injured. No one other than he who inflicted the wound can heal it.[17]

We note here the link between responsibility and existential guilt. Each person is called to answer the claim on him or her to promote the good of the order-of-being. The morally good person, far from neglecting or simply doing the minimum in personal relations, will act to bring richness, depth and vitality to them. The person of good character will avoid doing harm in the interpersonal and social spheres and will seek to make a positive contribution. When there is injury to the order-of-being, however, the appropriate response is to bring healing and renewal.

The therapist, observes Buber, cannot teach her client the way of responsibility, healing and reconciliation.[18] This is the task of the religious leader. She can, nonetheless, lead her client to the point where he catches a glimpse of the vision.

Buber notes that there are three spheres in which existential guilt is an important consideration.[19] The first is the justice system sponsored by the State. The third sphere, the 'highest', is that of faith. It is the middle sphere, however, which is relevant to psychotherapy. In between the judicial system and the realm of faith is the individual and her *conscience*. There is, of course, an overlap between the second and third spheres. Conscience is also a very important theological concept. 'For the sincere man of faith, the two spheres are so referred to each other in the practice of his life, and most especially when he has gone through existential guilt, that he cannot entrust himself exclusively to either of them.'[20] Buber, though, confines himself to the natural dimension of conscience (below we will explore the theological context).

Conscience is defined by Buber as 'the capacity and tendency of man radically to distinguish between those of his past and future actions which should be approved and those which should be disapproved'.[21] It refers not only to deeds but also to omissions, not only to decisions but to failures to decide. Buber is well aware of the destructive potential in an overweening conscience. A person may tyrannise herself through attempting to live with unrealistic or distorted ideals. There is a 'vulgar' conscience which torments and harasses but which cannot lead a person to 'the ground and abyss of guilt'.[22] What is required is a 'greater' conscience which moves a person to the point where she can take responsibility for her relationship to the order-of-being and to her own being. This higher form of conscience is not, however, only for the spiritual elite. Any person, contends Buber, with the vision and courage to transcend the lower conscience can achieve this level of personal authenticity and moral sensitivity.

The dynamics associated with conscience can be described with reference to three events: *self-illumination, perseverance,* and *reconciliation.* We have already mentioned the last of these three events; it refers to the call on a person to heal the wound he has caused in the order-of-being. Reconciliation is the attempt 'to restore the order-of-being injured by him through the relation of an active devotion to the world—for the wounds of the order-of-being can be healed in infinitely many other places than those at which they were inflicted'.[23]

It may be that a person recognises his moral failure, but it is only through illumination that he grasps the essence of his existential guilt and its meaning for his life. This movement of conscience can only take place in 'the abyss of I-with-me'.[24] Self-illumination refers to a profound moment of silence in the inner spaces in which the only sound is that of honesty and truth. It is

> not even a monologue, much less a real conversation between an 'ego' and a 'superego': all speech is exhausted, what takes place here is the mute shudder of self-being. But without this powerful wave of light which illuminates the abyss of mortality, the legal confession of guilt remains without substance in the inner life of the guilty man, no matter how weighty its consequences may be, and the religious confession is only a pathetic prattle that no one hears.[25]

The key concepts are self-illumination and reconciliation. Perseverance simply indicates the need for an on-going commitment to illumination. Even though one may have become stronger in moral character, there is a need to maintain an awareness of the identity of the new person with the old. Where such awareness is lacking, a person may become closed-off to the guilt of the present moment.

Buber concludes his reflection with the observation that there is an 'inner resistance' to illumination in modern humanity. He uses two characters from classic literature to illustrate his conviction, namely Nikolai Starogin in Dostoevski's novel *The Possessed*, and Joseph K in Kafka's *The Trial*.[26]

In a chapter which was later omitted from the book, Dostoevski describes a scene in which Stavrogin goes to a priest with the intention of confessing a shameful act, the rape of a young girl. This, however, was only a 'confession in words'. Stavrogin, comments Buber, 'lacks the small light of humility that alone can illuminate the abyss of the guilty self in broad waves'.[27] The feelings this feeble, pathetic character has are too weak and too shallow for genuine confession. He attempts to snatch in a moment the authentic existence which could only come through long, hard and painful work.

Joseph K, suggests Buber, fits even more closely with the modern ethos. He stands before the court convinced that he is completely without guilt. This character functions as a symbol of a generation for which 'no real guilt exists; only guilt-feeling and guilt convention'.[28]

The inner resistance to illumination may not be in general as strong as it is with these two characters. Nevertheless, it is true that for a whole range of reasons - the establishment of a therapeutic culture being prime amongst them - the modern person has a tendency to ignore, rationalise and minimise his guilt. The church has, of course, been significantly influenced by the contemporary cultural ethos. In my view, illumination and reconciliation are of crucial importance in the moral context of pastoral care. Too little attention has been given to stimulation of conscience in discussions of the relationship between counselling and ethics. The reasons for this neglect are not hard to find. One can point, for example, to a fear of moralising and judgmentalism. Then there is the fact that many have had negative experiences of an overweening conscience. These concerns are legitimate, but, as we will see, they can be adequately addressed. Most theorists in pastoral care concerned with the moral dimension, however, seem not to agree with this judgement. They are wary to the point that conscience is not even mentioned. They prefer to concentrate on questions of method in ethical decision-making.

TWO APPROACHES TO ESTABLISHING THE MORAL CONTEXT OF PASTORAL CARE: METHOD AND CONSCIENCE

We will discuss briefly the work of three theorists who have endeavoured to provide us with an effective methodology for working through ethical issues in pastoral counselling, namely Don Browning, James Poling and Donald Capps. John Hoffman and Alastair Campbell are representative of an alternative approach. A look at their reflections will help us as we begin to think about the role of conscience in pastoral work.

The most eloquent and persistent advocate for a renewal of a concern with ethical issues in pastoral care is Don Browning. In his early work, *The Moral Context of Care*,[29] Browning argues that care should not be confined to the embodiment of love, forgiveness and grace, but should also involve a practical moral inquiry into the normative shape of the various expressions of everyday life. Pastoral counselling is more than simply assisting persons in coping with various interpersonal, existential and developmental crises. It also involves providing a person with 'a structure, a character, an identity, a religiocultural value system out of which to live'.[30]

In order to develop this model of care, Browning retrieves the Hebrew images of the sage, the scribe, and the Pharisee. He relies on Max Weber's interpretation of ancient Judaism.[31] Ancient Judaism was a distinctively ethical type of religion. Human action was understood to have a vital role in transforming the world. The priest, the wise man, and the scribe, each in their different ways, were directors of the soul. Their 'cure of souls' was oriented to the *torah*.

The Levitical priests, for example, led in a cultic activity aimed at addressing breeches of the covenant law. The cultus worked to both inculcate and explate a sense of guilt. In a sense, the Levites exercised a rational, educational role. In post-exilic times, the expositors of the covenant law operated in a context further and further removed from the cultus. The group of *torah* experts formed in this time passed on a tradition shared in by the scribes and the Pharisees. In contrast with the magical and mystical techniques characterising the priestly activity in other religions, these mediators of the covenant law relied on practical rationality. They used a casuistic approach to the law in order to help others deal with the guilt, anxiety and need for forgiveness associated with everyday life. Browning identifies these scribes and Pharisees as 'practitioners of pastoral care par excellence'.[32]

Jesus, observes Browning, continues in this tradition but also transcends it. He was neither a legalist nor an antilegalist, but rather a 'supra-legalist'.[33] He showed a creative genius in being able to idealise certain aspects of the tradition, while simplifying or casting off other aspects. While a legalist is confined by the letter of the law, a supra-legalist such as Jesus is able to identify its inner meaning, its deeper objective.

A church which is in touch with these roots - the practical moral rationality of the *torah* experts and the supra-legalism of Jesus - will have a vision of itself as a 'centre for moral discourse'.[34] Whereas the task of religion is to construct a world of meaning, the specific task of the church is to construct an ethical world. The theological and ethical perspectives generated on issues such as work, sex, marriage and family life, child rearing, and ageing form the context for the ministry of care.

Given that one accepts that there is an important place for 'practical moral rationality' in the life of the church in general and in the practice of care in particular, the question that quickly comes to mind is: How do we go about the task of practical moral inquiry? That is, if one is persuaded by the argument in *The Moral Context* one will soon be asking the methodological question. Browning does not, as it turns out, leave us stranded. In his later work, he sets about working up just such a methodology. Five levels of practical moral rationality are identified: the metaphorical or visional, the obligational, the tendency-need, the environmental-social, and the rule-role.[35]

The symbolic or metaphorical level of human experience is of prime importance in the religious life. We do not know the ultimate dimension of experience directly; metaphors are the means of constructing our thought about this ultimate horizon. The particular metaphors we appropriate determine our fundamental vision of the universe. Browning, following Reinhold Niebuhr, identifies the vision of God as Creator, Governor, and Redeemer as fundamental in Christianity. It is these metaphors which shape our vision of the way we should think and act in the world.

Theological metaphors, however, cannot fully determine our moral thinking. The idea of the governance of God, for example, cannot in itself fund a position on abortion, on homosexuality, or on industrial relations. The obligational level is the most overtly moral dimension of the five. It is here that those carrying out practical theological inquiry will make use of deontological, utilitarian or narrativist moral systems. For example, as Browning suggests, one may look to John Rawls' principle of impartiality or justice as fairness (representing a deontological approach). This principle may be integrated with fundamental Christian notions of love and justice.

The difficulty in using 'impartiality' to interpret the Christian vision of love and justice is that impartiality is an abstract concept. Thus, argues Browning, it needs to be supplemented by a generic theory of human nature. Once we are able to establish the various tendencies and needs humans actually have, it is possible in situations of conflict or scarcity to use the principle of impartiality to effect an arbitration.

The social-environmental level introduces into our thinking the vital role played by social systems and the ecology in moral decision-making. There are social-systemic and environmental constraints on the way moral goods should be ordered.

Finally, the rule-role level indicates the enactment of the principles established through the thinking defined by the previous four levels. The purpose of moral reasoning is to establish certain concrete rules which shape our living in the world.

While Browning's methodological construct has the advantage of being comprehensive, its disadvantage is its complexity. It seems to demand a level of intellectual rigour which most pastoral counsellors would not aspire to. A simpler method, also with five levels, has been proposed by James Poling.[36] The levels are as follows: context, decision, rules, norms and story.[37] Ethical interpretation in a pastoral context needs to begin with the counsellor gathering data on the background and history of the relevant personal and institutional relationships. Establishing the context for the ethical dilemma is of prime importance. 'We cannot afford a return to a kind of ethics that treats decisions without regard for the complex intra-psychic dynamics of individuals or for the sociological web within which people live.'[38]

While recognising the personal and social complexity associated with ethical reflection, the counsellor cannot allow herself to become paralysed. She needs to reach a point of decision. In making her best assessment of what constitutes the good in this particular situation, she has moved to a new level, namely that of rules (cf. Browning's fifth level).

Rules are both specific to a particular situation and universal in nature. They are 'guidelines which transcend any particular situation but which give concrete help in deciding normal decisions'.[39] Examples would be these: pre-marital sex is wrong; marriage is good; cheating is bad. Rules need to be very concrete and specific. There can, of course, be contradictions. Poling uses the case of a couple contemplating divorce.[40] The rule 'divorce is bad' may be in tension with the rule which indicates personal happiness and growth as goods. In this situation, one is forced to choose one rule over another. Here we are introduced to the level of norms. Norms are 'community property'.[41] To speak of private norms is to introduce a contradiction in terms. Values *are* internalised by individuals, but the salient fact is that these values represent the consensus view, the moral wisdom, of a particular community or culture.

In the pastoral context, the moral wisdom of the community has as its source the Christian story.[42] The counsellor needs to identify the metaphors and symbols in the biblical narratives which inform the issue under consideration (cf. Browning's first level, the 'visional'). She needs to exegete the relevant texts in order to establish a biblical and theological framework in which to situate her ethical reflection.

As one would expect and as is indicated above, we see some of Browning's themes repeated in Poling's model. Christian ethical thinking is necessarily concerned with a biblical and theological context and with norms and rules. However, most pastoral counsellors, I suggest, would be attracted by the simplicity of method and clarity of presentation in Poling's system.

Donald Capps takes a very different approach to these two theorists in an attempt to equip pastors methodologically for the task of ethical reflection.[43] He observes that parishioners frequently come for counsel with themes of personal fulfilment and self-actualisation running through their minds. As a consequence, they may have overlooked the moral dilemma underlying the psychological distress. With this is mind, Capps sets out to provide pastors with a *diagnostic tool* for use in working through moral disorientation.[44] His focus is not, as it is for Browning and Poling, on norms and rules but on particular *virtues* and on the *vices* which are correlated with them.

Capps works within an Eriksonian framework. In the early sixties, Erikson developed a schedule of virtues to correspond to his eight stages in the life cycle. The eight virtues are as follows: hope, will, purpose, competence, fidelity, love, care and wisdom. Capps attempts to correlate these psychosocial strengths with the traditional list of deadly sins. The common list, of course, has only seven sins. He takes up a very early list in which sloth was viewed in terms of two separate sins, namely indifference and melancholy.[45] The complete list, then, is this: gluttony, anger, greed, envy, pride, lust, indifference and melancholy. Capps works with Erikson's idea that while a given virtue (or in the original theory, crisis) can feature at any point in the life cycle, it nevertheless has a particular time of ascendancy. That is, at each stage in human development there is one virtue or crisis which is focal. With this idea before him, Capps assigns the vices as follows.[46] Gluttony, anger, greed and envy develop in childhood; pride emerges in adolescence; and lust, indifference and melancholy arise in adulthood.

In this way, Capps provides the pastoral counsellor with a set of matching vices and virtues to be used as a diagnostic aid. Having identified the particular vice gripping a person, the counsellor has at her disposal a knowledge of the virtue which has the power to break its deadly hold. The crucial issue of course, something which unfortunately Capps does not address, is how to help a person strengthen a virtue in herself. This is the question which has exercised the minds of virtue ethicists from Aristotle and Aquinas through to contemporary figures such as Stanley Hauerwas.[47]

Leaving aside some of the problems with the way some of the theorists go about their work, they are surely right to draw attention to the prime importance of method and diagnosis in moral guidance. The concern that I have, however, is that a category which is of prime importance in the moral life, namely conscience, has been almost entirely overlooked by the advocates of the 'ethics in pastoral care' school.

John Hoffman[48] is one, however, who is not guilty of this oversight. His primary concern is to describe how a 'non-moralistic morality' functions in the counselling relationship. He begins the task by differentiating between a positive and a negative conscience.[49] The former corresponds to the Freudian notion of the ego ideal.[50] Through this structure of the personality, values and ideals to which one aspires are identified and pursued. The contents of the ego ideal develop through a process of autonomous choice and desire. Superego contents, on the other hand, are introjects of parental and societal injunctions and taboos. A negative conscience, being an expression of the superego, is characterised by imposition and heteronomy; a positive conscience is associated with aspiration and autonomy.[51]

A non-moralistic morality, it goes without saying, is oriented to the positive conscience. Appropriate ethical challenge in counselling is focused on aspiration rather than condemnation. It is grounded in the conviction that 'the individual's right to be [is] prior to any moral achievement'.[52] What Hoffman seems to be pointing to in this phrase 'the right to be' (which he uses repeatedly and without definition) is that the dignity of a person is derived fundamentally from her status as a child of God and therefore someone created, sustained and redeemed by God in love, grace and mercy. He is right to assert that it is of prime importance to communicate to the counsellee that she is accepted not on the basis of any goodness she has achieved but rather simply because she is God's child.

Like Hoffman, Alastair Campbell identifies a positive conscience. He also begins by acknowledging both the destructive potential in a tyrannical conscience and the importance of Freud's discovery of the dynamics associated with it.[53] In light of this, he points to the value in Carl Rogers' advocacy of the quest for the true self. Rogers believed that we tend to be so dominated and controlled by the 'conditions of worth' imposed by parents and other authority figures that we live out of a 'self-concept' rather than out of the more authentic 'organismic self'. Through self-trust, self-acceptance and the exercise of autonomy, though, it is possible to find and establish the true self.

However, despite the fact that these two important psychotherapeutic thinkers had some very significant things to say about guilt and conscience, we must, Campbell rightly points out, go beyond their formulations.[54] On the one hand, Freud's gloomy picture of humanity as a seething cauldron of sexual and aggressive desires restrained only by societal prohibitions and injunctions leaves us without hope. While on the other hand, Rogers' overestimation of the place of autonomy and self-interpretation leads the individual to cut herself off from the potentially positive influence of others. Put differently, the interpretations of both Freud and Rogers lack the transcendent dimension which orients us to the lostness and alienation in the human condition (sin in the Christian tradition).

In moving the discussion forward, Campbell offers his vision of the positive conscience. We can use guilt to lead us into our possibilities. In this way guilt can prepare us for grace 'because it tells us what we might be, if only we will seek to break open the shell of our subjectivity'.[55]

The role of the person offering pastoral care becomes one of an *embodiment* of grace. The helper seeks to incarnate love and grace as he contributes to the other's growth into her potential. This interpretation of the healing dialogue is, I think, quite similar to Buber's. For Buber, as we have seen, confirmation involves helping the other reach for her God-given psychological, moral and spiritual potential.

In the discussion below, I will attempt to build on the insights offered by both Hoffman and Campbell. However, I will be adding a Buberian perspective. Like the other two thinkers, Buber is concerned with transcending a negative (or 'vulgar') conscience in order to critically examine one's relationship to one's own being. What is distinctive in his analysis is the way in which he links responsibility and conscience. Each person bears a responsibility for the health of the human order-of-being. In the life of dialogue, others address us with claims for love, care, trust, respect and justice. A failure to answer those claims results in a wounding of the human order. Before the inner tribunal of conscience, we are convicted of our guilt in this wounding. Following Buber's lead, I contend that calling the other to responsibility is a key to stimulating conscience. In developing this notion, it will be instructive to explore the ways in which certain moral theologians have endeavoured to connect responsibility and conscience.

RESPONSIBILITY AND CONSCIENCE

In his classic study entitled *The Responsible Self*, H. Richard Niebuhr, inspired by Buber, identified answerability as the key modality associated with responsibility: 'What is implicit in the idea of responsibility is the image of man-the-answerer, man engaged in dialogue, man acting in response to action upon him.'[56] Conscience viewed from a dialogical perspective refers to a person confronting in the inner spaces not a law or an ideal but other persons and their claims on her.[57] The reflective life of conscience is 'life in relation to companions; it is I-Thou, I-You existence. It is existence in response to action upon us'.[58] Here, notes Niebuhr, one is placing oneself in the company of those who adhere to a social theory of conscience. In this theory, the idea is projected of the self in its critical examination adopting the view of an 'impartial spectator' (Adam Smith) or a 'generalised other' (George Herbert Mead). This 'partner' in the inner dialogue represents the social group and its moral consensus. The point at which Niebuhr parts company with the advocates of a social theory of conscience, however, is precisely in relation to this abstraction from the social milieu in the form of a generalised other. For him, it is real, concrete individuals who speak the words which echo around the inner chamber of conscience.[59] This approach is reflected by the eminent Roman Catholic moral theologian, Bernard Häring, in his notion of a *reciprocity of consciences*.[60] The self-examination and self-awareness associated with conscience are only possible existentially through encounter with the other. 'The person comes to his or her identity and integrity only in the reciprocity of awareness and conscience. One knows about one's own unique self only through the experience of relationship between Thou and I, which leads to the experience of the We.'[61]

Neither Häring nor Niebuhr, however, would be prepared to accept this as the final statement on the dialogical nature of conscience. The latter rightly points out that the relation that a person in the act of self-examination has with significant others always involves a 'third reality'.[62] This third factor is on the one hand something personal, and on the other something transcendent. That is to say, the third always points beyond itself. Without this transcendent dimension, a social theory of conscience would be seriously flawed. It would necessarily suffer through relativism, tied as it would be to the limited vision of the contemporary social group. In the context of the Christian community, an encounter with other disciples is grounded in a third reality represented by the prophets and apostles.[63] They in turn point beyond themselves to Christ. In discovering that one can be responsible in the Church only as one responds to Jesus Christ, there is the discovery that he points beyond himself to the cause to which he is faithful, namely, the Father's creative, renewing and redemptive purposes in the world.

In a more recent attempt to establish the connection between responsibility and conscience, William Schweiker broadens the base of the analysis.[64] A responsible person, in Schweiker's view, is *accountable* for her decisions and actions (and for her failures to decide and to act), *answerable* to the claims of others with whom she shares life, and called to care for others through the *representative actions* required by her vocation.[65] These three dimensions - accountability, answerability and representative action - need to be integrated, he rightly points out, in an adequate ethical theory of responsibility.[66]

With this comprehensive understanding in mind, it can be said that to be responsible refers to a capacity to evaluate and to transform one's life in the light of the values one chooses to define one's moral identity. A responsible person asks, 'What are the values that I really care about in this life, in my life?' *Care* is one key term for Schweiker.[67] The other is *respect*.[68] We are called to view others as intrinsically worthy of respect. 'Respect is the recognition of and regard for what is other than the self and its projects.'[69] In critical self-examination, the goal is to align our fundamental moral option, what we really care about, with the demands of respect. This is central in the agapic life - the life of Christian love.

> The aim of moral self-criticism in Christian ethics is to make the source of human action, that is, what we care about, to be identical with the claim to respect the integrity of life perceived in others and ourselves. The responsible person or community is the one who cares about what ought to be respected. This is actually what Christian faith means by love; *agape* is the bestowal, the gift, of care based on the recognition of the goodness of what is.[70]

Schweiker defines self-criticism more precisely through what he calls *radical interpretation*. This penetrating form of self-interpretation is a 'hermeneutic of conscience' and is basic to an ethics of responsibility.[71]

> Radical interpretation is reflective, critical inquiry aimed at the question of what has constituted our lives in terms of what we care

about and what ought to guide our lives under the demand of respect for others. It is the form conscience takes in the lives of social, linguistic, self-interpreting agents. Such inquiry becomes 'radical' when it strikes at the root of who we are, our identity-conferring commitments, and the conceptual frameworks that we have used to understand ourselves and our world.[72]

This radical form of self-criticism has as its goal a closer imitation of the divine goodness. In a very real sense, God *is* responsibility. God is infinite love and care at work in the world God has called into being. Through the ongoing divine work of creation, sustenance and redemption, God defines responsibility. With this in mind, we may refer to radical interpretation as 'theocentric' conscience.[73]

STIMULATING CONSCIENCE IN PASTORAL CARE

Above we discussed the dialogical nature of conscience. In examining one's conscience, there is a sense in which, as Buber points out, one stands alone in 'the mute shudder of self being'. Ultimately, though, the moment of illumination is only possible because there is a dialogue with the consciences of others. There is a 'reciprocity of consciences' which begins with significant others and leads through the apostles and the prophets all the way back to God.

Challenging Others with the Demands of Respect

An important function in pastoral care, I contend, is a dialogical stimulation of conscience. Buber and Hoffman (and others) are right, let me say at the outset, to remind us of the destructive possibilities in an overweening conscience. A person can indeed fall under the tyranny of her own ideals. It is essential, as Hoffman points out, to promote a healthy attitude in which persons establish their right to be. That is, pastoral counsellors need to relate in such a way that their clients are encouraged to embrace the fact of their acceptance in and through grace prior to their moral achievements. Buber, however, reminds us that there is another end to the spectrum. There are those who are resistant to self-illumination, whose consciences are underdeveloped. A central aim in the moral life, as we saw above in discussing Schweiker's analysis, is to align what we care about in the ethical domain with the demands of respect for others. It is sometimes the case that there is too little respect shown and a failure to really care about it. When there is a resistance to illumination, pastoral care involves lighting up the dark spots. A basic way to stimulate conscience is to point up the effects the actions of a person has had on others. It is sometimes the case, sadly, that a person fails to recognise, or cannot allow himself to recognise, the deleterious consequences of his irresponsible, disrespectful actions. Calling a person to responsibility entails helping him become aware of the destructive effects of his words and deeds.

Ted, a man of about 70, was an elder and the treasurer in my former parish. He was a man of considerable influence in the parish, although he was not particularly well-liked on the whole. Ted could be aggressive and demeaning when a person disagreed with him or acted in a way which he considered inappropriate. Others were expected to fit in with his plans and expectations. If they did not, he usually reacted by bullying them through activating his fierce temper and unleashing a verbal barrage calculated to belittle and wound. In a special session of the Elders' Council aimed at working out some of our differences (his behaviour featuring high on the list), Ted failed to acknowledge his problem. He considered his angry outbursts to be entirely appropriate, an expression of 'righteous indignation'. Others needed to be called to account, and he was 'man' enough to do it. He explained that the besetting sin of the church was the tendency of everyone to be so 'nice' that the truth was never spoken.

On another occasion, there was an incident involving Ted and myself which sparked a very intense and, in the end, reasonably fruitful discussion. In the parish we had a pastoral care group. The members of the group provided practical expressions of care (delivering hot dinners after discharge from hospital and so on) and they engaged in pastoral conversation with those in need. I was asked by the leader of the group to give input at one of the regular meetings. I chose to conduct a workshop on basic communication skills. Ted was present at the meeting and obviously resented my choice of topic. I assumed he did not like what he perceived to be 'new-fangled' psychological approaches. During one of the exercises in which the participants were encouraged to make a response, Ted blurted out, totally out of context, 'What I really hate is half-smart upstarts half our age who think they know everything telling us what to do. We've got a lot of experience and we've forgotten more than they'll ever know.' Naturally I was shocked and thrown completely off balance. I did, however, manage to ignore the comment and continue with the rest of the session. As soon as it was finished, I lent over to Ted and said, 'We need to talk. I'll see you in my study in a few minutes.' Our conversation proceeded as follows.

NP: Ted, can you tell me exactly what was going on just now?
Ted: I don't understand. What do you mean?
NP: I mean your outrageous reference to me as a 'half-smart know-it-all'.

Ted: You've got it wrong. That was just a general reference.

NP: Oh, come on Ted. I'm not stupid. You obviously resented my approach and you wanted to let me know about it. Isn't that so?

Ted: Well, I hate all this modern psychology stuff.

NP: Okay, you hate it. So that gives you the right to make a personal attack on me?

Ted: You're too sensitive. You need to learn to take criticism on board.

NP: Constructive criticism is one thing. But do you really think your comments fit into that category?

Ted: Maybe I was a bit harsh.

NP: Yes, you were harsh. Let me tell you how your comments affected me. When you used terms such as 'half-smart' and 'know-it-all' I felt attacked and belittled. Your words were demeaning and they hurt. Now I feel alienated from you. I want to have a good relationship with you, but your aggressive behaviour is making that very difficult for me. And you know Ted, I'm not the only one who feels this way.

Ted: Yeah, I want to get on with you and with other people. I do have a problem with my temper. I have to do something about it. I'll have to count to ten when I get worked up.

We then proceeded to talk about how he might modify his aggressive behaviour. I was pleased to observe that in subsequent parish meetings Ted was restrained and co-operative. Predictably, though, the 'model' behaviour did not last. There were more personal attacks, and these were followed by more discussions. However, the fact that he was prepared to acknowledge his moral failure opened the way for some positive change in behaviour. Some months later, Ted acted characteristically and abused one of the other elders for what he saw as a major 'sin'. Mary had written a short article in the local newspaper advertising our upcoming dramatic presentation during the Easter Day service. Mention had been made of a member of the congregation who was a professional playwright. Obviously she thought a few details of his professional career would provoke some interest. Ted's next-door neighbour, however, was also providing some assistance. The fact that she was not mentioned constituted in his mind a major slap-in-the-face for his friend and neighbour. Mary was, of course, puzzled and very upset by Ted's attack. The next day, though, she was pleased to report that he had spoken to her again and apologised for his bad behaviour. The abuse was characteristic of Ted; the remorse and apology were not. He was at least making some progress, however limited, towards aligning what he cared about with the demands of respect for others.

Challenging Others with Second-Order Responsibility

Respect for others and their feelings, allowing others the freedom to hold a different opinion, refraining from angry, demeaning outbursts - these qualities are part of what defines basic responsibility. In the family, in the church, in the society there is a collection of core values on which there is a general consensus. On the whole, we value honesty and diligence in the workplace, love, care and respectful discipline in the home, and love of God and neighbour in the church. There is general agreement on what it is to be a responsible parent, employee, or Christian. As the Roman Catholic moral theologian, Anne Patrick, points out, many people consider that they are being responsible in passively assuming the role of the 'good homemaker', or the 'good Catholic' (or the 'good Christian').[74] This constitutes what might be called a *first-order responsibility*.[75] This is a form of responsibility which is characterised by *habit, convention*, and *security*. Faced with an ethical issue, a first-order response is shaped instinctively by the influence of attitudes and patterns of thought inherited from the family and church. The person acts responsibly but in a *conventional* manner. To observe that the response is habitual and conventional does not imply denigration. The fact that the person is concerned with the promotion of what is right and good is morally praiseworthy. What is lacking, however, is *initiative* and *creativity* in the process of ethical reflection. That is to say, there is no real attempt to stretch one's understanding of what constitutes responsibility in this particular situation. One simply acts, or rather *re*acts, in terms of the attitudes and ideas that one has inherited. It is safe, comfortable, to work within the limits defined by the consensus view in the family and in the church.

A *second-order* responsibility, on the other hand, is characterised by *conscientiousness, creativity*, and *risk*. In attempting to differentiate the two orders, it may be helpful to introduce a parallel with approaches commonly adopted by school students. There are those scholars who are responsible enough to do the work assigned to them and to exert a reasonable amount of effort in completing it. Some students, though, are more conscientious, more inclined to be creative in their studies. A student of the French language, for instance, explores the possibility of spending some time in a French-speaking country. In preparing a class presentation, to give another example, a lad goes beyond the standard 'talk-and-pictures' approach to a creative use of sight and sound technology.

A person guided by a second-order understanding of responsibility is not content to simply follow a conventional approach. She searches for a creative edge in her responses to the claims of others. Anne Patrick helpfully suggests that this involves being

> conscientious in preventing harm and promoting good through realistic appraisal of the likely consequences of our decisions, and it entails a willingness to act without absolute assurance of being right. Instead of relying entirely on others' formulas for behaviour, one does one's own interpreting of what is going on and one's own analysis of how to prevent or minimise harm and contribute to the betterment of life for oneself and one's neighbours.[76]

It would be wrong, however, to think that second-order responsibility is only available to the ethically elite. This is not an ethic which applies only to those rare individuals with a genius for personal relationships and/or social challenge. The call to be creative in responsible living is for every person of good will. To be sure, some people have a greater talent for seeing new possibilities *vis-à-vis* responsibility than others. Nonetheless, given the limits of their gifts and abilities, everyone should be prepared to stretch their understanding of what it means to be responsible.

Consider the following very ordinary situation. Within a particular family, the Brown family, there is a girl, Jane, who lacks social skills. Jane finds it very difficult to express herself and is deficient in the basic conversational skills appropriate to her age (she is 12). As a consequence, Jane is something of a loner, even in her own family. This particular day, the Brown family is out on a walk in the hills. Mr Brown observes that Jane, as is her tendency, is walking by herself and ignoring her three siblings. He is eager to help his daughter and so he takes her to one side. Quietly he says, 'Jane, you must mix in more with the others. I know you find it hard, but do make the effort.' Jane, however, fails to respond to her father's exhortation. Mr Brown thinks, 'Well, I did my best. You can lead a horse to water....' The father's concern and his attempt to help are commendable. He could have simply ignored the fact of his daughter's isolation. In describing his actions as an example of first-order responsibility, there is no desire to devalue or condemn his response. With a little thought and creativity, however, his desire to respond to his daughter's needs could have been converted into a more effective course of action. Mrs Brown, also concerned about the fact that Jane is not socialising, thinks beyond encouragement and comes up with a creative strategy. To the children she announces, 'On our walk today, we are going to do something a little different. I've got a fun activity in mind for us. I want you to pair up and tell your partner what you would like to be doing in ten years time and why. Then I want you to tell us what he or she said. Okay?' After an initial reluctance, the children, including

Jane, join in and quite enjoy it. Without this structure, Jane would not have extended herself to socialise.

There are deep theological reasons for a concern with second-order responsibility. Quite apart from the obvious fact that Christians should be motivated to find that course of action which is most likely to be effective in promoting the good of others, there should also be a concern to reflect in our lives the nature of God. God is the ultimate in creative love and care. John McIntyre expresses it well: 'Imagination is the medium of God's loving penetration into the world of the sinner.'[77] While they may be theologically correct, the classical dictums concerning creation - *creation ex nihilo*, *creatio per verbum*, and *creatio continua* - fail to convey any sense of God's imaginative artistry.[78] It is only as one is able to tune into God's artistic use of colour, fragrance, shape and proportion that one feels inspired by the full range of God's creative action. In the arresting smells and sounds, in the sunsets and snow landscapes, in the juxtaposition of reef and rainforest, of mountain and lake, one sees 'the expression of God in his own creation'.[79]

God's loving and imaginative penetration into our world is also seen in the doctrine of the Incarnation.[80] When the world failed to receive the prophets sent at the divine command, God found a bold and immensely innovative way to communicate God's love, mercy and justice. In the Word-among-us, the essence of God could be seen, heard, handled, and questioned. The being of God was in this way communicated at the uppermost limit of concreteness, clarity and reality.

God's imaginative love and care for us represents the limit case in creative responsibility (we are confronted once again with the infinite gap between the human and the divine). In keeping with a desire to imitate the divine goodness, each and every Christian, given the parameters established by gifts and abilities, should be concerned to extend the boundaries of her understanding of what constitutes the right and good response. In commenting on a hospital chaplaincy case study presented by John Hoffman,[81] I hope to further demonstrate this.

> Mrs B. was a thirty-nine-year-old divorcee, the mother of two young children and an advertising executive for a manufacturing company. To the patient, her occupation represented many positive values. She strongly identified with her father and with the masculine role in general; she disliked women's groups. She enjoyed the aggressive nature of the position and the power it gave her. In addition, the financial rewards were appealing.

However, despite her valuing certain aspects of her work, her concern for honesty and integrity left her feeling uneasy about what she saw as the corruption in her industry.

Chaplain: Do you like your work?

Patient: A great deal of it.

Chaplain: You sound like you have some reservations.

Patient: Oh, I do. There is a lot of dirty work goes on in the fashion industry. It is not the glamorous field you might think from the outside. I don't like that aspect of it.

Chaplain: What do you mean exactly?

Patient: Well, we sell to the mills which make our gray goods, the plain gray cloth woven from our fibres; these people sell to the printers who in turn sell to the clothing manufacturers. Our company helps each of these with advertising, but each is cut-throat and out to get all they can, not caring who gets hurt. I tell you, when I get home from work at night, I just want to take a shower to wash it off me. I just loathe that aspect of it all.

'The patient later revealed', recalls Hoffman, 'that her father had been an advertising executive but had had to quit because he could not stand the immoral business practices which he encountered.'

Hoffman tells us that it is important to discern whether Mrs B's ethical concern is associated with a negative or a positive conscience.[82] That is, is it the case that she is disturbed by the corrupt business practices because she has simply taken over her father's value system and is acting out of a need to gain his respect? Or is it, more positively, that she has owned the values of honesty and fairness and that her struggle over what, if anything, she should do is characterised by autonomy and freedom? Hoffman reflects on these questions this way:

> Had I encouraged Mrs B. not to feel guilty on the grounds that her role was simply part of the tough business world, then providing that she had been afflicted by pressures from the negative conscience, she might have felt truly liberated. If, however, her strong moral convictions were another aspect of her father that she wholeheartedly admired, such counsel could have been experienced as an assault upon her father and her own self-esteem.[83]

While one fully appreciates the import of the difference between a negative and positive conscience, the relevance of the distinction is not obvious in this case. The simple fact of the matter is that Mrs B. is a party to business practices which are unethical and she has a guilty conscience about that. She identifies positively with her father and is challenged by the fact that he acted on his convictions and got out.

Assuming Mrs B. is a parishioner, how might one go about providing appropriate moral counsel? Obviously one could explore with her the possibility of looking for alternative employment. In the terms we are using, such a decision would represent first-order responsibility. She has the precedent set by her father to follow. To leave would be a conventional response. In asserting this, one is not overlooking the fact that it would also be costly. She values the challenges, status, and financial rewards attaching to her current position. A decision to leave would involve nobility and moral conviction on the one hand, and sacrifice and uncertainty on the other. One significant indication against leaving, however, is the fact that Christians need to be *in* the world (though not, according to the oft-quoted verse, *of* it). It is important that disciples of Christ find themselves in the world of business. Indeed, in every sphere of human activity Christians are to be salt, light, leaven in the midst. While it may be that there are other areas of the business world where the practices are less morally questionable, it is probably the case that the quest for a niche where one is free from any contaminating influence will be a vain one. Be that as it may, it could be argued that it is right there in the middle of the fashion industry that a Christian witness is most needed. Second-order responsibility would indicate, I believe, *engagement* rather than *withdrawal*. Mrs. B could be encouraged, for example, to ask herself how she might begin to work for change in her industry. She might consider inviting other like-minded individuals to join her in a small group to discuss ways of challenging the unethical practices in the industry. There may, in fact, already be avenues for directing grievances and concerns. That is, there may be an industry 'watch-dog' in place.

It may be that Mrs B. feels unable to take on the demands and stresses associated with the role of advocate for reform in business practices. The point is, however, that constructive engagement needs to be explored as an alternative to both passive collusion and total withdrawal.

RECONCILING THE DEMANDS OF CONSCIENCE

One's conscience, as Buber reminds us, can be stirred as a result of both sins of commission and of omission. A failure to decide or act (as would be the case if Mrs B. continues in involuntary collusion) is just as guilt-producing as positive wrong-doing. When one is convicted of one's guilt, the demands of both mental health and the moral order require an act of, in Buber's terms, reconciliation. The moral philosopher, Bernard Williams, refers to this act as 'response'. He groups it with the three other terms which constitute a theory of responsibility, namely cause, intention, and state.[84]

In an attempt to establish whether or not a person is responsible for an injurious situation, the most basic question is: Did his action either directly or indirectly cause the injury? If the answer is 'no', clearly there can be no question of responsibility.

Intention is also important; it indicates the seriousness and extent of the moral failure involved. Consider these two incidents in which a mother and a child are run down and killed by a car. In the first case, a man is lighting a cigarette while driving. The cigarette falls onto his lap causing him to swerve off the road where he collides with the woman and her infant. In the second incident, the man driving the car is the husband of the woman. She has just told him that she is leaving him to be with her lover. In a fit of rage, he directs his car towards her and the child. Both men are clearly responsible for the deaths; they caused them. However, the degree of moral failure was relatively slight in the first case (the tragic outcome coming as a result of 'moral bad luck'); in the second case, it was extremely high.

Finally, a theory of responsibility needs to incorporate the element of mental state. A person who at the time of an incident was out of touch with reality, either through a temporary form of insanity or as a result of a psychotic condition, cannot be held responsible.

In assessing the degree of criminality in a case, the courts take these factors into account. The response demanded by the State is, of course, the sentence handed down. What is important in the context of our discussion is the fact that the degree to which an individual feels the need to respond *personally* to meet the demands of her conscience is not correlated in the same way to these three elements. It means little to the person who acts unintentionally in a seriously injurious situation that the degree of moral failure can be adjudged to be only slight. Similarly, a person who has recovered a rational mental state takes little comfort in the knowledge that others do not hold her responsible for the damage done while she was not in control of her mental faculties. The very fact that others have suffered grievously as a consequence of one's actions, regardless of mitigating circumstances, produces in the person of conscience a strongly felt need and desire to in some way make amends. It may be, of course, that the result of the action precludes any meaningful *direct* restitution. The man who accidentally ran over the woman and her child can do next to nothing to lessen the pain the family is suffering. Even here, though, a degree of reconciliation with the structure of being is possible. 'The wounds of the order-of-being can be healed in infinitely many other places than those at which they were inflicted.' The driver could, for instance, write 'letters to the editor' recounting his experience and warning motorists of the dangers of engaging in potentially distracting activities while driving. Or he may choose to train in defensive driving and volunteer his services to help others learn the skills of safe motoring. Buber's concern was to point up for psychotherapists the contribution reconciliation makes to mental health. It seems that pastoral counsellors, who one would expect to have a stronger background in ethics than their secular counterparts, sometimes need the same instruction. The following case study is illustrative of this fact.[85] A returned soldier, John, killed five Korean soldiers in hand-to-hand combat and is suffering deeply under a weight of guilt. He goes to his pastor for help. The pastor, instead of helping him think in terms of reconciliation, is passive and evasive of the real issues plaguing John. We pick up on the conversation after the opening dialogue.

John: ...Reverend, can God forgive people?

Pastor: I think he can. What do you think about it?

John: I don't know. I thought so too, but that was before. Now I don't know - I don't know.

Pastor: You have some doubts about the forgiving nature of God? [John acknowledges that he does and proceeds to tell the story of the killing of the soldiers. The pastor responds with....]

Pastor: This has caused you some amount of worry since you have come back?

John: Yeah. You know how I've been with the church. I started out worrying more and more all the time. God is supposed to be able to forgive people, but this is sort of different. This isn't the same thing as when you preach up there on Sunday morning. You sort of get up and tell about these people. The little things - cheating at business, a heavy finger on the scale, or something like that - but this is different. This is big business; this is murder.

Pastor: The experience in the army is a very big thing to you in relation to some of the things we preach about?

John: Not so much the experience, but the killing. I just killed these men. I know, it might have been them or me. Maybe it would have been better if it had been me. I don't know. I've just been waiting, waiting for something to happen. I don't think God can just come out and forgive this kind of thing. I don't know. Just seems - I don't know.

Pastor: Things have been building up inside of you, and you have begun to question God's activity in this?

John: Yeah, I guess, sort of. Well, God - he's running the universe you might say. You just can't go around killing people right and left without being punished for it. God just doesn't sit there and let you stab people and let you get away with it. In our society, just like a man kills somebody, we kill him sometimes. This is almost the same thing. I mean, you take a life. You just don't go out and do this. You say, "Well, it's over with, it's part of the war"; but it's more than that. It's a man you killed. Just like if I killed somebody now, it's the same thing.

Pastor: Then you are wondering now how God can forgive one who has killed?

John: Yeah, that's about it. I don't know. I've been waiting; I've been hoping; I've even been praying. But I don't think he's forgiven me. He - I just keep worrying. Now I think I'm going to get punished; I don't know. But I think this is it; this is what's bothering me. I just keep waiting, looking every day. I wake up and I look out and I think, well, maybe today he'll punish me so I can go on living like I should. But he hasn't punished me. He just keeps me waiting.

Pastor: Waiting for punishment is a terrible threat.

John: Yes. You just don't kill somebody and get away with it. I mean, it's different; it's not like these little things. It is vital, vital to people. They got to live.

Pastor: In other words, killing is a rather large issue in the world today. More so than some of the other things, some of the smaller things you feel we talk about. This would make a very large problem; this would make one worry.

John: Well, killing is taking away life.

Pastor: Life seems important to you?

John: Yeah. I guess so. You can't live without life. Without life, what is there? I mean, I live; I got life. Why shouldn't the next guy have life? Why shouldn't he live the same way? You know - but I, I don't know. When you do something wrong, you have to pay. You just can't forget about it, cast it off, and don't worry about it. You have to pay, God makes everyone pay.

Pastor: You feel that somehow God must have punishment for the wrong deeds of man?

John feels the full burden of the awful responsibility for the killings. He is not helped at all by the idea, 'Well, it was part of war'. In terms of Williams' third category, *state*, John gives no indication that at the time of the actions he was not in full command of his mental faculties. However, while he acted rationally, he did not act in full freedom. It was not his choice to kill; as a soldier he felt compelled to do his duty. This is what is conveyed in the statement, 'It was part of war'. The knowledge that he was compelled to kill, however, does not help to lift the burden.

And, unfortunately, neither does the pastor's attempt at counsel. He is so intent on being reflective and non-directive that he fails to engage in any meaningful way with the profound issues his parishioner raises. John tells his minister that he is convinced that God will punish him for the horrible thing he has done, and that he is just waiting for it to happen. The pastor could have responded by acknowledging that while divine judgement is a reality, it is not to be understood in terms of direct action in the here-and-now. God is not waiting 'to get us' for our sins. He could also have reminded John that what Jesus' death and resurrection achieves for the faithful one is freedom from the power of sin and an end to condemnation. What John needed to hear, I believe, was an acknowledgement of his deeply felt need to 'pay' for what he has done, along with a firm and clear statement of the word of grace which says that because of what Christ has done there will be no act of divine retribution 'around the corner'. Responding to John's need to pay - in our terms, to seek reconciliation with the human order-of-being - the pastor could have explored ways of going about this with him. Paul Johnson's comments on the case are aimed in this direction; they are wise and insightful.

> Remorse is a trap of self-pity that needs to yield to full repentance to renounce the sin and have a change of heart that will reverse the direction of his life. No longer a victim of an unknown penalty that will destroy him, [John] may now decide to volunteer active deeds of penance and dedicate himself to reparation for acknowledged sins.
>
> Then, with the counselor, he could explore how to overcome evil with good, to save life more effectively because he has destroyed it. He might decide with his family to adopt a Korean war orphan, or to undertake more substantial support for the Christian mission in Korea, or in various specific ways to give his own life daily to God in unfaltering service.[86]

'To overcome evil with good, to save life more effectively because he has destroyed it.' This statement captures beautifully the idea of reconciliation, of placing one's hand in the wound in the order-of-being to heal it. If John had followed this path, there is no doubt that he would have experienced over time at least a partial release from the awful torment he was suffering.

One final comment may be required. In applying Buber's notion of reconciliation in the context of pastoral care, there may be a question in some people's minds concerning the theological significance of the concept. From a Reformed perspective, acts aimed at repairing damage to the order-of-being cannot contribute in any way to a person's salvation. A person is justified by grace through faith. The significance of reconciliation is not found in the realm of soteriology; but rather in the moral and the psychological spheres. On the one hand, an attempt to heal the wound inflicted in the order-of-being is a moral imperative. On the other, it contributes to psychological well-being.

CONCLUSION

Over the last twenty or so years there has been a renewal of interest in the relationship between pastoral care and ethics. As we have seen, most of that interest has been channelled into developing an adequate method for ethical decision-making. While acknowledging that method is crucial, we have argued that attention to the role of conscience is no less important.

We have tackled the issue from two directions. First, our argument has been that the stimulation of conscience can be achieved through calling a person to responsibility. Here, we found the notions of first- and second-order responsibility helpful. Responsibility can either be defined by habit and convention, or by conscientiousness and creativity. Every Christian, to the extent of her gifts and abilities, should be prepared to stretch her understanding of what, in any given situation, constitutes a good and right response.

Secondly, we sought to demonstrate the truth in Buber's contention that the demands of both morality and mental health are met through reconciliation with the order-of-being. Not only is it good and right that one should attempt to heal the wound one has inflicted, it is also essential for the cure of the soul.

1 See Buber, 'Guilt and Guilt Feelings', *Psychiatry* 20 (1957), pp. 114-129.

2 Perhaps the main reason for this is that the conscience has been associated so strongly with repression, neurotic guilt and anxiety. Gerald May believes that the repression of conscience in psychotherapy and pastoral counselling is a mirror image of the repression of sexuality in Victorian society. He argues that 'the time is ripe' to move 'out of an age of Spiritual Victorianism, a Victorianism of conscience' (see his 'The Fate of Conscience in Psychotherapy: A Synthesis and A Challenge', *Journal of Pastoral Counselling* 13 [Spring-Summer 1978], pp. 12-17, p. 12). Another theorist/practitioner who argues for a rediscovery of the role of conscience in pastoral counselling is John Hoffman (see his *Ethical Confrontation in Counselling* [Chicago: University of Chicago Press, 1979]). Like May, he is aware of the problem

of repression and neurotic guilt (the 'negative conscience'). There is also, however, as we shall see below, the 'positive conscience'. This, says Hoffman, is characterised by aspiration to ideals rather than submission to the internalised commands of oppressive authorities.

3 See K. Potts, 'Martin Buber's "Healing Dialogue" in Marital Therapy: A Case Study', *The Journal of Pastoral Care* 48, no. 4 (Winter 1994), pp. 325-338.

4 Ibid., p. 331.

5 Ibid., p. 335.

6 Ibid., p. 335.

7 See ibid., p. 336.

8 While he does not suggest that Buber himself thought of confirmation as a moral act, Maurice Friedman does identify the moral dimension in confirming the other. After referring to the obligation to encourage the other to respond to the demands associated with her existential guilt, he says that 'the paradox of guilt must be understood in the broader context of the problematic of confirmation' (*The Healing Dialogue in Psychotherapy* [New York: Jason Aronson, 1985], p. 168).

9 See Buber, 'Guilt and Guilt Feelings', p. 118.

10 Ibid., p. 118.

11 Ibid., p. 118.

12 Ibid., p. 118.

13 Ibid., p. 118.

14 Buber, *The Knowledge of Man*, p. 182.

15 'Guilt and Guilt Feelings', pp. 118-119.

16 Ibid., p. 119.

17 Ibid., p. 120.

18 See ibid., p. 120.

19 See ibid., p 120.

20 Ibid., pp. 128-129.

21 Ibid., p. 121.

22 Ibid., p. 121.

23 Ibid., p. 122.

24 Ibid., p. 123.

25 Ibid., p. 123.

26 See ibid., p. 123 ff.

27 Ibid., p. 126.

28 Ibid., p. 127.

29 D. Browning, *The Moral Context of Care* (Philadelphia: The Westminister Press, 1976).

30 Ibid., p. 103.

31 Ibid., pp. 45-47.

32 Ibid., p. 46.

33 Ibid., p. 49.

34 Ibid., p. 91.

35 See D. Browning, *Religious Ethics and Pastoral Care* (Philadelphia: Fortress Press, 1983), pp. 57-71; and idem, *A Fundamental Practical Theology: Descriptive and Strategic Proposals* (Minneapolis: Fortress Press, 1991), pp. 99-107.

36 See J. Poling, 'Ethical Reflection and Pastoral Care, Part II', *Pastoral Psychology* 32, no. 3 (Spring 1984), pp. 160-170.

37 In a more recent article entitled, 'An Ethical Framework for Pastoral Care', Poling includes a liberationist perspective. He observes that the abuse of power is often the primary cause of human suffering. Thus, he suggests, it is necessary to add in another level, namely 'Social Analysis of Oppression and Power'. See *The Journal of Pastoral Care* 42, no. 4 (Winter 1988), pp. 299, 306, p. 304.

38 Poling, 'Ethical Reflection', p. 162.

39 Ibid., p. 163.

40 See ibid., p. 164.

41 Ibid., p. 165.

42 See ibid., p. 167ff.

43 See D. Capps, *Life Cycle Theory and Pastoral Care* (Philadelphia: Fortress Press, 1983), chp. 2.

44 See ibid., p. 48.

45 See ibid., p. 37.

46 See ibid., p. 37.

47 In his theory of the inculcation of the virtues, Aristotle emphasises *phronesis* and *training* (see his *Nichomachean Ethics*

in *The Complete Works of Aristotle*, the Revised Oxford Translation, vol. 2, J. Barnes ed. [Princeton, Princeton University Press, 1984]). The person of virtue uses reason to order and tame the passions and appetites. Reason can never be the slave of passion. The moral life is fundamentally about excellent deliberation ordering the passions and so moving the moral agent towards attainment of the good. Moral excellence and practical wisdom are indissolubly linked together. The former establishes the right end for the human, and the latter indicates the means for achieving that end (see *NE* 1145a4-6).

Through the use of practical wisdom the moral agent is able to establish those passions and actions which over time are formative of character. It is in acting virtuously that a person eventually comes to possess this or that virtue (the idea of training). Just as a person becomes a lyre player by playing the lyre, one becomes just by doing just acts, brave by doing courageous acts, and so on (*NE* 12103a31-1103b1).

In a similar vein to his teacher, Aquinas refers to a virtuous disposition as a *habit*. 'The rational powers, proper to a man...are not determined to one act, but rather in themselves are poised before many. It is through habits that they are set towards acts...Human virtues, therefore, are habits' (*Summa Theologiae* I-II.55.1). His understanding of a habit, however, is different from our modern one. When he speaks of a virtue as a habit, he refers to a well-established disposition to act for the good. Every time a person acts virtuously, the disposition is more firmly established in her.

Key categories for the important contemporary theological ethicist, Stanley Hauerwas, in relation to the inculcation of virtue are *vision* and

community. We form our characters through growing into a right vision of self, of life, of the Christian way. The challenge is 'to become as we see' (*Vision and Virtue* [Notre Dame: University of Notre Dame Press, 1981], p. 46). The formation of character, further, needs a virtuous community to support it. 'Our capacity to be virtuous', writes Hauerwas, 'depends on the existence of communities which have been formed by narratives faithful to the character of reality' (*A Community of Character* [Notre Dame: University of Notre Dame Press, 1981), p. 116].

48 See J. Hoffman, *Ethical Confrontation in Counselling*.

49 See ibid., p. 56ff.

50 Of course, Freud's view of the ego ideal changed throughout his career. Hoffman acknowledges this. Given the context of our discussion, it is not necessary for us to follow with Hoffman the development in Freud's thought. It is enough for us to simply identify the key fact that aspiration is associated with the ego ideal.

51 See Hoffman, *Ethical Confrontation*, p. 90.

52 Ibid., p. 94.

53 See A. Campbell, *Rediscovering Pastoral Care*, 2nd ed. (London: Darton, Longman & Todd, 1986), pp. 66-68.

54 See ibid., p. 70.

55 Ibid., pp. 71-72.

56 H. Richard Niebuhr, *The Responsible Self* (New York: Harper & Row, 1963), p. 56.

57 See ibid., p. 70.

58 Ibid., p. 76.

59 See ibid., pp. 78-79.

60 See B. Häring, *Free and Faithful in Christ*, vol. 1 (Middlegreen, Slough: St. Paul Publications, 1978), p. 265ff.

61 Ibid., p. 266.

62 See ibid., p. 79ff.

63 See ibid., p. 88.

138

64 See W. Schweiker, *Responsibility and Christian Ethics* (Cambridge: Cambridge University Press, 1995), chp. 7.

65 See ibid., pp. 74-76.

66 I would want to argue, in line with Buber's teaching, that answerability is the primary category in an understanding of responsibility. In the life of dialogue, the other makes claims on my life with respect to love, care, trust, fidelity and justice. This is the fundamental ethical reality for *homo dialogicus*. The other categories Schweiker identifies — accountability and representative actions —are derivative from the notion of answerability. When I fail to respond rightly to the moral claims of others, I am accountable. My representative responsibility for others as parent, teacher, minister etc. is also to be interpreted in terms established by answerability. Those in my care make certain claims on me which I must faithfully and creatively fulfil. Answerability is primary; accountability and representative action are interpreted in terms of it.

67 See Schweiker, *Responsibility and Christian Ethics*, pp. 170-173.

68 See ibid., pp. 173-175.

69 Ibid., p. 173.

70 Ibid., p. 175.

71 See ibid., p. 175.

72 Ibid., p. 176.

73 See ibid., p. 179.

74 See A. Patrick, *Liberating Conscience: Feminist Explorations in Catholic Moral Theology* (London: SCM Press, 1996), p. 184.

75 Patrick refers to *passive responsibility*. I use here the more general term *first-order responsibility* because I am describing a form of responsibility which is characterised not just by passivity but by a range of factors.

76 Patrick, *Liberating Conscience*, p. 184.

77 J. McIntyre, *Faith, Theology and Imagination* (Edinburgh: The Handsel Press, 1987), p. 48.

78 Cf. McIntyre, op. cit., pp. 49-50.

79 Ibid., p. 51.

80 Cf. McIntyre, op. cit., pp. 53-55.

81 See *Ethical Confrontation in Counselling*, p. 91ff.

82 See Ibid., p. 93.

83 Ibid., p. 93.

84 See B. Williams, *Shame and Necessity* (Berkeley: University of California Press, 1993), p. 55.

85 See 'A Soldier's War Guilt', in N. Cryer and J. Vayhinger, *Casebook in Pastoral Counselling* (Nashville: Abingdon Press, 1962), pp. 267-272.

86 Ibid., pp. 271-272.

Part 2

SHAME AND DISTORTED PRESENCE IN PASTORAL CARE AND COUNSELLING

In our reflections up to this point, we have been attempting to show how in pastoral care and counselling, genuine presence contributes to healing and wholeness. We have approached wholeness in terms of both its psychological and its moral dimensions. What happens, though, when the person offering care manifests a defective form of presence? Theologian and ethicist, James McClendon, makes the very important observation that the 'primal defection from presence is found in the experience of shame'.[1] Shame is 'a failed wholeness'.[2] Presence and wholeness is only one side of the story. We need also to develop an understanding of the fall from presence and the experience of shame.

It is important to follow through on McClendon's insight (which he offers in passing) and identify the dynamics associated with a 'failed wholeness'. How exactly, we need to ask, are defective presence and shame related? When a person is on the receiving end of derogatory or dismissive treatment her dominant feelings may be inferiority and weakness, or they may be anger and indignation. How she reacts will depend on her level of self-esteem and self-confidence. A person who is assured of her self-worth tends to refer the problem to the other person rather than to herself. That is, she believes herself to be worthy of respectful, attentive treatment; the fact that she is not receiving it she takes as an indication of a failing in the other person and may angrily tell him so. To be sure, the dismissive treatment will probably cause her a moment of self-doubt. It is likely that she will wonder whether she really is boring, uninteresting, not worthy of attention. There will be slight shame feelings. The moment will quickly pass, however, because she is confident of her worth as a person. Her dominant feelings will be anger, indignation, and disappointment with the other person.

On the other hand, a person who is prone to shame tends to expect poor handling and sees it as in some way justified. Not only does she construe it as justified, she sees it as confirming her worst fears about herself. Inattention is received as an affirmation that she is boring and uninteresting. Derogatory comments are registered as confirmation of her inferiority and inadequacy. And so on. Her shame feelings are heightened through the defective presence of the other person.

Now what happens to the offending party in the first case where there is an expression of anger and/or disgruntlement? How does he react when he registers the displeasure of the other person? To the extent that he cares about the feelings of others and values wholesome relationships he will feel ashamed of his fall into distorted presence. Of course, if he is insensitive, boorish, he will simply react aggressively to the challenge.

Our interest in this book, however, is not on relationships in general, but on the helping relationship. With reference to the link between defective presence and shame, I want to develop an understanding of what happens when the person offering care falls from genuine presence. This 'fall' I will interpret in terms of the key categories we have been using thus far, namely availability and confirmation. Thus, distorted presence will be construed as *non-availability* and as *disconfirmation*. The focus will be on the shame reactions in *both the person offering help and in the person receiving it*. I will be aiming to show precisely how the distorted presence of a pastor or counsellor heightens shame feelings in persons already prone to those feelings. And I will analyse the shame reaction of the helping person when he becomes aware of his tendency to non-availability and/or disconfirmation. My argument will be that his shame has a potentially positive function, namely, the stimulation of his conscience and 'conversion' to genuine presence. That is to say, in attending to the call of his conscience, he has the opportunity to make the changes which will produce a higher capacity for presence.

The first step in the treatment of the issues outlined above will be to describe as comprehensively as possible the nature of the shame experience (chapter 6).

Next, I will attempt to develop the links between non-availability in the person offering help and the shame reaction he may experience on the one hand, and the heightened sense of shame in the person in his care on the other (chapter 7). I will begin by reflecting on the way in which 'constancy', Marcel's term for a pretence of presence, reinforces shame feelings in the counsellee. The fact that the counsellor will also feel shame when he catches himself acting a role rather than being genuinely present will also be highlighted. Also in chapter 7, the issue of what I will call 'technocracy' in counselling will be addressed. I will offer the idea that when the counsellor is more in love with the technical side of her craft than with her client, there will be a 'failed wholeness' in the relationship and a sense of shame. Finally in this chapter, the focus will shift to the parish context. I will attempt to describe the shame dynamic associated with the inevitable lapses in availability on the part of ministers offering care.

In chapter 8, I will analyse three disconfirming stances the counsellor may unwittingly fall into. I will refer to intrusion, derogation (borrowing from the psychotherapists, R. Meares and R. Hobson) and reductionism (my own category). Each has the effect of heightening the shame feelings in the counsellee. As in the preceding chapter, there will be a shift to the local community situation. I will explore the way in which a minister's failure to enter into the struggle that is confirmation may result in her experiencing a sense of shame.

The goal of the final chapter is to identify the positive function shame has in converting a pastor or counsellor to a more authentic way of being-with those he seeks to help. My argument will be that when a person in a caring vocation becomes aware of his tendency to a distorted way of being present the shame feelings he experiences may serve to stimulate a period of critical introspection. Spurred on by a new vision of himself in relationship, and empowered by the Holy Spirit, he is able to enhance his capacity for genuine presence.

Chapter 6
SHAME

Shame arises when the self evaluates itself as flawed, defective, inferior. One judges that one has fallen short of a cherished ideal. One perceives a gap between the self as it really is and a desired identity. As Silvan Tomkins so neatly expresses it, 'desire has outrun fulfillment'.[1] It is possible to feel shame about almost anything. One condemns oneself as socially awkward, clumsy, gauche. One feels dull, incompetent, ignorant. Cowardice and betrayal are especially potent sources of shame. One may be ashamed of one's appearance, height (or lack of it), weight, disability, or disfigurement. In the following chapters, we will consider yet another source of shame. An attempt will be made to identify counsellor attitudes and behaviours which have the potential to embarrass, belittle or, worse, humiliate. Our aim in this chapter is to lay the groundwork for that investigation by describing the experience of shame.

Shame is commonly viewed as an exclusively negative emotion. This is understandable, given its potential for high emotional toxicity.[2] Current research links shame to aggression, addictions, obsessions, pathological narcissism, depression and a number of other psychiatric disorders. Even when it is disassociated from mental pathology, it is seen as an emotion one must overcome. In a society in which self-confidence, assertiveness and free expression are cherished by many, shame will be commonly viewed as an unhealthy source of inhibition. It is important to recognise, though, that shame has a positive value. There is a healthy form of shame. Shame, for example, forms the psychological base for humility.[3] Occasional experiences of failure serve to mitigate arrogance and haughtiness. There is also the fact that shame offers an innate protection against depersonalisation and violation in a society in which privacy is increasingly not being respected.[4] Finally, shame is a source of moral motivation and protects our relationships with valued others. This last observation will be amplified in the discussion on moral shame below, and will feature in chapter 9. The negative features of shame will come into play in chapters 7 and 8 where we focus on the ways in which a distorted pastoral presence is potentially shaming.

In order to prepare ourselves for these explorations of the links between shame and distorted presence, it is necessary to describe the shame dynamic as fully as possible. This involves three tasks. The first is to generate an adequate phenomenology of shame. Defining characteristics such as exposure, incongruence, threat to trust, the global nature of shame, and hiddenness will be investigated.

Shame, moving now to the second task, has a near relative, guilt. Given the fact that a good deal of confusion arises on both an existential and a theoretical level as a result of the overlap between these two dysphoric affects, it is important to attempt to disentangle them.

The third task may be introduced with the observation that any excursion into the area of inter-subjectivity necessarily involves a moral dimension. The shame a pastor or counsellor feels when she becomes aware that her way of being-with in the counselling relationship has been defective, and therefore harmful, is of a particular kind. It is not situational embarrassment (e.g. slurping one's soup in a fine restaurant); nor is it the kind of shame that is associated with incompetence or lack of ability (e.g. one makes a mess of a business presentation). Rather, it is moral shame. The shame a person feels, on the other hand, when she suffers under the distorted presence of pastor or counsellor is not of a moral type. She has done no wrong. Rather, it is the case that her sense of self-worth is brought into question. She may feel more inadequate, more flawed. This is an experience of 'inferiority shame'. All of this points to the fact that there are various types of shame. Below we will acquaint ourselves with the members of *the shame family*.

These, then, are our tasks in mapping the territory of shame. We begin with a phenomenological description.

A PHENOMENOLOGY OF SHAME

Shame researchers emphasise a variety of concomitants and characteristics of the shame experience. However, there are five aspects that take us to the essence of the shame experience, namely, exposure, incongruence, threat to trust, involvement of the whole self, and hiddenness.

Exposure

Shame occurs when particularly sensitive and vulnerable aspects of the self are exposed.[5] Exposure may be to others, or to oneself, or to both. Shame is registered as a painful emotional jolt when aspects of one's self that are considered unworthy and inferior are suddenly opened to the disapproving gaze of others. One wants to disappear, to 'sink through the floor'.

This public exposure is so commonly observed and so vivid that it seems that the attention of some researchers has been drawn away from the private dimension. The fact that a shame reaction is sometimes a very personal affair is overlooked. David Ausubel, in line with the anthropologists Margaret Mead and Ruth Benedict, argues that shame always demands an audience, real or presumed.[6] Helen Merrell Lynd, however, rightly points out that 'exposure to oneself is at the heart of shame'.[7] The shame one feels in deceiving others into believing something about oneself that is untrue is particularly intense and painful. Consider this scenario. A prominent businessman and community leader who enjoys the respect of his family and of all who know him harbours a shameful secret, namely his attraction to child pornographic material. His wife and children think of him as caring, reliable, industrious and a good provider. His business acumen and community-mindedness earn him the admiration of colleagues. While he will no doubt feel shame over the unsavoury way he gains sexual titillation, perhaps he is most intensely shamed by the double life he leads. Even if he is never publicly exposed, shame will burn secretly within him.

The psychoanalytic scholar, Léon Wurmser, suggests that there are intimate links between shame and exposure on the one hand, and shame and perception on the other.[8] 'Moments of self-exposure' and 'acts of perception' play important roles in the shaping of identity. Seeing/being seen and hearing/being heard are the modalities which facilitate a comparison of one's self-concept with the concept others have of one. 'The modes of attentive, curious grasping and of expressing oneself in non-verbal as well as verbal *communication* are the arena where in love and hatred, in mastery and defeat our self is forged and moulded' [emphasis in the original].[9] When the interchange is defective, the core of the self-concept is disturbed and becomes shame-laden.

Incongruence

A shame reaction occurs when a person is suddenly aware that her behaviour is incongruous with, inappropriate to, the situation she is in.[10] It is not that she has done something wrong; no sin has been committed. Rather, there is a painful awareness of a gap between her actions and the expectations of the environment. The person is acting on the assumption that a particular behaviour is appropriate, but in a moment of painful awareness he discovers that the assumption was false. It is the experience of suddenly finding oneself out of tune with one's environment. To illustrate this, let me refer to an experience in my last parish. The committee of the Men's Breakfast group invited a local Roman Catholic man to speak at their next gathering. He was a very humorous man and he 'spiced up' his stories with 'colourful' language. I really enjoyed him.

But I seemed to be in the minority. The majority of the men were from strict evangelical backgrounds and were quite offended by his bad language. Looking at his audience, he was expecting to see happy, laughing faces, but instead he was greeted with frowns of disapproval. His face suddenly went quite red and he lost his poise.

Threat to Trust

Lynd observes that this sudden awareness that one is out of key with one's environment results in a threat to trust.[11] One is led to question one's own adequacy and/or the reliability of the values of the world of reality. In order to supplement the illustration above, I will use a familiar domestic scenario. It also depicts the link between misplaced confidence and shame. A child has laboured long and hard in the kitchen preparing a feast for her mother. Where the child sees a labour of love and a delectable offering, her mother sees only a very messy kitchen and a waste of ingredients. Instead of the expected smile of appreciation, the would-be chef receives a glare of anger and reproach. Lynd sums up the situation in relation to misplaced confidence nicely, 'The rejected gift, the joke or the phrase that does not come off, the misunderstood gesture, the falling short of our own ideals, the expectation of response violated - such experiences mean that we have trusted ourselves to a situation that is not there.'[12] The jolt of shame is triggered by this sudden awareness that what one thought could be relied on has betrayed the confidence one had in it.

Involvement of the Whole Self

Shame researchers consistently use the global aspect of the shame experience to differentiate it from its cousin, guilt. A person feels guilty over actions (or omissions) which have caused harm to others. Guilt can be localised in a certain aspect of the self, namely, that which is associated with a particular moral transgression. A person with a gambling problem, for example, may say, 'I am basically a good person. I just get carried away when I go down to the racetrack.' Shame, though, cannot be located in a discrete act which can be separated off from the self. The difference may be expressed this way: 'I am guilty of this bad act; but I *am* my shame.'

As Wurmser accurately observes, shame has a global quality because it is evoked by a discrepancy between a tested self and an ideal image.[13] This image is not simply constructed out of a delimited reality such as actions, but out of all the components which define a self. It is through shameful events that the self is revealed. Personal identity is shaped in this way. The shame events throw up the contours of one's selfhood and of the world of reality one inhabits. Guilt may be assuaged by confession or restitution, but the experience of shame may be transcended only by a re-shaping of identity.

Hiddenness

Given that shame is acutely painful and is associated with the exposure of sensitive and vulnerable aspects of the self, we would expect that there would be a tendency to block the feeling from conscious awareness. W.H. Auden, in reviewing Stendahl's *Diaries*, expressed surprise that the latter found it so difficult to admit certain facts to himself: 'How can admitting anything to oneself be daring?'[14] This comment indicates an ignorance of shame dynamics. Our first reaction to shameful realities about ourselves is to hide from them.

In her ground-breaking phenomenological study of shame, Helen Block Lewis observes two distinct ways in which patients repress shame. First, there is the defence of 'by-passing' shame feeling.[15] The shame events are recognised, but shame feelings are blocked from entering consciousness. This is achieved by what she calls a 'distancing' manoeuvre. The self views itself through the eyes of the other, but without much affect. That is, the shame affect is bypassed and replaced by an impassive viewing of the self from a variety of perspectives. For example, a patient may speculate, in a quite dispassionate way, about what the therapist is thinking about him at the moment.

The second form of hidden shame Lewis labels 'overt, undifferentiated shame'.[16] Some patients in Lewis' study who manifested a high level of shame affect were unable to identify their feeling state as shame. Rather, they used words such as 'depressed', 'tense', 'lousy', or 'blank' to describe their psychological state.

Clinicians have observed that the tendency in patients to hide the real situation is not quite as pronounced in relation to guilt as it is to shame. Guilt seems to have more dignity about it than shame. And yet both affects produce a sharp drop in self-esteem. They are closely related, and any study of shame must include a careful attempt to differentiate it from guilt.

SHAME AND GUILT

Shame and guilt both produce dysphoria and theoretically, phenomenologically and clinically share a considerable area of overlap.[17] Reference to an overlap only makes sense, however, in a moral context. It is in moral failure that guilt and shame become entangled with each other. There is no guilt associated with embarrassment, for example. One does not feel guilty because one has tripped over a shoe-lace at an inopportune moment. Nor does one feel guilty over a body-shape, *per se*, that is less than ideal. There is no guilt linked to the fact that one was born without the blessing of certain talents and abilities. It is, of course, true that a person may experience both guilt and shame in relation to body-shape and talent. A woman may be ashamed of her unattractive figure, and guilty because she knows that her failure to restrain calorific intake is causing considerable distress to her husband. A person may be ashamed of a relatively unskilled occupation because of its low social status, and guilty because he has wasted both his considerable talent and his parents' tuition fees through laziness. The shame in these instances has a non-moral association; the moral dimension is introduced through guilt. In fact, this split is too simple. Tied in with the guilt related to over-eating and idleness will be shame feelings. This indicates the way in which the two feeling states are intricately woven together. It remains true, nonetheless, that it is only in relation to moral issues that this entanglement occurs. The fact that one is disfigured, or overweight, or is embarrassed does not *in itself* produce guilt feelings; though there may be other factors related to these experiences that produce a feeling of guiltiness.

As we have already seen, shame researchers typically differentiate shame from guilt in terms of the global nature of the former affect. Shame is a painful experience which involves a focus on the whole self. In the face of the negatively evaluated experience, it is the whole self which is devalued. Lynd expresses it well: 'I cannot have done this. But I have done it and I cannot undo it, because this is I.'[18] Guilt, on the other hand, is focused on a specific behaviour, on a particular moral transgression. It can be assuaged by confession and restitution; shame, on the other hand, requires a transformation of the self. 'I feel guilty', one may say, 'but I *am* my shame.' Shame is consequently more painful and debilitating than guilt.

The clearest approach to distinguishing the global dimension of shame from the act-and-consequences orientation of guilt comes, I think, from Helen Block Lewis.[19] She observes that the ideation of being ashamed of oneself runs simultaneously with that of guilty self-reproach. In moral failures, guilt and shame get tangled up together. In observing the pain and hurt one's actions have caused the other, one feels guilt. One feels remorse and begins to think of ways to make amends. Linked to the awareness of the damage to the other caused by one's actions will be a questioning of self-worth. Ideas of shame operate in conjunction with the recognition of one's guilt. 'What sort of person am I to have done this bad thing?' one thinks. Lewis brings out these distinctions very clearly when she compares the self-reproaches involved in situations of guilty feelings with those in situations of shameful feelings:

[Guilt-laden cognitions run thus:] 'how could I have *done that*; what an injurious *thing* to have done; how I *hurt so-and-so*, what a moral lapse that *act* was; what will become of *that* or of *him*, now that I have neglected to *do it*, or injured *him*. How should I be *punished* or *make amends*? Mea culpa!' Simultaneously, ashamed ideation says: 'how could *I* have done that; what an *idiot I am* - how humiliating; what a *fool*, what an *uncontrolled person* - how mortifying; how unlike so-and-so, who does not do such things; how *awful and worthless I am*. Shame!' [emphasis in the original][20]

In early anthropological and psychoanalytic formulations, shame and guilt were differentiated on the basis of the former's relationship to *external* sanctions (the shaming of the group) and the latter's connection with *internal* sanctions (conscience).[21] The philosopher, Agnes Heller, rightly questions this distinction.[22] If by sanctions punishment is implied, then it does not hold. Experiences which evoke shame are often not punished at all. Even if the sanction is understood in terms of torment of the self rather than punishment, the conceptualisation is still flawed. It is possible to have a clear conscience and still feel the pain of mortification (cf. the guiltless shame experiences identified above). This line of reasoning leads Heller to argue that it is the *authority* rather than the sanction that is external. This authority, though, can be internalised. In which case one experiences a loss of honour. The internalisation of moral authority points to the important role exposure to the self plays in the experience of shame, as we have already seen. Hence, the internal/external dichotomy is not a totally accurate way of differentiating shame and guilt. Internalisation plays an important role in both affects. For some people, a shameful secret is more painful than public shaming.

A more promising way of differentiating the two feeling states is through a strong-weak dichotomy. Guilt presents as a more dignified emotion because there is a certain sense of power that is associated with injuring another person. There are now a significant number of empirical studies which support this conceptualisation.[23] During guilty states, experimental subjects reported feeling more active and having a greater sense of control than when being shamed. In the shame state, they described feelings of being inhibited, lacking in power, standing, and self-confidence. When shamed, they felt 'weak, shy, helpless, and injured in relationship with someone who was powerful, ridiculing, and hurtful'.[24] Under conditions of shame, subjects reported a feeling of being the focus of ridicule and humiliation. When feeling guilty, a drop in self-esteem was felt, but there was also the feeling of being the source of a similar blow to self-esteem in the other person. There seems to often be, then, a kind of pride, albeit a perverse one, associated with guilt. No such pride is connected with shame.

Despite the fact that shame and guilt can be clearly distinguished in this way, the two affects do share a number of features. Both produce a drop in self-esteem. Whether one has made a number of embarrassing mistakes in an important speech or told a straight-out lie which protects one's own interests but is injurious to another person, the effect is much the same: a fall in one's sense of worth. Related to this is the fact that both guide future behaviour by selecting out actions which produce dysphoria. And finally, both are associated with the internalisation of parental and social norms, rules and prohibitions.

It is worth pursuing the question of why shame and guilt share this sizeable area of overlap. Silvan Tomkins believes that he has an economical way of explaining the link, namely that guilt is simply a shame variant.[25] He argues that the shame affect is identical in those experiences in which one feels embarrassed or inadequate and in those in which one feels guilty. Hence, he contends, the word 'guilt' was invented to distinguish shame from guilt. Donald Nathanson, an influential interpreter and advocate of Tomkins' views, suggests that guilt is simply shame about a violation of a moral rule.[26]

This insistence that shame and guilt are the same affect is inevitable given the dictates of Tomkins' affect theory. The theory holds that all known emotional states can be explained in terms of just nine innate affects.[27] These affects are described in terms of a mild to intense rating as follows: interest-excitement and enjoyment-joy (the positive affects); surprise-startle (the reset affect); distress-anguish, fear-terror, shame-humiliation, 'dis-smell', disgust, and anger-rage (the negative affects). Tomkins' theory is brain- rather than mind-centred. The affects, he contends, are triggered by neural firings associated with particular programs in the sub-cortical area of the brain. It is the density of the neural firings which determines which particular affect will be triggered. A sudden increase in stimulation, for example, will result in a person becoming startled, or afraid, or interested. The suddenness of the increase in neural firings per unit time determines which of these affects is triggered. If there is a high, constant level of stimulation a person will experience either anger or distress (depending on the level of stimulation). Finally, a sudden decrease in the density of neural firings produces enjoyment-joy.

Shame-humiliation is considered to be a drive auxiliary. Its function is to interrupt the affects *interest* and *enjoyment* at a time when the signal for these affects is still competent. That is, the shame affect is triggered in order to pull a person away from an enjoyable experience when there is every reason for it to continue. As the innate shame affect is co-assembled over time with the concomitants in the situations in which it was triggered, the shame emotion is established. Pure shame affect is meaning-free. It is only as the maturing individual adds her particular, unique interpretation to her shame experiences that the mature emotion known as shame develops.

Tomkins and his associates have been unable to find an innate guilt affect. Consequently, affect theory demands that guilt be understood - along with embarrassment, shyness, and inferiority feelings - as a variant of shame. It is the same innate affect, it is argued, which is triggered in all the various situations associated with these different feeling states. Each variant emotional state feels different simply because of differences in causes and consequences. It seems that the constraints of affect theory have led its adherents to ignore compelling evidence provided in the substantial body of empirical and clinical studies that shame and guilt are distinct emotions. While the two affects share a sizeable area of overlap, the fact that shame involves the whole self whereas guilt relates to discrete actions, coupled with evidence that guilt produces a feeling of power compared to the powerlessness associated with shame, is indicative of a clear distinction.

A more satisfactory approach, I believe, is offered by the psychoanalytic theorist, Susan Miller, in her suggestion that Erikson's conceptualisation of early contact between the two developmental lines for shame and guilt helps explain the entanglement.[28] One developmental line relates to self-esteem (shame), while the other is associated with the superego's generation of conscience (guilt). According to Erikson, the shame which is accrued in the autonomy crisis is absorbed by the guilt generated in the initiative phase.[29] Shame is linked to compulsion neurosis.[30] Parental over-control leads to the child feeling ashamed of her inadequacy. She begins to overvalue self-control and control of the environment. As a result, she develops a rigid, overweening conscience. The child's display of autonomy aimed at reducing the feeling of helplessness and shame is taken over by the need to conform to parental wishes. The recognition of a feeling of power associated with self-manipulation is lost to a feeling of needing to avoid parental disapproval and condemnation. In this way, there is a shift from an affective experience (shame) to a personality style (compulsion) which is the expression of an overweening conscience. Erikson thus shows the historical connectedness between shame and guilt. There is a dynamic interplay between the two feeling states as the child moves from the autonomy to the initiative crisis. This interplay is described in terms of the dynamics of self-manipulation and conscience.

Tomkins' dissolution of the guilt experience into shame affect fails to take account of the psychodynamic history of the two affects. There is a tendency early in the life cycle for shame to atrophy as guilt takes over. This helps to explain how the two affects become entangled. Consider the case of a young man brought up with a strict code of moral conduct. He goes off to university and is confronted with more liberal and daring approaches to life. He begins to feel ashamed of his 'straight' life-style. 'Perhaps the set of values I was raised with are in fact narrow and inhibiting as my friends suggest', he begins to think. As he begins to try on new behaviours he feels a burden of guilt over what feels like a rejection of parental values. The fact that he has not been able to completely disassociate himself from his familial values means that he also feels some shame over falling short of internalised ideals.

Miller gives the example of an adolescent girl who fantasised over the degree of her 'badness' as an infant in order to compensate for her feelings of helplessness and abandonment.[31] In exaggerating her badness she seemed to experience genuine guilt. This illustrates a 'shame-based motivation for the over-development of guilt-producing self-concepts'.[32] This self-image of a bad baby who persecuted her parents provided a fantasy of power and strength in her past to compensate for the feeling of helplessness she felt as an infant, and continues to feel as an adolescent. She needed, observes Miller, this attack on self ('I was a horrible baby') despite its guilt-producing effect to compensate for a sense of smallness and insignificance (shame).

In summary, guilt is much more than a word invented to describe the shame associated with moral lapses. Shame and guilt have their own distinctive developmental histories. The historical interplay between the two affects has lasting implications for the way in which they influence each other. There is an almost infinite variety of situations in which shame and guilt become entangled.

In the above discussion reference has been made to different forms of shame: embarrassment, inferiority, shame over one's appearance and moral shame. Shame is clearly not a unitary concept. This variety in shame reactions sometimes causes a great deal of confusion. Two authors may both be discussing shame and yet it may seem as if they are talking about almost entirely different things. It seems that a typology for shame is needed to bring some clarity to the discussion.

INTRODUCING THE SHAME FAMILY

The shame label is used to describe experiences as diverse as a social gaffe and an act of cowardice while in the line of fire. Clearly there are many different experiences which generate a sense of shame. In this second part of the book, we will involve ourselves with shame related both to moral failure and to a sense of inferiority. These refer to the person giving help and to the person receiving it, respectively. Every person engaged in a helping vocation at some point encounters limitations in his way of being present to others. We do our best, and yet we still fall short. There need be no guilt or shame in this situation. But when a pastor or counsellor, through a lack of courage, honesty or commitment, allows himself to fall into distorted forms of presence which either mitigate or halt the improvement of the person in his care, he should feel a sense of shame. On the other hand, his failure in presence will, in most cases, heighten feelings of inadequacy in the counsellee. It is necessary, then, to discuss these two different forms of shame. We will set them beside other common varieties of shame in order to bring them into sharp focus.

An attempt to categorise the different shame variants should bring some clarity to our discussion. Typologies, however, may obscure as well as clarify. A helpful typology utilises appropriate categories and distinctions. With this in mind, the following structure for the shame family is proposed: *situational shame, aesthetic shame, inherited identity shame, inferiority shame,* and *moral shame.*[33]

Situational Shame

The term 'situational shame' comes from Robert Karen.[34] It describes those embarrassing moments - slurping one's soup in polite company, tripping over one's shoe-laces at an inopportune moment, a joke falling flat - which come to us all at some time. 'Situational shame keeps us bathing regularly, dressing appropriately, eating with utensils, and able to work in close proximity to others without acting on every aggressive or sexual impulse.'[35] Clearly, we are dealing here with the low toxicity end of the shame spectrum.

Babcock and Sabini define embarrassment as that emotion which is evoked by a perceived discrepancy between one's behaviour and one's conception of one's 'persona'.[36] A persona is 'a self-imposed standard or model for action'.[37] While this definition is a helpful way of conceptualising what constitutes an embarrassing situation, Babcock and Sabini take the unwarranted step of distinguishing embarrassment and shame as distinct emotions.[38]

Embarrassment, however we may wish to define it, is an unavoidable part of life. The fact that we have certain standards for our social presence, coupled with the fact of our human fallibility, means that inevitably we all end up at some time or other 'red-faced' and feeling rather silly.

Aesthetic Shame

In a culture which places such a high value on physical beauty, there is a great potential for those who fall short of the ideal to feel shame. Whereas the ideal in other forms of shame may relate to intelligence, social skill, or moral strength, here we are dealing with an aesthetic ideal. When one perceives a gap between the real self and the desired physical ideal, shame is the painful result.

Aesthetic shame can vary from relatively slight discomfort over one's appearance to a sense of horror and self-loathing. The latter experience is associated with profound disfigurement. An attractive, unmarried twenty-five-year-old woman poignantly describes her reaction to life with a colostomy after having her colon surgically removed:

> I feel so embarrassed by this - this thing. It seems so unnatural, so dirty. I can't get used to the smell of it. I'm so scared of soiling myself. Then I'd be so ashamed I couldn't look at anyone else. I've met four or five colostomy patients. They seem to be doing so well. But none was my age and unmarried. Who would want a wife like this? How can I go out and not feel unable to look people in the eyes and tell them the truth? Once I do, who would want to develop a friendship, I mean a close one? How can I even consider showing my body to someone else, having sex? Now they tell me the colitis is gone, together with my bowel, but what is this I'm left with? It's a disaster for me. I feel terrible, like a monster.[39]

In every other way a person may feel a sense of healthy pride, and yet disfigurement, as in this sad case, or other forms of dissatisfaction with body-image, have the potential to all but destroy emotional well-being.

Inherited Identity Shame

We are all born into a particular family, class and culture. Our inherited identity may be a source of pride. Sometimes, though, it carries with it a burden of shame. Members of ethnic minority groups may internalise the prejudicial stereotypes of the dominant culture. They may come to condemn themselves as 'dirty', 'ignorant', or 'lazy'. Even when a person begins to be successful according to the standards of the dominant majority, a lingering feeling of inferiority may plague her. James Fowler calls this 'ascribed shame'.[40]

It may seem irrational to feel shame simply because one happens to be born into a particular class or culture. After all, everyone is an individual with his own unique set of gifts, abilities and personal qualities. However, it is not possible to define personal identity in terms of an 'atomistic' self.[41] I am who I am, in part, because I was born in *this* particular family, in *this* social class, in *this* country. My identity is defined, to a significant extent, by Australian culture, mainstream Protestant Christian ethos, and middle-class values. Culture, class, nationality are all given expression in and through me. The identity ascribed to a person by class and culture may generate pride, or it may result in a feeling of defect and inferiority.

Inferiority Shame

Cultural identity is sometimes a source of shame. In the literature, however, shame is more commonly related to feelings of inadequacy arising purely out of personal experience. In broad terms, a sense of inferiority may be related either to talents and abilities or to personal qualities. A person may feel shame because she judges herself to be incompetent. She may also feel shame because she considers she is boring, timid, socially inept, lacks a sense of humour, and so on. Or she may feel ashamed on both counts.

It is common for people to feel that something is lacking in their personality. Most of us have a desire to enhance our personal qualities. We would like to be more assertive, more in control, more engaging and lively in relationships, more articulate, etc., etc. The problem is not necessarily a lack of intelligence or ability. A person may judge himself to be very successful in his chosen vocation and be quite comfortable in that setting (designing engine parts or fixing plumbing problems). In a social situation, however, he feels out of place and silly. He thinks that others find him 'stiff' and uninteresting. Another person may be able to put together perceptive, highly articulate pieces of writing, but feels small because she constantly allows others to dominate and control her.

A sense of shame may, on the other hand, be related to feelings of incompetence. Almost everything a person does, from cooking lasagne to giving an important business presentation at work, turns out less well than he would like. Another person would like to have the ability to even get into a position of having to give such a presentation.

The reflections on shame by the psychotherapist Donald Nathanson[42] and the moral philosopher John Rawls[43] take into account both lack of achievement and personality failures. The emphasis in both treatments, though, is on the former. Nathanson works with the relationship of shame to its counterpart, pride. Shame and pride are tracked through a series of developmental stages defined in terms of size and strength, dexterity and physical skill, dependence vs. independence, cognitive ability, communication, the sense of self, gender identity and sexuality, and, finally, interpersonal skills. The issues raised in this discussion rotate around one pole defined by skills, abilities, competence and success, and another described by failure, a sense of inferiority, and assaults on self-esteem. When one has moved through a stage relatively successfully one accrues a sense of personal competence, self-worth, and healthy pride. Failures along the way, on the other hand, may coalesce to shape an identity defined by a sense of inferiority and shame.

Rawls' reflections have a similar orientation. Shame is related to a failure in a person's plan of life. Associated with this failure is a loss of self-respect. Rawls uses the term 'excellences' to describe naturally endowed gifts such as imagination, wit, grace and other talents and abilities. Self-respect is posited as the most important primary good. Respect for oneself has two essential conditions. First, a person must believe that his plan of life is worth pursuing. He must, second, have the confidence in his abilities required to fulfil his intentions. That is, he must believe that he really has been endowed with excellences, and that they are adequate for the tasks at hand. Self-respect will be injured when, either, one feels that one's life-project is of limited value, or, one is assailed by self-doubt and fear of failure such that it is impossible to successfully carry out the project. It may, of course, be the case that one values one's plan of life but the choice of that particular plan was overly ambitious. Failure is then related not so much to self-doubt as to lack of ability. Rawls characterises shame as 'the feeling that someone has when he experiences an injury to his self-respect or suffers a blow to his self-esteem'.[44]

Increasingly, people in modern industrialised societies, dominated as they are by a preoccupation with success, concentrate almost exclusively on incompetence and failure as the locus of shame. With this in mind, Agnes Heller refers to a 'one-dimensionality' in the western (or as we tend to say now, northern) experience of shame.[45] In the competitive, highly structured workaday world, we never really confront others with our global personalities. Other persons only see the particular roles we are called on to play. 'We wear our "roles" outside and our shabby incognito inside.'[46] In this context, shame is evoked by an evaluation by the self and by others that a role has been performed incompetently. Interestingly, Heller observes that it is only at war that a person is known as a total personality.[47] Here the real self, in all its many facets, is put to the test. In the firing line, skill, competence and success are no longer the only channels for approval or disapproval. One is judged in terms of courage, ingenuity, goodness of heart and solidarity with fellow soldiers.

Moral Shame

This last observation points to the fact that shame and pride have a moral reference. Moral lapses produce a sense of shame.

Following Kant, Gary Thrane contends that a sense of honour derived from a sensitivity to shame is the only truly moral motivation.[48] The link between the moral personality and shame is established in terms of autonomy and identity. An important dimension in autonomy is the capacity for embracing the ideals and standards that are truly one's own. Autonomy is a personal good because it requires 'freedom, courage and self-command'.[49] When a person follows externally determined standards, he feels a sense of shame. The loss of autonomy produces a loss of dignity and sense of worth.

A sense of identity is established when a person integrates internalised attitudes and values into a stable configuration which continues over time. When a person falls short of her ideals, there is inevitably a degree of identity confusion. This is the result of the disorienting effect of perceiving a discrepancy between her tested self and her ideal identity. She comes to the shameful realisation that she is not the person she thought she was. On the other hand, to live without any standards or values is to live in a state of anomie. It is impossible to establish a sense of identity. One cannot feel 'real' in a social sense because it is not possible to connect with others in any meaningful way. This is so because they cannot fix on an identity that is stable and dependable.

Thrane argues that shame rather than guilt is the truly moral feeling. 'Those who merely dread the punishing voice of conscience (guilt) are not moral. Only those who love their virtue and dread its loss (shame) are moral.'[50] If the only motivation one has for moral behaviour is the fear of guilty feelings, one's performance of good actions will be marred by the grudging spirit behind them. A person influenced by shame feelings, on the other hand, derives satisfaction from fulfilling his duty. The sense of freedom and of self-worth associated with having nothing to be ashamed of motivates moral behaviour. Further, the capacity to live according to principles is evidence of a firm character. One needs self-command and willpower to act in accord with high ideals.

I consider that Thrane is overly negative in his assessment of the role of guilt and conscience. Buber, as we saw in chapter 5, quite rightly identifies existential guilt as a genuine source of moral motivation. He is careful to point out that a 'vulgar' conscience, one controlled by anxiety and tyrannical demands, is unworthy. His 'greater conscience', the call to act for the good of the social order-of-being, is shaped by a sense of honour and duty. It thus describes a moral life very close to what Thrane has in mind. Existential guilt is, I suggest, an authentic moral feeling.

A sense of honour and responsibility drives moral behaviour, but shame is always lurking in the shadows. As soon as one establishes high standards, moral failure and the associated shame reaction are ever-present possibilities. The idea of liability to shame as a motivation for moral behaviour is closely associated with Carl Schneider's notion of 'discretion-shame'.[51] Discretion-shame is contrasted with 'disgrace-shame'. When a person has done something that she considers unworthy of her best character, there is a feeling of disgrace. She judges that she has acted badly and this is followed by a shame reaction. However, observes Schneider, there is also an experience of 'shame felt before'. If discretion-shame is to have ethical value it must be something more than mere emotion. After all, an emotion hardly qualifies as a virtue. Feelings are changeable and unpredictable; the virtues are settled dispositions, character traits. Since discretion-shame, observes Schneider, is closely linked to modesty, there is some suggestion that a sense of shame is more than an emotion. Modesty is usually considered to be a virtue. A highly developed sensitivity to shame may be thought of as an enduring attitude or character trait. 'Shame, then, is not "just a feeling," but reflects an *order of things*. Furthermore, discretion-shame not only reflects, but sustains, our personal and social ordering of the world' [emphasis in the original].[52]

James Fowler uses the notion of a sense of shame as sustaining social order to link it with conscience.[53] Discretionary shame allows us to maintain our bond with the valued members of a group or community. It funds a capacity for sensitivity, tact and respect for others. The feeling of shame is a peremptory warning against behaviour which will lower one's sense of worth and threaten one's valued place in the group. Over time, one learns to identify the kinds of infringements which trigger shame feelings. In this way, an instinctive tendency to refrain from unworthy actions develops. Since discretionary shame incorporates these instinctive evaluative responses and the moral imagination, it plays an important role, concludes Fowler, in the formation of conscience. It is interesting to note that while Buber links the formation of conscience to existential guilt, Fowler associates it with shame. This serves to reinforce a fact we identified above, namely that in the moral sphere there is a good deal of overlap between guilt and shame. Buber's 'greater' conscience, shame and guilt are all inextricably bound together.

In general, it may be said that the conscience is formed by the internalisation of a particular configuration of moral values. There is, however, a form of moral shame which is non-internalised.[54] A person may feel dysphoric because others have cast the withering eye of disapproval on him. This is despite the fact that he has not internalised the moral value lying behind the judgmental reaction. For example, a child may lower her head in shame when her teacher berates her for lying. Yet she can see nothing really wrong with taking liberties with the truth. After all, it usually avoids the kind of unpleasant situation she currently finds herself in!

It is also the case that one may feel shame without internalising the judgement of moral failure communicated by the group. The moral philosopher, John Deigh, uses the case of Crito (from the *Dialogues* of Plato) to illustrate this situation.[55] Crito is anxious about what the good citizens of Athens will think of him for failing to stop Socrates from killing himself. This is in spite of the fact that he considered Socrates' course of action to be the right one. Not only that, but he did everything that could be expected of a friend in this kind of tragic situation. Nevertheless, he still feels a sense of shame when he is reproached by his fellow citizens for cowardice.

In summary, moral shame has both internalised and non-internalised forms. When one lives according to externally determined values, one forfeits autonomy and suffers a blow to one's dignity and honour. Discretion-shame (along with existential guilt) is a worthy moral feeling; neurotic guilt - guilt induced by anxiety and associated with external expectations and controls - is not. Discretionary shame functions to safeguard one's valued place in the group. While moral lapses tend to undermine one's sense of identity, the absence of discretion-shame means that it is impossible to establish an identity.

With this map of the territory of shame in hand, we are ready to set out on our journey. The 'journey' in the concluding chapters will look like this. I will be attempting to show, firstly, how defective presence in a caregiver is shaming both for herself and for the recipient of care (although in quite different ways), and secondly, how the caregiver can use her shame to grow into more authentic ways of being present.

1 S. Tomkins, 'Shame', in D. Nathanson ed., *The Many Faces of Shame* (New York: Guilford Press, 1987), pp. 133-161, p.155.

2 See R. Karen, 'Shame', *The Atlantic Monthly* (February 1992), pp.40-70, p. 40.

3 Cf. S.M. Hines, 'Shame-Based Families', *Review and Expositor* 91 (1994), pp. 19-30, p. 20.

4 This is the thesis C. Schneider argues in *Shame, Exposure, and Privacy* (New York: W.W. Norton, 1992).

5 Exposure is an important theme in the studies by Helen Merrell Lynd and Carl Schneider. See H.M. Lynd, *On Shame and the Search for Identity* (New York: Harcourt, Brace & World, Inc., 1958) and C. Schneider, *Shame, Exposure and Privacy*.

6 See D. Ausubel, 'Relationships Between Shame and Guilt in the Socialising Process', *Psychological Review* 62, no.15 (1955), pp. 379-390, p. 382.

7 H.M. Lynd, *On Shame*, p. 32.

8 See L. Wurmser, 'Shame: The Veiled Companion of Narcissism', in D. Nathanson ed., *The Many Faces of Shame*, pp. 64-92, p. 82.

9 Ibid., p. 83.

10 This discussion of the link between shame and incongruence is informed by H.M. Lynd, *On Shame*, pp. 34-42.

11 See ibid., p. 43.

12 Ibid., p. 46.

13 See L. Wurmser, 'Shame: The Veiled Companion', p. 86.

14 W.H. Auden, the *New Yorker*, Dec. 18, 1954, pp.142-143. Cited in Lynd, *On Shame*, p. 32.

15 See H.B.Lewis, *Shame and Guilt in Neurosis* (New York: International Universities Press, 1971), p. 38.

16 See ibid., p. 53.

17 See D. Harder and A. Zalma, 'Two Promising Shame and Guilt Scales: A Construct Validity Comparison', *Journal of Personality Assessment* 55, nos 3 &4 (1990), pp. 729-745, pp. 741-742.

18 H.M. Lynd, *On Shame*, p. 50.

19 See H.B. Lewis, *Shame and Guilt in Neurosis*.

20 Ibid., p. 36.

21 See D. Ausubel, 'Relationships Between Shame and Guilt', p. 383.

22 See A. Heller, *The Power of Shame: A Rational Perspective* (London: Routledge & Kegan Paul, 1985), p. 4.

23 See C. Goldberg, *Understanding Shame* (Northvale NJ: Jason Aronson Inc., 1991), p. 50.

24 Ibid., p. 50.

25 See S. Tomkins, 'Shame', in *The Many Faces of Shame*, p. 135.

26 See D. Nathanson, *Shame and Pride: Affect, Sex, and the Birth of the Self* (New York: W.W. Norton & Co., 1992), p. 144.

27 See S. Tomkins, 'Shame', in *The Many Faces of Shame*; and idem, 'The Quest for Primary Motives: Biography and Autobiography of an Idea', *Journal of Personality and Social Psychology* 41, no.2 (1981), pp. 306-329.

28 See S. Miller, 'Shame as an Impetus to the Creation of Conscience', *International Journal of Psychoanalysis* 70 (1989), pp. 231-243.

29 See E. Erikson, *Childhood and Society*, p. 227.

30 See ibid., pp. 226-227.

31 See S. Miller, 'Shame as an Impetus', p. 239.

32 Ibid., p. 239.

33 Two leading shame researchers who have developed typologies are Robert Karen and James Fowler. The former suggests four categories, namely *existential shame* (the individual suddenly becomes aware of his failings), *class shame* (related to my category of *inherited identity shame*), *narcissistic shame* (one's personal identity is shame-based), and *situational shame* (a category I also use).

See his 'Shame', p. 58. Moving from 'normal' shame to increasingly pathological variations, James Fowler describes five types and degrees. These are: *healthy shame* (we referred to this in the introductory section above), *perfectionist shame, shame due to enforced minority shame* (cf. my *inherited identity shame*), *toxic shame* (cf. Karen's *narcissistic shame*), and *shamelessness*. See Fowler's *Faithful Change: The Personal and Public Challenges of Post-modern Life* (Nashville: Abingdon Press, 1996), chapter 7.

34 See R. Karen, 'Shame', p. 58.

35 Ibid., p. 58.

36 See M. Babcock and J. Sabini, 'On Differentiating Embarrassment from Shame', *European Journal of Social Psychology* 20 (1990), pp. 151-169, p. 153.

37 Ibid., p. 154.

38 The vast majority of shame researchers are rightly content to view embarrassment as a shame variant. Babcock and Sabini argue, however, that the two feeling states should be differentiated on the basis of the different nature of the standards involved. Embarrassment is evoked when there is a discrepancy between one's actual behaviour and one's standard for behaviour (usually idiosyncratic). Shame, on the other hand, results from a failure to reach an ideal (one that has universal acceptance). The fact that embarrassment is usually correlated with idiosyncratic standards, whereas shame is associated with universal ones is sufficient warrant, argue Babcock and Sabini, for the view that we are dealing with distinct emotions. This, I contend, involves an unnecessarily fine distinction. Both feelings of embarrassment and more intense shame feelings (such as humiliation and mortification) are evoked by a sense of falling short of an ideal. The ideal may, of course, be defined in a number of different ways. It may have a reference to social poise, to personal appearance, or to moral strength. This accounts for the variety of feeling states associated with the shame family of emotions. It does not, however, indicate a need to break up the family into separate emotions.

39 Cited in L. A. Burton, 'Respect: Response to Shame in Health Care', *Journal of Religion and Health* 30, no.2 (Summer 1991), pp. 139-148, p. 142.

40 See J. Fowler, *Faithful Change*, p. 119.

41 See G. Thrane, 'Shame', *Journal for the Theory of Social Behaviour* 92 (1979), pp. 139-166,
 p. 144.

42 See D. Nathanson, *Shame and Pride*.

43 See J. Rawls, *A Theory of Justice* (Oxford: Oxford University Press, 1973), pp. 440-444.

44 Ibid., p. 442.

45 See A. Heller, *The Power of Shame*, p. 17.

46 A. Heller, ibid., p. 19.

47 See ibid., p. 20.

48 See G. Thrane, 'Shame', pp. 139-166, esp. pp. 139, 152-154, 157-158.

49 Ibid., p. 152.

50 Ibid., p. 154.

51 See C. Schneider, *Shame, Exposure, and Privacy*, pp. 18-20.

52 Ibid., p. 20.

53 See J. Fowler, *Faithful Change*, pp. 104-105.

54 See D. Ausubel, 'Relationships Between Shame and Guilt', p. 382.

55 See J. Deigh, 'Shame and Self-Esteem: A Critique'

Chapter 7

SHAME AND FAILURES IN AVAILABILITY IN COUNSELLING AND IN CARE

Availability in a relationship produces a sense of well-being and wholeness; it promotes healing and growth. There is, however, another side to the coin. Where there is a distorted presence, a failure to be available, there is a potential for a high level of embarrassment and shame. The level of shame varies in inverse proportion to the level of self esteem. When a shame-prone personality experiences a lack of attention, a failure in self-giving, she is confirmed in her sense of inferiority and worthlessness. Sadly, she is quite used to having to suffer a non-disposing presence. She tends to expect it; she takes it as confirmation of her inferiority and worthlessness. 'Why should anyone bother extending themselves for my sake?' she thinks. The reaction of a person with a healthy sense of self-worth and a high degree of self-confidence on the receiving end of inattention and a lack of respect is quite different. She may experience a moment of self-doubt and the associated shame feelings, but because she is assured of her worth as a person she will eventually refer the problem to the other person. The slight feeling of shame will soon be overcome by a strong sense of indignation and anger. She does not expect this sort of treatment and she will tell the offender so. She will tend to think less of the other, not of herself. All this indicates the importance of the shame prone personality - sometimes referred to as a narcissistic personality[1] - for our discussion. While shame is a factor in every experience of non-disposability, it looms large when the person on the receiving end is a narcissist.

In this chapter, we will begin by reflecting on a report of therapeutic work with an obese woman called 'Betty'. The therapist has a particularly strong prejudice against overweight persons and as a consequence he is anything but empathic in his relationship with her. We will see that in trying to hide his negative feelings about her and her obesity, far from maintaining rapport, he weakens it. His 'constancy', to use Marcel's term for a pretence of presence, reinforces Betty's belief that she is inferior, flawed. And when he becomes aware of his failing, he too feels shame (although his shame is moral in nature, whereas hers is an inferiority shame).

We will next consider the way in which a preoccupation with counselling technique can sometimes mitigate availability. When a counsellor is more in love with theory, it will be argued, than with his clients, he falls into what might be called 'technocracy'. When technology rules, self-giving fails. And where there is a failure in availability, the shame feelings in the counsellee are reinforced. 'Of course', she thinks, 'he wouldn't really care about someone like me.'

Having reflected on failures in availability in counselling, we will move to a consideration of the dynamics associated with a non-available presence in pastoral visitation. Here our emphasis will shift from the shame of the recipient of care to that of the care-giver. I will offer the idea that in experiencing a wane in compassion, and being reduced to the level of a pretence of availability (Marcel's problem of fidelity in care), a pastor may feel the pangs of shame. Nevertheless, the fact that he has expressed his faithfulness, I will further suggest, through providing the best care he can in spite of not feeling particularly compassionate, is reason for a counter-balancing sense of pride.

We begin our explorations, though, in the realm of counselling process. Here we will attempt to learn, first of all, from the candid report of certain 'blind spots' from a therapist who is usually empathic and compassionate.

IN BETTY'S CASE: THE SHAME POTENTIAL IN CONSTANCY

Counsellors are, of course, expected to be supportive and affirming. Indeed, they expect this of themselves. Given this, when a counsellor feels a block with his client there is a temptation to feign empathy, to pretend that he prizes the counsellee. In Marcel's language, a pretence of presence is constancy. Constancy in a counsellor is almost always easily picked up by the client and will disrupt the rapport in the counselling relationship.

The person featured in our case study, Betty[2] (see chapter 4 above), has low self-esteem and suffers from depression and feelings of inferiority. Her distress and psychological dysfunction is related largely to her obesity. Persons like Betty who have a high propensity for shame do not expect to be valued and admired. Depending on the company they are in, they tend to anticipate either blunt rejection or polite attempts to feign interest. With reference to the latter case, they develop a particularly keen sense for signals indicating boredom and inattention. When a counsellor attempts to fake presence, the shame-prone counsellee will very easily and very quickly see through it. The realisation of pretence, of course, reinforces her tendency to shame. Marcel poignantly expresses the loss associated with this experience: 'Something has been shattered [in the person], a certain value has been lost and... what remains is only straw....'[3]

Irvin Yalom is committed to a relational approach to counselling. In his writings, he emphasises the therapeutic value in compassion, presence and availability. He describes his commitment thus:

> Once I accept someone for treatment, I commit myself to stand by that person: to spend all the time and all the energy that proves necessary for the patient's improvement; and most of all, to relate to the patient in an intimate, authentic manner.[4]

To his great credit, he has been brave enough to record a case in which for a good deal of time he was anything but intimate and authentic. In his work with Betty he tries to hide the fact that he finds obesity deeply offensive and disgusting. He realises that while he is not alone in his bias, '[his] contempt surpasses all cultural norms'. 'When I see a fat lady eat', he says, 'I move down a couple of rungs on the ladder of human understanding. I want to tear the food away. To push her face into the ice cream. "Stop stuffing yourself! Haven't you had enough, for Chrissakes?" I'd like to wire her jaws shut!'[5]

It is not surprising that Betty received a less than warm and intimate reception from her new therapist when she arrived! She had been referred by Dr. Farber, who felt that 'she was not receptive to psychotherapeutic intervention'. Actually, he found her so boring that he would frequently fall asleep during sessions! Initially, Yalom had a similar experience:

> Every one of my notes of these early sessions contains phrases such as: "Another boring session"; "Looked at the clock about every three minutes today"; "The most boring patient I have ever seen"; "Almost fell asleep today - had to sit up in my chair to stay awake"; "Almost fell off my chair today."[6]

In a desperate attempt to gain the interest of her therapist, or anyone else for that matter, Betty seeks to entertain with (unfunny) jokes and a host of (dull) stories 'spiced up' with various accents and impersonations.[7] Here is a classic 'jolly fat lady' routine. Tragically, Betty is socially isolated and prone to deep depression.[8]

In the initial stages of the therapy, Yalom feigned compassion and interest. I would term this stage *the period of constancy*. There would come, however, *a time of availability*. The change was precipitated by

Yalom's challenge to Betty concerning her insistence on keeping their conversations at the level of 'cocktail chatter'. She had the courage to respond to the confrontation, and as she began to attempt disclosure, to share her pain in a real way (she dropped the accents and the giggling), her therapist found himself engaging with her; he was even able to find a degree of empathy.

> I was less bored now. I looked at the clock less frequently and once in a while checked the time during Betty's hour not, as before, to count the number of minutes I had yet to endure, but to see whether sufficient time remained to open up a new issue.
>
> Nor was it necessary to sweep from my mind derogatory thoughts about her appearance. I no longer noticed her body and, instead, looked into her eyes. In fact, I noted with surprise the first stirrings of empathy within me. When Betty told me about going to a western bar where two rednecks sidled up behind her and mocked her by mooing like a cow, I felt outraged for her and told her so.[9]

The dialogue between Betty and Yalom deepened over time, and together they worked through the issues which were causing her so much distress: shame, social isolation, depression and her obesity. Along with a boost to Betty's self-esteem came a very significant weight-loss. A course of therapy which had such an unpromising beginning, ended most satisfactorily.

What is particularly significant about this case from our point of view is the fact that Yalom, in the initial stages, tried to act the part of the empathic, authentic, intimate therapist. Further, he would later pride himself on the fact that he had actually carried off his charade. It is no mean feat to dress up constancy in the guise of the real thing, availability. Yalom records that he felt a sense of elation and relief; he really had got away with it. Or so he thought.

> Our final three hours were devoted to work on Betty's distress at our impending separation. What she had feared at the very onset of treatment had come to pass: she had allowed herself to feel deeply about me and was now going to lose me... I attempted to address Betty's despair, and her belief that once she left me all our work would come to naught, by reminding her that her growth resided neither in me nor in any outside object, but was a part of her, a part she would take with her... To drive my point home, I attempted, in our final session, to use myself as an example.
>
> "It's the same with me, Betty. I'll miss our meetings. But I'm changed as a result of knowing you..."

She had been crying, her eyes downcast, but at my words she stopped sobbing and looked toward me, expectantly.

"And, even, though we won't meet again, I'll still retain that change."

"What change?"

"Well, as I mentioned to you, I hadn't had much professional experience with....er....with the problem of obesity..." I noted Betty's eyes drop with disappointment and silently berated myself for being so impersonal.

"Well, what I mean is that I hadn't worked before with heavy patients, and I've gotten a new appreciation for the problems of....." I could see from her expression that she was sinking even deeper into disappointment. "What I mean is that my attitude about obesity has changed a lot. When we started I personally didn't feel comfortable with obese people...."

In unusually feisty terms, Betty interrupted me. "Ho! ho! ho! Didn't feel comfortable.... that's putting it mildly. Do you know that for the first six months you hardly ever looked at me? And in a whole year and a half you've never - not once - touched me? Not even for a handshake!"

My heart sank. My God, she's right! I *have* never touched her. *I simply hadn't realised it. And I guess I didn't look at her very often, either. I hadn't expected her to notice!* [emphasis added][10]

The expression 'my heart sank' says it all. Here is a therapist who prides himself on his genuineness, presence and empathy, and his client is laughing at his pitiful attempt to hide his true feelings and to act the part of the caring therapist. Yalom is clearly ashamed of himself and his play-acting.

Given the fact that she saw through the charade, why, one might ask, did Betty continue to hand over good money. There are other therapists around. When Yalom asked Betty why she stayed, one reason was her low expectancy of what others will give to her.

"....Remember that I'm used to it. It's not like I expect anything more. Everyone treats me that way. People hate my looks. No one *ever* touches me.... And, even though you wouldn't look at me, you at least seemed interested in what I had to say - no, no, that's not right - you were interested in what I *could* or *might* say if I stopped being so jolly. Actually, that was helpful. Also, you didn't fall asleep. That was an improvement on Dr. Farber."[11]

There are at least *four important insights* which can be gleaned from this case. The first is that shame-prone persons expect to be treated badly. Consequently, Betty's expectancy of what Yalom would and should give her was initially very low. While he was more absent than present during the first six months, the fact that he could at least keep his eyes open was encouraging! Constancy, a pretence of self-giving, may be enough to keep a shame-dominated person in a counselling relationship, but it is not enough to facilitate the overcoming of her deep feelings of inferiority and worthlessness. It was Yalom's movement from constancy to availability which facilitated a healing dialogue. The whole complexion of the relationship changed when he found himself able to prize Betty.

It is instructive, secondly, to reflect on the impetus for this progression to genuine presence. Yalom found himself able to engage more fully with Betty when she was prepared to risk disclosure, to drop the 'jolly fat lady' act and be honest and authentic. The positive change in Betty awakened Yalom's 'presential' (a word coined by Marcel) capacities. His repulsion with obese women, together with his client's talent for boring chatter, resulted in a solid block to his natural tendency to be available. Betty's movement towards real presence helped clear away this obstruction to the flow of Yalom's compassion, empathy and intimacy.

It is interesting to contrast this change with the movement in another leading psychotherapist, Heinz Kohut, in the course of his involvement in the treatment of a man with narcissistic personality disorder.[12] The case study refers to his supervision of an analyst in training whose patient was a lonely man suffering from deep feelings of shame and emptiness. In his childhood, the man had to contend with a 'bizarre and unpredictable yet powerful mother' and 'the emotional distance of his more humanly predictable but weak and retiring father'. At one point in the analysis, the patient gave accounts of his profound cruelty to animals. This was something which, Kohut reports, 'strained our empathic capacity, our tolerance, to the utmost'. While the patient usually pampered his cats, on occasion he would throw them against the wall. Kohut interpreted this bizarre and cruel behaviour as 'a wordless description of how he had felt as a child'. He had been cruelly tossed around by an unpredictable and, at times, deeply hurtful mother. Just when he would expect understanding and support, which she could sometimes give, she would react with ridicule and contempt. This interpretation of the behaviour was affirming or 'mirroring' for the patient. It also, I think, helped the analysts in their attempts to affirm a man whose actions they found repulsive. The extent of their struggle to understand is indicated by Kohut when he reports:

> We felt close to abandoning the analyst's tolerant attitude of readiness for empathic comprehension. We felt close, in other words, to following the example of those therapists who have reported wholesome consequences when, in analogous circumstances, they

openly expressed their indignation and, as they saw it, reacted honestly and appropriately to a patient's wrongdoings. We did not take this road, but gritted our teeth and continued to attempt to understand...[13]

In this instance, the change took place *entirely within the therapist*. Initially, Kohut was almost overwhelmed by his feelings of revulsion and indignation. In his attempt to mirror he found himself 'gritting his teeth'. His formulation of an empathic interpretation helped him reframe his view of his patient. Seeing the behaviour of this lonely, wounded man as an acting-out of the cruel 'tossing about' he had experienced as a child made it easier for him to understand. Although Kohut does not explicitly say so, it is reasonable to think that after this insight empathic responses would come more freely and spontaneously. Nothing had changed in the patient. He had not given up his cruelty to his cats. It was Kohut's capacity for empathic reframing which helped him move beyond his feelings of revulsion to a genuine desire to mirror.

Kohut's gritting of the teeth, progressing now to our third insight, is matched by Yalom's 'inner groans'[14] in listening to Betty's surface chatter. Attempting to hide one's negative reactions, far from maintaining rapport, will weaken it. The act of concealment will rarely, if ever, be successful. The chances are, then, that the counsellee will lose confidence in the counsellor as a person of honesty and integrity. Further, it is very likely that the aim of protecting the feelings of the counsellee will fail. Sensing the displeasure of the counsellor, shame feelings will be reinforced in the counsellee. She will take it as yet another indication of her inferiority.

As we have seen, shame-prone persons develop a keen sense for veiled signals of disinterest or disapproval. It is really not possible to hide behind a pretence of availability when one is with a narcissist (or anyone else for that matter). 'Ho! ho! ho!', says Betty in response to Yalom's careless handling of the truth concerning his presence with her. An experienced and gifted therapist he may be, but he still felt the need to attempt a concealment of his true feelings about his client. He was afraid of broaching the issue of his prejudice against overweight women. We have all been exposed to Rogers' relentless insistence on congruence; cases like this, along with our own counselling and relational experiences, remind us just how difficult it can be sometimes.

While Yalom was unable to raise the shameful fact of his own prejudices, he did tackle the difficult issue of Betty's dull, surface conversation. It is instructive to follow Yalom's mental processes as he attempts to formulate a line of approach.

I dared not use the word *boring* - far too vague and too pejorative. I needed to be precise and constructive. I asked myself what, exactly, was boring about Betty, and identified two obvious characteristics. First of all, she never revealed anything intimate about herself. Second, there was her damned giggling, her forced gaiety, her reluctance to be appropriately serious.

It would be difficult to make her aware of these characteristics without hurting her. I decided upon a general strategy: my basic position would be that I wanted to get closer to her but that her behavioural traits got in the way. I thought it would be difficult for her to take offence with my criticism of her behaviour in that context.[15]

One can understand Yalom's fear of hurting Betty. A counsellor, and this brings us to our fourth and final insight, will naturally be reluctant to probe those issues which go to the heart of the counsellee's shame experience. It seems that in addressing the behaviours which manifest the inadequacy and failings of the person, her shame will be heightened rather than healed. The paradox in the situation is, however, that in temporarily intensifying shame the way is opened to overcome it.[16] When a person is brave enough to respond to the challenge and expose her shameful self to the counsellor, and he in turn responds with acceptance, affirmation, and admiration, the deadly grip of shame is forced open.

I am reminded of the fact that Jesus was secure enough in himself, and confident enough in the healing power of his presence, to go directly to a person's sense of shame. The woman at the well (Jn. 4:3-30) comes alone at noon to collect water. Women would typically come in groups and at an earlier or later hour. Perhaps, as a result of her morally suspect past, she experiences a public shame and the sense of isolation that goes with it. She clearly wants to avoid the taunts of those who think of themselves as morally superior. Jesus wastes little time in going right to the heart of her guilt and shame: 'Go and bring your husband', he says (v.16). The New Testament scholar, Don Carson, observes that this fact is sometimes overlooked in treatments of this well-known passage. Having noted the flexibility in Jesus' dialogical approach, he comments that 'no less startling (though more often overlooked) is the manner in which Jesus commonly drives to the individual's greatest sin, hopelessness, guilt, despair, need.'[17]

To return to our counselling 'text', we can sum up this way. In trying to hide his negative feelings about Betty and her obesity, Yalom, far from maintaining rapport, actually weakened it. His constancy reinforced

Betty's feelings of inferiority and worthlessness. And when he became aware of his failing, he too felt shame, in his case moral shame. In a counselling relationship *there is nowhere to hide*. It is destructive to the counselling process to attempt to hide one's blind spots and to hide from painful issues. Both genuineness and the exposure of shame are essential in the work of healing narcissistic injury.

Above we worked with a report by a secular therapist. We now turn our attention to counselling in a congregational context. Here we will explore the shame-inducing potential in 'technocracy'.

COUNSELLING 'TECHNOCRACY' AS A FORM OF NON-AVAILABILITY

Given that we live in a 'therapeutic culture', it is to be expected that some ministers at least will want to develop good counselling skills. In itself, this is a good thing. It becomes problematical, however, when a minister becomes so intent on the technical side of his counselling that he fails to tune-in to the very basic needs of those he seeks to help. In this case, the minister's presence is distorted. A 'failed wholeness' and shame rather than unity and a sense of hope characterise the pastoral relationship. In the following case study,[18] the pastor wonders whether the failure in rapport with his parishioner, Mrs. T., was caused by his faulty counselling technique. The question he should have asked, I suggest, is, Did I give enough of myself? What she needed from him was empathy, compassion, and presence.

Mrs. T. has undergone three or four operations in the past three years. She has to cope with the fact that at almost any time she may have to face surgery again.

Pastor: Mrs. T., it's good to see you again. I had just heard that you had gone to C_____ to the hospital, and the next day heard that you were home again. Are you feeling pretty well again?

Mrs. T.: Oh, I'm as well as I can ever expect to be, I guess. Pete told me I ought to let you know I was going into hospital, but I said never mind. This hospital business is getting to be an old thing with me, it seems like.

Pastor: Don't tell me you're getting used to being in the hospital!

Mrs. T.: Oh, no, nothing like that. But I just didn't want to bother you with all my troubles. And to tell you the truth, I didn't feel as if it would do much good whether you knew it or not. I've just about lost all my faith, after all those operations, all I've been through.

Pastor: You've suffered so much that now it's hard to believe in God, is that it?

Mrs. T.: Well, sort of. Of course, I believe there is a God - I just don't feel much like having faith in God, though. I've had so much trouble, seems like, and I wonder what all this stuff about faith in God - what good it has done me.

Pastor: It makes you feel as if God has let you down.

Mrs. T.: That's about it. I just began feeling as if I wasn't going to ask him to make me well again. I've prayed so much and it didn't do much good. We're supposed to have faith, and all that, but I still haven't got my real health. But you know, I did pray in the hospital. There was another woman there, she had it so much worse than I did, I prayed for her all the time - I couldn't help it.

Pastor: So you found someone who seemed to be suffering more than you and found that you had to pray for her. This was a kind of faith that seemed even bigger than your doubts, wasn't it?

Mrs. T.: I suppose so. But I still didn't - I still don't have any faith for myself. You know what I mean. It don't seem real for me. Why should I have to suffer so? Then there's Julie. It seems now like she will be able to see pretty good, but why did I have to worry about her for so long?

Pastor: You feel as if you've had more than your share of worry and pain.

Mrs. T.: Well, I've had a lot of it. Oh, the pain isn't so bad, but it's just knowing I might have to go back and have it done all over again; that's the discouraging part. That's why I've lost my faith. Then there's Pete. You know, Mr. T., you wouldn't believe it, but that man used to be in church every Sunday. Now he don't go hardly at all, and he acts like I'm a burden to him, with all these doctor and hospital bills. He used to be a real help to me, but now I guess he thinks I cost him too much money. (*Here she seemed close to tears.*) The girls and I try to get him to go to church, but he just won't do it. And it's pretty hard for me to go by myself.

Pastor: You feel then that Pete resents all your medical expenses.

Mrs. T: Yes, and Julie's too.

Pastor: And you wonder why he no longer seems to want to go to church.

Mrs. T.: Yes. He just sort of laughs at church now, and he used to go every Sunday. Sometimes he'd make me go when I'd thought I'd stay home, and now I can't get him to go hardly at all. He doesn't seem to have faith anymore. Maybe that's why I've lost mine. Gee, it used to be so much better! When the girls were little and before Julie's eyes went bad and before I was sick so much. Seemed like we were closer then, and now I don't know what's going to happen to us.

Pastor: Things seem pretty dark to you now.

Mrs. T.: Yes, they do. Oh, of course, I'll get to feeling better, and then I won't be so gloomy. Thank you for calling, Pastor. You'll be sorry you came, I was so down in the dumps.

Pastor: That's all right, Mrs. T. Feel free to call on me any time, and I'd be glad to talk with you or Pete in my study any time you like.

Mrs. T.: Oh, you'll never get Pete there. Me, I'll be all right, when I get to feeling better. Good-bye.

The pastor made a second call two weeks later. He reports that Mrs. T. made only small talk, and that when he asked her about her faith she responded by commenting that she thought it was 'going to be all right'. 'I got the feeling', says the pastor, 'that she was uneasy and unwilling to talk with me, so after a few more remarks, I left.'[19] In reflecting on the two visits, the pastor has this to say:

> I felt as if I had a good rapport with Mrs. T. during that first call, but the second call seemed to me to be a complete failure. Why this failure? ....Very probably.... my technique was somewhat faulty, or I may have been overly anxious to help her. My second question, however, is theoretical. Must we not allow for human freedom and agree that there are those who will refuse help, be it ever so skillfully offered?[20]

The pastor wonders whether the failed relationship can be put down to faulty technique. He seems to be suggesting, on the other hand, that he is actually a skilled counsellor and that the visits were unsatisfactory because Mrs. T. simply did not want help. He would be better served, perhaps, to focus on whether or not he allowed himself to become aware of the claim Mrs. T. was making on him. She was asking him, I believe, to be prepared to enter into her pain and struggle, and into the associated faith crisis, in a real way. She needed him to give of himself in the dialogue rather than simply offering stock-standard counselling responses in a detached manner. He is clearly very intent on picking up on Mrs. T's feelings and reflecting them back to her, but his responses seem to lack 'heart'. It is of course impossible to be sure about this with only the printed page to work with. Still, I wonder if it is the case that while feelings have been identified and appropriate responses offered, there has been no genuine meeting between Mrs. T. and the pastor. Carroll Wise's comments on this case reflect my intuition. He poses these questions:

'Were [the pastor's] reflections of feeling, and other comments, just mechanical statements, or in responding in this way, did he give something of himself? Did he feel a deep love for this woman and a deep concern about her problems, and did he have any confidence in her inner capacities to grow to the place where she could deal more creatively with her situation?'[21]

It is a very good thing for pastors and counsellors to reflect from time to time about their technique and their application of personality theory. If, however, they are more in love with theory than with their clients, they will fall into what might be called 'technocracy'. They have allowed technique and theory to dominate their work. When technology rules, there cannot be real compassion and empathy.

There is no indication of whether or not Mrs. T. has a propensity for shame. She may simply have been annoyed by her pastor's detached, almost mechanical, way of responding to her pain. In a person with low self-esteem, however, there is a tendency to refer a lack of warmth and caring to the self and its failings. 'Of course he wouldn't care', she thinks, 'about a person like me. No one really cares about me.' The pastor's failure to dispose of himself serves to reinforce her tendency to shame.

We now shift our attention from the counselling context to that of pastoral visitation. Whereas above we were directing our attention primarily to the shame of the recipient of care, now we focus on non-availability as a source of shame feelings for the care-giver.

THE PROBLEM OF FIDELITY AND THE SHAME OF THE PASTOR

The main idea we are working with in this chapter is that where there is a failure in availability on the part of the provider of care there is a potential for shame. Thus far, we have emphasised the shame reaction in the recipient of care. When a counsellor is inattentive and/or feigns affirmation it is likely that the tendency to shame in the counsellee will be strengthened. The negative feelings she struggles with - inferiority, inadequacy, and worthlessness - will be reinforced.

What about the counsellor? When he becomes aware of his distorted presence, as Irvin Yalom did, he may well feel shame also. It is a different variety of shame, though, to that experienced by the counsellee. Hers is inferiority shame; his is moral shame. He realises that he has fallen short of his ideal of genuine presence, has harmed his client, and consequently feels ashamed.

I want at this point to explore further the shame dynamics in the care provider by referring to a specific case, namely the emotional reaction a pastor may feel as a consequence of being caught in Marcel's 'problem of fidelity'. Our attention here is given to pastoral visitation. I will suggest that as a result of the ebb and flow of compassion a pastoral visitor inevitably experiences, she is prone to a shame reaction. However, I will also contend that in being faithful to her pastoral calling and in endeavouring to be fully available even though her feelings of compassion may not be particularly strong, she is entitled to feel good about herself.

Let us cast our minds back to chapter 1 where we reflected on Marcel's struggle to reconcile himself to the fact that a promise of presence is sometimes followed by a drop in one's level of disposability. This is the problem of fidelity. How is it possible, he asks, to make a promise of availability when one knows that the compassionate feelings one has today may all but be gone tomorrow? We saw how he uses the example of a promise of a return visit to a friend who is dying in a nursing home. It is a commitment 'moved by a wave of pity'. By the time he is ready for the next visit, however, the wave has subsided. This fact produces in Marcel an inner struggle. At first, he reflects, 'my whole being was concentrated into an irresistible impulse towards him, a wild longing to help him, to show him that I was on his side, that his sufferings were mine.'[22] But how different he feels now. 'I have to recognise that this impulse no longer exists, and it is no longer in my power to do more than imitate it by a pretence which some part of me refuses to swallow.'[23]

This last expression indicates constancy. His reflection that it is a pretence which he cannot swallow points to the experience of shame. He feels a sense of unworthiness in acting out before his friend a show of compassion. Indeed, Marcel actually uses the word 'shame' to describe this distressing ebb and flow of moods.

> The silence I feel within me is strangely different from that other cry of pity from the heart; yet it does not seem to me altogether mysterious. I can find a good enough explanation for it in myself and the rhythm of my moods. But what is the good? Proust was right: we are not at our own disposal. There is a part of our being to which strange, perhaps not altogether conceivable, conditions give us sudden access; the key is in our hands for a second; and a few minutes later the door is shut again and the key disappears. I must accept this fact *with shame and sorrow* [emphasis added].[24]

I believe that most, if not all, pastors struggle with this problem of fidelity as described by Marcel. We are not at our own disposal; the key is in the hand for just a second and then the door closes. There may be those with a rare capacity for compassion who feel the tension only slightly and on rare occasions. Most of us engaged in the ministry of care, though, find ourselves plagued by a nagging, often non-thematised, sense of unworthiness. The shame feeling, I suggest, is usually not identified. A minister will experience a vague feeling of uneasiness associated with the sense that his act of care lacks authenticity, and at the same time may be unable to explore clearly the dynamics associated with the distress. Marcel's analysis provides us with the insight we need. There is for those engaged in pastoral care an unavoidable 'rhythm of moods' which necessitates a pretence of availability. It is this sham form of being-with-the-other which generates the shame feelings.

Insight is always liberating. The fact that one is aware of the dynamics behind these vague and unsettling feelings of unworthiness helps to keep them within appropriate limits. A pastor's sense of shame, moreover, should be balanced by an awareness that she is in fact expressing faithfulness despite the fact that her feeling-state militates against a caring presence. It may be that the level of compassion she is feeling is low at the moment, but nevertheless she is offering the best care she can. This should provide a boost to her self-esteem.

The problem of fidelity, as it relates to acts of care, carries with it what might be called a *bipolar affective dynamic*. On the one hand, the recession in the tide of compassion, carrying with it as it does a fall into a pretence of availability, may produce a sense of shame. However, there is also a wholesome sense of pride associated with the fact that one has been faithful, despite the counter-urges, to one's commitment to the provision of care.

The focus in this chapter has been on the link between shame and non-availability in therapeutic and in pastoral settings. In the next chapter we will track the shame dynamic in those same contexts but this time our attention will be directed to a disconfirming presence.

CONCLUSION

We began by reflecting on the movement in a therapeutic relationship from constancy to availability. In trying to hide his negative feelings about Betty and her obesity, Yalom, far from maintaining rapport, actually weakened it. His constancy reinforced Betty's belief that she is inferior, defective. And when he became aware of his failing, he too felt shame. It is destructive to the counselling process to attempt to hide one's blind spots and to hide from painful issues. Both genuineness and the exposure of shame are essential in the work of healing narcissistic injury.

Next, we identified 'technocracy', a preoccupation with counselling technique, as a form of nondisposability. A pastor may fall in love with the latest therapeutic techniques, but may forget to love his people. Where there should be an experience of unity and hope in his pastoral relationships, he will find only the 'failed wholeness' that is shame.

We also discussed the relationship between shame and non-availability in the context of pastoral visitation. Connections were made between Marcel's reflections on the problem of fidelity and what we called a bipolar affective dynamic. A recession in the tide of compassion results in a pretence of availability. This may produce feelings of inauthenticity and unworthiness. Constancy generates shame. On the other hand, a recognition of the fact that one has dismissed all counter-urges and has chosen to be with the other in her need produces a boost to self-esteem.

1 There is a substantial body of literature in which shame is identified as one of the prominent features of the narcissistic personality disorder. See H.B. Lewis, 'Shame and the Narcissistic Personality', in D. Nathanson ed., *The Many Faces of Shame* (London: The Guilford Press, 1987), pp. 93-132; H. Kohut, 'Forms and Transformations of Narcissism', in P. Orstein ed., *The Search for the Self*, vol. 1 (New York: International Universities Press, 1978), pp. 427-460, idem, *The Analysis of the Self* (New York : International Universities Press, 1971), pp. 144, 192, and idem, *The Restoration of the Self* (New York: International Universities Press, 1977), p. 241; A. Morrison, 'Shame, Ideal Self and Narcissism', in A. Morrison ed., *Essential Papers on Narcissism* (New York: New York University Press, 1986), pp. 348-371; L. Wurmser, 'Shame: The Veiled Companion of Narcissism', in *The Many Faces of Shame*, pp. 64-92; and R. Hutch, 'Confessing the Dying Within', *Journal of Pastoral Care* 48, no. 4 (Winter 1994), pp. 341-354.
2 See I. Yalom, *Love's Executioner* (London: Penguin Books, 1987), chp 3.
3 Marcel, 'Creative Fidelity', in *Creative Fidelity*, p. 155.
4 Yalom, *Love's Executioner*, p. 91.
5 Ibid., pp. 88-89.
6 Ibid., p. 92.
7 See ibid., p. 92.
8 See ibid., pp. 90, 97.
9 Ibid., p. 99.
10 Ibid., pp. 114-116.
11 Ibid., p. 116.

12 See Kohut, 'The Psychoanalyst in the Community of Scholars', in P. Ornstein ed., *The Search for the Self*, vol. 2, pp. 685-724, p. 710ff.

13 Ibid., p. 710.

14 Ibid., p. 92.

15 Ibid., p. 95.

16 Cf. D. Capps, *Life Cycle Theory and Pastoral Care* (Philadelphia: Fortress Press, 1983), pp. 91-92.

17 D. Carson, *The Gospel According to John* (Grand Rapids: Eerdmanns, 1991), p. 221.

18 The case study is taken from N. Cryer and J. Vanhinger eds., *Casebook in Pastoral Counselling* (Nashville: Abingdon Press, 1962), pp. 167-171.

19 Ibid., p. 169.

20 Ibid., p. 169.

21 Ibid., p. 170.

22 Marcel, *Being and Having*, p. 48.

23 Ibid., p. 48.

24 Ibid., p. 48.

Chapter 8
SHAME AND DISCONFIRMATION IN COUNSELLING AND IN CARE

There are those who hold the view that while counselling may sometimes not do any good, it cannot hurt. In fact, a counsellor, even an experienced one, *can* do harm to her clients. Psychotherapists Russell Meares and Robert Hobson have identified and discussed this possibility, and have coined the term, *the persecutory therapist*.[1] They use the following categories to describe this lamentable phenomenon in therapy: intrusion, derogation, invalidation of experience, opaqueness of the therapist, the untenable situation, and the persecutory spiral. Our major concern in this chapter is the establishment of links between various forms of disconfirming presence on the part of the counsellor and shame reactions in the counsellee. With reference to the six features identified by Meares and Hobson, the first two are immediately suggestive of shame inducement. Probing into hidden secrets (intrusion) and launching covert attacks on a person's worth (derogation) are obviously shaming. I intend to develop and expand these categories by connecting them with the notion of disconfirmation.

I also want to complement the work of Meares and Hobson by adding a category, namely, *reductionism*. Confirmation involves a capacity to appreciate and affirm uniqueness. There is a tendency in some counsellors to view those they see through a grid of personality theory. It will be argued that this approach results in reductionism; the particularity of the counsellee is lost. Further, we will discuss the fact that the counsellee records this subjection to ready-made psychological categories as a devaluing of his worth as a person.

In the final section of the chapter, we will shift our attention from the counselling context to that of care in the parish or local situation. Our focus will be on the shame associated with a turning away from the struggle of a confirming dialogue. Whereas in discussing counselling we will be concerning ourselves with the shame feelings of the recipient of care, here we will concentrate on the shame of the person offering care, *viz.*, the pastor.

Before proceeding to a discussion of shame and a disconfirming therapeutic style, a word needs to be said about the primary case study material we will be using. Meares and Hobson point out that it is rare to find a client's account of her experience with therapy. They do, however, identify one such source, namely, the journals of Anaïs Nin.[2] Since we will be making extensive use of her reflections on her treatments by Drs. René Allendy (founder of the French Psychoanalytic Society) and Otto Rank (a one time special protégé of Freud), it will be well to begin with a portrait of this interesting and insightful woman.

SHAME AND 'PERSECUTION' IN COUNSELLING

A Biographical and Psychological Sketch of Anaïs Nin

Anaïs Nin was born in Neuilly, a suburb of Paris. As a child she accompanied her father, the famous Spanish composer-pianist Joaquin Nin, on concert tours all over Europe. In her teens, long after her father had left the family, she broke out of the demoralising confines of a poor existence with her Danish-born mother in New York to become an artists' model and later, a Spanish dancer. As a novice writer, she made her way back to Paris with its literary and cultural atmosphere. In 1929 she settled at Louveciennes and there, as after the outbreak of World War II in her apartment in New York's Greenwich Village, she welcomed a host of little known, but destined to be famous, creative people.

Anaïs was the friend and confidante to important literary figures such as Henry Miller and Antonin Artaud. In the case of the former, she was more than a friend; she was also a lover. Her relationship with Miller was taut and volatile. Anaïs lived an intense and multi-dimensional life, moving with zest and vitality through the cosmopolitan world of art and society.

While one recognises that it is not possible to develop psychological categories with any degree of certainty from a collection of remarks and reflections in a personal journal (even one as detailed as Nin's), it does seem possible to identify a number of quite clear indications by Anaïs of (a mild at least) narcissistic disturbance. A leading theorist of narcissistic personality disorder is Heinz Kohut.[3] Kohut describes the symptoms of the disorder as inferiority feelings, propensity for embarrassment, shame, depression, and a feeling of not being fully real. He attributes the condition to acute empathic failures on the part of 'self-objects' (parents and caregivers). His clinical experience led him to the conclusion that what narcissists most need is to admire (or idealise) and to be admired (or 'mirrored'). An indication that Anaïs suffered with narcissistic personality disorder is found in an entry in her journal referring to inferiority feelings. She identifies a lack of self-confidence as a major source of distress in her life:

> [With Dr Allendy] I talked about my work, and my life in general. I said I had always been very independent and had never leaned on anyone.
>
> Dr Allendy said, "In spite of that, you seem to lack confidence." He had touched a sensitive spot. Confidence![4]

This lack of confidence she relates to her figure. She feels inferior when she compares herself to women who are well-endowed. Men only love 'big, healthy women with enormous breasts', she laments.[5] She recalls the Spanish proverb quoted often by her mother, 'Bones are for the dogs.' To compensate for what she perceives as physical undesirability, she decided early to shape her persona around her artistic gifts. 'It was to forget this [a petite body] that I decided to be an artist, or writer, to be interesting, charming, accomplished. I was not sure of being beautiful enough...'[6]

A further indication of narcissism is the way in which Anaïs recalls for her analyst the painful experience associated with the extreme empathic failures of her father:

> My father did not want a girl. My father was over-critical. He was never satisfied, never pleased. I never remember a compliment or a caress from him. At home, only scenes, quarrels, beatings. And his hard blue eyes on us, looking for flaws. When I was ill with typhoid fever, almost dying, all he could say was: "Now you are ugly, how ugly you are."[7]

As writers on narcissism repeatedly observe, in reaction to these traumatic childhood narcissistic injuries a person usually develops an intense craving for affirmation and approval.[8] This was certainly the case with Anaïs. She acknowledges her fear of being hurt and laments over the associated need for constant confirmation of affection. 'I despise my own hyper-sensitiveness', she writes, 'which requires so much reassurance. It is certainly abnormal to crave so much to be loved and understood.'[9]

In order to develop a full and accurate picture of a person's psychopathology it is necessary to spend many hours in face-to-face conversation. All we have before us is a small collection of personal, psychologically-oriented reflections. And yet one cannot help but be struck by the appearance of a number of classic symptoms of narcissistic personality disorder. The notes of a propensity for shame seem to be sounded clearly enough to be recognised. We turn now to a consideration of the way Anaïs felt shamed by the intrusive presence of Dr Allendy.

Intrusion: Shame and 'The Look' of the Counsellor

Psychotherapists have long recognised the existence of what might be called a 'pathogenic secret'. 'As soon as man was capable of conceiving the idea of sin', writes Carl Jung, 'he had recourse to psychic concealment - or, to put it in analytical language, repressions arose. Anything that is concealed is a secret. The maintenance of secrets acts like a psychic poison which alienates their possessor from the community.'[10] Such a secret is harmful because it is guilt-laden. The 'cathartic method' consists in helping a person bring the repressed material to the surface. When it is exposed, the pathological force of the secret is weakened and emotional healing begins.

There is, however, as Russell Meares[11] has observed, another kind of secret. This secret is not guilt-laden ideo-affective content but rather a constellation of ideas that the person feels constitutes the substance of the self. To share these intimate thoughts is somehow to lose the self. Meares uses the words of a shy, ill-educated and somewhat depressed woman to illustrate the concept.

> I suppose I'm scared that if I talk, there'll be nothing left to say. Say I told you all my thoughts, ideas and whatsit, it'd be like me piled up beside us, with nothing left to say.[12]

She seems to be afraid of somehow becoming invisible. Meares refers to the fear and anxiety a person like this young woman feels when 'the secret is out'.[13] Now a part of the self is outside and vulnerable. Others may damage it and then it would be almost like suffering bodily harm. The inner secret is not thought of as something dark which must be hidden (the pathogenic secret), but rather as a cluster of precious ideas which is the substance of one's existence.

To expose one's substance to another is to take a great risk. If it is handled roughly, without proper respect and sensitivity, irreparable damage is done to the self. In Buber's language, the being of the other is disconfirmed. Confirmation involves a double movement of distancing and relating.[14] The distance pole indicates the independence, uniqueness, and particularity of the other. Intimacy, the I-Thou relation, is a togetherness which respects otherness. Confirmation, then, involves respecting, valuing and affirming otherness. In repaying with respect the trust the other places in one by sharing her secret, one confirms her personhood. Confirmation of the other through a sensitive handling of her secret is the fundamental act in establishing intimacy. 'Secrets are disclosed with care', writes Meares, 'in a developing dialogue with others who can be trusted to share and respect them. They then become the coins of intimacy, and the currency of its transactions.'[15] (One is reminded of Marcel's idea that the sharing of the secret is 'the mainspring of inter-subjectivity'.)

A shame-prone person finds intimacy profoundly threatening. She experiences a desperate need to keep the secret which is her inner core hidden away from what is potentially the critical gaze of the other. To be exposed to the judgmental, condemning *look* of another is mortifying. Anaïs remembers with pain the experience of her father's 'hard blue *eyes* on us, looking for flaws'[emphasis added]. She felt oppressed and dominated by his critical eye. Admiration was only ever indirect. He could never look her straight in the face and speak gentle, affectionate words of affirmation. His communication of his appreciation of her was refracted through a camera lens. '[My father] liked', she writes, 'to take photos of me while I bathed. He always wanted me naked. All his admiration came by way of the camera. His eyes were partly concealed by heavy glasses (he was myopic) and then by the camera lens.'[16]

This partial and inadequate attempt at confirmation could never, however, compensate for his repeated and devastating attacks on her. The 'eyes' would sometimes 'appear' when she was feeling exposed and vulnerable; she felt under attack even when he was not physically present.

> When I gave a concert of Spanish dances in Paris, I imagined I saw his face in the audience. It seemed pale and stern. I stopped in the middle of my dance, frozen, and for an instant I thought I could not continue. The guitarist playing behind me thought I had stage fright and he began to encourage me with shouts and clapping. Later, when I saw my father again, I asked him if he had been at this concert.
>
> He answered me, "No, I was not there, but if I had been I would have disapproved absolutely. I disapprove of a lady being a dancer. Dancing is for prostitutes, professionals."[17]

Sadly, Joaquin's gaze brought a sense of shame rather than fatherly support and encouragement. The lack of self-confidence associated with his judgmentalism meant, as we shall soon see, that Anaïs was extremely reluctant to share her secrets with others, including her analyst.

There is an intimate connection between exposure to the other and shame. Jean-Paul Sartre has produced a perceptive and interesting analysis of this link.[18] For Sartre, to be exposed to 'the look' is to suffer the degradation of becoming an object.

> Pure shame is not a feeling of being this or that guilty object but in general of being *an* object; that is, of *recognizing myself* in this degraded, fixed, and dependent being which I am for the Other. Shame is the feeling of an *original fall*, not because of the fact that I may have committed this or that particular fault but simply that I have "fallen" into the world in the midst of things and that I need the mediation of the Other in order to be what I am [emphasis in the original].[19]

Sartre begins his reflections with the example of a person seated in a public park and observing a man.[20] Through the person's look, he becomes 'the man-as-object'. That is to say, he becomes part of the onlooker's world. He is defined by her spatial categories (he is over there, 20 paces away) and is subject to her reflections and judgements ('I wonder what that briefcase is for?.....The hair-cut and the stud in the ear look silly on a man his age!'). An object, moreover, is defined by its relationship to a subject. The fact of his being-as-object implies her being-as-subject. The degradation of the look consists in the other's capacity to take control, to 'transcend one's transcendence'. To be caught in the gaze of another is to experience a fall from freedom and a sense of alienation from the self.

These implications Sartre works out in his 'spying through the keyhole' construction.[21] For some compelling reason - morbid curiosity, jealousy, etc. - I am looking through a keyhole at the goings-on in a room. I am in control; my 'free selfness' is expressed through the way in which I freely go about my tasks. But then I hear footsteps in the hallway. Someone is looking at me! My experience-of-being-there is suddenly and radically modified. A sense of freedom is replaced by feelings of shame. I become self-conscious. That is, 'I see *myself* because *somebody* sees me...'[22] It is shame 'which reveals to me the Other's look and myself at the end of the look'.[23] I become the object of his observations and judgements. My intrusion into the lives of others in turn becomes subject to his intrusion. Associated with the shame I feel is a loss of freedom and a sense of alienation from the self. The look has delivered me into the hands of the Other. He is in control. 'The Other as a look is only that - my transcendence transcended.'[24] My 'possibles' are always conditioned by his; I have lost my freedom. I have the possibility of using a dark corner to hide but am threatened by the possibility that his torch-light will expose me. A more profound threat comes from the fact that I have now become subject to his categories, values and judgements. I stand in the light of his critical gaze. (One thinks of Anaïs' feelings of attack and oppression under the look of her father's 'hard blue eyes'.) Sartre observes that to be looked at is to apprehend oneself as the unknown object of unknowable appraisals - in particular, of value judgments. But at the same time that in shame or pride I recognize the justice of these appraisals, I do not cease to take them for what they are - a free surpassing of the given toward possibilities. A judgment is the transcendental act of a free being. Thus being-seen constitutes me as a defenceless being for a freedom which is not my freedom. It is in this sense that we can consider ourselves as "slaves" in so far as we appear to the Other.[25]

While one appreciates the depth of perception in Sartre's analysis, it seems to be overly pessimistic. The gaze of the Other may be shaming, but it may also be affirming. Recall, for example, Buber's reference to the confirming glance of the stranger (chapter 2).

Sartre's gloominess deepens when he reflects on the look of the divine. He contends that the ultimate experience of bondage is to be caught in the gaze of God, 'the concept of the Other pushed to the limit'.[26] To be known by the omniscient One is to be trapped in a state of eternal shame. Shame before God is

the recognition of my being-an-object before a subject which can never become an object. By the same stroke I *realise* my object-state in the absolute and hypostasise it. The position of God is accomplished by a reification of my object-ness.[27]

This situation Sartre considers to be intolerable. In one's relationship with the human Other it is always possible to effect a reversal. My shame becomes a motivation to 'turn the tables' by establishing the other as object under my subjectivity.[28] It is impossible, however, to make God an object. The only way in which one can secure one's free selfness is, as Nietzsche also saw, to put God to death.

How does one respond to Sartre's challenge? Is it in fact the case that the gaze of the omniscient God represents a degrading intrusion into one's being? This would indeed be the reality if it were not for the fact of God's absolute benevolence.[29] God's wholly benevolent intention means that our openness before God is beneficial rather than degrading. We are able to trust God in the penetration into our secret places, our hidden recesses, because we believe in God's total goodness and love.

There is a parallel in the counselling relationship. Sharing the secret self only feels safe when the counsellor has established her trustworthiness. Openness and honesty are beneficial in the presence of a person whose heart is good, who is by nature disposed to a care-ful and sensitive handling of the revealed self. The human person can never, of course, be *wholly* good and benevolent. Buber, in recognition of this, points to the

fact that there is a bipolarity in the self, a 'yes' and a 'no'. In his attempt
to be responsive to the address of the other, a person is caught in a struggle
between loyalty and disloyalty. The responsible person is the one in
whom loyalty wins out.

> Responsibility presupposes one who addresses me primarily, that is,
> from a realm independent of myself, and to whom I am answerable.
> He addresses me about something that he has entrusted to me and that
> I am bound to take care of loyally. He addresses me from his trust and
> I respond in my loyalty or refuse to respond in my disloyalty, or I
> have fallen into disloyalty and wrestle free of it by the loyalty of the
> response. To be so answerable to a trusting person about an entrusted
> matter that loyalty and disloyalty step into the light of day (but both
> are not of the same right, for now loyalty, born again is permitted to
> conquer disloyalty) - this is the reality of responsibility.[30]

The persecuting counsellor manifests his disloyalty through his rough
handling of the secret entrusted to him. Under his gaze, the counsellee
suffers 'the transcendence of her transcendence'. She is made into an
object through his intrusive approach. It seems that he is forcing the
confession of hidden ideas and feelings. When respect for, and a valuing
of, closely guarded ideo-affective content is lacking, 'a therapeutic
intervention is felt as a mutilation of the confessed experience - as a
destructive persecution'.[31] Anaïs had experienced the 'destructive
persecution' of Joaquin Nin, and now she wonders whether Dr Allendy
could really have 'freed me of the EYE of the father, of the eye of the
camera which I have always feared and disliked as an *exposure*'.[32] Sadly,
she has in therapy yet another experience of the look which shames.
'Enter this laboratory of the soul where every feeling will be *X-rayed* by
Dr Allendy to *expose* the blocks, the twists, the deformations, the scars
which interfere with the flow of life' [emphasis added].[33] Under Allendy's
probing, she feels 'oppressed'; his questions are like 'thrusts'. It is as if she
were 'a criminal in court'.[34] Finally, she can take it no longer.

> Anaïs: "Today, I frankly hate you. I am against you."
>
> Dr Allendy: "But why?"
>
> Anaïs: "I feel that you have taken away from me the little confidence
> I did have. I feel humiliated to have confessed to you. I have rarely
> confessed."[35]

To receive the secret which is offered with deep respect and great care is
to confirm the counsellee. An intrusion into her independent space, on
the other hand, is a persecution. Far from being therapeutic, it produces
shame and humiliation.

Derogation: The Shame of Being Set Apart

The image that many have of a counsellor is of a person who is caring and sensitive, who guards against any comment which may be received by the counsellee as pejorative. Counsellors, though, share in the common humanity of the psychologically less aware. They are locked in a struggle with the same destructive urges. Like everyone else, they sometimes want to dominate, to feel superior, to be in control, to attack and so on. To be sure, one of the reasons that many professionals choose to go through a period of therapy is to gain insight into their own particular ways of acting on these negative urges. Insight, however, does not guarantee a complete cleansing of the soul. The dark desires have a way of finding a covert avenue for expression. For example, as Meares and Hobson point out, the provision of insight by the counsellor may in fact be a subtle form of name-calling. Telling a counsellee that he has an arrogant sense of entitlement ('You project the doting behaviour of your mother onto your wife, your friends, and your co-workers.') or that he is passive-aggressive ('Whenever you feel angry and hostile your Child gets hooked and you punish others with your sulking.') may constitute a personal attack smuggled into the conversation under the guise of interpretation. As Meares and Hobson express it, '...an angry, destructive and manipulative person feels that the therapist is confirming what he, the patient, feels that he is - bad and worthless.'[36] Insight-giving which is poorly formulated or motivated by a destructive urge on the part of the counsellor is shame inducing.

This does not mean, of course, that a counsellor should never confront. In chapters 4 and 7 we discussed appropriate forms of challenge. Irvin Yalom's approach to the issue of Betty's boring chatter is a good example of constructive confrontation. Recall that he told her that he wanted to get close to her but her insistence on keeping the conversation on a surface level prevented him from doing that. Yalom was motivated not by an urge to attack or belittle, but rather by a desire for an authentic relationship.

A repressed hostility towards the client is one urge that may negatively affect the counselling relationship. Another is a desire to feel superior, to place oneself on a level higher than the client. When this dynamic is operating, a sense of alienation is the inevitable result.

> By subtle means, the patient is made to feel that he is 'bad', 'ill' and 'abnormal'; and, hence, completely different from the therapist. Such patronising intimations, implying 'It is all your problem which I do not share' induce a sense of alienation.[37]

The shame dynamic operates within a strong-weak polarity. When a person compares himself to another and makes a judgement of inferiority he feels shame. 'Patronising intimations' by a counsellor evoke feelings of worthlessness and a sense of alienation. Anaïs was quite distressed by the fact that Allendy could be dismissive of her and yet would establish an unassailable position for himself in the face of her challenges.

> Today I find flaws in Dr Allendy's formulas. I am irritated by his quick categorising of my dreams and feelings. When he is silent I do my own analysis. If I do, he will say I am trying to find him defective, inadequate, to revenge his forcing me to confess my jealousy of his wife. At that moment he was much stronger than I.[38]

It is interesting to reflect on what may lie behind this tendency to set the client at a distance, to assert superiority. There are no doubt a number of reasons. Let us start, though, with the observation that counsellors and psychotherapists are, by definition, very committed to the cause of mental health. They are especially concerned with their own level of psychological integration. Many have worked conscientiously in their own therapy, and continue to diligently address dysfunctional attitudes and behaviours. There is, however, a negative side to all forms of zeal, namely, a tendency to feel superior. It is quite difficult to avoid a patronising approach to those lower down on the ladder of success.

One immediately thinks of the New Testament parallel, the Pharisees. They have functioned for generations as the symbol of derogation (although there are New Testament scholars who believe that the gospel image of the Pharisaic movement is something of a distortion[39]). The paradigmatic example is found in Luke 18:9-14. Jesus tells the story of two men going up to the Temple to pray, one a Pharisee and the other a tax collector. The former stands up and prays about himself: 'God, I thank you that I am not like all other men - robbers, evildoers, adulterers - or even like this tax collector. I fast twice a week and give a tenth of all I get' (vv. 11-12).

Granted, most counsellors would not be as extreme as the Pharisee in their feelings of superiority. And yet there are those who do not have the capacity to include themselves in the experience of their clients. Inclusion in the inner reality of the client obviously does not often refer to *direct* experience. While there are recovering alcoholics and substance abusers who counsel addicts, and quite a few counsellors suffer from some form of anxiety, depression or phobia, it is often the case that the counsellee's ailment is completely outside the counsellor's personal experience. Buber recognised the fact that in dialogue the partners must contend with their fundamental and sometimes substantial differences. One must recognise 'that this one or that one does not have merely a different mind, or way of thinking or feeling, or a different conviction or attitude, but has also a different perception of the world, a different recognition and order of meaning, a different touch from the regions of existence, a different faith, a different soil...'[40] Given these very significant differences in the thoughts, feelings, perceptions, values and convictions which define each other's being, there needs to be an imaginative capacity which facilitates a bridging of the gap. This, as we have seen, Buber calls 'imagining the real'. It is an 'intensive stirring of one's being' in which one swings into the life of the other.[41] Imagining the real is of the essence of confirmation. One needs to imaginatively include oneself in the inner reality of the other in order to recognise and validate her personhood. The patronising stance of the counsellor, the tendency to set himself apart from the counsellee, represents a failure in inclusion.

Buber also uses the expression 'experiencing from the other side' to describe inclusion.[42] He gives the example of a man caressing a woman. He feels the contact from two sides: with the palm of his hand and also with the woman's skin. Experience of the other side has both 'abstract' and 'concrete' forms. The former Buber illustrates with reference to two persons engaged in a disputation.[43] They have a very different vision of life, of the world. At first, they are preoccupied with their own arguments. But then, in an instant, each one becomes aware of the other's 'full legitimacy' as a person. There is an immediate grasp of the spiritual dimension which grounds the other in 'the Present Being', and as such is the source of both his particularity and his validation. Buber uses the word 'abstract' to describe this experience because while there is a recognition of the other as a spiritual being, there is no swinging into his concrete experience of life (very little may be known of this).

In the context of education, a *concrete* form of inclusion is required.[44] The educator, says Buber, must be over there, standing with the student she is communicating with, as well as standing in her place on the rostrum. It is not enough to simply grasp the spiritual dimension in the student - as important as this is - the teacher must also be able to concretely feel what it is like to be taught. The inclusion, however, (as, one might add, in the counselling context) is not mutual. '[The teacher] stands at both ends of the common situation, the pupil only at one end. In the moment when the pupil is able to throw herself across and experience from over there, the educative relation would be burst asunder, or change into friendship.'[45]

The derogatory counsellor fails at the level of both abstract and concrete inclusion. She is incapable of orienting herself fully to the spiritual dimension in the client. It is this inclusive act which sparks a profound recognition of a common humanity and dignity. Derogation arises in the counselling relationship when the counsellor is oriented to the dysfunctional behaviour which defines difference rather than to the spiritual dimension which is the source of commonality.

The derogatory counsellor is also incapable of standing concretely over there with the client. She cannot enter fully enough into the experience of bringing to another the secret which is the self. While she has some grasp of what that is like - perhaps she has been in therapy herself - she cannot reach deeply enough into the reality of exposing one's pain and chaos to another person. In the end, she stands apart from the client and he feels belittled and alienated.

Reductionism: The Shame of Being Categorised

Confirmation involves a validation of otherness. Buber writes, 'This person is other, essentially other than myself, and this otherness of his is what I mean, because I mean him; I confirm it; I wish his otherness to exist, because I wish his particular being to exist.'[46] As has already been noted, in order to reach into otherness we need the capacity to imagine the real. When this capacity is lacking, we see the other, as Maurice Friedman puts it, 'in our own image or in terms of our ready-made categories'.[47] The reduction of one's feelings, thoughts and values by a counsellor, I suggest, to fit his ready-made categories is a form of persecution. One feels misunderstood and devalued; it is as if one only exists in the terms defined by the counsellor. To be understood in one's own terms is confirming; to have one's personhood compressed to fit another's mould is shaming.

There is a warning here for counsellors, I think, against sitting too closely to any particular personality theory. In those who have a doctrinaire approach to their chosen school of psychotherapeutic thought there is an almost irresistible temptation to view all counsellees through a theoretical grid. In this situation, one cannot see the person for the theory, so to speak. What is the root of this tunnel vision? It is to be found, I think, in the universal human tendency to use an ideology to establish a sense of security. To turn again to our New Testament parallel, we see it very clearly in the Pharisees. They looked for safety and certainty in the application of the Law. All of life is defined and shaped by their understanding of the divine commandments. People and relationships are constructed in terms of *torah* categories. Jesus, on the other hand, wanted to assert God's confirming grace and love in the divine-human relationship. God did not intend the covenantal boundaries to be oppressive. The aim was not to take away human initiative, to deprive people of the possibility of creative thought and action. 'The Sabbath', Jesus teaches, 'was made for the human, not the human for the Sabbath' (Mk 2:27). Counsellors do well to remember that theories of personality and psychotherapeutic technique need to be applied within a person-centred orientation. When Anaïs finally gave up on Dr Allendy, she found in Otto Rank an analyst who valued her freedom and dignity as a person. In their first meeting, she shared with her new analyst her dissatisfaction over Allendy's categorisation. Rank, in turn, communicated his valuing of particularity.

> "I felt that Dr Allendy's formulas did not fit my life. I have read all your books. I felt that there is *more* in my relationship to my father than the desire of a victory over my mother."
>
> By his smile I knew he understood the *more* and my objection to oversimplification.....
>
> Immediately I knew that we talked the same language. He said, "I go beyond the psychoanalytical. Psychoanalysis emphasises the resemblance between people; I emphasise the differences between people. They try to bring everybody to a certain normal level. I try to adapt each person to his own kind of universe."[48]

In counselling we do need maps to guide us around the psychological territory. They are, however, *only* guides. A person is more than the sum of the psychodynamic interpretations we can apply to her life. The reductionistic counsellor attempts to fit the person into a theory, rather than to locate her in her 'own kind of universe'. To have one's particularity recognised and validated is an experience of grace; to be categorised is to be reduced to the status of an object and to suffer under a disgrace.

There is, of course, a place in counselling for theory-informed analysis. It is appropriate and helpful for the counsellor to work with the categories developed in the leading personality theories. In every relationship, the Thou must at some point revert to being an It. Buber recognised the important and essential role played by the I-It modality. Our world is the world of space and time, of cause and effect. A movement into a spatio-temporal-causal context is an entry into the realm of the It. A Thou analysed, categorised and described becomes an It. That this transition takes place is not cause for regret; it is as it should be. A vital balance is kept, though, through the immediacy and directness of the I-Thou meeting. The confirming glance of the other person brings vitality, meaning, joy and hope to our existence. In a counselling relationship, there will be moments of reflection and analysis. However, it is only when the counsellor is able to make his presence felt, to establish the creative tension of the 'between', that the counsellee feels confirmed at the deepest level. One hears notes of joy and pride sounded in Anaïs' recollection of her first impressions of Dr. Rank: 'He was agile, quick, as if each word I uttered were a precious object he had excavated and was delighted to find. He acted as if I were unique, as if this were a unique adventure, not a phenomenon to be categorised.'[49] In stark contrast, her lamentations concerning her experience with Dr Allendy have the tone of sorrow and shame. By way of introduction to these sad reflections, it needs to be noted that what Anaïs particularly appreciated about Rank was the way he viewed neurosis as a distortion in the creative spirit. She was in his eyes not a sick, disturbed person, but rather an artist whose creative energies have been wrongly directed. Allendy, on the other hand, had no appreciation of the value she attached to creativity and imagination; he could not fit these things into his ready-made categories. Anaïs writes:

> The scientific rigidity acts very much like a trap, a trap of rationalisation. The patient who is a hypersensitive person cannot help being influenced by what he is expected to say, by the quick classification baring the structure too obviously. The neurotic feels his next statement is expected to fit into a logical continuity whose pressure he finally succumbs to.
>
> The more this process becomes clear to him, the more he experiences *a kind of discouragement* with the banality of it. The 'naming' of his trouble, being in itself prosaic, links it to his physical diseases, and deprives him of that very illusion and creative halo which is necessary to the re-creation of a human being. Instead of discovering the poetic, imaginative, creative potentialities of his disease (since every neurotic fantasy is really a twisted, aborted work of art), he discovers the de-poetisation of it, which makes of him *a cripple* instead of a potential artist...
>
> To raise the drama instead of *diminishing it*, by linking it to the past, to collective history, to literature, achieves two things: one, to remove it from the too-near, personal realm where it causes pain; the other, to place the neurotic as a part of a collective drama, recurrent through the ages, so that he *may cease regarding himself as a cripple, as a degenerate type......*
>
> It is in this difference between individual expression that we find a new dimension, a new climate, a new vision. To reduce a fantasy is only a means of *dredging the neurotic imagination, of diminishing the stage* on which the neurotic must live out his drama with the maximum of intensity, for the sake of catharsis [emphasis added].[50]

The confirming counsellor has a broad vision. He is able to see a creative potential in a person. In contrast, the counsellor controlled by psychodynamic theory and its neat categories runs the risk of shaming his client. Note the shame cognates Anaïs uses in her reflections: 'discouragement', 'a cripple', 'a degenerate type', and 'diminishing the drama'. A counsellor with a big vision of life and of humanity will find a way to frame the story he hears in a way which communicates admiration and approval (Rank focused on Anaïs' artistic gifts). The reductionistic counsellor, on the other hand, allows himself to be blinkered by his theoretical constructs. While he thinks he is providing insight, he succeeds only in discouraging and diminishing his client. Technical prowess without a capacity for confirming dialogue is of very limited value.

In the above discussion on intrusion, derogation and reductionism, the focus has been on the shame feelings induced in the recipient of care. Obviously, the counsellor may also feel shame as a result of her failures in presence. It will be, though, a moral shame, and thus different from the type of shame the counsellee feels. He has done no wrong. It is simply the case that he found himself in the unfortunate situation of being 'persecuted' by his counsellor. As a result his tendency to feel inferior and inadequate has been reinforced. The counsellor, on the other hand, has failed herself and harmed her client. In reflecting on that fact, she may feel ashamed.

I wish to explore this type of shame reaction further by referring to pastoral care in a parish context. In turning from the challenge of a confirming dialogue, a pastor may feel a sense of moral failure.

THE SHAME OF THE PASTOR IN TURNING FROM THE STRUGGLE

While the situation in a parish is usually quite different from that of a counselling centre, ministers - or some at least - share the tendency to intrude, to subtly belittle people, and to put them in boxes. There is another way, too, in which they fall into disconfirming others. Quite simply, they opt out of the struggle that is confirmation. Rather than engage in genuine dialogue, they take the easy route and avoid difficult issues.

As we saw in chapter 2, confirming the other involves struggling with him, often against himself, as he reaches for his psychological, moral and spiritual potential. In our pastoral relationships, we are constantly receiving a call to enter into a confirming dialogue. Sometimes we respond and sometimes we do not. While there may be a valid reason for turning away from the struggle (e.g. one makes the judgement that at this point one does not have the time and/or the energy to commit to an intense relationship), it may also be that behind the turning away is some personal failing. Some of us, for example, like life and our relationships to be clearly defined, relatively predictable and under control. As soon as one begins to wrestle with another person who is caught between a 'yes' and a 'no', between wanting to find a positive direction and wanting to hold on to the status quo, one is plunged into uncertainty, confusion, and ambiguity. The thought of trying to bring order to the chaos is too unpleasant, too daunting, and so one turns away.

There is clearly a significant cost for us in committing ourselves to the struggle that is confirmation. Let us look at other 'cost factors'. To begin with the obvious, time must be made available. Then there is the fact that we will have to expend mental and emotional energy. And finally, we will have to deal with the negative and/or frustrating reactions from the person we are trying to help (anger, 'game-playing', rationalisations etc.).

I found Janice to be most interesting on the one hand, and confusing and annoying on the other. Quite early on, I picked up that she was constantly projecting an image, a persona. She was clearly quite intelligent, witty and creative. And she used her talents to weave together the most fascinating stories about her past. Unfortunately, many of them were simply untrue. She told me, for example, that she had played tennis for her State. As a young lad, I played in tournaments, including State titles, on a regular basis; so I know something about the game. I invited Janice to join in a game of doubles with two of my children. I can tell you, she can hit a ball, but she has never represented her State! Janice also had stories about her many overseas trips, but when I asked her about some of the cities she was supposed to have seen (and which I had visited), it was evident that she had never been in them. I could go on and on about Janice's stories.

She needed the grandiose tales, I supposed, to compensate for her lack of self-confidence and her sense of inferiority. As a teenager, she got caught up with the wrong crowd and fell into petty crime. As a consequence, she found herself in a residential institution for delinquents. When she left there, she began experimenting with Eastern religions in order to 'find herself'. She married a young man on the same journey of spiritual exploration. Sadly however, like most of the things she had tried, the marriage failed.

More recently, she had found Christianity and arrived at my church. She was full of enthusiasm and very quickly began to suggest ways that she might serve God and our parish. It seems that she had helped a minister in another city in his ministry with the homeless. I was understandably wary, so I contacted the minister. 'Off the record', said James, 'don't touch her. She's more trouble than she's worth.' I found a strategic way to decline her offer of assistance.

Occasionally I would gently challenge Janice. Once, for example, she saw me after a service to 'correct' a mistake in the pronunciation in a Greek phrase I had used in my sermon. She had been studying NT Greek by extension for three weeks now, and due to her 'extraordinary facility' with languages had 'just about mastered it'. Hence, she could tell me where I was going wrong. My pronunciation probably left something to be desired, but hers was just ludicrous. At first, I thought I would simply let it slip by. I had a quick re-think, though, and decided that as I had been thinking that I should begin challenging her stories and begin to help her face up to some of the underlying issues, here would be a place to start. I told her that her suggestion was way off. But I did not go further and tell her that no one, no matter how gifted, could possibly master Greek or any other language in a matter of weeks.

Unfortunately, this was my pattern in relating to Janice. I suppose I just did not want to get into the struggle with her. I did not want to pay the price. She used to tell me how she had overcome her violent temper and her tendency to revert to physical violence when angered. Indeed, I had seen her anger begin to flare on occasion, and it was not a pretty sight. It seemed safer to humour her. I was also concerned about what might happen to her emotionally if I stripped off her masks. Mostly though, I was concerned about my own emotional equilibrium.

When I reflected on my unwillingness to really engage with Janice I realised that I could not justify it. It was simply the case that I was not prepared to give the mental and emotional effort required, nor was I prepared to deal with (what would almost certainly be) her angry reaction. I was aware that I could help Janice, or at the very least, relate to her in a more authentic manner. What was I feeling when I reflected this way? Well, I felt guilty. The dominant feeling, though, was shame. I pride myself on my integrity and courage, but when I admitted to myself that these qualities were nowhere to be seen in my relationship with Janice, I was ashamed of myself.

What did I do with these shame feelings? The answer is, 'not much'. I simply let them sit there and continued to relate to Janice in 'bad faith' because it was easy.

If I had attended to my shame and responded to the prompting of my conscience I would have made a positive change. Sadly for Janice and for me, I chose to turn away from the call to enter the struggle. We will take up this theme of shame and a movement towards genuine presence in the final chapter. Shame feelings alert us to our failures in presence. The challenge is to find the courage and the commitment, under God, to change.

CONCLUSION

In this chapter, we began by considering the ways in which counsellors may harm their clients. While a confirming presence validates particularity and enhances a sense of worth, a distorted presence is persecutory and reinforces a sense of inferiority. We have identified three forms of distorted presence which induce shame, namely, intrusion, derogation (from Meares and Hobson) and reductionism (our own).

The intrusive counsellor handles the secret which is the self roughly. His clients feel as though they are being attacked; it is as though he is trying to force a confession out of them. Under the intrusive gaze of the counsellor, the client feels 'objectified' and humiliated.

Psycho-dynamic interpretation, moving to the second category, can be a covert form of name-calling. The various labels applied to the counsellee reinforce his sense of being a defective, inferior person. The fact that the counsellor sets herself apart from the counsellee and his psychological dysfunction adds to the sense of shame.

The reductionistic counsellor tends to view the client through a grid of personality theory. He is unable to grasp the fact that a person is more than the sum of psycho-dynamic interpretations. As her thoughts, feelings and values are shrunk down to fit into a theoretical container, the counsellee finds her self-esteem diminishing along with them. Counsellors need to be aware of these and other 'persecutory' attitudes and behaviours. With awareness comes the possibility of transcending the tendency to distorted presence.

Finally, we turned our attention to the shame a pastor feels when he turns aware from the challenge of a confirming dialogue. It is possible to use those shame feelings to set a course towards genuine presence. However, one must find the courage and the determination, in the power of the Holy Spirit, to change one's behaviour.

1 See R. Meares and R. Hobson, 'The Persecutory Therapist', *British Journal of Medical Psychology* 50 (1977), pp. 349-359.

2 A. Nin, *The Journals of Anaïs Nin, 1931-1934*, G. Stuhlmann ed. (London: Peter Owen, 1966).

3 See H. Kohut, *The Analysis of the Self* (New York: International Universities Press, 1971); idem, *The Restoration of the Self* (New York: International Universities Press, 1977); and idem, *How Does Analysis Cure?* (Chicago: University of Chicago Press, 1984).

4 A. Nin, *The Journals*, pp. 75-76.

5 Ibid., p. 81.

6 Ibid., p. 81.

7 Ibid., p. 76.

8 See, for example, D. Capps, *The Depleted Self* (Minneapolis: Fortress Press, 1993), pp. 14-15; R. Hutch, 'Confessing the Dying Within', pp. 347-348; H. Kohut, *The Analysis of the Self*, chp. 5, esp. pp. 114-116, and idem, *The Restoration of the Self*, chp. 4.

9 A. Nin, *The Journals*, p. 77.

10 C.G. Jung, *Modern Man in Search of a Soul* (London: Kegan Paul, Trench, Trubner & Co., 1945), p. 35.

11 See R. Meares, 'The Secret', *Psychiatry* 39 (Aug. 1976), pp. 258-265.

12 Ibid., p. 258.

13 See ibid., p. 259.

14 Cf. M. Friedman, *The Confirmation of Otherness in Family, Community and Society* (New York: The Pilgrim Press, 1983), p. 29.

15 R. Meares, 'The Secret', p. 259.

16 A. Nin, *The Journals*, p. 87.

17 Ibid., p. 87.

18 See Sartre, *Being and Nothingness*, pp. 252-302.

19 Ibid., pp. 288-289.

20 See ibid., p. 254 ff.

21 See ibid., p. 260 ff.

22 Ibid., p. 260.

23 Ibid., p. 261.

24 Ibid., p. 263.

25 Ibid., p. 267.

26 Ibid., p. 266.

27 Ibid., p. 290.

28 The whole point of the analyses of Buber and Marcel, of course, is to describe that form of presence which rules out any need to seek control and mastery over the other. 'Inter-*subjec*tivity' is Marcel's preferred term for genuine being-together. When two subjects are relating, when an I is in communion with a Thou, the threat of a degrading 'objectification' is removed.

29 Cf. C. Schneider, *Shame, Exposure and Privacy*, p. 133. He quotes the contemporary philosopher, John Sibler: 'Complete openness and honesty are wholly beneficial in relation with a wholly benevolent Other.' (From his 'Masks and Fig Leaves', in J. Roland Pennock and J. Chapman eds., *Privacy, Nomos 13: Yearbook of the American Society for Political and Legal Philosophy* [New York: Atherton Press, 1971], p. 234.)

30 Buber, 'The Question to the Single One', in *Between Man and Man*, p. 45.

31 Meares and Hobson, 'The Persecutory Therapist', p. 350.

32 A. Nin, *The Journals*, p. 88.

33 Ibid., p. 105.

34 Ibid., p. 82.

35 Ibid., p. 85.

36 Meares and Hobson, 'The Persecutory Therapist', p. 350.

37 Ibid., p. 350.

38 A. Nin, *The Journals*, p. 108.

39 James Dunn observes that there is a widespread consensus in NT and in Jewish scholarship that the Pharisees have been misrepresented in at least some degree in the Gospels. See his 'Pharisees, Sinners, and Jesus', in J. Neusner et al. eds., *The Social World of Formative Christianity and Judaism* (Philadelphia: Fortress Press, 1988), pp. 264-289, pp. 264-265. The NT scholar who has most vigorously and comprehensively challenged the negative image of the Pharisees in the gospels is E.P. Sanders. See his *Jesus and Judaism* (Philadelphia: Fortress Press, 1985) and idem, *Jewish Law from Jesus to the Mishnah* (London: SCM Press, 1990). Sanders argues that the Pharisees would not have been critical of those who were not as strict as themselves in Torah observance. He also contends that they would not have condemned the ordinary people as 'sinners' because they failed to incorporate a number of the *halakoth* advocated by them, the Pharisees, in their daily activities. Attacked also by Sanders is the view of the Pharisees as exclusivist. While they had a positive concern for purity (the ritual cleanliness rules were applied to daily living) they would not separate themselves from the less scrupulous. Finally, he argues that while they no doubt considered themselves to be stricter and holier than most, they did not claim to be the only true Israel. While one accepts that the gospel accounts have been coloured by post-70CE antagonism between earliest Christianity and Judaism, it may well be the case that Sanders has over-corrected for the distortion (cf. Dunn, op. cit., p. 275). In any case, the fact that the movement sponsored by the Pharisees had many positive features not mentioned in the gospels does not exclude the possibility that there was within that movement a small group which was in fact characterised by self-righteousness and exclusivism.

40 Buber, 'The Question to the Single One', in *Between Man and Man*, pp. 61-62.

41 Buber, 'Elements of the Interhuman', *Psychiatry* 20 (1957), pp. 105-113, p. 110.

42 See Buber, 'Education', in *Between Man and Man*, p. 96.

43 See ibid., p. 99.

44 See ibid., p. 100.

45 Ibid., p. 100.

46 Buber, 'The Question to the Single One', in *Between Man and Man*, p. 61.

47 M. Friedman, *The Confirmation of Otherness*, p. 43.

48 A. Nin, *The Journals*, p. 271.

49 Ibid., p. 272.

50 Ibid., pp. 298-299.

Chapter 9

SHAME, SIN AND CONVERSION TO GENUINE PRESENCE

In the previous two chapters, while we have made references to the shame of the person offering help our major focus has been on the shame of the person receiving help. Here our attention shifts to the affective reactions in the pastor or counsellor. Our aim is to identify a positive function for shame in relation to their ministries. The idea that shame feelings may serve as a stimulus to a critical evaluation of one's capacity for presence will be developed. In working with this notion, we will need to carefully work out the relationship between shame, sin and conscience.

In his book *The Depleted Self*,[1] Donald Capps shows a deep sensitivity to the pain and distress suffered by shame-prone personalities. He argues that in what may be called a narcissistic age, a 'sense of wrongfulness' (sin) is more likely to be experienced in terms of shame than guilt. The narcissist senses the distortion in her way of being in the world and it causes her pain. She connects this distortion and pain, however, not with moral failure but rather with personal inferiority and worthlessness. Capps claims that we need a shamed-based understanding of sin if we are to connect with the suffering in the narcissistic culture. In a radical move, he reinterprets sin in terms of self-injury. The victim when the shame dynamic dominates is the self.

While I appreciate the importance of linking sin to the shame experience, the problem I have is that construing sin as self disesteem and self-victimisation constitutes a radical discontinuity with virtually every major theology of sin. The greats in the theological tradition, in talking about sin, always focus on the human's relationship with God. As Cornelius Plantinga puts it so neatly, sin has 'first and finally a Godward force'. An interpretation of sin as self-victimisation necessarily lacks this 'Godward force'.[2] In seeking guidance on the relationship between sin and shame we will turn to Karl Barth's more conventional treatment. Barth's[3] analysis, characteristically, has a christological orientation. He argues that Christ's exemplification of human existence shames us. When we are open and truthful we internalise Christ's shaming and we feel ashamed. Ashamed, we are aware of our need of conversion.

This saving conversion has a parallel in another kind of conversion. Marcel refers to the way in which contemplation of one's way of being in the world can lead to a conversion to a more authentic existence.[4] The main aim in this chapter is to show that *shame provides an impetus to conversion to genuine presence*. In order to develop this idea, use will be made of James Fowler's observation that both discretion-shame and disgrace-shame have an important function in the operation of conscience (as discussed briefly in chapter 6). While a number of writers on shame are concerned exclusively with the negative dimension in shame, our argument is that *shame, when it is associated with conscience, also has a positive function*.

SHAME, SIN AND CONSCIENCE

Capps' primary aim in his book, *The Depleted Self*, is to demonstrate that in the narcissistic culture of the modern industrialised nations persons are more likely to experience a sense of 'wrongfulness' (sin) in terms of shame rather than guilt. He suggests that if people are asked to talk about feelings of pride, envy, and anger most would use guilt language.[5] His contention, however, is that while some guilt is no doubt involved, the 'deeper layer of emotion' is in fact shame. 'For the victim in each of these cases is felt to be the self, and the feelings involved express and even contribute to a sense of self-depletion, of self-diminishment.'[6] In experiencing these feelings we feel small, vulnerable, empty. We may recognise that others are indirectly hurt by our feelings and attitudes, and for this we should feel sorrowful and repentant. 'But the primary victim of such feelings and attitudes is the self.'[7]

Donald Capps is one of the most interesting and important contemporary thinkers in the field of pastoral care, and I have learnt a great deal from everything he has written. I have to say, though, that I find it difficult to accept that it is legitimate to construe self-victimisation in terms of sin. This is so because here the Godward orientation fundamental in the doctrine of sin is necessarily missing. While sin does involve damage to self and others, the primary focus in most, if not all, major interpretations of sin is on a distortion in the relationship with God. Here is not the place to attempt an historical study of the doctrine of sin. However, even a cursory survey will indicate that theologians have always stressed the importance of the Godward force.

A key category for theologians in interpreting sin is pride. For Augustine, sin is pride in which the mind is fixed on the standard of the self rather than on the standard of God.[8] We attempt to determine how we should live, rather than allowing the divine will and purpose to shape our living. Pride is also a central feature in the doctrines of sin developed by Reinhold Niebuhr[9] and Paul Tillich.[10] In a misguided attempt to overcome our *angst*, we seek to elevate ourselves to the sphere of the divine. This 'will-to-power' (Niebuhr) expresses itself in the pride of power, knowledge, and virtue.

Karl Barth identifies a form of sin which in comparison to 'the heroic form of pride' is somewhat mundane and trivial, but for all that is no less toxic, namely sin as sloth.[11] This form of sin is associated with disobedience and, even more seriously, with unbelief. God has graciously offered salvation in Christ, through his sloth the human hardens himself against this offer. This 'no' to God's offer of grace is also at the heart of Karl Rahner's interpretation of sin. 'Guilt', he writes, 'in the concrete order as "sin" is the free no to God's direct, intimate love in the offer of his self-communication by uncreated divinising grace.....'[12]

The liberation theologians refer the 'no' to God to oppressive, unjust socio-political structures.[13] They describe structural sin as a process in which personal egoisms, manifested through a lust for power and for material things, are crystallised into permanent structures designed to maintain the privileges of the elite at the expense of the suffering majorities. The damage to others caused through injustice, J.I.G. Faus rightly points out, is also an offence against God.[14]

This survey has been all too brief. But it does indicate that in a number of significant interpretations of sin from Augustine through to the liberation theologians a Godward orientation is primary. There is a recognition of the hurt caused to both the sinner and those sinned against, but the primary focus is on the damage to the relationship with God.

In seeking guidance on the relationship between shame and sin I find myself looking to a more conventional source, namely Karl Barth.[15] An important difference between the approaches by Barth and Capps is that the former works with moral shame, while the latter focuses on inferiority shame. It is impossible, I think, to stretch the theology of sin to the point where it can include the self-victimisation associated with feelings of inadequacy and incompetence. To start as Barth does with disgrace-shame (Carl Schneider's term) opens the way for creative thought about sin which maintains the all-important Godward orientation.

Barth structures his reflections around the fact that in the context of the person and work of Christ a person is able to see herself, her existence, her life as it truly is - morally and spiritually flawed.

> Jesus is distinguished from all other men, and the knowledge of Jesus from that of all other men, from that of all real or possible objects of knowledge, by the fact that they involve our incontestable shaming.

When we say this we affirm in the first instance the purely factual element in the relationship between Him and us that He is the One who shames us and we are those who are shamed, quite irrespective of whether we are aware of the fact and are ashamed of ourselves, or still close our eyes or close them again to that which has happened and still does so.[16]

The human person is shamed, despite all attempts to hide or repress the fact, because she is in the position of being compared to God. Some may object that it is inappropriate, unfair or even nonsensical to compare the human with the divine. All these objections, though, overlook the fact (from a faith perspective) that God took on the form of a human in and through Jesus. Whether or not we accept it, we all stand in relation to Christ. We cannot avoid a comparison of our lives with his. Alongside the life of Christ we must place our thoughts, feelings, and actions. Against his we must measure how well we have used the time and talents given to us. By his standard we must judge our ordering of our relations to God, neighbour and self. When we measure our lives against that of Christ we are put to shame. 'In this comparison with His', writes Barth, 'of our actions and achievements, our possibilities and actualisations, the true expression of that which is within us, and the inwardness of that which we express, our whole whence and whither, the root and crown of our existence, we are genuinely shamed.'[17]

The fact that Christ shames us can neither be denied nor avoided. We may attempt to close our eyes to this unpleasant reality, but where does it get us? Our freedom and reconciliation depends on opening our eyes, on accepting the fact that we compare poorly with Christ, on allowing ourselves to *feel ashamed*. An acceptance of one's shame opens the way to repentance and the joy and freedom of reconciliation. Barth uses the parable of the Pharisee and the tax collector (Lk 18:9ff) to illustrate the possibility of both pride and humility in the face of our shaming by Christ. The parable, he says,

speaks of two men who are both equally shamed before God but who are completely different because of their knowledge or ignorance of the fact.....The shame of both is already disclosed. But the one knows that this is the case and the other does not. The one can only humble himself whereas the other sees many things which encourage him to exalt himself. It is by this problem of shaming, whether it becomes acute or remains latent, that the decision is made and the ways divide.[18]

Barth's analysis, I suggest, helps us see the relationship between shame and sin in its proper perspective. *To feel shame is not in itself sinful; but it is a sin not to feel ashamed in the light of Christ's life.*

Barth's use of disgrace-shame moves us into the realm of *conscience*. In the depths of our being we honestly compare ourselves to Christ and we feel ashamed. This is another reason why Barth's analysis is attractive to us. Our focus in this chapter is on counsellors and pastors and the work they do. In the course of their ministry, they sometimes have feelings of failure and inadequacy. They will from time to time experience a strong sense of shame associated with the feeling that they have failed those in their care.[19] While some writers on shame orientate themselves exclusively to the negative side of shame, we are interested in the positive function of shame. *It can stimulate conscience*. In the context of pastoral care and counselling, conscience can lead a person to a conversion to genuine presence.

In the work of James Fowler we find a helpful analysis of the interlinking between sin, shame and conscience.[20] He offers insights which we will be able to make good use of in describing the process of conversion to pastoral presence. Fowler asserts that shame is not itself sin, but rather an innate affect which activates the conscience and interrupts the pursuit of sin. '*Shame is not the act of sin*', he writes. '*Rather, it is the subjective amplification of the objective fact of the potential for separation or destruction of relation involved in the sinful act*' (his emphasis).[21] Fowler here uses the key notions of both Silvan Tomkins and Carl Schneider (see chapter 6 above). Tomkins views the affects as the primary psychological motivating mechanisms. When an affect is triggered it *amplifies* that with which it is associated (e.g. hunger pains, sexual urges, an interest in history). As Tomkins puts it: 'Without [the affect's] amplification, nothing else matters, and with its amplification anything can matter.'[22] With this in mind, Fowler asserts that the shame affect has the function of amplifying one's awareness that a current course of action has the potential to cause a serious breech in a relationship. The shame experience thus has a pre-emptive or anticipatory function. Fowler is referring, then, to the notion of shame-felt-before, *discretion-shame*, developed by Schneider. He, Schneider, connects it with the French concept of *pudeur* which refers to modesty or propriety.[23] Shame feelings can be anticipatory; we use them to protect ourselves from exposure and embarrassment. We take precautions in private activities such as intimate conversations and sexual intercourse to avoid unwelcome intrusion. To take the first case, two people wanting to talk confidentially will seek out a private place and they will converse in hushed tones. Discretion-shame functions here to guide the choices of where and how to speak. Now it may be that a third party walks in on the conversation and overhears part of it. Discretion-shame operates at this point to bring the conversation to an immediate halt. Both the partners in the previously private *tête-à-tête* naturally wish to limit the damage done. It is this experience - damage limitation - which Fowler is particularly interested in. In the context of relations with valued others, discretionary shame functions to interrupt an action or a particular line of conversation which may weaken the relationship. Consider, for example, this scenario. While in conversation with a friend, one is criticising a mutual acquaintance. The look on the friend's face, though, indicates that he disapproves of the attack on the other person. One feels ashamed and, wishing to limit the damage to the friendship, cuts short the critical rendition and changes the topic. In this kind of setting, observes Fowler, discretion-shame involves both 'instinctual evaluative responses' and the use of the 'moral imagination'.[24] Discretionary shame, he concludes, is clearly important in the operation of *conscience*. Below we will explore the way in which a counsellor may use discretion-shame to avoid a fall into distorted presence.

Above we saw how Barth associates disgrace-shame, shame-after-the-event, with a humble turning toward God and God's gracious offer of healing. Disgrace-shame, however, has links with sanctification as well as with justification. Here again, Fowler's thought is helpful. A person may feel ashamed of an isolated word or deed. More seriously, he may feel a sense of disgrace concerning an overall pattern of distorted attitudes and behaviours. Fowler observes that release from a sense of disgrace-shame involves revealing one's defects to a trusted person. One can work with a friend, pastor or counsellor in an attempt to change the destructive pattern defining one's way of being in the world. Thus, he concludes, disgrace-shame plays an important role in 'the punitive and self-reformative aspect of conscience'.[25]

Fowler has helpfully identified the intimate connection between, on the one hand, both discretion- and disgrace-shame, and on the other, conscience. Alongside the negative aspect of the shame dynamic is its positive role in activating conscience and promoting wholesome, constructive ways of relating to others. This observation will be used to demonstrate the important role of both discretion- and disgrace-shame in converting pastors and counsellors to genuine presence.

THE DISCRETIONARY FUNCTION OF SHAME IN COUNSELLING

Discretion-shame is shame-felt-before. A counsellor may experience shame feelings even though she has not at this point in time done anything wrong. A feeling of unworthiness may come, for example, because she is contemplating taking an easy, non-threatening route in the counselling process. That is, an awareness that opting for avoidance rather than constructive confrontation is a very real possibility leads to shame feelings. Counsellors avoid issues because, like anyone else, they wish to spare themselves the anxiety associated with tackling a difficult problem. It may be, say, that a counsellee has an aggressive tendency. In challenging him to work on attitudes and behaviours he feels defensive about it is likely that he will initially react angrily. If the counsellor feels especially vulnerable in the face of angry outbursts, she will be tempted to avoid areas about which the counsellee is sensitive. She knows, though, that to save herself means sacrificing his improvement. Even the thought of avoidance shames her.

The counsellor may attempt to defend against the shame feelings with rationalisations. For example: 'We need more time to develop trust and rapport'. Or: 'A non-directive approach is what is required here; confronting him will be counterproductive'. The rationalisations may succeed in holding off shame feelings for a time, but it is likely that eventually the counsellor will have to face the fact that she is failing in her covenant of care. Reaching a point of honesty, she will be able to acknowledge that her subtle approach is not so much, as she would like to think, an indication of sensitivity and patience, but more a strategy for self-protection. As she grows in the conviction that her inaction is a sign that she cares more about 'self-defence' than client-improvement the shame feelings will intensify.

Fowler's analysis shows us that a shame reaction is an innate mechanism which has the purpose of changing a pattern of relating before serious damage is done to the relationship. In the context of counselling this means, I suggest, that *discretion-shame has the function of bringing a counsellor to a point of crisis*. As is often noted, the Chinese character for 'crisis' indicates both opportunity and danger. Associated with the shame feelings will be, on the one hand, a tingle of excitement, and on the other, a sense of apprehension. With reference to the present scenario, the sense of excitement, faint though it may be, arises out of an awareness in the counsellor that she has within her the strength to override her anxiety and to do that which is right for her client. The benefits in finding the courage to move with the client into difficult areas are twofold. First, for the counsellor there is an opportunity to strengthen in herself the virtue of presence. Every time she acts in accordance with the requirements of genuine dialogue she grows in the virtue. To use the language of the virtue ethicists, the habit of presence grows stronger with each positive expression.[26] The faint stirrings of excitement are, of course, not only self-referential. They are associated with an awareness in the counsellor that she has an opportunity to do that which has the potential to move the counsellee in the direction of growth

The danger signal is associated, first, with an awareness that to follow one's conscience may lead to emotional suffering. The counsellor is aware that she may have to absorb some aggression. This suggests another source of danger. There is a very real possibility that she will not be able to resist taking the easy path. It is very tempting to structure the relationship solely around empathy and acceptance. She is rewarded for that by the counsellee. 'Speaking the truth in love', on the other hand, is a scary thought. She senses danger because she realises that she just may not be able to resist sinning against the counsellee and against herself.

Discretion-shame will bring a counsellor to a point of crisis. There is a critical period in the counselling process in which she must choose whether she is prepared to take 'the road less travelled'. Every time a counsellor acts in accordance with the requirements of genuine presence the virtue is strengthened in her. Conversely, every time she opts for the less demanding route the virtue is weakened. Everything depends on how she handles the crisis moment associated with discretionary shame.

Theologically, the crisis moment may be interpreted as a time for a 'yes' or a 'no' to God's leading and empowering. The Spirit is prompting the counsellor to seize the moment of opportunity. The courage needed to act rightly may be found in the Paraclete, the One who comes to our side in power and possibility.

Above we have been referring to the feelings of shame associated with the contemplation of avoidance behaviour. There is, however, another situation in the counselling process in which discretion-shame plays a vital role. Recall Fowler's observation that shame operates to interrupt a behaviour which is potentially damaging to a relationship. It may be, for example, that a counsellor catches himself engaging in a persecutory style of relating (chapter 8). Perhaps he has a tendency to reductionism. He enjoys the search for the neat categories which will capture his client so satisfactorily. At a point in a particular counselling relationship he cannot resist the temptation to share his clever interpretations. The disappointment and anger he senses in the counsellee, however, serve to wrench him out of his intellectual game. In that moment he is reminded that counselling is not primarily about cleverness and theory. He finds himself in touch again with his best wisdom, namely that it is the relationship that helps and heals. He feels shamed by his dialogical failure and immediately sets about restoring the empathic flow in the relationship. Discretion-shame functions in this kind of setting to interrupt a style of being-with the client which is damaging to the relationship.

It is worth pointing out that the discretionary function of shame is only a possibility when the counsellor is *aware* of his tendency to distorted forms of presence. Consider the categories associated with a persecutory presence, namely intrusion, derogation and reductionism. A counsellor may not realise that he is actually guilty of relating in these destructive modes. He may think that he is being brave and direct when in fact he is actually manifesting his lack of sensitivity. He perhaps continues to unwittingly derogate clients through what he judges on a conscious level to be helpful insights. Or he may pride himself on his technical skill, overlooking to a large degree the importance of wisdom, empathy and compassion. It will be quite difficult for him, however, to maintain his delusions indefinitely. There will be some clients who will challenge his relational failures. It may be that he is able to blunt these challenges by relegating them to categories such as 'resistance' and 'shame defence'. If, on the other hand, he finds the courage, openness and honesty to let the confrontational word address him, if he is able to let it into his life, conversion is possible. It is the case now that shame feelings will be associated with his failures to be 'present'. He can no longer use insight-giving as a subtle means of asserting his superiority without feeling the pangs of shame. Whenever he finds himself handling the secret of the other roughly, he will be troubled by a sense of unworthiness. And so on. Openness, honesty and self-awareness, then, are necessary if discretion-shame is to function to interrupt a dysfunctional behaviour and prevent a serious dialogical failure.

DISGRACE-SHAME AND 'CONVERSION' TO GENUINE PRESENCE

Fowler points out that shame functions not only to interrupt behaviour which is potentially damaging to a valued relationship, it also has a role in changing persistent and destructive patterns of relating to others. When a person becomes aware of a personality trait which mitigates presence, he may experience disgrace-shame. If he does, his shame feelings will activate the reforming function of the conscience. It is this idea that we will develop below. To help us, we will make use of both Barth's idea of shame through comparison with Christ and Marcel's idea of contemplation leading to 'conversion'.

Barth argues that because we are asked to compare ourselves with Christ we are necessarily shamed. Two reactions to this fact are possible. We may close our eyes to our shame and attempt to exalt ourselves, as the Pharisee in the parable did. Or we can, like the tax collector, face the reality openly and honestly and allow ourselves to feel ashamed. Barth sees in the feeling of disgrace-shame following a comparison with Christ the beginnings of faith and the possibility of reconciliation. Here, however, we are interested not in conversion to Christ but in conversion to genuine presence. For us too, though, the idea of a comparison with Christ is important.

It is, among other things, the affirming presence of Christ against which we who are counsellors and providers of pastoral care must measure ourselves. I have queried his reflections on the link between sin and shame, but Donald Capps is at his best when he describes Jesus' way of mirroring (recall that mirroring is Kohut's term for affirmation and approval). Capps refers to two biblical stories which we have also discussed, though from very different perspectives, namely, the account of the woman who anointed Jesus' feet (Lk. 7:36-50) and the Johannine crucifixion scene (19:26-27).[27]

In and through her intimate actions, observes Capps, the woman risked being belittled and rejected. Instead of being ground down even further, she is uplifted and affirmed by Jesus. Her sensuous acts - the wetting of his feet with her tears and the wiping of them with her hair, followed by the anointing - left her wide open for rejection. She risked, she exposed herself, she made herself vulnerable. In order to do that she needed to trust herself, and she needed to trust Jesus. Her act of trust was rewarded; there was a very positive outcome. Capps perceptively comments: 'What could do more to lift her spirits.... than this response to [the] critics: "Why do you trouble the woman? For she has done a beautiful thing to me" (Matt. 26:12). What could do more to inspire her to a life no longer dominated by shame and insatiable neediness than his prediction, "Wherever this gospel is preached in the whole world, what she has done will be told in memory of her" (Matt. 26:13)...'[28]

Capps, secondly, sees in the crucifixion scene as it is described by the fourth evangelist Jesus' facilitation of positive mirroring between Mary and the beloved disciple.[29] He invites them to behold each other and a 'bond of love', the stuff of community, is established. In the beholding there is mirroring. Jesus enabled the man and the woman to see what he saw in each of them. In this way, he modelled a new style of relating. Capps comments:

> It is often suggested that the Christian community began with the resurrection of Christ, with the disciples' realisation that he who was dead is now alive. But, according to the Gospel of John, for those who loved Jesus the most deeply - the group of mourners gathered around the cross - it began before he breathed his last breath, as a woman and a man beheld one another, and saw, in that moment, what the one on

the cross had seen in the other. In that moment, a bond of love was established, a bond much stronger than shame, the death we die daily. By inviting them to behold one another, even as he was, even then, beholding them, Jesus exercised a new kind of authority, and *ushered in a new era in human relating* [emphasis added].[30]

Along with his compassion, sensitivity and a willingness to affirm and encourage, we find in Jesus the courage to speak the hard word when required. In the dialogue with the woman at the well (see chapter 7 above), for example, he was not afraid to confront her concerning her inability to sustain a married relationship and the irregularity in her current relationship. Jesus could be tender, and when the situation required it, he could be firm and direct. Further, as is made clear in numerous biblical stories, his style of relating is characterised by a willingness to make himself fully available. He exemplifies what it means to be-there-for-the-other. Not only is he present in terms of the gift of himself, he also makes time for others. The gospel accounts show how he manages to achieve the proper balance between making himself available and withdrawing for prayer and personal renewal. When it is appropriate, he does not jealously guard his time and his personal space. On other occasions, he temporarily drops the demands of his ministry in search of emotional, physical and spiritual renewal. Of course, for those of us who are married and have families there can be no question of a straight comparison with Jesus in terms of being generous with one's time. The whole question of the management of time for those in ministry is a complex one. Balancing one's time with one's commitments is a particularly challenging task for most. One thing is certainly clear, and that is that those of us in ministry are not called to sacrifice our families and ourselves on the altar of service. We cannot take on an impossible burden; we need to choose which calls for help we can and must respond to and which ones we are able to pass on to others. Having made a choice, sitting now with this particular person, we are obliged to give him what he needs and deserves, namely our availability. He needs to feel that his minister has time for him, that his concerns are important and not simply one more thing to be squeezed into a busy schedule.

Though Jesus' situation and experience are in some respects different to ours, he nevertheless sets the standard for us in how to relate to others. Whether the reference is to mirroring, or to compassion and availability, or to constructive confrontation, he establishes an ideal to which we aspire. Inevitably we fall short of the ideal and feel unworthy. It is important to recognise, though, that our shame feelings have a positive function. They are an impetus to conversion to genuine presence.

In order to carry forward our reflections on the relationship between feeling ashamed and growing into genuine presence, we will at this point construct two typical scenarios in ministry. While these are not actual case studies, they are shaped around real personalities and real events. The first scenario involves a minister who allows his tendency to be task-oriented to militate against effective pastoral care. The second refers to a counsellor who is reluctant to broach sensitive moral issues because she is afraid of displeasing her clients.

Scenario 1. The Revd Tony Smith is highly organised and takes pride in his ability to achieve a great deal in any given day. He is a diligent visitor to the homes of his parishioners. However, in his visits he is always conscious of time and attempts to keep firm control of the visit. When a person raises a concern his tendency is to close-off exploration of the issue prematurely. Rather than patiently sit with the parishioner in order to allow the personal story to naturally unfold, Tony grabs at the issues and hastily pursues solutions.

Not surprisingly, some of his parishioners have reacted to this rough handling of their personal concerns by emotionally withdrawing. Mary Thompson is a case in point. She was recently diagnosed with breast cancer. She spoke in a very candid and open way with her elder, Bill Johnson, about her fears and anxieties. When her minister called, however, she spoke only briefly and superficially about her problem. Bill, unsure whether Tony Smith had heard about Mary's problem, mentioned their long and quite intense conversation. The minister wondered why Mary had failed to open-up to him during his visit and felt more than a little hurt. He decided to visit Mary again the next week. He would not, of course, mention the fact that he had heard from Bill that she was much more troubled than she had indicated to him. He simply wanted to give her the chance to share on a deep level with him. 'Mary', he said after a time of light conversation, 'I guess you must be feeling pretty worried just now. We didn't really get a chance to talk about it last week, did we?' Mary's response was polite, but it had an edge to it: 'Well, I know you're a busy man. I don't want to take up too much of your time with my problems. You're got so many other things to worry about.' Tony was stung by her dismissive remarks. He responded, however, by assuring her that he had all the time in the world just now to listen. Mary did in fact share some of her thoughts and feelings, but it was evident to her listener that she was still holding back from him.

Mary's cutting comment had the effect of bringing Tony face to face with a reality he had been ignoring. He was forced to accept the fact that he valued getting things done more highly than being-with-others. The sad truth that he has a tendency to squeeze the pain of others into his carefully controlled schedule was now forcing in on him. And he felt ashamed.

Scenario 2. Margaret Jones is a Christian who works as a student counsellor at the local university. She is firmly committed to the non-directive approach and believes that unconditional positive regard is the most significant factor in the promotion of healing and personal growth. She is currently working with John, a medical student in his early twenties. He is feeling dissatisfied both with his studies and with the prospect of becoming a doctor. He wants to clarify the issues and his feelings. John hates the way in which his father is always pushing him to be successful in his medical studies. He wonders if the calling to be a doctor is his or his father's. It could be, he realises, that his disaffection with his course is not so much a genuine realisation that he is in the wrong slot as a reaction to his father's constant pressure.

During the third counselling session, John mentions that the young woman he is living with, Jenny, is encouraging him to continue. 'She thinks', he says, 'that I would make an excellent doctor. She's madly in love with me and likes to see herself in a support role down the track.' John goes on to say that, 'What she doesn't realise is that out relationship probably won't go on forever.' 'Well', observes his counsellor, 'no one can be sure that their love is forever.' 'No, what I mean is that I only see myself sticking around for another couple of years. Jenny's pretty immature and lacks confidence in herself. I want to help her get her head together and then I'll probably move on.' As John sees it, he 'can do a good thing for Jenny right now, but will eventually outgrow her'. When asked whether he has raised with Jenny any of his concerns about their relationship, he simply replies, 'No, I'll just let it ride for the moment. She couldn't handle it.'

Understandably, Margaret is troubled by John's paternalistic approach. She is also concerned that he is not prepared to be open with Jenny. However, she is very gentle in her comments: 'While you can't commit to Jenny for the long-term, you do care about her and want to help her to grow. At this point you don't think it's right to raise your concerns with her.' 'Yeah', John responds, 'that's about it. I'll know when its time to move on. I'm just going to do my best for her right now and let the future take care of itself.' After a short silence, John switches the conversation back to his concerns over his father's relentless pressure.

Later, Margaret is reflecting on the session. She wonders whether she should have challenged John in relation to his paternalistic and condescending approach to his relationship with Jenny, on the one hand, and his failure to raise with her his concerns about it, on the other. As she considers why she was so soft with her client, she begins to feel distinctly uncomfortable. The reality that she has been trying to hide behind her commitment to acceptance and the non-directive approach is showing itself. Her tendency to bracket out moral issues is not so much a consequence of her commitment to the person-centred approach as an expression of her own need to please, to be liked by her clients. She needs and enjoys the warm reaction to her affirming, accepting style. The fact that her clients would likely be displeased with a challenge to their value systems is something she feels very uncomfortable about. Seeing the situation as it really is, facing up to her own insecurities and the way in which she allows them to militate against effective counselling, she feels unworthy.

Both Tony Smith and Margaret Jones have begun a process of introspection which Marcel calls 'contemplation' (see chapter 1). To contemplate is to engage in 'a kind of inward regrouping of one's resources, or a kind of ingatheredness; to contemplate is to ingather oneself in the presence of whatever is being contemplated, and this in such a fashion that the reality, confronting which one ingathers oneself, itself becomes a factor in the ingathering'.[31] Ingathering describes a process in which one draws near to the reality one contemplates and allows it to impact on one's life. That reality may be a landscape, a poem, or a work of art. It may also be a character trait which distorts one's relations with others.

In order to illustrate the last mentioned possibility, Marcel refers to Emperor Augustus' struggle with his dark side as it is described in Corneille's tragedy, *Cinna*.[32] Augustus is a tyrant who ruthlessly dispatches any opposition. He has just discovered that one of his subjects, a man on whom he has previously showered favours, is leading a plot against his life. At first the emperor is overcome by indignation, rage, and a lust for vengeance. There is, though, something in Augustus which refuses to yield to these vengeful urges. He forces himself to look honestly at himself; he enters his inner depths where the voice of truth can be heard.

> Cease to complain, but lay thy conscience bare:
> One who spared none, how now should any spare?......
> Durst then tax Fate with an unjust decree,
> Now, if thy friends aspire to see *thee* bleed,
> Breaking those ties to which *thou* paid'st no heed?

Just is such treason, and the Gods approve!.......
As easy lost as won, thy state remove,
See traitors' swords in treacherous blood imbued,
And die, thou ingrate, by ingratitude![33]

Marcel suggests that the soliloquy, taken in the context of the reflections preceding it, reveals *two modalities of the self* in Augustus. There is the self which lusts after vengeance; and there is the self which is capable of seeing the justice in the traitorous plot. Marcel goes on to observe that while in this act of contemplation Augustus turns inward his awareness of the outer world, what is happening in him is not so much introversion as *conversion*.[34] He does not use the word in a religious sense; Augustus is not converted to faith in God. Rather, Marcel refers to a conversion which is 'an act of inner creativity or transmutation'.[35] It has the character of a *return*, 'a return in which what is given *after* the return is not identical with what is given before'.[36] The terms 'transmutation' and 'a return' indicate the fact that ingathering involves a *withdrawing of oneself from one's own life*.[37] That is to say, it produces a gap between one's being and one's life. Paradoxically, 'I am not my life, but in another sense, I am my life'. The two modalities of the self refer, then, to the *actual life* I have been leading, on the one hand, and to the *potential life* I carry within me, on the other. I am not my actual life without remainder; I am also the life I can be through creative development.

While the experiences of Tony Smith and Margaret Jones are much less intense than that of Augustus, it is evident that the same dynamic is operating for all three. They are, each in their different ways, faced with the possibilities and the challenges of growth. *A sense of shame becomes the catalyst for contemplation. Contemplation, in turn, opens the way for conversion.* Neither Tony nor Margaret need remain confined by their actual way of being with the other. They have within them the potential for a new, more authentic, way of being present. Within them also, and most importantly, is the power of the Holy Spirit moving them to change and to grow. The real question is, will they seize hold of the opportunity put before them?

CONCLUSION

We began this chapter with an attempt to find an adequate description of the relationship between shame, sin and conscience. Donald Capps' argument that sin needs to be interpreted in terms of self-victimisation was judged to be flawed. Though there is always self-injury associated with sin, the concept requires a Godward orientation. There is no offence against God associated with the experience of inferiority. God is not offended (though God is grieved) by feelings of incompetence and defectiveness. We found in Karl Barth's orientation to moral shame a more adequate treatment of the relationship between sin and shame. We are all shamed through a comparison with the person and work of Jesus Christ. In this way, Barth points us in the direction of conscience. In James Fowler's analysis we found a helpful way of linking shame and conscience. He suggests that discretion-shame has the function of interrupting behaviour which is potentially damaging to a valued relationship. Observing the disapproval of the other, one's conscience is activated. It reminds one that the behaviour is wrong and needs to be immediately dropped. Disgrace-shame, on the other hand, serves to alert a person to the fact that not just an isolated act but, more seriously, an overall pattern of life is destructive and needs to be changed.

These insights of Fowler's were applied in the context of pastoral care and counselling. We attempted to demonstrate, first, how discretion-shame works to prevent a fall into distorted presence. It leads a person to a crisis point. In the moment of crisis, he has the opportunity to turn his behaviour in the direction of genuine presence. Then we tried to show how disgrace-shame also has this positive function in modifying distorted ways of being with others. Shame feelings, arising out of the awareness that one has a character trait which militates against effective care, provide an impetus to contemplation. Through contemplation and openness to God's reforming power there is conversion to genuine presence.

1 D. Capps, *The Depleted Self: Sin in a Narcissistic Age* (Minneapolis: Fortress Press, 1993).

2 C. Plantinga, 'Not the Way It's S'pposed to Be: A Breviary of Sin', *Theology Today* 50, no. 2 (1993), pp. 179-192, p. 184.

3 See Barth, *Church Dogmatics* IV, 2 (Edinburgh: T & T Clark, 1958), p. 405ff.

4 See Marcel, *The Mystery of Being*, vol. 1, p. 126ff.

5 See Capps, *The Depleted Self*, p. 71.

6 Ibid., p. 71.

7 Ibid., p. 71.

8 See Augustine, *The City of God*, Bk XIV, chp. 13.

9 See R. Niebuhr, *The Nature and Destiny of Man*, vol. 1 (London: Nisbet & Co., 1941), chp. VII.

10 See P. Tillich, *Systematic Theology*, vol. 2 (London: Nisbet & Co., 1957), chp. XIV.

11 See K. Barth, *Church Dogmatics* IV, 2, p. 403ff.

12 K. Rahner, 'The Need of Redemption', in K. Lehmann et al eds., *The Content of Faith* (New York: Crossroad, 1992), p. 200.

13 See, for example, J.I.G. Faus, 'Sin', in J. Sobrino and I. Ellacuria eds., *Systematic Theology: Perspectives from Liberation Theology* (New York: Orbis Books, 1996), pp. 194-206.

14 See ibid., p. 202.

15 See Barth, *Church Dogmatics* IV, 2, p. 384 ff.

16 Ibid., p. 384.

17 Ibid., p. 386.

18 Ibid., p. 385.

19 No doubt, they will sometimes also feel some guilt. Shame and guilt tend to get tangled up together. Nonetheless, I believe it is right to identify shame as the dominant affect associated with 'presence' failures by pastors and counsellors. Due to personal shortcomings, a helper sometimes falls into inauthentic ways of relating to those in his care. When he becomes aware of the fact that he has allowed his personal failings to impede the healing process, he will feel, I suggest, mainly shame. The shame ideation might, for example, run like this, 'What sort of counsellor am I when I am so often distracted and find it so difficult to be warm and empathic?' He will probably also feel some guilt: 'I feel bad that I said some things that were insensitive and obviously hurt Joe Bloggs' feelings'. However, in the context of failures in presence guilt tends to be somewhat in the background. The dominant feeling will be shame. The helper has not acted intentionally to hurt; rather, he has fallen short of his ideal for authentic relating and that has mitigated against his helping intention. He feels ashamed that he has not been able to transcend his fears and flaws. In contrast, think of a case of sexual abuse by a pastor or counsellor. Then guilt would be felt at least as strongly as, and probably more strongly than, shame. The primary reality confronting him is the fact that he is guilty of serious wrongdoing and has deeply hurt and traumatised the woman in his care.

20 See J. Fowler, *Faithful Change*, chps. 6-8.

21 J. Fowler, *Faithful Change*, p. 136.

22 S. Tomkins, 'Shame', in *The Many Faces of Shame*, p. 137.

23 See C. Schneider, *Shame, Exposure and Privacy*, p. 18.

24 See Fowler, *Faithful Change*, p. 105.

25 Ibid., p. 107.

26 Reference was made above, in footnote 47 in chapter 7, to Aquinas' notion of virtue as a habit. In saying that a virtue is a habit, he means that it is a well-established disposition to act for the good. Every time a person acts virtuously, the disposition is more firmly established in her. She is developing a readiness to act virtuously when a situation calls for it.

27 See D. Capps, *The Depleted Self*, pp. 162-165.

28 Ibid., p. 163.

29 See ibid., pp. 165-166.

30 Ibid., pp. 165-166.

31 Marcel, *The Mystery of Being*, vol. 1, p. 126.

32 See ibid., pp. 129-132.

33 Corneille, *Cinna*, Act IV, scene 2; cited in Marcel, op. cit., pp. 129-130.

34 Marcel, *The Mystery of Being*, vol. 1, p. 131.

35 Ibid., p. 132.

36 Ibid., p. 132.

37 See ibid., p. 136.

SUMMARY

The primary thesis that I have argued is that *in pastoral relationships availability is before skills and techniques and confirmation is beyond empathy and acceptance*. While it is acknowledged that techniques certainly have a place in pastoral care and may be used to good effect, in the absence of giving of self, of real emotional availability, of genuine love and fidelity, they will be only minimally effective in facilitating healing and growth. Put differently, a person feels genuinely cared for not so much because she has received expert psychological assistance, as important as this is, but rather because she has received a gift of self from her pastor or counsellor. To be sure, too many pastors operate with a woeful lack of psychological and therapeutic knowledge. There are also counsellors who pay too little attention to skills training. It goes without saying that those offering care need to have a good grasp of available theories and techniques. However, in pastoral care and counselling availability is the *foundation* which supports skills and techniques. Without this solid base, the edifice of care is very shaky indeed.

In order to demonstrate that in Marcel's concept of *disponibilité* we have the foundation for pastoral care, I attempted to establish its affinities with the biblical notion of compassion. Some writers have suggested that the biblical notion of compassion is captured by the Rogerian terms acceptance and empathy. No doubt, in being accepting and empathic one is showing compassion. However, I have argued that beyond these core relational attitudes and skills, is a more profound communication of self. In the Old Testament, compassion is understood as an expression of an intimate attachment to the other. The seat of this emotion is identified as the womb or the heart. For Paul, compassion is more than the registering of emotion, it is an expression of one's total being at the deepest level. The Greek word he uses, *splánchnon*, originally referred to the 'inward parts of the body', or to the womb. These two terms, the womb and the heart, are very closely linked to Marcel's idea of the 'home-space'. To receive the hurt and distress of another is to receive her *chez soi*, at home. I argued on this basis that availability is a cognate term for the biblical notion of compassion and therefore qualifies as a foundational quality in pastoral care.

I developed the notion of disposability as foundational in pastoral care by referring to the important Marcelian concepts of *belonging* and *substitution*. 'Belonging' is also a rich biblical and theological term. Marcel refers to belonging to Christ - the key fact in a life of faith. For the Hebrew people, personhood was defined through the belonging established in a covenantal relationship. Using the theology of covenant as a framework, we extended our understanding of the foundational role availability plays in pastoral care and counselling. The willingness to substitute the other's freedom for one's own is an important dimension in a covenantal relationship. It constitutes a fundamental attitude for the pastor and the pastoral counsellor.

A commitment to extend oneself in a relationship of belonging is foundational in pastoral care. Beyond this foundational moment, however, is an engagement with the other in her struggle to realise her God-endowed psychological, spiritual, and moral potentialities. We construed growth towards psychological wholeness in terms of a reclaiming of disavowed sub-selves. Beyond empathy and acceptance in the counselling relationship there is a need to sensitively confront the counsellee. In this case, the need is to confront him with his disowned polarities. The process does not stop there, however. It is necessary for the counsellor to facilitate an inner dialogue, a dialogue within the community of the Self, through which disavowed selves are integrated.

We have also developed an understanding of the explicitly moral dimension in confirmation. It was contended that there needs to be a greater role assigned in the theory and practice of pastoral care to conscience. In stimulating the conscience, the pastor or counsellor calls the person in her care to responsibility. Here, we found it helpful to differentiate between first- and second-order responsibility. First-order responsibility refers to those responses which are commonly embraced, conventional, in the family, in the church, and in the society. Creativity and conscientiousness define second-order responsibility. Pastors and counsellors, it was suggested, need to promote both as they each have a role to play. An active conscience, though, brings into play the disquieting, disturbing impact of shame and guilt. An important part of the minister's or the counsellor's role is helping the person find avenues for effecting *reconciliation*. In a Reformed understanding, acts aimed at repairing damage to the order-of-being cannot justify a person. The significance of reconciliation is not found in the realm of soteriology, but rather in the moral and the psychological spheres. An attempt to heal the wound inflicted in the order-of-being is a moral imperative; it is one's duty. It also contributes to psychological well-being.

The overall aim in the first part of the book was to describe, on the one hand, what genuine presence looks like, and, on the other, how it functions in pastoral practice to assist a person towards healing, growth and wholeness. There is, of course, another side to the coin. Pastors and counsellors may subvert their intention to help and to heal through distortions in their way of being present. This we explored in part 2. My argument was that when this happens, there is a potential for shame in *both* the provider and the recipient of care.

So that we could be clear about our terms, it was necessary to differentiate shame from guilt. In the moral sphere, the two affects get tangled up together. It is possible, nonetheless, to distinguish one from the other. Shame has a global reference, whereas guilt is connected to particular transgressions. In observing the pain and hurt one's actions have caused the other, one feels guilt. One feels remorse and begins to think of ways to make amends. However, in thinking of the damage to the other caused by one's actions, one immediately begins to question one's worth as a person. In other words, shame ideation operates in conjunction with the recognition of one's guilt. 'What sort of person am I to have done this bad thing?' one thinks. That is to say, I *do* things which cause me to feel guilty, but I *am* my shame. In essence, shame is a failure in valuing of the self.

Shame was linked to two forms of distorted presence, namely non-availability and disconfirmation. In relation to the former, we made use of Marcel's concept of constancy. Constancy refers to a pretence of presence. In company with a pastor or counsellor who is only shaming availability, one's sense of self-worth may drop. His lack of commitment may be received as a confirmation of the feeling that one does not really deserve a full expression of self-giving.

We also discussed the relationship between shame and non-availability in the context of pastoral visitation. Connections were made between Marcel's reflections on the problem of fidelity and what I called a bipolar affective dynamic. A recession in the tide of compassion results in a pretence of availability. This may produce feelings of inauthenticity and unworthiness. Constancy generates shame. On the other hand, a recognition of the fact that one has dismissed all counter-urges and has chosen to be with the other in her need produces a boost to self-esteem.

In continuing the investigation of defective pastoral presence, I described three expressions of disconfirmation: intrusion, derogation, and reductionism. All of these tendencies in counsellors have a potential to heighten a person's feelings of inferiority and inadequacy.

I also applied the concept of disconfirmation in the context of care in the parish. It was observed that in our pastoral relationships we are constantly receiving a call to enter into a confirming dialogue. Sometimes we respond and sometimes we do not. While there may be a valid reason for turning away from the struggle, it may also be that behind the turning away is some personal failing. When a pastor cannot find the courage and commitment to engage in the wrestling which is confirmation, there is a potential for shame.

While some writers emphasise the debilitating effects of shame, even going to the point of relating the self-victimisation associated with shame feelings to sin (D. Capps), I endeavoured to point-up a positive role for shame. Shame feelings, I argued, should not be construed in terms of sin, but rather linked to the reforming function of the conscience. The secondary thesis argued was that *the shame feelings a pastor or counsellor experiences as a result of his distorted way of being present have a potentially positive function, namely, moving him to a period of critical introspection in which he may grasp a vision of a higher capacity for genuine presence.* Shame feelings may lead a care provider to a time of *contemplation*. In contemplation, a person is faced with two modalities of being. On the one hand, there is the actual self with its flaws and defects. On the other hand, there is the potential self: the new person one can become if one is prepared to make certain decisive changes. Looking squarely at his tendency to defective forms of presence, a pastor or counsellor may also see a vision of himself in which he is more available, more ready for the demands associated with confirming others. In a theological interpretation, the Holy Spirit has moved him to contemplation, and now empowers him for growth towards genuine presence.

I wish to conclude with this thought. While not wanting to underestimate the complexities involved, it seems to me that the various theories and techniques associated with the psychotherapeutic schools can be learned relatively easily. Whatever difficulties there may be in appropriating healing techniques, they are small compared to those associated with living a life of presence. A person with the requisite ability and diligence can master interventions in a few short years. It takes a life-time, however, to even begin to grasp what it means to share in a real meeting with another human being.